SCRATCH

TROON McALLISTER

Also by

TROON McALLISTER

Barranca

The Kid Who Batted 1.000

The Foursome

The Green

RUGGED LAND | 276 CANAL STREET · FIFTH FLOOR · NEW YORK CITY · NY 10013 · USA

RuggedLand

PUBLISHED BY RUGGED LAND, LLC

276 CANAL STREET · NEW YORK · NEW YORK · 10013 · USA

RUGGED LAND AND COLOPHON ARE TRADEMARKS OF RUGGED LAND, LLC.

PUBLISHER'S CATALOGING-IN-PUBLICATION

McAllister, Troon.
Scratch / Troon McAllister.
p. cm.
"An Eddie Caminetti novel."
ISBN 1-590-71021-5
1. Golf--Fiction. 2. Golf stories. I. Title.
PS3557.R8S37 2003   813'.54

Book Design by Hsu + Associates

RUGGED LAND WEBSITE ADDRESS: WWW.RUGGEDLAND.COM

FIRST RUGGED LAND TRADE PAPERBACK EDITION MARCH 2004

1   3   5   7   9   10   8   6   4   2

Scratch is dedicated to the participants of
the 2002 edition of **The Caminetti Cup**, an annual event that pits
eight U.S. mainland golfers against eight from Puerto Rico.

The tournament is named for Eddie Caminetti, who first appeared
in *The Green*. A key requirement for participation is that each player
has read that book and passed a test on its contents.

The 2002 event, which was held at the Doral Golf Resort in
Miami, Florida, was won by the U.S. team, 10–6.

(The Puerto Rican participants have assured their opponents that
at the 2003 event to be held in the Dominican Republic,
drinking water provided on the course will be spiked with
a potion not seen on the mainland since
Benjamin Franklin sampled a bit
and then went kite-flying in a thunderstorm.)

SCRATCH

Golfers are funny damned people.
What does every golfer in the world do when somebody hands him
a club that's supposed to hit farther?
He swings it harder. Every damned time.

—*Eddie Caminetti*

PROLOGUE

He was a physicist, Norman Standish was. A *physicist*. That's like a rocket scientist, only smarter.

And make no mistake about it: Norman Standish was one smart puppy, the kind of guy who liked to do partial differentials in his head. Once, while traveling by train with a Nobel laureate colleague from Caltech, Standish said, "I'm bored. Give me something difficult."

They were heading into Kansas, which is as good a reason for being bored as any. The Nobelist, who dreaded flying and wasn't all that fond of train trips either, wanted nothing more than to sleep for a few hours. "Tell me the first five partial derivatives of the natural log," he responded. Then he nodded off, because it had taken him five months to work the answer out himself when he'd tackled it during his post-doc.

Somewhere near Salinas he felt something tugging at his pant leg. His eyelids fluttered open to see that it was Standish. Had a year passed? He looked outside. Still nothing but wheat flashing past the window. "What?"

"I got em. Want to hear?"

The eminent professor shook his head; he didn't need to hear. If Norman Standish said he had the derivatives worked out, he did. Standish was that smart, and everyone in the department knew it.

Problem was, he just wasn't very creative. He understood everything about everything that others had come up with, sometimes better than the creators themselves. His mind jumped miles ahead to unforeseen implications, and if there was a flaw in a new theory, he saw it instantly, which is why all the other brainiacs came to him before they dared publish. If you could get it past Standish, the rest was easy.

He just couldn't seem to come up with brand new stuff himself. In fact, he hadn't contributed a single original concept in the twenty-odd years he'd been a physicist. The only way he'd survived "publish or perish" was by critiquing or extending the work of others, or by sharing publication credit with colleagues whom he'd saved from acute embarrassment by catching problems before official peer reviewers did.

So here he was in his mid-forties, long past prime productive age for physicists, nearly all of whom did their best work by the time they were thirty-five. Einstein was twenty-six when he came up with his first theory of relativity, for Pete's sake. Standish's Caltech colleagues appreciated him, his peers at other universities respected him, students flocked to his classes, but the physicist himself went around in a perpetual and increasingly public funk: depressed, unfulfilled, full of self-doubt, ever hopeful of the blinding insight that would make his name in the world and progressively less confident that it would ever happen.

"Let's play some golf," another professor said one day, trying to cheer him up.

"Why?"

"Long as you already feel like shit, that's the game for you."

So off they went, to the Indian Wells Country Club in Rancho Mirage, Standish awkwardly dragging a set of borrowed clubs and doing his best to learn golf the same way he'd learned chess: by watching other people play. Except he wasn't exactly on the links with Bobby Jones or Jack Nicklaus. Learning golf from the guys he was with was like trying to learn the theory of flight by watching a pigeon that had just been hit by a truck.

Standish was particularly intrigued by his friend's brother-in-law, Jerome Traumerai. About forty years of age, six foot three and getting thick around the middle, Jerome handled his clubs the way a French poodle would handle a Harley. On the first tee he wound up into a tremendous backswing and brought the club down at blinding speed, smashing the golf ball a solid thirty yards. The chunk of dirt he brought up from underneath the ball went about ten yards further than that.

"It happens," the brother-in-law said with perfect equanimity, then trudged to his ball and leaned into it with a three-wood, missing it completely. "Shit!" he cursed, then looked at his club with curiosity. Standish would soon learn that this was a standard reaction to a complete miss, as if the golfer was looking for the hole through which the ball had cleanly passed.

Standish had it wrong, of course. He didn't know that Jerome was a student of the game and believed that the shaft was the engine that really powered the club. If Jerome missed the ball completely, his wisdom told him that the fault was in the shaft, not the head. Standish, of course, being a novice, wasn't yet attuned to these fine distinctions.

Jerome's next shot was better, a five-iron that went fifty yards, albeit from left to right rather than straight ahead. But let's move ahead, because it's really not worth belaboring every shot the guy took on this challenging par-four hole before scoring a twelve.

"How the hell'd you get a twelve?" his brother-in-law asked.

"Missed my putt for an eleven," Jerome replied.

It went on like this for the front nine, Jerome sending balls in so many directions it was starting to look like he was running out of ways to keep it away from the hole. Despite his considerable bulk and what looked like reasonable coordination and some athletic ability, he hadn't hit a single shot over a hundred yards nor scored less than eight on any hole, and the eight was on a par-three.

It wasn't until the fourteenth hole, though, that The Thing happened that would change Norman Standish's life forever.

Jerome finally got hold of one, a three-wood off the tee. His satisfaction with the *click* that signified a clean shot was short-lived, though, because his inside-out swing had imparted about 12,000 rpm of sideways spin to the ball, which veered alarmingly as soon as it left the teeing area and headed into a mini-forest of old-growth something-or-other trees lining the fairway.

The foursome dutifully trudged into the local *Schwarzwald* and began tramping around in search of Jerome's errant ball, which was doubtless huddling beneath some thick moss and praying for a quiet death rather than more pummeling at the hands of its inept owner. After about ten minutes of the statutory five-minute search, Jerome popped up in the vicinity of a pile of rotting leaves, holding aloft a golf ball.

"Hey, look what I found!" he shouted gleefully. "A Z Tamale!" At least that's what it sounded like to Standish. He took it to be some type of ball that was different than the one Jerome had hit.

As the four of them stumbled out of the forest, Jerome stared down at his new find and uttered the words that would lead to the complete overhaul of Norman Standish's life.

"I *love* this ball!"

Standish stopped dead in his tracks, utterly dumbfounded.

Jerome *loved* this ball? What did that mean? That was like Standish saying he preferred the F-15 fighter jet to the Phantom 5, or the Oonsfutten bobsled to the Farshluginner. How could a golfer like Jerome possibly perceive a difference between one golf ball and another?

The good professor had spent the better part of the past three hours trying to understand what was going on around him. How come a big guy like Jerome could barely hit a ball past the red tees, but guys he saw on other holes, like a snippet of a man who couldn't have weighed in at more than a hundred and forty, could hit over two-thirty without seeming to half try? What were the differences among all those clubs in the bag? How come one guy's putter head looked like the tail section of a stealth bomber and the one in Standish's own bag was nothing more than a simple block of brass?

He was okay with all those mysteries, and assumed that answers would drift in slowly if he observed patiently, but Jerome claiming to *love* the Z Tamale (or whatever)—that was just too much. What on earth could that guy possibly love about a golf ball?

"Just curious," Standish said to Jerome when he was able to compose himself. "What is it about this, this..." He pointed to the ball Jerome was cupping lovingly in his hand. "What's so good about that particular ball?"

Jerome grinned a conspiratorial grin at his brother-in-law, as if the two of them were privy to some awesome secret they were now willing to impart to an eager novice.

"See this cover?" Jerome said as he held the ball out.

As he took the ball, Standish could indeed see the cover. It was white, with dimples. "What about it?"

"Made outta this stuff, it's got a really soft feel but outstanding spin characteristics. Dimple pattern's part of it, but it's the material, too. And it's got a two-piece core with barterminium surrounding an antideluvian smeroid, see?"

Standish nodded. "And that means...?"

"First of all, it holds the green," the other scientist jumped in. "Lob it up with backspin and it grips the surface so it stays put where you want it to. But at the same time it has tremendous distance off the tee, and tends to mitigate the effects of a slice or a hook. It's also very true on the putting surface."

Standish felt as if he'd fallen down a rabbit hole. What did extra distance mean to Jerome, exactly? That he could hit the ball a hundred yards into a lake instead of ninety? And as for holding the green, wasn't there some implication that you had to actually *hit* the green before the aforesaid holding could take place? Then there was the alleged putting prowess of the super ball. What was the point of true-ness—that it would truly go three feet to the side of the hole Jerome was aiming for?

And if the ball was so damned good, how come somebody had lost it in the first place?

But...maybe he wasn't being fair. These guys had played golf for years, whereas Standish had been at it for half an afternoon. Maybe they really did know what they were talking about. Maybe he was about to witness a miraculous transformation in the hapless Jerome's game for the final four holes.

He handed the ball back. Jerome accepted it, then turned and dropped it into a pocket in his bag.

"Aren't you going to use it?" Standish asked, perplexed.

"Use it?" Jerome looked up in surprise. "Why would I risk losing a ball like that?"

The other physicist smiled and nodded in complete understanding.

"Fuhgeddaboudit!" Jerome proclaimed as he pulled an old ball from his bag and five-ironed it right back into the woods.

Back at the lab, Standish emptied some new golf balls he'd just bought onto a table. He looked at them through a magnifying glass, weighed them and sent them down inclines at various angles of elevation. He scraped at the covers with a file, then cut into them with a scalpel, peeling back the various layers and carefully separating the individual materials.

He took samples over to the experimental operations building and placed them under a scanning electron microscope. He kept very detailed notes, Norman Standish did, and when he'd seen all he thought there was to see, he begged some time on the cyclotron and put various combinations of materials in the target chambers to flood them with a riot of exotic particles that exploded away from the colliding beams of the giant machine.

After the better part of a week in the labs, he headed for another building, this one a classified research center requiring special clearances. There, he parked himself in front of a computer terminal with access to a web of information somewhat more extensive than that available to the uncleared public. He searched and read for hours but found nothing useful. The next day he stayed at home and got onto the Internet and read some more. The day after that he did the same. Then he went back to the lab for a few more hours.

Two weeks after his first and only round of golf, he stood over a white, faintly iridescent golf ball. It had 418 dimples but no logo. He picked it up and walked over to the only window in his office, holding the ball aloft so the late-afternoon sun could fall full on it.

He stared at it for a minute, then softly muttered, "Fuck *me*."

Professor Norman Standish, Ph.D., was ready.

CHAPTER ONE

O'BANYAN'S CASINO
FREMONT STREET, LAS VEGAS

They'd been at it now for thirty-two hours straight. That's a long damned time to be playing poker with nothing but the occasional pee break and a few quick bites of sandwich here and there. After that amount of time it was easy to let your concentration wane, easy to lose focus, and that meant a slow and painful death to a card player. Pros already know what garage amateurs are still learning: that winning in poker has precious little to do with the cards you get, which is why the good players usually win and the bad ones usually lose, even though neither of those camps gets better or worse cards than the other over the long run.

In Texas Hold 'Em, which is what Elmore "No Butt" Whitman was playing right now because it's the only game serious poker players play, you only get two cards to call your own. The other five are community cards, which all the players share. Two cards doesn't give you a lot of options, so they're actually not all that important. What *is* important is what you've learned about how your opponents play the game.

Whitman had the accountant from Pennsylvania figured out in less than two hours. The guy bet small when he had lousy cards, huge when he had good ones. He might as well have turned his cards face up for everyone else to see, and he hadn't lasted past the first morning.

The obstetrician from Atlanta was just as bad. He played "tight," folding unless he had a sure winner, but it was astonishing how fast your stake could get whittled down just by losing antes and blinds, especially when your cards were so transparent that nobody stayed in with you when you finally got around to making a bet.

The New York taxi driver took a little longer. He kept bluffing his way through bad cards, making absurdly huge bets, daring the others to challenge him. The first few times it worked, nobody else being willing to gamble as much as ten grand that the guy didn't have anything. Then one time when he'd shoved $20,000 into the middle, the guy sitting opposite Whitman met the $20,000 and raised another $20,000. The taxi driver only had about $16,000 left. Under table stakes rules he wasn't obligated to put up more than he had, but his options were limited to either betting his last $16,000 or folding. Since he didn't have shit in his hand, and since he didn't have enough money to re-raise and try to scare the big bettor into folding instead, he went out, losing the $20,000 plus the $12,000 he'd already bet. He was so devastated he crumbled completely, and was gone four hands later.

Whitman had eyed the fellow who'd called that bluff with more than a little interest, having barely noticed him before. At about five-ten, with barely a distinguishing feature worth mentioning, he was the most utterly nondescript human being Whitman had ever seen. Average build, average coloring, neatly dressed, but if you turned your head for a second you couldn't recall a single thing he was wearing. And the guy had barely said a word since he first sat down.

The other seven players were knocked out one by one, and most of the other action in the casino had come to a halt as the patrons swarmed to the poker pit to watch the action. Whitman was lapping it up, relishing with anticipation how the admiring throng would watch him take the sheep to the slaughter.

The casino manager was less amused. O'Banyan's didn't make money off an audience, and for all he knew, these two poker players could be at it for another twelve hours, and that wouldn't do at all, which was about the time the quiet player waved him over and said, "Mind if we move this into a private room?" The manager lifted his eyebrows questioningly at Whitman to see if it was okay with him. Whitman didn't have to agree, but he liked O'Banyan's, with its low ceilings, absence of distracting entertainment, cast-off cocktail waitresses and bad lighting. Up on the Strip the suckers treated gambling losses as the price they willingly paid for erupting volcanoes, water fountain ballets and circus acts flying around overhead. O'Banyan's catered to pure gamblers. Among the things they didn't have were house limits. If you wanted to bet a million bucks on a single roll of the dice, you didn't need permission, you just needed the cash. Whitman liked O'Banyan's, and he wanted to be welcomed back, so he nodded his agreement to take the game private, shrugging helplessly toward the disappointed crowd to make sure they understood this wasn't his fault.

Since then it had been just Whitman against this strange guy, and Whitman had no doubt he was going to beat him. It wasn't simply that Whitman was a good poker player; he was damned good, but while that meant that against lesser players he'd come out ahead over the long run, it guaranteed nothing about what would happen on any given day. On any given day he could lose his shirt. Such were the laws of probability.

The reason he knew he was going to beat the other guy was that he'd discovered a tell. A "tell" was a giveaway, a signal given off by a player without his being aware of it that indicated what he was holding. Professional poker players assumed everybody had one and that it was just a matter of figuring out what it was. It was usually something in the eyes, which was why so many players wore sunglasses at the table, but there were other things. The nail salon owner from Thousand Oaks who'd gotten knocked out earlier in the day tugged at her sleeves whenever she had the "nuts," a hand that couldn't be beaten. The importer from Seattle cleared his throat when he was bluffing, and so on.

It had taken a long time for Whitman to read this other guy, though, and when he finally caught on it was like the heavens had opened and rays of light were pouring into his brain. Every time the guy had hot cards, the little finger on his left hand would rub the one next to it. It wasn't a real big movement, barely detectable, in fact, but it was enough. Whitman wore sunglasses and could look at the guy's hand without being noticed. It was important that the guy not see his eyes flick, because that would be a dead giveaway that he'd discovered a tell and the sucker would work to suppress it.

When the last of the other players had left the table, the stranger had about $340,000 in front of him, and Whitman had $140,000. Three hours later, when they agreed to move to the back room, they were even, Whitman having patiently whittled his disadvantage down to nothing. "Patiently" was the key, because he had to purposely lose the occasional hand. If he folded every time he saw the little finger move and raised when it was still, the guy would know he'd been figured out. He might not know exactly how, but he would know he'd been made and he'd take his dough and split.

There was nothing that said he had to stay. In an organized freeze-out tournament you stayed until either all your chips were gone or you'd won everybody else's, but this wasn't a tournament. It was just high-stakes poker under ordinary house rules.

"Say, what's your name?" Whitman asked the stranger as they rose to head for the back room. They ignored their chips, knowing that floor men would scoop them up and move them, and would be completely honest when they did. Without that kind of assurance, there would be no O'Banyan's.

"Eddie," the guy said, taking Whitman's offered hand but not bothering to ask his name in return. Whitman was experienced enough to let that go. Some guys used conversational ploys to throw other players off, annoying them with boring tales about their grandkids or the latest problems with their lawn mowers, but Whitman prided himself on playing a purer kind of poker, one that relied on only two things: knowing the odds and knowing your opponents. The bullshit he could leave to lesser players who had to compensate for their shortcomings with cheap tricks.

Once they were seated the game resumed without delay. The only other person at the table was the dealer, who didn't participate in the game itself but was part of the service provided by the house in exchange for a small "rake" taken periodically from the pots. Seated away from the table were half a dozen onlookers, employees and friends of the house who stayed dead silent and just watched.

The dealer dealt two cards to each man, the "hole" cards, and then five cards into the middle face down. Whitman picked up his hole cards, a pair of threes, and bet $5,000. Eddie met the bet but didn't raise, and then the dealer flipped over three of the community cards, called the "flop," a three, a six, and a seven. Whitman now had three of a kind, a very strong hand. Eddie hesitated, then bet $10,000. Whitman met it and raised another $10,000. Eddie hesitated again and then matched the raise.

The dealer flipped over the fourth card on the table, the "turn" card. It was a deuce, which did nothing for Whitman, but he bet another $10,000. Eddie met it and came back with a $20,000 raise.

Pretending to think, Whitman ducked his head slightly and watched Eddie's hand.

Nothing.

He watched some more. At these kinds of stakes, nobody was going to rush him. Still nothing.

He shook his head, as if to say *I don't believe you got em*, and re-raised another twenty. He watched with satisfaction as his opponent pressed his lips together and then threw down his cards. It was a big pot, and Whitman took the next one, too, and then he let a couple go by. After two hours they were still pretty much even.

There might not have been an advantage in money, but Whitman was starting to get one in stamina. He'd stayed patient, waiting for Eddie to wilt, and it was beginning to pay off. He'd watched as the guy stifled a few yawns and rubbed his eyes occasionally, and as Eddie grew more worn out his tell got more pronounced.

It was time.

Whitman carefully grew his stack of chips to about \$280,000 against Eddie's \$200,000. To have more money on his side was absolutely critical when he went in for the kill. If he had that advantage, there was no way he could get wiped out in a single hand, no matter how much Eddie wagered, because even if Eddie went "all in"—bet everything he had—it would still leave Whitman some money if he met the bet and lost. That would put him one up if it came down to them bluffing against each other. He'd be way down, but he'd be alive, and could patiently work back up again. But if Eddie went all in and lost just one hand, he'd be out of money and that would be the end of it.

On the next hand Whitman drew a six and seven of clubs, and checked: no bet. To his surprise, Eddie didn't offer a bet of his own, a free ride, and the dealer turned up the flop to show two sevens and a nine. The nine and one of the sevens were diamonds. Just like that Whitman had three of a kind. He concentrated on staying perfectly still, not giving anything away.

Eddie threw in \$10,000, a fairly modest wager at this point, and that gave Whitman some pause: What had the guy liked about the flop that made him bet? He probably didn't have a pair in the hole, or he would have bet earlier, so three of a kind was unlikely, but was it possible he was holding two other diamonds? If so, he had a reasonable shot at a flush on the next two cards, whereas Whitman's chances of making a full house to beat it were somewhat less. Eddie's little finger wasn't moving, so he didn't have much else going, and was probably banking on filling in the hand.

Whitman bet $20,000, hoping that would be too rich for Eddie, but it wasn't. Eddie didn't re-raise, but he did meet the bet. The dealer flipped over the turn card: jack of clubs. Couldn't help either of them, and now Eddie was down to a one-in-four chance of buying the flush whereas Whitman was already holding three of a kind. Except that the little finger had begun to twitch, so Eddie thought he had a winning hand. But what the hell was it?

It couldn't be all that strong, based on how Eddie was betting, so that probably meant that he figured Whitman for an even lousier hand, and that he could be beaten with only...two pair! That had to be it! Eddie had two pair and thought it was a winner.

Whitman bet twenty grand to scare him out and now Eddie hesitated. Maybe he'd buy the flush, maybe he'd fill in the full house or trips, but he had to know he was at a disadvantage. The finger was still twitching, though, so the guy was certainly confident, and that was proven when he met the bet, although he didn't raise.

The river card came up queen of hearts. No improvement for Whitman, but he still had three sevens, a pretty good Hold 'Em hand, especially with only two players in the game. But it was probably not good enough to really go to town on, so he checked.

Eddie pushed $150,000 into the pot.

Whitman felt his bowels explode. What the hell was the sonofabitch holding! Had he just bought a third queen—"six tits"—a winning hand? Did he have three nines, and had just gone easy not knowing what would happen to his opponent's hand until now? If so, how did he know Whitman hadn't just bought a third queen? There was only one way he could know that, and that was if he himself was holding two queens and therefore knew Whitman couldn't be. That had to be it.

The worst part when he folded and conceded the pot to Eddie was not knowing for sure what the guy had been holding. The finger told him Eddie had a real hand, that it wasn't a pure bluff, but for all he knew it was two lousy pair and he could have beaten him.

Now it was Eddie who had the money advantage, and Whitman got nervous. One big fuckup and he'd lose it all. Even though he had Eddie's "tell" down pat, there was still a problem: The giveaway finger told him whether Eddie *thought* he had a winning hand, but it didn't tell him if Eddie was *right*. Sure, the guy was a hell of a poker player but he wasn't psychic, for chrissakes. Once in a while he just had to be wrong.

Whitman drew a two and a jack on the next deal and folded immediately when Eddie bet into him, losing his $5,000 ante. Next he drew a pair of threes, bet the now-standard $10,000, and folded when Eddie re-raised. Then it was a pair of kings, and it was Eddie's turn to fold when Whitman hit him hard. It went on like that for a few more hands, both players suddenly ultra-conservative and unwilling to take big chances.

Then Whitman drew a pair of bullets, "pocket aces," the sweetest hole cards in the game. He feigned hesitation, then checked. No way did he want to scare Eddie out this early. This was the one he'd been waiting for ever since he'd arrived in Vegas, and he was going to milk it for all it was worth, maybe even end the game right on this hand.

Eddie bet $50,000, and Whitman nearly fainted. It was pure bullshit! That's the kind of bet you make on two aces and the odds against Eddie having the other two in the deck were astronomical. Yet Eddie's finger was twitching like mad now.

Oh, bliss! Oh, joy! The stupid sonofabitch had a pair of kings and was convinced he was sitting in the catbird's seat! It was the kind of situation Whitman had dreamed about: playing in O'Banyan's, one-on-one with another great player, leading the poor sap to the slaughterhouse. All that was missing was the crowd that was no longer there to watch.

He waited, then waited some more. He fiddled with his cards, scratched his nose, scratched his ass, and finally met the $50,000 bet and hit it back another $50,000, hoping Eddie would see it as a bluff but not surprised when Eddie just matched it and didn't raise.

The flop came up two nines and a jack. Even if Eddie had two pair, they couldn't be higher than his. There was no way Eddie had four nines, because if he'd been holding two to start with he wouldn't have dared bet like that. Nines weren't strong enough. Or maybe he would have bet the first fifty grand as a bluff but he never would have met the re-raise.

Couldn't have three nines either, because that would mean he'd had absolutely nothing to start with, and that also meant he didn't have three jacks. This was getting better all the time.

And then he noticed Eddie's little finger. It was lying still as a dead mackerel. Whatever the dumb jerk had been hoping for on the flop, he hadn't gotten it, and now he was out the hundred large he'd already bet and he was in very serious trouble. If he lost this hand, it would be tough to come back from $140,000 against Whitman's $340,000 but it could be done, with patience and if the asshole didn't fall asleep in the process. More than likely he'd just scoop up his money, still a mighty tidy profit, and slink away, knowing that abandoning the game after nearly two days of play without seeing it to its conclusion would mean he'd get laughed out of O'Banyan's the next time he showed his face. Despite the guy's monumental error, Whitman didn't figure him for a quitter, and he settled in for what was sure to be a few tedious hours of Eddie trying to claw his way back, which wasn't bloody likely given the guy's worn and ashen appearance. So maybe after he folded he would just quit the game after all.

Eddie pushed the rest of his chips into the pot.

Behind his dark glasses Whitman blinked. Usually when you wanted to cash out you stood up and pointed to your stack, a signal to the floor guys to come get your chips and walk you to the cage. Jesus, you don't push them into the middle of the goddamned table and risk getting them mixed up with the pot. Guy like this, he should know better, and Whitman didn't care how tired the dumb sonofabitch was.

Then again, it wasn't possible that he was actually making a bet, was it?

"What've you got left?" Eddie asked quietly.

Unbelievable. After all these hours, did this guy really think he was going to bluff his way into the biggest pot of the game?

Whitman ran his fingers across his stacks of chips and said, "About eighty grand." He moved them into the pot as Eddie took back some of the chips he'd pushed in so that his bet was equal to the $80,000 Whitman had left.

There was no more necessity for bullshit. Since Whitman was out of money, there would be no more betting, and therefore no folding, and therefore no need to hide any cards. The dealer would flip up the turn and river cards, the two players would reveal their hole cards, and the two hands would simply speak for themselves.

With a slight shrug and a sheepish look on his face, as if saying to Eddie, *Gosh, I'm sorry, but you asked for it, buddy,* Elmore "No Butt" Whitman flipped over his bullets. Two pair, aces and nines.

Eddie Caminetti turned up his hole cards to show two nines. Together with the two others already showing on the table, he had four of a kind.

He didn't gloat or smile, or react outwardly in any way at all, just waited politely for Whitman to acknowledge the hand and concede the pot. But nothing happened. So he stood up and held out his hand, and still nothing happened. Eddie had no way of knowing, but Whitman wasn't being rude. He was simply preoccupied with how to re-inflate a pair of lungs that had suddenly collapsed. Unable to breathe, and too stunned even to gasp, he just sat there, looking for all the world like a beached cod in sunglasses whose face was slowly turning blue.

As the casino manager came over to see if oxygen might be required, Eddie signaled the floor men to rack his chips, then walked out of the room, stretching his arms over his head and yawning. For real, this time.

Out in the main casino, Vernon O'Banyan watched from a barstool as Eddie headed for the cashier's cage, two floor men behind him carrying racks full of his chips. O'Banyan waved over the pit boss. "Where's Whitman?"

The pit boss jerked a thumb at the door to the private room. "He's gonna need a minute or two. Couple of the boys'll stay with him."

O'Banyan nodded his approval, then stiffly got to his feet and made his way over to the cage. "Whaddaya say, Eddie?"

Eddie turned at the sound of the familiar voice and smiled. "Hey, Vernon. How's it goin?"

"Good. What the hell'd you do to No Butt?"

"Just played a little poker. So how's Shirley?"

"Good, good. Arthritis actin up a bit, you know how it goes, but she's okay."

"Glad to hear it. Give her my love, will ya?"

"You bet."

O'Banyan watched as his cashier counted up the chips and made notations on a slip of paper, which she then turned around and showed to O'Banyan.

"Nearly half a mill," the owner said. "Leave it on account?"

"Yeah," Eddie replied as he stretched and yawned again. "Take fifty large and hand it around to the boys."

"Thanks, Eddie," one of the floor men said. "Sure appreciate it."

O'Banyan walked Eddie out, the two of them blinking back the bright morning sun. As they shook hands, O'Banyan held on and wouldn't let go. "Don't tell me you used that old pinkie finger bullshit again, Caminetti."

Eddie pulled his hand free, then grabbed O'Banyan's nose and tweaked it lightly. "No idea what the hell you're talking about, Vernon. Now can a guy f'chrissakes go get some sleep?"

CHAPTER TWO

SWITHEN BAIRN
ON AN ISLAND IN SOME OCEAN

There couldn't be a more inviting spot on the planet. An emerald island in an opalescent sea, striped with beaches of crushed pink coral, dotted with palm trees and scattered explosions of bougainvillea, and all of that just a background setting for a golf course so heartbreakingly beautiful you didn't know what you wanted to do more, play it or sleep with it.

"This place gi's me the creeps," Jasper Kronauer muttered.

Winston Jerome Paddington shook his head. "Whole goddamned trouble with you," he said to his corporate counsel, "you're always looking for the bushel insteada the light. How can you gaze upon all this freakin splendor and get the creeps?"

"I'm your lawyer," Kronauer answered. "It's my job to see the bad in everything. Except in this case I'm not making it up."

"Ah, horse-pucky." Paddington dug into his waffle and held a piece up in front of his face. "Only trouble with this place is that this Caminetto character hasn't shown his face."

"Caminetti," Kronauer corrected him.

"Whatever." Paddington popped the waffle chunk into his mouth and began chewing violently. "We bring thirty people for a weeklong confab at huge expense and this host, this *mook,* holes up like a bear in winter."

Kronauer picked disconsolately at his fruit plate. "What I hear, it's better off he does."

"Oh, yeah? Whyzzat?"

Maybe it had to do with Eddie Caminetti's rumored but undocumented meting out of righteous comeuppance to all manner of sinners who'd come to the fabled Swithen Bairn expecting anything but. A "Venus flytrap of a vacation spot," as one of Kronauer's old clients had put it. The client had made millions with an insurance-scamming occupational therapy center, but after a weeklong getaway in the clutches of Caminetti he'd returned home to sell the place and use the funds to establish a string of community medical clinics in some of the poorest neighborhoods in Detroit. And there were other stories as well.

"He didn't get where he is by losing money matches, Winston. He's a very good golfer."

"You miss the whole point, Jasper. Guys *love* to lose to Caminetto."

"Caminetti."

"Whatever. Jacko Trautmann, president of Trans-United? Crazy bastard's been bragging for a year how he lost fifty large on a single hole."

"One hole?"

"Yeah. Caminetto, he says to Trautmann, he says, 'Gimme two strokes on a par-five for fifty grand,' and Trautmann asks him is he nuts, and Caminetto says, 'I'll play the hole with a shovel and a rake.'"

"You mean instead of clubs?"

"Zackly. Trautmann pars, Caminetto shoots bogey and wins."

"That's nuts. Still, no rule says he's got to play with our crew."

"You got any idea how much dough we spent here this week, Jasper?"

"To the penny, Winston."

Their company, Premiere Golf, in the last stage of its $90 million campaign to promote a new golf ball, was hosting two dozen of the most influential sports journalists, on-air commentators and magazine publishers on a no-expense-spared junket of unprecedented scope and opulence. Transportation was by corporate jet, everybody got a private suite, the food was prepared by two French chefs flown in for the occasion, and party favors included handmade and individually inscribed leather golf bags, a set of custom-fitted clubs, three pairs of golf shoes each, and personalized instruction from two currently touring PGA pros. All of this, as Paddington had put it when graciously waving away the inevitable outpourings of gratitude, "just to give you guys the opportunity to write objectively about this great new ball." Which they could do after the unlimited free golf they'd enjoy on the too-gorgeous-for-words Swithen Bairn course.

But influential sports journalists, on-air commentators and magazine publishers got stuff like this all the time. Maybe not quite of this caliber, but all of them had become extremely adept at navigating their way around eBay as they sold off thousands of dollars' worth of corporate freebies under assumed names like "Won-a-Sweepstakes" and "Got-it-in-the-Divorce" and "Had-to-give-up-golf-due-to-illness."

What made this trip different was the unmistakably implied promise of meeting Eddie Caminetti, the low-life hustler from South Florida who'd wound up on the U.S. Ryder Cup team several years ago and pretty much scammed the entire golf world on his way to helping the American team retain the Cup. After that extraordinary tournament, which to the intensely private Eddie had been just another day at the office, so many people had beaten a path to his door he'd had to fake his own death to escape the unwanted glare. He'd resurfaced a year ago at Swithen Bairn, the only place on earth that could absolutely guarantee his privacy because he had total control over who was allowed to set foot on the island. Compared to being invited to play a money round of golf with Eddie Caminetti, getting an audience with the pope was like getting an appointment for a haircut.

"Wasn't part of the deal," Kronauer reminded his boss, "anybody gets to meet Caminetti."

"Fuck that," Paddington mumbled around another chunk of waffle. "Coulda gone to friggin Palm Springs for a third the cost, and on top of—"

"You want your money back?" came a voice from somewhere behind him.

Paddington stopped chewing and looked up at Kronauer, confused. "Whuzzat?"

Kronauer was looking over Paddington's shoulder, and pointed.

"I said," the voice repeated, "do you want your money back?"

The confused CEO spun around. "Holy shit." He swallowed and scrambled to wipe his hands before standing up. "Mr. Caminetto, I'm—"

"Camin—" Kronauer started to correct him, but Eddie held up a hand to stop him and to stop Paddington from standing up.

"Anybody thinks he didn't get his money's worth, he can have his dough back. All of it, no questions asked. Standing rule around here."

"Aw, shit," Paddington said as he sank back onto his seat and smiled a touch too brightly. "Just two crusty old farts bullshitting."

Eddie grabbed a chair from an adjoining table, spun it around and sat down on it backwards. "So what's the problem? Can't be the food, on accounta you brought your own chefs. Your rooms okay? Maybe the golf course?"

"No, no, nothing like that at...jeez, the place is incredible. Hell, you know that already, Mr.—"

"Eddie."

"Yeah. Eddie. It's just that..."

"Just what? C'mon, we're here to please. What's on your mind?"

Paddington slumped back in his seat and surreptitiously took a look around to see if any of his guests were in the vicinity. He wanted it known to as many people as possible that he was having a cuppa with the proprietor of Swithen Bairn. "Thing is, we were kinda hoping that, uh, that maybe you'd play a little golf with some of the guys. You know, a couple bucks here and there, no big deal, just to say we did, see?"

Eddie went stock still for a few seconds. "You want to play a match with me?"

Paddington shifted uncomfortably. "Well, yes...no, no...I mean, yeah sure, not a *match* match, like nothing real formal or anything. Just thinking, you know, you being Eddie Caminetto and all..."

"You were thinking maybe some of your guests might get a kick out of it, that about it?"

The CEO took a breath, looked at Kronauer, then looked down at the table and shrugged. "Just thought it might be nice. You know."

"Chrissakes, Paddington..." Eddie signaled a waiter with a pouring motion, then put his arms on the back of his chair. "Why the hell didn't you say something? What do you think I do around here, clean the fucking toilets? Hell yes, let's play some golf!"

Paddington's mood went from deflated to elated in about a nanosecond. "Square shit?"

"You bet. Whadja have in mind...just wanna hand me the dough right now and save yourself the trouble, or you actually want to play?"

"Fuck you!" Paddington laughed. "Hey, listen, fuck you! I'll kick your ass from the first tee to the last green!"

"Right. Maybe use that piece-a-junk new ball of yours, is that it? What is it, what's it called, Jerkolo?"

"*Circolo*. Like you didn't know damn well. Hey!"

Paddington had yelled out to a pair of men passing by the dining room. They turned at the sound, spotted Eddie and came hurrying over.

"Uh, Winston, listen here," Eddie said in a low voice. "I think maybe we should keep this just between you and me, okay?"

"What are you, kidding me? No way am I gonna—yo, Billy! Steven!" Two more of Paddington's guests came scurrying over.

"What I'm saying," Eddie urged, "you don't want to go public here. Trust me on this."

The CEO ignored him, and within five minutes some fourteen guests of the Premiere Golf Corporation were gathered around, pumping Eddie's hand, getting his autograph and asking him to pose with them for pictures.

"The man offered me a match!" Paddington announced with undisguised glee.

"What's the bet?" someone yelled out.

"Who gives a shit?" someone else responded, and there was congenial laughter all around.

Eddie leaned in close to the host of the affair. "Winston, I'm telling you, you don't want to have all these guys around when we—"

"Hell, I'll play the guy straight up," Paddington bellowed, completely ignoring Eddie, "and all I gotta do is use the Circolo to win!"

More laughter, backslapping, friendly insults flying through the air.

"You use that ball yet, Caminetti?" a voice called out.

"Can't say that I have," Eddie responded. "Not really familiar with what it's all about."

"It's round, Eddie," Paddington announced.

"Round."

"Yep. Now this may come as a surprise, but every damned golf ball up until the Circolo has been *spherical*, see, meaning round-*ish*, but when I say round I'm talking one hunnerd percent goddamned perfectly freakin round. Straighter and farther, both in the air and on the putting green. It's flawless, Eddie, and if I told you how many strokes were lost on account of defects in the shape of golf balls, why, you wouldn't believe it."

"Well, I'll be damned. Wonder why nobody'd ever thought of that before."

"Between you and me?" Paddington leaned in closer so only those within eight miles could hear him. "Nobody knew *how* before, that's why. The technology to make a perfectly round ball? Daunting is what it is. And the cost is astronomical."

"You don't say. So what's a dozen of these babies go for?"

"At retail? About fifty bucks."

"Fifty bucks! And people are buying these things?"

"They will when we release it to the public. But judging by the advance buzz? They'll be lining up."

"Amazing!"

"So what ball do you use, Eddie?" asked Steven Cronenberg, president of the Denver Don's chain of discount golf shops.

"Any soft two-piece that's on sale. Can't tell one from the other."

More laughter. "You can't be serious!" someone said.

"I'm dead serious. Can't tell two brands apart, and never met anybody who could. Never once saw somebody change balls and improve his score. Golf balls are like gasoline: It's all the same stuff, and all that's different is the label and the advertising."

"Well, you're wrong, my friend," Paddington said. "I'll play you straight up, you let me use my ball."

"You got it, Winston."

Paddington slapped his hand on his new buddy's shoulder. "So whaddaya say, Eddie...how much we gonna bet?"

A waiter set a cup in front of Eddie and began filling it with coffee. "How about an even million?"

Paddington's smile faltered for the briefest of seconds as the excited shuffling and chatter from the onlookers died, then came back up to full wattage. "You serious?"

The waiter, whose hand had yet to show the slightest tremor, finished pouring and left. "I'm always serious when it comes to betting on golf, Winston. But really, we should discuss this in private, because—"

"These are my friends, Eddie. These are the people who can make or break a revolutionary product like the Circolo. I have faith in my ball and I'm not afraid to put my money where my mouth is."

"You sure?"

"Absolutely."

Eddie hesitated as the crowd held its breath, fearful that they might get cut out of the excitement. "Suit yourself," he said at last, and a relieved collective sigh went up.

Eddie waved to a nondescript man who'd quietly come into the room some minutes before. He was holding two boxes, each about the size of a thick novel. He handed the boxes to Eddie, who said, "This here's The Piper."

"Like in 'pay the piper,' right?" said Artie Fillmore, golf reporter for *USA Today*. "I heard about him."

"That's the guy." Eddie set the boxes on the table and opened the lids. Each held a dozen golf balls.

As the guests pressed forward for a closer look, Fillmore said, "What are they? I don't see any labels, just letters."

Eddie nodded. "They don't have any labels. One box has all the balls marked with the letter A, and the other, they're all marked B."

"I don't get it," Paddington said.

"Simple. One box came from Kmart, the others are yours. These are what we're gonna use."

"Which is which?" asked Mike McGinty, equipment reviewer for *Golf Weekly*.

"Damned if I know," Eddie replied. "We asked your production supervisor to prepare em."

"Which one do I use?" Paddington asked.

"Either one you want. And I'll use either one you want me to. You can even change yours or mine from shot to shot. It's your call."

Paddington smiled. "You must be kidding. I'll put my ball up against any in the world. It's perfectly round, like I told you. Nothing else can touch it."

"I understand."

"So how's the bet work?" McGinty asked.

"A five-dollar Nassau," Eddie replied.

Silence. Then Artie Fillmore said, "Five bucks? That's the big deal bet here?"

"Yep."

Paddington frowned. "I don't get it. Where does the million come in?"

"Oh, yeah," Eddie said, slapping his head. "Almost forgot about that."

"Okay!" Paddington straightened up, relishing the excitement beaming in from his onlooking guests.

Eddie looked around at the guests. "You sure you want to do this in front of—"

"Absolutely! So what are we betting a million bucks on?"

"Pretty simple, really." Eddie pushed the two boxes toward the CEO. "At the end of the round, just tell me which ones are yours."

CHAPTER THREE

THE NISSAN PRUDENTIAL FRUIT OF THE LOOM TEXACO
WASTE MANAGEMENT (FORMERLY THE VALLEY VIEW)
OPEN EAU CLAIRE, WISCONSIN

What do you think, Bill?" Steve Farley said as the tee box introductions were being made for the next pairing (in which there were three players). "Is this young man a question of too much, too soon, or does he really have what it takes to make it on the PGA Tour in the long term?"

"Well, I'll tell you," Bill Winters replied, "that's about the dumbest fucking question I've ever heard a golf reporter ask, and I've heard some pretty dumb fucking questions. How in the hell can I or anybody else have the slightest goddamned clue what's going on in this guy's head or what he's going to do on tour, and who gives a rat's ass what we think anyway? Watch the fucking match, watch the next *ten* fucking matches, and then you'll know, and what I have to say on the matter is about as relevant as a goddamned—"

At least that's what Winters would like to have said. His face was half-obscured by an absurdly large headset and a boom mike the size of a zucchini, making it largely beside the point that his image was going out over the airwaves at all, never mind that his face was the least interesting thing on the golf course and that he was nowhere near the first tee to begin with but in a booth high up in a tree somewhere on the back nine. He could as easily have done all of this from his office in New York.

That's what he would like to have said, but, being on the air and not wishing to lose his network its license, he replied instead, "That's a most intriguing question, and one that I'm sure is much on people's minds. It's possible we're seeing the future of golf in Albert Auberlain, a virtual nobody who shows up at Q School, blows away the field of would-be pro golfers and then winds up in the top forty of the PGA Tour after his first four tournaments. On the other hand, maybe the real pressure just hasn't sunk in yet, and when it does we'll see some chinks in the armor."

"I think you hit it right on the head, Bill," Farley came back into his own zucchini, nodding so assiduously that his headset slipped forward and covered his eyes.

As the director quickly cut away to a shot of the first tee, Winters muttered, "How can I hit it on the head when all I said was he could go either way?"

Farley turned to him and mouthed *What?* but Winters didn't see it because, now that the reporting duo wasn't video-hot for a few seconds, a production assistant slipped him a note reading, "Don't say *chink* on the air." He balled up the note and threw it away, deciding not to make an issue of it considering how close he'd come to being fired only a year before when he'd referred to the first cut of grass surrounding the green as "frog hair" when French pro Jacques St. Villard was putting.

"Auberlain is coming to the first tee now, Bill."

Winters turned away and sighed. How many times had he told Farley that he was supposed to be talking to the fourteen million people watching on television, not the guy sitting next to him, and why in God's name did he insist on describing for those fourteen million viewers what they could bloody well see for themselves? That conversation had followed Farley's blow-by-blow of the scene on the eighteenth green at the British after Alan Bellamy sank his putt for the win. 'He's turning and hugging his caddy, he's got his arms raised in the air, here comes his wife, a great big hug and he lifts her right off the ground, now here's Joel Fleckheimer grabbing his shoulder in heartfelt congratulations...' Winters had turned to the director, pointed to Farley's boom mike and run his finger across his throat. As soon as the audio had been cut off, he'd grabbed Farley, spun him around and said, 'Will you shut the fuck up!'

Five seconds later the producer called on the hotline and said, "Hey, how come you guys aren't talking?" and afterward tried to explain that on-air reporters didn't just report the game, they themselves were the draw. They had to be. 'Elsewise,' he'd said, 'why in God's name would I pay you assholes three mill a year when I could hire some goddamned radio school student at minimum wage?' Not a bad point, as Winters, a sucker for clear-eyed logic, had been forced to concede.

He sighed again and keyed his mike. "What confidence in a rookie, folks.

This young man carries himself like a veteran, no sign of nerves, keeping up an amiable stream of chatter with fans pressed in against the ropes."

"I don't think Auberlain has forgotten how recently he caddied for Eddie Caminetti at that memorable Ryder Cup, Bill. The man knows his roots, and with all his self-possession, hasn't forgotten that he was just like one of those people behind the ropes not too long ago. And, as you put it so succinctly, he could be back there again in a heartbeat."

Or not, *I also said*. "I think everybody's pulling for him. It's a great story."

"You bet. Just looking at him, you know, there's no swagger. No swagger at all. Confident, for sure, but he's not swaggering a bit."

"You're right, there. There's not a—"

"Let's go to Yasmina down on the turf. Yasmina, what do you think...see any swagger in Auberlain?"

"This is Yasmina down on the first tee here at the Nissan Prudential Fruit of the Loom Texaco Waste Management Open. No, Steve, I don't see an ounce of swagger. Back to you and Bill up in the booth."

"That confirms it, Bill, whadda you think?"

"You bet."

"Just as you said, and you were so right: It's a great story."

It *was* a great story. At least to news reporters it was a story. To Albert Auberlain, it was his life.

When he'd caddied for Eddie Caminetti at the Ryder, he'd been a brown beach ball of a 280-pound high school kid fresh out of the toughest section of East Los Angeles. Eddie didn't like caddies; all he needed was his bag carried, and he wasn't looking for any advice or support or companionship. "Fat Albert" Auberlain had come out to the desert as part of a charity gig where he and several dozen of his inner-city high school classmates, not one of whom had ever touched a golf club before, would get to spend a few hours being taught by a handful of the best golfers in the world. While his friends flailed about helplessly, sending balls dangerously close to the half dozen television cameras in attendance, Auberlain had been taken aside by Eddie and given some serious instruction. Observing the grossly overweight kid's intensity, Eddie had made an on-the-spot decision not to use the caddy that the Ryder organization had dug up for him, instead giving the job to "Fat Albert." The kid didn't even know enough to pull the stick out while Eddie putted, but when a 30-footer came rolling into the hole he exploded into an impromptu dance of such unbridled, blissful joy that the staid crowd, initially shocked into near catatonia, had fallen instantly and madly in love with him.

He'd gone back with Eddie to the hustler's shithole of a home club, the old Ambassador Golf Course in Hallandale, Florida, and dived into learning golf as though his life depended on it, which to some extent it did. Devastated when Eddie faked his own death without telling him, he was on the verge of caving in, giving up, going home, but had somehow managed to discover that he didn't need to depend on anyone else, that he was a whole human being in his own right. He got a job at the shithole club, lost a hundred pounds, caddied for free for anyone who might have something to teach him, and eventually turned himself into an extraordinarily skilled golfer of uncommon consistency and poise.

The people he'd met and learned from in south Florida were constantly extolling his prowess, bragging about him, showing him off to visitors and using him in countless hustles. Finally, after one particularly lucrative outing when he and his pals were in the bar of the old Ambassador, laughing and endlessly recounting every one of his spectacular shots, Auberlain stood up and said, 'Gentlemen, I have a business proposition.'

This was greeted with a chorus of derisive hoots and catcalls, but when Auberlain didn't smile, the room quieted down. 'What I'm proposing is that you guys form a syndicate.'

Marvin Kaminsky banged his beer to the table as he sneered derisively. As a noted trial attorney whose entire practice was devoted to the defense of drug smugglers, sneering derisively was as natural to him as belching was to a college student on spring break in nearby Ft. Lauderdale. 'Yeah, good idea there, Albert,' Kaminsky chortled. 'What're we gonna syndicate?'

As the lawyer turned to milk some laughs from his buddies, Auberlain said, 'Me.'

'Hell you talking about, Albert?'

Auberlain stayed on his feet and picked up his glass of scotch. 'All you pudknockin duffers keep tellin me how godawful good I am. So what I'm sayin here, I got a way we can all make some money off it.'

'Shit,' somebody said, 'we *been* making money off you already!'

That was met with a rousing chorus of cheers, but Auberlain held up his hands for silence. 'I'm not talking about forty, fifty bucks at a time foolin outatowners who don't think a ghetto kid can play golf.'

'So what *are* you talking about?'

'What I'm talking about,' Auberlain replied, 'is me goin on the tour.'

'What tour?' Kaminsky said. 'You mean like a cruise? 'Cause I know some guys can get you a discount on a nice, five-day Caribbean—'

'Not *a* tour, Marvin. *The* tour.'

Silence.

'The PGA Tour,' Auberlain explained.

It was a simple plan he then laid out. Auberlain figured he needed a solid, uninterrupted year to work on his game. He'd need money to house, clothe and feed himself and for incidental expenses and, most importantly, for lessons, from whoever he damned well thought he needed them from, no matter where they were. 'I'm figurin I need a hundred grand,' he said in conclusion.

'Which comes from where?' a voice called out.

'You guys. That's what the syndicate is. We form a corporation whose purpose is to get me on the tour. Y'all fund it with a hundred grand.'

'And?' Kaminsky prompted him. 'What do we get in return?'

'If I get through Q School and qualify for the tour,' Auberlain answered, 'the syndicate gets half my first year's earnings.'

'Oh, that's rich, Al!' Joey Burkhardt yelled out. 'Like we're gonna fork over a hundred large to some kid who says he—'

Burkhardt stopped when he realized nobody else was joining in on his razzing.

Larry deVito, a retired investment banker from Jersey City, tapped at his chin with a forefinger. 'Your earnings...that include endorsement deals?'

'You gotta be kidding!' Burkhardt choked. 'Are you seriously—'

'Hey, Larry,' Kaminsky said softly. 'Do us a favor and shut the fuck up for a second. For the rest of your life, now that I think about it.' He turned back toward Auberlain. 'You were saying?'

Auberlain nodded. 'Includes everything. Somebody cuts a check to me, half goes to the syndicate.'

'What about multiyear endorsements?' Neil Osterrung asked.

'One year's worth. And if there's a signing bonus, we amortize it evenly over the life of the deal to figure the value of a year.'

And so it went. Kaminsky took notes, and after well over an hour somebody asked how shares were to be allocated.

'Straightforward share price,' Osterrung suggested. 'The more you put in, the more you own.'

As others chimed in to consider the implications, Auberlain shook his head. 'No. Leads to complications and bad feelings. Everybody who wants in steps up. We divide a hundred g's by that number of guys, and everybody has an equal chunk.'

'Sounds fair,' deVito agreed. 'But what happens if you don't qualify?'

'Then you lose all your dough,' Auberlain answered.

'Nope,' Kaminsky declared. 'You gotta give us an option on another year. Make that two more years.'

'What's that mean?' Osterrung asked.

'Means we get to fork up another hundred large and Albert here gets another year to try.'

'Okay,' Burkhardt, of all people, said, 'what happens if, after let's say halfway through the second year, Albert decides he's had it and doesn't want to—'

And so it went for another two hours, ironing out the details, considering all the implications and what-if's, getting interim agreements between the syndicators and the syndicatee. At the end, when the conversation had petered out, Kaminsky pulled out a fresh sheet of paper, drew some lines on it and asked, 'So who's in?' and nearly got trampled to death as forty guys scrambled to get their names on that sheet at $2,500 a pop.

Less than a year later Auberlain had plunged into the brackish and terrifying waters of Q School, which wasn't a school at all but a torturous, agonizing and supremely ego-deflating six-round tournament intended to give 133 spent and beaten contenders a one-way ticket straight to the gates of Loser Hell and a handful of lucky bastards (the others always said they were lucky) a pass to a year on the PGA Tour.

Auberlain got the pass. Then he exploded out of the gate and acquitted himself beautifully in his first four pro starts, so endearing himself to the crowd that he wound up with several endorsement deals which, while quite modest by top-ten standards, were nevertheless the stuff of which most unsung rookies couldn't even begin to dream. By the time those were added to his tournament winnings, "Fat Albert" returned to his syndicate participants a staggering 460 percent return on investment, which prompted Joey Burkhardt to lament, "We shoulda given him *two* hundred grand and gotten two years out of him steada just one."

And now here he was at the Nissan Prudential Fruit of the Loom Texaco Waste Management (formerly the Valley View) Open. He ranked thirty-eighth on the money list, but was so rock-solid, consistent and unflappable that there was talk that Ryder Cup U.S. team captain Joel Fleckheimer might seriously consider him as one of his discretionary picks for that biennial United States-versus-Europe contest. The Ryder put such enormous pressure on the participants that mental fortitude was valued at least as much as pure golf skill. Besides, Auberlain was such a personable crowd-pleaser that no one would decry the choice...unless of course the U.S. team lost, in which case they'd call for Fleckheimer's head on a stick.

"Coming to the first tee with the ten-twenty starting time," the announcer intoned, "Mr. Albert Auberlain of Hallandale, Florida!"

Wild applause and shouts erupted from the crowd. Auberlain, as was customary, showed his ball to the other two members of his pairing and then teed it up before acknowledging the enthusiastic spectators with the standard two-fingered half-salute off his cap. He stood back from the ball and swung his driver a few times, not so much to loosen up but to give the enraptured crowd a chance to settle down. When the noise had pretty much abated and only the shuffling of feet and fabric remained to attest to the presence of the onlookers, Auberlain walked back to the ball and took his stance.

Setting the club head down behind the ball somewhat carelessly, he looked to his left and surveyed the fairway, planting firmly in his mind the image of his intended landing spot, first visualizing precisely how each part of his body would move to get it there, then shoving that aside and mentally stepping back to see the movement as a single integrated, indivisible and exquisitely coordinated whole. Then he turned back to the ball and this time positioned the club face exactly where he liked it, half an inch behind and resting lightly on the grass. He exhaled, and as his breath left him, he completely suppressed every detail of what he'd just spent time envisioning, turning the task over to the muscles, neurons and synapses that had been through this a million times and knew exactly what to do.

Keeping his head so still it looked like it had been painted against the sky, Auberlain brought the club slowly back and up and around. When it seemed impossible that it could go back any further, it did, and still kept going, finally pointing almost at his left foot before he clicked into reverse, and then slowness was no longer part of the equation. By the time the club was once again straight up over his head it had already begun to blur, and when it was to his side and parallel to the ground it was essentially invisible, moving so fast it made a ripping sound through the air trying in vain to get out of its way, and still it accelerated. As it finally got ready to slam into the hapless ball, the club head was moving at over 120 miles per hour.

The awestruck crowd gasped as club head and ball at last made contact, whipped their heads to the side to watch it scream away like an asteroid in reverse, frowned in puzzlement and shielded their eyes with their programs as it failed to materialize along the expected trajectory, gasped again as, one by one, they caught sight of it, a pathetic, wobbling glob of dimpled Surlyn giving a passable impression of a detached hemorrhoid rather than a professional golf shot.

"You da—!"

"Get in the—!"

Half-completed cries of the idiotic standards shouted out by the token brain-damage patients that seemed to show up at every golf tournament were the first external stimuli Auberlain noticed after he realized his ball was about to dribble into the fringes of the crowd with so little momentum people weren't even scrambling to get out of its way. It plopped onto the soft ground with an ignominious sound not unlike that of a diarrheic cow going poo on fresh mud, a sound that was clearly audible around the tee box because it was coming from less than fifty yards away.

Auberlain remained poised in his follow-through. The crowd slowly turned back to look at him, in much the same way one turns to view a train wreck or a sudden eruption of boils. He stayed that way, elbows high in the air, the club hanging over his left shoulder, for an excruciatingly long time. He just didn't know what to do. He'd never had to uncoil from his follow-through after hitting a drive like that before, and it was a totally alien feeling to have to acknowledge that the shot was now over even though the ball was still right over *there* when it should have been far enough away to be visible only with the Hubble.

He couldn't stand there like that all day, so he slowly let his arms drop, and the club with it, acutely aware that every slight move he made was drawing more and more eyes to him.

He'd damned near missed the ball altogether, barely catching it with the toe of the club head. It would have been better if he *had* missed, because then he could have passed it off as a practice shot, or a little joke with the crowd, there being not a single sentient entity within eight light-years of the tee box who would have considered for even a nanosecond that Albert Auberlain had actually intended to hit the ball.

"What in the flaming hell was that?" Steve Farley asked of fourteen million viewers.

"Damned if I know, Steve," Bill Winters responded.

Auberlain felt the same way as he had when he'd first found out that his Aunt Roberta used to be his Uncle Robert.

There were no words to convey that feeling and therefore no way to cope with it. It was as if his entire universe had suddenly shifted a few degrees sideways, except that, since he'd never paid much attention to how it had been oriented in the first place, he wasn't quite sure what had happened. All he knew was that something had, and whatever it was, it was awful. Terrible.

Disoriented and suddenly afraid, he tried to shift into autopilot. *What is it you do after you've hit your shot? Oh yeah*...He handed the driver to his caddy and put his left foot in front of his right, then his right in front of his left. *That's called, uh, walking! Good! I'm making progress.*

Now that he pretty much had walking down pat, it was time to steer. *Toward the ball, that's it. Easy, now...*

"Shake it off, Albert!" he heard an unfamiliar voice call out.

Am I supposed to know who that was?

"Don't mean shit, Albert!" another voice cried. "Seventy-one holes still to go!"

"You can do it!" a whole choir began babbling in chaotic dyssynchrony.

Do it? Do what? Oh, yeah...I'm in a golf tournament.

"It's just one shot, Auberlain!"

"Nerves, baby! You'll get over it!"

"That one's history! Brand new shot comin up!"

Auberlain stopped dead. *What was it that last guy said?* He turned, and saw the guy. "What?"

The guy's smile, nervous to begin with, devolved into an upside-down happy face that threatened to break out into trembling sobs at any moment. The number thirty-eight professional golfer in the world, after hitting the number one worst professional golf shot in the world, had stopped walking and was looking at him, asking him what he'd said.

"I...jeez...didn't mean to...Criminy, Mr. Auberlain!"

But Auberlain was no longer listening. His caddy had pushed lightly on his arm, propelling him forward.

New shot comin up!

That was it. *Ohchristalmighty!*

"Come on, Albert," the caddy was saying. "Let's think about the next shot."

The next shot? The next shot?

"Come on now..."

Fuck the next shot! Fuck you! Fuck this whole fucking game...!

But there was no way around it. Whatever small piece of Auberlain's brain was responsible for protecting the rest of its host was telling him that the stuff of tabloid news was in the making here. That every two-bit, sit-on-your-ass-and-pretend-you're-a-real-reporter television news reader was going to endlessly replay that shot until a war or a car chase came around to displace it was a sure-bet given. All that mattered now was how he handled himself once the damage was done. If he smashed a monster out of this mess, parred the hole and then went on to win the tournament, they'd kid him about it, sure, but always in the context of a historically titanic, up-by-his-own-bootstraps feat of mental strength and self-discipline that would be an inspiration for motivational locker room speeches for centuries to come. 'Remember the time Albert Auberlain duffed one on the first shot of the tournament, roused himself, dug deep down to a hidden place only true champions know, shook it off and came back to...' etc., etc.

Yeah! That's how he'd play it! Like a real champion! *All those on-the-sideline bastards asking all those dumb-ass questions about do I got it or don't? Let em eat my shit!*

Auberlain straightened up and stiffened his spine and walked about ten paces like that, and then his erect posture turned back into a question mark because an awful reality hit him—hard—just as his ball came into view.

He had no goddamned idea why he'd hit that shot so bad.

None. Nada. Zip.

He was sure that, were he to watch an ultra-slo-mo replay, every centimeter and microsecond of that swing would be exactly where and how it was supposed to be. It had felt perfect. It *was* perfect. In fact, Auberlain knew with a dead certainty that everything about that shot was perfect except one thing, and that was that it hadn't worked. The ball had met the club face at the toe—the very edge of the toe—instead of in the middle.

He hadn't a clue why.

And therefore he had no way to fix it. How do you fix something that had nothing wrong with it except that it hadn't worked?

"Okay, what are you thinking?"

Huh? What?

"Might be a three-iron, pick it up outta that rough stuff, but on the other hand, still bein so far from the green, maybe a five-wood, on accounta why play it safe at this point, knowmsayin? Wait! Seven-wood! Yeah, that'd—

whoops, we ain't carryin a seven-wood. Okay...what'll it be?"

It was his caddy. They'd stopped walking, somehow having arrived at the ball. Spectators were shoving each other trying to get into position to see his next shot.

My next shot...

"Whaddaya say, Albert?"

"I don't know what to do."

"Okay, look, it's still early. Just take the three-iron, let's get it the hell back onto the fairway, you'll have about one-eighty in and the way you approach, why I bet you can—"

Listen, don't you get it? I. Don't. Know. What. To. Do!

"Albert?"

I don't know how to swing. If I swing the way I just did, I'll duff it again, but I don't know what to change because I don't know what went wrong!

The caddy laughed nervously and looked around, then leaned in close to his man. "Listen, goddamnit," he hissed as he tried to maintain his smile. He had no doubt that every television camera in the vicinity had full-framed the two of them, and those guys in the broadcast booth had fourteen million people on three continents holding their collective breath as though the next thirty seconds would rank with that kid stuck down a well fifty years ago on the Hushed Expectation scale. "You gotta hit this shot, Albert. It don't hardly matter, you hit it good or not, but if you don't at least try, a couple million people gonna think Albert Auberlain his own self is a *pussy*, you hear what I'm tellin you? A coast-to-coast, network-class *pussy!*"

The caddy yanked a three-iron out of the bag, opened Auberlain's hand and slapped the grip into it. "And I ain't goin down in golf history as the guy who caddied for no *pussy*".

The caddy took a half step to the side, folded his arms, rubbed at his chin, rocked his head back and forth and then nodded. Frowning in thoughtfulness he muttered something to Albert that was inaudible to television viewers but looked like, "I agree, that's the way to go," but in fact was "Hit the goddamned ball, motherfucker! Nod your goddamned head!"

Auberlain dutifully nodded, without knowing quite why, and the caddy stepped back. A murmur swept over the crowd.

"Looks like he's made up his mind, Bill," Steve Farley said into his zucchini.

"Sure does," Bill Winters said into his, but it didn't look like that to him at all. He knew this golfer well and to him it looked like space aliens had just stolen his pancreas, and Auberlain, not knowing what a pancreas was, kind of sensed something was missing but wasn't quite sure what.

Auberlain autonomically took up a position over the ball and swung the three-iron a few times, then stopped when he realized he didn't know how it had gotten into his hands. For the first time he took a look at the fairway and green from this angle, then took note of how the ball was sitting. He was in terrible position but knew this was no time to be conservative. *What the hell am I doing holding a—*

He stepped back and turned to his bag, which was resting upright on the ground next to the caddy. He held the iron out and the caddy grabbed it, then Auberlain reached into the bag himself and pulled out a three-wood.

"Now you talkin!" the caddy said encouragingly.

But Auberlain didn't hear him.

"What's he got there, Bill...zat a three-wood?"

"I do believe it—"

"Yasmina, what's he got there, a three-wood?"

"Stand by a second while I...yes, Steve, I can confirm that with certainty. It is a three-wood. I repeat, Albert Auberlain has taken out a three-wood!"

"Well, whaddaya know. He's going for it! How about that! What d'you think, Bill?"

I think I'll wait until he hits *it, is what I think. Any schmuck can take it out, despite Yasmina making it sound like he'd taken out a cure for cancer.* "You have to admire that kind of courage, folks. Reminds me of the time Mack Merriwell used a putter out of a sand trap back in—"

"I'd say he's pretty much made up his mind here, Bill. Yasmina, down on the course, does it look to you like—"

Auberlain took a deep breath and set back up over the ball. Nerves he never even knew he had were screaming at him. He hefted the club a few times, trying to get the feel of it, then took one last look at the target area, set the club head down behind the ball and let it gently settle onto the grass.

Nothing left to do but swing.

But swing how? He only knew one way, which he'd always thought was the right way. It had worked a million times before, so just do it again and all will be well.

But hang on a second. Isn't that what he'd just done back on the tee? Swung like he'd always done? And look what had happened!

Fine. So do something else.

But what? He still didn't know what he'd done wrong. So what could he change?

Don't change anything! Just look at it statistically: A million times it worked like a charm, and once it didn't. Those are pretty good odds, no? So you've got a million good ones coming before you screw up again. Can't beat that.

Yeah! He waggled his hips and craned his neck a little to loosen it up, then got ready to swing.

But wait: Sounds good on paper, but isn't that the same logic you used back on the tee? And look where that got you.

But what else can I do!

Change something.

Change what?

"Come on, Albert!"

Change what?

Don't change anything! You don't need to!

Yeah! Except...

"Albert, goddamnit!"

The caddy was right. *Doesn't matter anymore how I do it, I gotta just do it!*

Albert gritted his teeth, steadied himself as best he could, then took the club back and swung.

In the broadcast booth up in the tree, even Steve Farley had stopped speaking as he waited for Auberlain to hit the ball. When he saw the club go up and pause at the top, he unconsciously grabbed Bill Winters' forearm and squeezed, not letting up until the club had come all the way down and through.

"Holy fuck," he mumbled before a technician could hit the kill switch.

Next to him Winters, who prior to becoming a sportscaster had covered civil insurrection in Uganda, an outbreak of Ebola virus in Manchuria and a public beheading in Yemen, couldn't bear to watch the aftermath of Auberlain's atrocious shot and turned away from his monitor.

"Ain't seen nothin that ugly since my three-year-old threw up dog food," Yasmina said, not realizing that the same technician who'd killed Farley's zucchini had patched hers in instead.

But no viewers phoned in to complain.

How could you blame someone who'd only spoken the truth?

CHAPTER FOUR

THE CATHEDRAL CANYON COUNTRY CLUB
CATHEDRAL CITY, CALIFORNIA

Guy's absolutely amazing," club pro Terry Cleghorn said, watching a member practicing chip shots just below the clubhouse.

"Oh, yeah?" Eddie Caminetti had watched the man hit about two dozen shots onto the green from the other side of a practice bunker. He'd gotten a goodly number of them very close. "Whyzzat?"

"Nothing rattles him," Cleghorn answered. "He was a Marine chopper pilot. Somalia, Afghanistan, rescue missions in the Himalayas. You can talk on your cell phone while he's hitting and he doesn't even hear it."

"No shit."

"God's truth. Concentration of a Tibetan monk."

"What's his name?"

"Travis Woodhaven. And he loves to bet."

"Does he now."

"Yeah. But this is one guy you're not gonna shake up, Caminetti. Hell, he *loves* distractions. Prides himself on ignoring them."

"You don't say."

"I do say. Wanna set something up? Man's got dough."

"From where?"

"Lecture circuit. They call him The Rock."

"Gimme a break."

"Didn't say he calls *himself* that. C'mon."

A smallish man in a tweed beret stood close by. He wasn't holding any clubs, wasn't even dressed for golf. Just standing there. Eddie gave him a quick glance, and then he and Cleghorn made their way across the cart staging area and down a short hill to the practice green. Woodhaven had his back to them as they drew close, and was in the middle of his back swing when Cleghorn yelled, "Travis!"

Woodhaven never broke his fluid swing, and popped a ball up to within two feet of the pin. "You know better, Cleg." He turned and flashed a tight-lipped, military smile, crow's feet wrinkling up his craggy, weather-beaten face.

"One's these days, boy. Want you to meet a friend of—"

"You serious, son? I know who this is." Woodhaven stuck out his hand. "Travis Woodhaven."

Eddie took his hand, expecting to have his fingers crushed, and he wasn't disappointed. "Pleased to meet you. Cleg here says you like to lay a few bucks down now and again. I'm here alone and looking for a friendly bet, if you're up for it."

"Always up for it. What'd you have in mind, dollar-wise?"

"Up to you."

Woodhaven put his wedge up behind his shoulders and rested his arms on it, his hands dangling forward. "Gotta tell you, Eddie: I'm not one of those guys willing to lose a bunch of money just for the privilege of playing the legendary Eddie Caminetti."

Eddie grinned. "Glad to hear it. Those kinda guys, what a bore." He looked around, then leaned in closer to Woodhaven. "I beg em to just wire me the dough in exchange for me swearing to their buddies they really played me!"

Woodhaven, unable to hide his gratification at being taken into Eddie's confidence, chuckled appreciatively. "So we understand each other. What kind of index you play?"

"He's scratch," Cleg volunteered. "You can take my word for it. And you're still a six, right?"

"Right. So whaddaya say, Eddie...give me three a side, five hundred bucks three ways?" Woodhaven was proposing a standard Nassau, $500 for whoever won the most holes on the front, $500 for the most on the back, and $500 for the most overall.

"Sounds good," Eddie answered easily.

"Great."

"Only..."

Woodhaven took the club off his shoulder and stepped back. "Oh, here comes the malarkey!"

Eddie shook his head. "No malarkey. I was just thinking..."

"Thinking what?" Woodhaven prompted, on guard and wary.

Eddie folded his arms and scratched his chin with a thumb. "Cleg here says you're a real steady golfer. Don't get rattled much, that right?"

Woodhaven looked down modestly. "Been in a lot of combat. Shot at, shot up, shot down...somebody sneezing in the middle of my swing isn't going to jar me much."

"Yeah." Eddie thought for a few seconds. "Say, I got an idea, make this a little more fun."

Alert to shenanigans, Woodhaven said, "I'm listening."

"Okay, how's this: First off, I'll spot you four strokes a side instead of three."

"And in exchange?"

Eddie smiled broadly and held out his hands. "You let me scream at you in the middle of your swing."

Woodhaven said, "Going to make for a rather noisy—"

"Not every time. Just twice, whenever I want."

Woodhaven waited for the rest, and when no more came he said, "That's it?"

"That's it."

"You get to yell twice in the whole round and I get two extra strokes?"

"You got it."

Woodhaven thought about it, examined it from every angle, looked for loopholes and misleading language. "I don't get it," he finally announced.

"Get what?"

"Any of it. You're just handing me two strokes. Even if you do shake me up, which you won't, all it costs me is two strokes at the most, so where's your upside? I just don't get it. What's the gimmick?"

"No gimmick, Travis."

"I don't know. Sounds fishy to me."

"One thing I can tell you, Travis," Cleghorn said. "I've known this guy for a long time. He's one sly, too-clever sonofabitch but he never, and I mean *never*, bullshits you."

Woodhaven looked unconvinced.

"Tell you what, Travis..." Eddie began.

"Oh, boy, here it comes!" Cleghorn said, rolling his eyes.

"Real simple. You think I lied or left something out or misled you in any way, you don't have to pay up at the end."

"You're kidding."

Eddie shook his head. "No questions asked. You think I'm full of shit, you don't pay."

"And if I win?"

"I pay up on the spot."

"He's not pulling your leg," Cleghorn said. "He makes the same offer to every person he bets, no exceptions."

"That true?"

"I'm your witness," Cleghorn assured him.

"Hard to argue with a guarantee like that," Woodhaven had to agree.

"Reputation like mine?" Eddie said. "Who the hell would play me without it, am I right?"

"Good point. Okay, let's do it! Cleg, what nines are we playing?"

"Arroyo and Mountain," Cleghorn answered. "I'll make sure you go out as a twosome."

"Thanks. You all set, Eddie? I got my own cart, and you're welcome to ride with me."

"Sounds good."

As Woodhaven went off to get the cart, Eddie turned to Cleghorn and pointed back toward the clubhouse with his elbow. "Who's that little guy with the hat?"

Cleghorn turned and looked where Eddie was pointing. "Beats me. Never seen him before. Why?"

"No reason. Thought he was looking our way."

Cleghorn grinned and gave Eddie a playful shove. "Hell, Caminetti. You're famous, remember?"

"He's not looking at me like I'm famous."

"Forget him. Go have your round, and don't forget to tell me what happens."

Eddie walked back up to the cart area and looked hard at the little man, who turned away in embarrassment at having been found out.

When Eddie was in the cart with Woodhaven and heading for the first tee, he turned back to see the little guy follow Cleghorn into the clubhouse and tap him on the shoulder.

"Let me ask you something, Eddie," Woodhaven said as they drove down to the first tee.

"Shoot."

"Why do you think people love this game so much? I mean, chasing a little white ball around trying to put it in a hole? How stupid can it get?"

"Most games are stupid," Eddie replied. "The only ones that aren't are the ones that came outta real work kinds of stuff."

"Such as?"

"Well, take log-rolling. Hey, don't laugh. Log-rolling makes sense on account of it's based on something some guys really do for a living. Same thing for auto racing, and even shooting with bow and arrows. Those are useful skills in real life. Or were once. Running, weightlifting, target shooting..."

"Okay..."

"But baseball? Basketball, bowling, golf? They're all stupid. They're all based on made-up rules that have nothing to do with real life. But the thing is, they're all fun, and the only thing that's really stupid is askin, 'Isn't golf a stupid game.'"

"All true. Except it doesn't get to my question, which is how come we love it so much, often to the point of unhealthy obsession."

"I know. So what do you think?"

Woodhaven looked around, taking in the stark and dramatic scenery, which was dominated by San Jacinto, one of the steepest mountains in North America. It sprang up out of the flat desert floor and slashed its way over two miles straight up, a looming presence that seemed to be the only thing in the area connecting the sky to the earth.

"I think it's because it's outdoors," Woodhaven said. "It's played in the open, in fresh air, at least if you don't count Rancho Park in L.A. or Van Cortlandt in the Bronx."

Eddie smiled, but didn't let the joke get in the way. "That's true of baseball and football, too. Those're played outside, so that doesn't answer your question."

"Guess not."

They drew up to the par-five first hole of the Arroyo course, one of three nines comprising the twenty-seven holes at Cathedral Canyon. Woodhaven pulled a driver out of his bag and took a few easy practice swings. "Just to make sure I understand," he said, "I get four strokes a side and you get to yell twice during the round, that right?"

"That's it," Eddie answered. "Don't look for any tricks, Travis. You already know you can call bullshit on me at the end so why would I mess around?"

"I still don't get it, but what the hell. Want me to hit first?"

"Be my guest." Eddie also took a driver and followed Woodhaven to the tee box, taking up a position about ten feet back and a few feet to the left of him. Woodhaven bent over to tee up his ball, stepped back and took a few vigorous practice swings, then gripped his club carefully and got into his stance. Calming himself, he took one last look down the fairway to fix his target area in his mind, then set the club behind the ball and willed himself to stillness. Wasting little time, he took the club back smoothly, then brought it up and around his left shoulder, pausing momentarily at the top.

At the exact moment he started his downswing, Eddie let loose a scream so loud and bloodcurdling it turned heads as far away as the tee box of the fourth hole on the Mountain nine.

But it didn't turn Woodhaven's. His composure didn't waver one bit, and he drove his ball some 260 yards, setting it down in the middle of the fairway just left of a bunker and with a clear line toward the green.

Smiling at Eddie, he picked up his tee and walked away from the tee markers.

"Beauty!" Eddie said with genuine admiration.

"You got one left now, right?"

"That's it. Just one."

Eddie's own shot was some fifteen yards short of Woodhaven's but was also very well struck and in excellent position.

"Nice one yourself." Woodhaven stuck his driver back in the bag, waited for Eddie to do the same, and then they were off down the fairway.

Eddie was away, and too far from the tricky and well-protected green to risk trying to get there in two shots, so he laid up about forty yards in front.

"Smart play," Woodhaven said.

"Thanks. What're you gonna do?"

Woodhaven eyed his shot as they drove up to his ball. "Well, I think I can make it. Give it a go, anyway."

"Hit it smooth," Eddie said encouragingly.

Woodhaven stopped the cart and grabbed a three-wood as he came around the back. He didn't break his stride when he noticed Eddie getting out of the cart as well, but checked from the corner of his eye to see where he was standing before turning his concentration back to the ball. Trying not to be obvious, he checked once more without turning his head, then let loose.

"Not a bad try," Eddie said as the ball faded away from the green and landed well to the right and short. "Least you didn't catch the bunker."

"Yeah."

Eddie was away once more and hit a soft sand wedge to within eight feet of the pin. Woodhaven used a sand wedge as well, but landed only about four feet away. Eddie missed his putt by less than two inches. Woodhaven conceded the par, then sank his own putt for a birdie.

"Nice!" Eddie said. "Hell, you stroked this hole and didn't even need it."

"Take em any way I can," Woodhaven replied amiably.

On the tee box of the par-four number two hole, Woodhaven, who had the honors, made sure to gauge where Eddie was standing before he swung. On that last three-wood shot, he'd caught him out of the corner of his eye just as he'd reached the top of his backswing, and hadn't expected it. As he turned slightly this time, he thought he saw Eddie somewhat poised—crouched, maybe—rather than just relaxed. But he pushed it out of his mind and forced his full attention to his shot, and swung, perhaps just a tad too hurriedly so as not to let the thought of what Eddie might be doing intrude.

Eddie winced as he watched the ball sail into a bunker just shy of the

150-yard stake. "Rats! Tough break."

"I think I can get out of it pretty good," Woodhaven said jauntily as he retrieved his tee.

"Yeah. Looks like you got a pretty good lie."

Eddie teed up and hit one 225 down the middle.

"Three-wood, eh?" Woodhaven said.

"Yeah. Kinda narrow for me, and it's not that long, so I figure, play it safe."

"Not a bad strategy."

At the bunker, Woodhaven assessed the lie, the height of the trap's edge and the distance to the green. "Four-iron, I'm thinking."

"Makes sense. Keep it smooth."

As Woodhaven stepped into the bunker and got set up, Eddie got out of the cart and walked over to the edge, directly behind Woodhaven but well out of his way. Woodhaven hesitated, not wanting to turn around and see where he was. He was sure Eddie wasn't standing too close, or anywhere near too close, but he would like to have known exactly where he was. And what he was doing, or was getting ready to do.

Taking a deep breath and letting it out slowly, he settled down over the ball, swung, hit too far down into the sand and sent the ball thudding into the forward edge of the trap.

"Fuck!" he spat.

Eddie, as was the only proper course of action when another golfer was angry with himself, stayed silent. Woodhaven used a sand wedge to get the ball safely out of the trap, and still had eighty yards to go, lying three. Eddie put his ball on the green, then they drove up to Woodhaven's. He took a lob wedge and spent a long time trying to gauge the shot. There was a breeze from the east, the flag was up on the back tier of the green and he had a slight downhill lie. He made up his mind how he intended to swing, and this time tried to figure out what Eddie was doing by just listening. But Eddie, unfailingly polite, didn't make a sound.

Woodhaven backed away from his shot. "Now, just so I understand," he said, turning to Eddie and letting the club head drop to the ground. "You've got one yell coming, but you're not allowed to make any small noises, are you? Rattling clubs or change in your pocket, anything like that?"

"Damn, Travis!" Eddie said, looking genuinely horror-stricken as he dropped back onto the passenger seat of the cart. "Have I been making any—"

"No! No!" Woodhaven rushed to reassure him. "Not at all! I'm just saying...for the future, you know. Here on in. Can you—"

"No way in the world!" Eddie exclaimed. "Hell no, Travis! Strict etiquette all the way. Jeez, I'm sorry. I should've made it clear that there's absolutely no other—"

Woodhaven quickly held up a hand to stop the apologetic flood. "I get it, Eddie. Didn't at all mean to imply that you were, you know...I was just—"

"Sure, I get you. Glad we got that squared away early."

"Me, too."

"You bet."

"Right. Well, all right then. Okay."

Woodhaven turned back to his ball, and tried to remember how he'd planned to hit it. Wind, second tier, downhill lie... okay, he remembered, and started to settle down over his ball.

Eddie quietly got out of the cart.

Woodhaven took a shuddering breath and hit the ball forty yards left of the green. "Fuck!" he hissed, and conceded the hole.

"Bad luck," Eddie said as they drove to the par-three third.

Woodhaven picked up after landing his tee shot in the water.

"Tough break, Travis," Eddie sympathized on their way to the fourth.

Woodhaven three-putted from twelve feet away.

Eddie thought it best to stay quiet on the way to the fifth, which he bogeyed and Woodhaven tripled.

On the par-three sixth hole, a difficult 170-yard downhill to a well-protected green, Woodhaven took a towel clipped to his bag and rubbed his face—hard—then re-clipped the towel and looked at the green. The blue flag indicated that the hole was toward the back. He fingered his clubs, unable to decide between a seven and a six. He kept still when he sensed Eddie was about to swing, but didn't look toward the tee box. When the sweet click of a well-struck ball reached his ears, he glanced at the green and saw a ball settle softly onto the front section.

"Damn," Eddie said. "Got about a fifty footer there." He stooped to pick up his tee. "Ah, well... at least it's uphill, right?"

Woodhaven didn't answer. He didn't feel like speaking. On the other hand... "Mind, if I, uh, ask you..."

"Huh? Oh, yeah, sure." Eddie held out his club. "Seven-iron. Musta teed it up too high. I hit it pretty good and only caught the front."

Woodhaven nodded, touched his six-iron, touched the seven, touched the six again, unable to decide.

If Eddie was annoyed or puzzled, he didn't say anything, just stayed quiet.

"Can't seem to...can't decide..."

"Yeah," Eddie responded sympathetically. "Between clubs, eh? Well, there's no hurry. Just take your time."

It wasn't that. Woodhaven wouldn't have been able say what it was, if asked, but it wasn't that. There was just something so nice about standing there, leafing through his irons, trying to make up his mind, thinking about the shot. Something so nice about...

...not having to hit just yet.

But he was The Rock. And this was ridiculous.

He played with guys who got cell phone calls, blew their noses, yelled out to friends three holes away and belched three beers at once in the middle of his backswing. None of it ever bothered him, *ever*.

He was The Rock, and this was getting goddamned ridiculous.

He yanked a six-iron out of his bag and strode purposefully to the tee box. He smacked his club into the ground, raising a small welt of soft earth, and set his ball on it instead of using a tee. He worked the grip in his hands and cast a baleful eye at the beckoning green, then hitched his shoulders, took his stance, and nailed his eyes to the ball.

In the corner of his vision, he saw Eddie's feet a respectful fifteen feet away.

Woodhaven sniffled, stood up, then bent back down and put the club head behind the ball.

Eddie didn't move.

Woodhaven focused his vision back to the ball, then wiggled his feet and re-set them. Eddie was safely out of his field of view.

He re-gripped, just to make a hundred percent sure his hands were locked in and correctly positioned. Yep, right smack on the money, totally comfortable.

He sensed no movement behind him. Absolutely nothing. Couldn't even hear breathing.

Okay, then. Adjust a little, and slowly lower the club until the head barely touches the grass.

Woodhaven took a deep breath and let it out. *Feet shoulder-width apart,* he said to himself. *Hands slightly behind the ball, knees bent, shoulders square to the target...*

He took one last look at the green.

What could possibly go wrong?

He swung.

By the time they finished up, there was barely enough left of Woodhaven's brain to allow him to write a check for $1,500 without throwing up all over his golf cart.

Cleghorn came out of the clubhouse, took one look at Woodhaven and waved for a cart boy to come and drive him back to his condo near the eighth hole on the Lake nine. "And don't leave until he's inside the house and sitting down."

"What about his cart?" the kid asked as he undid a strap and lifted Eddie's bag off.

Cleghorn looked over at Woodhaven, who was well within earshot but might as well have been on Neptune. "Stick it in the cart barn," the pro replied. "He won't be needing it for a while."

Eddie had a cigarette halfway to his mouth when he spotted the guy with the tweed beret. He decided maybe it was time to confront him, but as he started forward the little man did the same and headed his way. Eddie lit the cigarette and waited for him.

"Mr. Caminetti?" the guy said tentatively.

Eddie nodded.

"Yes. Well, I'm Norman Standish."

"Good for you."

Standish smiled shyly. "Suppose I must apologize. Please forgive me for seeming to stalk you. I assure you I had no intention of giving offense."

Eddie decided to give the guy a break. "None taken."

Standish tilted his chin at Woodhaven's cart, which was disappearing toward the parking lot. "I take it you screamed at him only once."

Eddie had started to shake out the match but stopped. "Scuse me?"

"Mr. Cleghorn told me about your wager. Most clever. I'm assuming you yelled at him once, then never did it again, correct?"

Eddie finished shaking out the match. "On his first swing."

Standish grinned. "Splendid!"

"Listen, don't mean to be rude here, but was there something—"

"Ah! Yes, I'm sorry. As I said, my name is—"

"Norman Standish. I got that part."

"Sorry. I'm a professor of physics, and—"

"Really. Where at?"

"Caltech. That's the California Institute of—"

"I know what it is."

"Sorry again. You being from the East, I wasn't sure—"

"I could be from the Congo and know what Caltech is. And how come you know where I'm from?"

"Did a little research. After all, well, that is my forte, isn't it? Research?"

"I'm sure it is. Now—"

"I have a business proposition for you, Mr. Caminetti."

Well, there it was. "You play golf, do you?"

"Golf? Me? Heavens, no. Well, once I did. Recently, in fact. Which is rather why I'm here, as it happens."

"Uh huh. So...?"

"Right. Well, I invented something, Mr. Caminetti. Something I think you might be interested in."

"Uhhright. And that would be...?"

"Well, actually, it's a golf ball."

Oh, Christ... "Yeah. Very interesting. Look, uh, Professor Standish..."

Standish smiled. "I know exactly what you're thinking, Mr. Caminetti."

"I doubt it."

"No, I do. The word *bullshit* comes to mind. Am I close?"

"Remarkably."

Standish spread his hands. "So you see?"

"Not really. What do you need from me?"

"There are one or two things I still don't understand. I'm told you might have some insight."

Standish saw that Eddie, his mind already having gone on to different things, was just standing there to be polite. "Mr. Caminetti, I know a good deal about physics. Much more than most of the so-called technical people working for the major golf equipment manufacturers. I assure you that—"

"Do you know anything about the USGA rules for golf balls, Professor? Not to dash your hopes or anything, but do you know that any kid with a high school education can make a golf ball that can go four hundred yards? It's easy. There's nothing to it. But the USGA has a set of pretty strict rules about how far a ball can go, and in the entire history of the sport there's never been—"

"Mr. Caminetti," Standish interrupted, "I can recite for you by memory the entire technical manual of the United States Golf Association. I know the specifications of every one of their testing machines right down to what material the smallest screws are made of. I even know how often they're lubricated and precisely what the range of allowable temperatures, humidity and air pressure are for their operation. I can tell you what kind of grass they use on their testing grounds, how often it's watered and mowed, even the brand name of the fertilizer they use, and I know the results of every test they ever conducted on every ball since the organization was first established. Now..." Standish folded his arms across his chest. "Do you suppose you might manage to give me twenty minutes of your time?"

Eddie blinked a few times, trying to figure out what this guy could possibly be up to, then gave up. "I'm sorry," he said. "Were you talking to me?"

Standish's eyes grew wide, and then he burst into laughter. Eddie took one last hit off his cigarette and then led the professor into the lounge, which they didn't leave until well after midnight when Cleghorn came by at the bartender's insistence and threw them out.

"Tell me," Standish said as they watched the moon perched just off the peak of Mount San Jacinto, "what is it about this game that gets people so obsessed?"

"What do you think?"

"I don't know, really. But I suspect it's because it can be played by individuals at all skill levels. Because of the handicapping system, people can compete regardless of how well they play with respect to one another."

"But that goes for bowling, too."

"Bowling?" Standish exclaimed.

"Don't knock it. Shares a lot in common with golf."

"Surely you're not serious."

"Both scoring systems let you track your progress over time. They're both very friendly—there's nothing your opponent can do to screw up your play, so the only way you can win is by elevating your own game, which makes it very civilized. And now that I think about it, bowling and golf are also two of the few sports in which you can have a good time and not compete at all—just go out and play. Even alone, if you want."

"Yes, I see. So that doesn't really explain the obsession, does it."

"Nope."

CHAPTER FIVE

CATHEDRAL CANYON COUNTRY CLUB
ONE MONTH LATER

Norm Standish stood about thirty yards from the first tee of the Lake nine and watched as the next group drove up. Four pretty ordinary-looking golfers, men in their fifties, three with slight paunches, one not so slight. None having hit any shots yet, they were in a pretty good mood, but Standish, after ninety minutes spent observing the previous eight foursomes, knew that by the time this bunch drove off the first tee, at least two would wish they'd gone for root canal instead.

He looked over at his assistant, patted the canvas bag slung over his shoulder and lifted an inquiring eyebrow.

The assistant, who was seated in a golf cart, didn't respond right away but kept his eyes on the foursome. Three of them were fairly subdued, but one guy, a florid-faced, midlevel aerospace manager–type, was cracking jokes and laughing loudly at them, good-naturedly chiding his buddies over how badly he was going to wax their tails, engaging in friendly banter with the starter, and generally demonstrating that he was one happy-go-lucky, hugely entertaining, so-goddamned-tickled-just-to-be-alive sonofagun.

"Dudn't get much better'n this, boys!" the man exclaimed with primal joy as he yanked a driver out of his bag and took the tee box.

"Go for it, Flackman!" one of his bunch called out.

"Make us proud, Chester!" another said.

The man took careful aim between the water on the left and the out-of-bounds on the right. Unable to completely suppress his smile, he nevertheless managed to still himself as he stood over the ball, then brought the club up and into a deep backswing, hesitated for a fraction of a second and whipped it down toward the ball.

"*FUCK!*" screamed the so-goddamned-tickled-just-to-be-alive sonofagun. *"Fuck me up the ass! Sonofabitch bastard cock-sucking motherfucking blue-balled..."*

Not even bothering to watch his ball as it sliced its way toward—*over*—a row of condos formerly considered a safe place for children to play, he slammed his club into the ground with such force it splattered the carts with bits of grass, clods of dirt and several small stones. "Goddamnit goddamnit goddamnit...!" he hissed through clenched teeth as he stomped his way off the tee box, his suddenly quiet and subdued friends sidling quickly out of his way. After he jammed the offending club back into his bag, each of the waiting golfers began urging the others to please go ahead and hit next, none willing to step immediately into the still-swirling maelstrom of Flackman's toxic fury.

Finally, one of the group inched timidly toward the markers and leaned down to tee up his ball, then pulled it back up and moved away, in order to put as much distance as possible between it and the newly minted impact crater that looked like it had been made by a meteor. His shot traveled a reasonable distance and set down softly just to the right of the centerline.

"Fuck," muttered the sonofagun, an epithet he repeated with equal venom as the remaining two golfers also kept their balls safely in play. Resigned to hitting what would now have to be scored as his third shot, he pulled his driver back out of his bag, then grabbed a damp rag to clean it, not bothering with bits that had been driven into the grooves with such force they'd likely metamorphosed into substances heretofore not known to exist in the Southern California desert.

Somewhere behind him, Norm Standish's assistant touched the side of his nose, then got into his cart and began driving down toward the fairway.

"Fuck's he goin?" the florid-faced spreader of good cheer spat.

"Excuse me..."

Flackman turned at the sound of a timid voice. "What." Not a question, but a demand to please state your business and then get the hell out of the way. Putting his attention back on the task of cleaning his club, Flackman didn't fully take in the short-statured man, who was wearing a corduroy jacket, gray slacks, a tweed skimmer, horn-rimmed glasses and a bow tie, a ridiculous getup that made Norm Standish feel like an idiot but which the assistant had been adamant that he wear. Flackman didn't pay attention to him, or to the canvas bag he was carrying because, when you got right down to it, Chester Flackman's universe pretty much ended at the boundary of his own skin.

"I wonder..." the professor began, then cleared his throat and tried again. "Would you be so kind...your next shot..."

"What?" Flackman demanded gruffly.

"Yes, well, it would seem your first attempt was somewhat, shall we say...errant? So I'm given to believe you're required to—"

"Yeah, I gotta hit a provisional."

"Sorry?"

"A provisional! Just in case!"

Standish turned toward where Flackman's ball had last been visible before disappearing. "I think not."

"What the hell do you mean, you think not?"

"Well, do forgive my impertinence, but isn't the purpose of a provisional, as you say, *just in case* a ball cannot be located in a playable position?"

"Yeah, so what of it?"

"Well...how shall I put this..."

"You ain't hittin a provisional," one of Flackman's buddies said. "First shot was OB, not MIA."

"My sentiments precisely," Standish concurred.

"Says who?" Flackman demanded.

"Only way that ball is playable," another of the foursome said, "is if it landed on another golf course. You're hittin your third shot, Chester."

Standish waited a decent interval for Flackman to resign himself to the inevitable, then said, "Would you mind hitting one of my balls for your next shot?"

Flackman walked to the markers and surveyed the fairway before him, as though to assess whether any profound changes had occurred since last he'd seen it. "Hell for?"

"Well..." Standish stepped forward, shrugging the bag off his shoulder. "It's rather a special ball."

"Yeah, I bet."

Standish could hear knowing sniggering from the other three golfers. "I'm quite serious."

"Mister," Flackman said as he teed up his ball, took a step backwards and pointed his club toward the ground, "that there is whatcha call a Pericles X-9. Fifty bucks a dozen, and in the history of this sport there's never been a better pill. And that's a fact."

"I see," Standish said.

Flackman waggled his club in preparation for bringing it to rest behind the ball. "You bet."

"Interesting."

"Don't come no better, buddy."

"Indeed."

Flackman waited until the cart driven by Standish's assistant had receded to a safe distance, then settled the club head down and steadied himself. He turned his head slightly and aligned himself by using just his right eye to look down the length of the shaft. His friends grew quiet and ceased all motion.

"So it's designed to veer off to the right when struck, is that correct?"

The golfers standing off to the side turned toward Standish. Flackman backed off his shot and straightened up. "Excuse me?" he intoned ominously as he looked at the little man.

"The Pericles X-9. That was, um, a *slice*, I believe is the correct term? When it, ah"—Standish made a swerving motion with his hand—"when it moves precipitously to the right like that?"

"Hey, fellas," the starter called out. "Got some folks behind you waiting to tee off."

Flackman turned back to his ball and tapped his club against the ground several times, as if trying to decide between lining up his shot again or ramming the club down the tweedy little guy's throat. "Listen, pal..."

"Please." Standish reached into the canvas bag. "Indulge me."

He withdrew a polished wooden box about three inches on a side, dropped the bag and walked toward the tee box. "Take your shot with my ball," he said, holding up the box.

Curiosity got the better of Flackman's friends, who drifted in for a closer look. But Standish wouldn't open the box until Flackman himself finally relented and drew closer.

"Seen a lotta bullshit in my day, buster. Whudda you got that's so special?"

"The future," Standish answered, then flipped up the lid.

The inside of the box was lined with inky blue velvet. Nestled in a depression in the middle was a single golf ball. It was white, but with a hint of iridescence that was only perceptible at just the right angle. In the middle of that strangely disconcerting surface was the image of a buxom she-devil, provocatively recumbent in red stockings and arm-length gloves, a golf ball clutched in one elegant hand. Her expression was enigmatic, but she seemed to be daring someone off to her right to take the ball. Stretching across her uplifted left leg was a banner reading SCRATCH.

"Damn," one of the onlookers breathed.

"Scratch?" another said. "That's what it's called?"

Flackman couldn't take his eyes off of it.

"Come on, guys!" the starter demanded. There were now four carts standing at the little shack behind the tee box, and two more were on their way down from the clubhouse.

"Hey, Marty," another golfer said. "C'mere and look at this, wouldja?"

The starter huffed in annoyance and strode over to see what the big deal was just as Flackman reached for the ball.

"Whup!" Standish yelped, snatching the box away and snapping the lid shut.

"Thought you wanted me to hit it," Flackman growled, his eyes following the box hungrily.

"Hit it, yes. But please don't touch it."

"F'cryin out loud!"

"Hit it, kiss it, shove it where the sun don't shine," the starter said, "but whaddaya say we shake a leg here, eh?"

Flackman, somewhat subdued now, looked questioningly at Standish, who blinked uncomfortably and inclined his chin toward the starter. "Seems perhaps there isn't time. I guess you should just go ahead and hit your own—"

"No!" Flackman gasped, then caught himself. "No. I mean, you want me to test that ball...that *is* what you want me to do, right? Give it a whirl?" He ended on an almost pleading note.

"If you'd be so very kind."

"If you'd be so very *fast*, Flackman," the starter snarled.

"Yeah, yeah, keep your shirt on." Flackman pointed to the closed box. "So, uh..."

Standish walked to the tee and set the box down next to the closest marker, then opened the lid. He took Flackman's ball off the tee and tossed it behind him, then, almost reverentially, lifted the new ball out of the box and set it softly down on the wooden peg. After a few more seconds, he leaned back on his haunches and, reluctantly, it seemed, stood up and stepped back. Then he waved his hand toward the ground, said, "Please" to Flackman, and walked off the tee box.

Flackman, acutely aware that there were now some two dozen people watching him, including two foursomes on the first tee of the Arroyo nine who had paused to see what was going on, drew himself up to full height and returned to the tee box for the third time. Once again he took up his stance, waggled the club head a few times, and set it down behind the ball, which he noticed Standish had turned so the little she-devil faced toward the ideal landing area for the hole. When he was comfortable, he took a last look out at the fairway. Way in the distance was the cart that he'd seen leaving the teeing area a few minutes before, but it was well out of his range and he put it out of his mind, turning once more to the ball.

Motionless now, Flackman took a deep breath and let it out slowly. Then he took the club away, let it pause at the top of his backswing, and brought it back down in one smooth, elegant, powerfully accelerating arc. His head as still as a cheetah's, he concentrated on the rearmost part of the ball and saw with crystal clarity the exact instant that the club face, perfectly perpendicular to the path he intended the ball to take, slammed into it with a solid, satisfying and startlingly loud *cra-a-a-ck!*

The club spent its remaining momentum whipping itself over his left shoulder, and he stayed poised in a classic finish as he watched the glistening ball rise against the Santa Rosa Mountains, and keep rising, not turning left or right but tracking straight ahead with laser-guided precision, reaching its peak altitude and hanging apparently motionless for a second before deciding reluctantly to begin its descent.

Flackman didn't even notice the awed exhalations behind him because when the ball crossed the point on the fairway at which his tee shots usually came to rest if he hit them well, it was still some twenty feet in the air. It was heading for the cart in which sat Standish's assistant.

"No way that guy was in your range," someone said.

"Nuh uh," someone else agreed. "Don't worry about it."

Flackman didn't answer, but watched as the ball landed about thirty feet short of the cart, rolled another few yards, and then came to rest within two club lengths of the front bumper.

An eerie, stunned silence hung in the air as Flackman finally took the club off his shoulder. Even the starter had momentarily forgotten what he was doing there. He'd seen golfers hit that far before, plenty of them, but this was Chester-freakin-*Flackman*, for God's sake. The starter had probably seen him on this tee a thousand times, and knew with the precision of a seasoned observer exactly what his capabilities were, just as he knew those of every other member at the Cathedral Canyon Country Club. And one thing he knew for absolutely goddamned certain was that there was no way Chester-freakin-Flackman could hit a shot like that. No way in hell.

As the onlookers roused themselves back to reality, Flackman turned slowly to Norman Standish, who was smiling in satisfaction and nodding his approval, whether of Flackman's prowess or the performance of the ball, no one could say.

Standish turned to regard Flackman, who blinked a few times, scratched the side of his head and said, "Fuck me."

There was some minor pandemonium as the assistant in the cart some 260 yards distant got out, picked up the ball and marked its location with a tee.

"What the hell's he doing!" Flackman screamed.

"He's just retrieving the ball," Standish said. "Don't worry: He's marked the spot with a—"

"Bullshit! That's bullshit!"

"Hey..." the starter cautioned.

"You can't do that!" Flackman spluttered. "I...the rules...you can't switch balls unless it's cut! Yeah, yeah, you can't replace a ball unless—"

"It's okay, Chester," one of his friends said. "We'll let you—"

"Fuck that, Louie!"

"But—"

"And fuck *you*, too." Flackman whipped around to Standish. "Listen here, you sawed-off piece of...goddamnit, you gave me that ball to play! Damned near begged me, and now—"

He caught a movement out of the side of his eye and turned to see the assistant's cart halfway back to the tee.

"Put it back!" he screamed. "Put it *back*, you sonofabitch!"

He dropped his driver and began running down to the fairway, but his friends leaped after him and managed to stop his forward motion.

"The rules!" Flackman choked out pathetically. "We gotta play by the—"

"According to the rules you couldna hit that ball in the first place!" the starter called out. "You can't switch brands in the middle of a round."

"What?" Flackman looked at him, then back out toward the fairway. "But...shit..."

The starter turned toward Standish. "Who you tryin to kid with this, mister? Any *jamoke* can make a ball that goes half a mile."

A man from one of the waiting foursomes got out of a cart near the shack. "He's right. It's gotta be USGA approved before anybody can use it." He pointed toward the assistant's cart, now pulling up near the ball washer. "And that juiced-up piece of hard rubber will never be certified."

"They've already finished testing it," Standish replied, as he walked toward the cart. "And thus far there appears to be little doubt of its eventual certification."

"Sorry?"

The assistant handed back the ball. "Thank you," Standish said, wiping it with his handkerchief before returning it to the box. "It's being certified by the USGA right now."

The assistant got out of the cart and the two of them began walking off toward the parking lot. "Thanks very much for your help," Standish said to Flackman.

"Hey, where you going?" someone called out.

"Have to run."

The starter said, "Aren't you trying to sell us the ball?"

"Indeed not. As I said, just doing a little testing. Have a nice day, everybody."

Standish and his assistant ignored the stupefied expressions that arose on faces turning to track their exit, and also ignored the starter and two large men trying to hold back a near-berserk Chester Flackman. Once in the parking lot, they got into their car, waved and drove off.

"Where to now?" Standish asked as they exited the main gate and made a right turn onto the street.

Eddie Caminetti pulled a cigarette from a pack in his shirt pocket and pressed in the lighter below the dashboard. "PGA West," he said as he glanced at his watch. "They got six courses. We can hit em all and be outta there in time for dinner."

CHAPTER SIX

Jack McGrange cocked a skeptical eye at Eddie. "If I'm gonna hand you ten million bucks, you gotta hire somebody I trust as the chief financial officer."

"I don't need a chief financial officer."

"The hell you don't."

"The hell I do! Another mouth to feed? What for?"

"I'll tell you what for: Because a guy who knows how to handle money—"

"I know how to handle money."

"Corporate money, Eddie. Not like the chump change you and I bet with. The guy who manages the company's dough is almost as important as your lawyer. And it's gotta be a guy I can trust."

Eddie leaned back on the seat of the golf cart and put a foot up on the cup holder. "Jack, when was the last time I cheated you?"

"Never."

"When have I ever lied to you?"

"Not once."

"Not once, right. So how the hell come all of a sudden you're—"

McGrange stepped out of the cart, came around the front and stood facing the passenger seat. "Eddie, how much you figure you've taken from me playing golf?"

Eddie reached into his shirt pocket for a pack of cigarettes. "No damned idea."

"Well, I do have a damned idea. Over three hundred grand, that's how much."

"Gee whiz. Sounds like a lot."

"Fuck you, it sounds like a lot. And you know what? In all that time you never cheated or lied to me."

"Like I said—"

"Shut up and listen. Remember when you bet me an even grand you could hit a ball at the bottom of a paper cup over two-ten down the fairway?"

"Helluva shot, that one."

"Yeah. You hit it over two-thirty. What you didn't tell me was that the paper cup actually makes the shot easier, and that you'd practiced it about eight thousand times before making the bet."

"Never said I didn't. All I did was make a simple bet. You're the one who assumed—"

"That's just the thing, Eddie. You knew I would assume you'd just thought of it on the spot."

"Why is that my problem? Besides, you know my standing offer: If you think I cheated, all you have to do—"

"Yeah, I know. You'll give me back my dough."

"No questions asked."

"You gonna give me back ten million if I ask for it?" McGrange folded his arms across his chest, expecting no reply and not getting one. "Got a piece of advice for you, Caminetti: You ask a guy for that kinda scratch, don't sit there and throw bullshit at him. Last thing you wanna do right now is make me uncomfortable."

Eddie smiled and shook a cigarette out of the pack. "Okay. You got me."

McGrange didn't smile back. "Now I'm really worried."

"Chrissakes, Jack! Six years we've known each other and you've never won a single bet offa me, but you keep coming back for more! Me, I figure you just like pissing money away. So what's the big deal, you piss away ten mill in one shot?"

"So you *are* going to scam me somehow."

"Nossir. I'm gonna give it back to you double, just like I said." Eddie put the pack to his mouth and pulled the cigarette out with his teeth. "Just trying to give it a little perspective. You're so worried, why're you even talking to me about the deal?"

McGrange pulled a disposable Bic out of his pants pocket. "Because," he said, lighting it and holding it toward Eddie, "you know that if you fuck me,

I'll have you killed."

"Well, there you go," Eddie replied easily, leaning forward toward the flame. "What a basis for a trusting partnership."

"Except I don't want to have to do that."

"Makes two of us. So you see?" He touched the tip of the cigarette to the flame and took a long puff. "Something else we agree on."

"Fine." McGrange lifted his thumb and let the flame go out. "So I'll send around a guy for you to interview."

"Just one? Don't I get to choose?"

"Absolutely." McGrange dropped the lighter back into his pocket. "But ten grand says you hire this guy."

Eddie blew out a stream of smoke that billowed into a bluish cloud and hovered in the still air. "Ten grand."

"Yep."

"All I have to do is not hire the guy and I win ten grand."

"That's it. And if you think I cheated, you don't have to pay."

Eddie's eyes grew wide, and then he laughed. "What's this here...a taste of my own medicine?"

McGrange held his arms out a little ways and then let them drop back down. "I'm just telling you the deal."

Eddie eyed him for a few more seconds, then shook his head. "No bet."

"Didn't think so. Noon tomorrow okay?"

"Sure."

"Great. Say, lemme ask you something."

"This gonna be like a pop quiz?"

"No, nothing like that. Just wanted to know...what do you figure's the reason we're all so nuts about this game?"

"What do you think?"

"Me? I always figure it's all those gorgeous courses out there. Palm Springs, Hawaii..."

"I'll tell you something, Jack: I play a lot of gorgeous courses all over the world—hell, I *own* a gorgeous course—but every once in a while? And a lot, lately?" Eddie leaned in, almost conspiratorially. "I find myself at really scraggly, beat-up muni tracks with nothing but crabgrass to play on."

"No shit? Me too, Eddie!"

"How come?"

"Hard to explain. Usually happens after I go to a tournament where I see pros bitch and moan on accounta the rough is too high or somebody didn't rake the sand properly or the green wasn't mowed low enough or the pin placement is unfair. Shit, guys at my home club go completely batshit cause there's a patch of yellow grass somewhere on the fairway. That's when I like to hit some of them scrubby courses and go a few rounds with short-order cooks and plumbers. Guys who're like I was... before..." McGrange shook his head. "I take that back. Guys who're just like I still am."

"Well, it's the same with me, which proves my point."

"What point?"

"About why beautiful courses doesn't explain the obsession. If all we had were those scrubby munis, we'd still be out there every chance we get, am I right?"

"No question about it."

Eddie took another hit off his cigarette. "So lemme ask you something."

"Shoot."

"How come you keep betting with me? I mean, three hundred g's, come on! Don't you think there's, like, a *pattern* here?"

McGrange came around the cart and dropped onto the driver's seat. "Eddie," he said as he hit the pedal to release the toe brake, "every time I lose a bet to you, I go back home and make it back ten times over pulling the same shit on other guys that you pulled on me."

He pressed the accelerator and the cart gave a small lurch before picking up speed. "Way I look at it," McGrange said as he steered around some overhanging bougainvillea, "I'm not paying you for lost bets."

"Oh yeah? So what are you paying me for?"

McGrange turned toward Eddie and grinned.

"Tuition," he answered.

The man was barely distinguishable from the wallpaper next to him. Average height, average weight, medium build, brown hair, brown eyes. He

wore a plaid shirt, gray slacks, brown loafers, and could have passed for an
accountant, a lawyer, a street sweeper, terrorist, barber, hit man or florist.

To Eddie Caminetti, it was like looking in a mirror.

"Eddie?" The man held out his hand. "I'm Oscar Petanque. Come on
in."

Eddie accepted the man's hand and stepped inside. He'd never conducted
a business interview before—the only interview line of any kind he was
familiar with was "For how much?"—and didn't know any of the rules or
protocols. It only made sense to him that if you were going to try to find
out something about someone you were thinking of hiring, the best place to
talk to him was right in his house, so that's where he was now.

He liked the house immediately, and got a good feeling about Petanque's wife from it, too. No professional decorator had come anywhere
near it; the furniture wasn't coordinated to any specific theme, although
there was little of anything modern present. Each piece had a likeability
about it, as though chosen for the pleasure of its owners rather than the
admiration of visitors. It was stuff you were supposed to use, not look at,
and as Petanque motioned him to a place on a wonderfully comfortable-
looking couch, Eddie also noticed that everything was of exceptionally
high quality. He also noticed a complex but ancient machine resting on a
lace doily on a sideboard.

"That what I think it is?" he asked instead of sitting down.

"Probably," Petanque responded as the two of them walked over to the
sideboard to have a closer look. "A Norden bombsight." As Eddie bent
down for a closer look, Petanque added, "Go ahead and fool with it if you
want."

Reluctant to tinker with the World War II–vintage device, Eddie asked,
"How come there's one sitting in your living room? You a war buff or
something?"

"Not really." He turned away and explained as Eddie followed him back
toward the couch. "I saw it sitting on a workbench at one of those bullshit
art walkabouts in California where you go into the artist's house and ooh
and ahh at some bored housewife who dribbles Cream of Wheat on a coat
rack and applies for an NEA grant to support her creative expression."

Eddie nodded. "Venice, right?"

Petanque pointed a finger at him. "You got it exactly. So here's this *sculptor,* an unemployed past-lives therapist or something, and he's got this thing sitting on his workbench. I recognize it immediately, but I say, hey, what's that? And this fella scratches himself for a couple of seconds and he says, I swear, he says he's going to use it in a piece celebrating the revolutionary idealism of garment workers in Sri Lanka. Or something like that. So I ask him how he's going to do that, and he says he's going to cut it up and hang the pieces from the ceiling in the shape of a business suit."

Eddie said, "You're pulling my leg," and dropped onto the couch.

Petanque held up his hands and sat down on a hand-carved oak rocker facing him. "Swear to God. Now I know it's a Norden, right, and I'm picturing some nineteen-year-old bombardier frantically unscrewing one of these things from its mount while his plane is burning all around him and spiraling straight down, trying to get it loose and take it with him when he bails out so he can drop it in some bog because he's right over Berlin and he knows it's the first thing the Nazis are going to be looking for when they locate the crash site, and he'd rather go down in flames and die than let those guys get their hands on it." He paused, whether for breath or because he felt himself getting carried away in front of someone he was asking for a job, Eddie couldn't tell.

"And then you see some clown thinks he's Michelangelo getting ready to chop it up into little pieces."

"Right. So I tell him, boy, that sounds fantastic. What do you figure that *sculpture* is going to fetch? And he scratches himself a little more and he says, probably around ten thousand, and I nod and look real thoughtful and I say, I'll give you a hundred dollars for that thing right now. You would have thought it was carrying plague, how fast he carried it out to my car."

Eddie laughed and shifted around a little to make himself comfortable. "Guess we oughta talk about this job."

"Sure. Would you like something to drink?"

"I'm good. So: You done any work like this before?"

"A few times." Petanque settled back on his chair. "I don't like the front lines, you know, making products or selling. What I'm good at is the back room, supporting the people who are doing those front-line things."

"Administration, you mean."

Petanque winced. "That usually implies pushing paper around, not help-ing the cause. The way I look at it, my job is to see to it that people like you don't have to worry about anything except what you're in business for. If you're making widgets, the only thing you should be doing is making them better, faster and cheaper, and selling as many as you can for as much as you can. Every minute you spend on shipping, receivables, payroll, things like that, is a minute you're not doing the company much good."

"And the company's money?"

Petanque rubbed the side of his head. "I'm going to be straight with you, Eddie. I've seen a lot of geniuses go bankrupt because they assumed that if they're geniuses in one area they must be geniuses in all of them. Just because a guy can make an integrated circuit out of tinfoil and an old brassiere doesn't mean he knows how to invest cash, control expenses, speed up receivables, stretch out payables and fire bad apples without getting sued."

"And you do."

"I do. And I'm a lot more creative than I look."

Eddie wasn't quite sure what to make of this guy. He was confident as hell and talked a good game, but how do you go about telling if he's really got the goods? "About that drink, got a glass of ice water handy?"

"You bet." Petanque jumped up, pointing to Eddie's jacket pocket as he walked past him toward the kitchen. "And if you want to smoke, let's go out in back. Too nice to sit inside anyway."

As soon as they were ensconced in two well-cushioned chairs amid fra-grant lemon trees in the backyard, Eddie said, "So tell me, Oscar: What's the most creative thing you've ever done for a company?"

Petanque nodded, approving of the question, then thought for a second and smiled. Mostly to himself, it seemed to Eddie. "Ever hear of the Champ d'Lawndale Shopping Mall?"

Eddie frowned in concentration. "In Nebraska somewhere?"

"That's the one. My proudest moment."

Eddie tried hard to conjure up the memory of some news stories.

"But...I thought those guys...wait a minute. They nearly went bankrupt two years ago."

"Yes." Petanque had a wistful, nostalgic look in his eyes. "My best work, that."

Eddie didn't even pretend to understand. "The owners came this close to losing their shirts"—he held up a thumb and forefinger—"and you were *proud?*"

Petanque reached for his water glass and took his time taking a sip. "I wasn't working for the owners," he said slyly.

"Ah." Intrigued now, Eddie grabbed his cigarettes and motioned for Petanque to continue.

"I was working for Jack McGrange. We'd known each other for a while and he was involved in a complex deal and needed some help. This was back when the shopping mall was still being built."

Eddie lit his cigarette and let his lighter snap shut. "Coming back to me now. The Champ d'What the Hell Ever, it sat around half built for something like a year, right?"

"Yeah. They ran out of money and needed about eight million to finish it, but they'd tapped out all their money sources. They decided to set up the parking garage as a concession operation and let somebody else run it and kick part of the profits back to the mall. They figured that once they had that deal nailed down, they could take it to the banks and borrow against the expected revenue."

"So where did McGrange fit in?"

"He was negotiating for the concession rights, except the owners were nickel-and-diming him to death, demanding outrageous percentages that would have made it almost impossible for him to turn any profit at all. In fact, when I ran the numbers, it looked to me like he'd have to keep paying them even if he was actually losing money."

"So how come he didn't just tell them to stick it in their ear?"

"Because they were negotiating like rug merchants. They'd tell him it was a done deal, shake hands, then come back the next day and say, gee, they're sorry, but their lawyers wouldn't let them do this or that, so we've got to start again. Which Jack knew was nonsense because four of the seven owners *were* lawyers and weren't consulting anybody on the outside at all. And all this time he's wondering how they can keep dragging this out and making all these demands when they're on the verge of losing the whole project altogether because they're eight million short, and then he finds out that for three months they'd been talking to a Saudi prince about the parking rights, the idea being to drag Jack to the wall and then point to this Arab and say that if Jack doesn't want the deal, this guy does, so take it or leave it."

Eddie flicked some ashes onto the grass and reached for his water glass. "But why would the Saudi go for a bad business deal?"

"Why? Because he was so damned arrogant he wouldn't have an accountant look over the numbers for him. The owners had him convinced it was a great deal, and by the time Daddy found out what was really going on, it would be too late. But the owners didn't really want troubles with non-citizens and so they were just using it to pressure Jack into signing. When he found out about it, he got angry as only Jack McGrange can get angry."

"And how's that?"

"He gets quiet. Really quiet, and thoughtful, and he says to me, he says, Oscar...what do you think?"

Petanque paused, and Eddie took the bait. "What'd you tell him?"

"I told him to buy the whole garage outright, offer them eight million, cash, take it or leave it right on the spot, or he walks."

Eddie had been about to take a hit off his cigarette but paused with it halfway to his mouth. "You're shitting me."

"Nope. And I told him to write into the deal that the garage gets split off into a completely separate business entity, even the title to the land it was on gets re-filed into its own self-standing plot, and nowhere on any piece of paper connected to the garage does the shopping mall even get mentioned. No discussions, no more bargaining, and then I have him draw down a bank draft for the full amount and take it to the meeting. Jack, I said, come back with a contract or come back with the draft torn up. One way or the other, end it today. Would you like some more water?"

"No. So he bought the thing?"

"He bought it. The owners got the cash to finish building, the mall opened, it was a smashing success, and as soon as they started making money hand over fist they sued Jack."

"Sued him! On what grounds?"

"Some legal gobbledygook, 'contract of adhesion' or something along those lines. I didn't even understand it, really, but what they were saying was that Jack'd had them up against a wall and forced them into a bad deal they didn't really want but had to take because they had no choice and therefore it should be declared null and void."

"I don't believe it."

"Believe it. After all the papers were filed they came to us and said, look, neither of us wants a long, drawn-out trial, so why don't you just agree to give us twenty-five percent of your gross receipts and we'll settle the matter?"

Eddie shook his head. "Woulda been all I could do not to choke the livin shit out of those guys with my bare hands. What did you do?"

"I told Jack to take the deal."

Eddie shook his head again. "Oscar, I gotta tell you: So far it sounds to me like you were really working for the other side. Aren't you supposed to be tryna impress me or something?"

"I'm just being dramatic. Trust me, what Jack tells me about you, you're going to love this. So I tell Jack to take the deal, give them the twenty-five percent of the *gross*, not the net, which you and I both know is not only highway robbery on their part but suicide on Jack's. I also told him to make sure that it was *their* lawyer who wrote up the deal, not ours, so they couldn't come back later and say we tried to slip something in without them noticing. I called that lawyer and dictated a couple of innocuous paragraphs, about how this is a settlement of a lawsuit and they agree to forever hold us harmless and never sue us over this deal and so forth, and they're so greedy and proud of themselves for pulling this off, they agree right away because what could possibly go wrong, and two days later it's all signed and done and filed with the court."

Petanque paused again, and took another sip of his water. "And you're thinking, why am I even talking to this head case, right?"

"Nah. I'm guessing we're coming to the good part."

"You're right."

"So what happened?"

"Jack paid the twenty-five percent, every penny, right on time, month after month. The mall was phenomenally successful, the owners were drowning in cash, and Jack was barely breaking even."

"And this went on for how long?"

"About a year."

"Then what?"

"Then I told Jack to raise the prices in the parking garage."

Eddie blinked, waited for Petanque to continue, then blinked again. "Yeah, so?"

"To thirty dollars an hour."

"What the hell are you talking about?"

"He raised the prices to thirty dollars an hour. Not much to it, really. Change a few signs, hit a few buttons on the computer...new prices go into effect."

Eddie was having trouble following, and didn't bother trying to hide it. "Who in the hell's gonna pay thirty bucks an hour to park at a goddamned shopping mall!"

"Nobody in his right mind, that's for damned sure. And overnight this hotsy-totsy shopping mall goes from looking like LaGuardia at five o'clock on a Friday to Forest Lawn at midnight."

"Ahhh..."

"Yeah." Petanque crossed his legs and continued. "It was only hours afterwards that all the shop owners in the place started coming unglued. These were the kind of places, if business dropped off, you didn't just not make money, you started losing it by the fistful. The mall owners got busy and arranged for buses to ship customers in without charge, and that helped a little, but then Jack closed off the garage lanes, which were the only way in, cutting off all the access for the buses."

"Hold it a second." Eddie sat up straight and gestured with his hands. "Can you get away with that? I thought...I ran into something like that with a guy once...he tried to trick me out of some money he owed me on a bet. I thought that if you own the only access to some guy's property, law says you can't block it off. You've got to let people in and out."

"That's true, Jack knew that good and well beforehand, and boy, did he grouse up a storm when he lost that battle in court and got hit with an injunction. That was four days later, though, and by that time the regular clientele was so disgusted most of them were damned if they were going to get on some smelly bus just to spend money at a mall with the nerve to charge that kind of money for cars, and who the heck did those owners think they were trying to kid?"

"But it wasn't the owners," Eddie protested. "It was—"

"Jack, right. Like the people who buy Gap jeans and Sharper Image cell phone—egg beater combos care who owns what. All they are, they're angry, and like somebody once put it, they started staying away in droves. Meanwhile, the mall owners have Jack in court every other day, arguing that it's extortion this and tortious that, and Jack keeps pointing to this agreement, written by the mall's own lawyer, saying in crystal-clear language that he owns the garage outright, not even mentioning the mall, and he can do anything he wants with it, including tearing it down and building a cemetery, and, by the way, they agreed not to sue him over it so what are we doing in court in the first place?"

"And...?"

"And, he's right. There's nothing they can do, and while they're trying to do it anyway, their business is going down the shitter."

Eddie heaved a sigh and exhaled slowly. "You mean to tell me Jack McGrange was willing to lose eight million bucks just to get back at these guys?"

Now it was Petanque's turn to look surprised. "Are you kidding me? You think I'm going to sit here and brag about how I helped my boss drop eight million dollars just to get his rocks off?"

"Good point. And since I know that mall is still in business, what'd you end up doing?"

"Simple." Petanque lifted his shoulders and let them drop. "Sold the garage back to the owners for forty million dollars."

Two hours later the sun started to go down, and they went back inside the house to escape the chilling air.

"We both know my real job would be to protect Jack's investment, right?"

Eddie said he understood. "Sounds to me like you could only do that if you did right by the company."

"That I would."

"So how come you haven't even asked me what the job pays?"

"What's it pay?"

"I have no idea."

"That's fine with me."

"You know, I'm getting the definite impression you don't really much care what it pays."

"I don't."

"And why is that?"

"Two reasons. The first is that Jack will make sure I make money if he makes money. Always has. He figures, what sense is there in giving a guy a job without also giving him an incentive to do it well?"

"Makes sense. And the second reason?"

"I don't need the money."

"So why take the job?"

"Because I like the game."

"Speaking of that, do you play golf?"

"Just started. I'm taking lessons."

"How's it going?"

"So far all I can hit is my ankle, but I'm having a ball."

Eddie stood up and headed for the door, and started laughing about halfway there.

"What's funny?" Petanque asked.

Eddie, still chuckling, turned to face him. "I saved ten thousand dollars since I got here today."

"How'd you do that?"

"By not making a certain bet with Jack McGrange." He stuck out his hand. "Glad to have you aboard, Oscar."

CHAPTER SEVEN

"**Fat Albert**" **Auberlain looked out** over the impossibly beautiful golf course at Swithen Bairn, somewhere in the middle of the Pacific. "Is this the most gorgeous place you've ever seen in your entire life?" he asked.

"No," replied the owner as he fished a ball out of his pocket. "So what's your problem?"

They were standing on the first tee, between two planters full of black orchids that marked the back tees. Up ahead some thirty yards was a second set of planters, this time of yellow roses, and still farther ahead violets marked the forward tees.

"My problem? Not much, really. I play golf for a living and my game is shot to hell. Other than that? Car runs nice, my crabgrass is just about gone..."

"Game is shot. Why's that?"

"Very funny."

"I don't get you."

"How the hell am I supposed to know why!" Auberlain spat back.

"Who the hell else is? You're the one's playin it. What's wrong?"

"I don't know. Was hoping you could tell me."

"How many other guys you already ask?"

"Two, three dozen."

"Guys on the tour?"

"Yeah. Didn't do shit for me."

"And you think I can. Well." Eddie bent to tee up the ball. "Seein as how someone beat you with the stupid stick this morning, how much're we playin for?"

"How many strokes you want?"

"None."

"Very funny. How many?"

"I told you, none."

Auberlain cocked his head and looked at Eddie suspiciously. "Kinda shit you gonna pull on me?"

"Hey, you wanna play or what?"

"I'm number forty-five on the PGA money list and you're gonna play me straight up?"

"Why the hell not? You just got finished telling me your game's gone to shit. Mine hasn't changed a bit, so I'll win. Grand a side?"

"Your funeral."

"Right. So don't worry about me."

Eddie turned back to his ball. Having only hit this particular tee shot eight or nine thousand times before, he paused to study the curve and drop of the near-phosphorescent fairway as it boldly slashed its way down a gentle slope, turned right at the bottom around a stand of palm trees, and finally ended at a peninsula of a green surrounded on three sides by the ocean. The cobalt blue of the sea was separated from the deep jade green by an arc of crushed coral, giving the target area the look of a giant eye. The white flag fluttering dead center was a gleam that completed the illusion perfectly.

Auberlain snickered as he watched Eddie. "Why don't you just save us both some time and walk it out to the middle of the fairway about two-fifty?"

Eddie ignored him and took up his stance, then swung smoothly. The ball had a very slight fade that kicked in about halfway through its flight and guided it to a gentle touchdown in the center of the fairway 250 yards away.

Auberlain muttered something about what a shocking surprise *that* was, then bent to tee up his own ball. Standing up he took a moment to breathe deeply of hyacinth and honeysuckle. "Well, it's the most beautiful place *I* ever seen, that's for damned sure."

Barely pausing to get lined up, he hauled back and let loose with an explosion of controlled power and exquisite technique that sent his ball rocketing away at an almost frightening velocity. It was still high in the air when it sailed over Eddie's ball, fading a bit before settling out of its glide in preparation for reentry into the lower atmosphere. It finally came to rest midway between rose bushes comprising the 100-yard markers, a 300-yard drive.

"So how was it before your game went down the crapper?" Eddie cracked.

"Got lucky," Auberlain said as he knelt down to retrieve his tee. They picked up their bags and headed for the fairway.

"So where's the problem?" Eddie asked as they walked.

"Everywhere. Shanking tee shots, misjudging chips, putting like a spastic blind man..."

They stopped at Eddie's ball. Auberlain kept his bag on his back as Eddie doffed his and pulled out an eight-iron. He took an easy swing and set the ball down on the front of the green, where it released and rolled about halfway to the pin.

"Not bad," Auberlain said. "Still not doing much with backspin, I see."

"Not too much. Kills me on greens that slope away."

"Yeah." They arrived at Auberlain's ball. He chose a sand wedge and lofted it high in the air. It landed less than ten feet from the flag, and had just enough reverse spin to come to a dead stop rather than roll further away.

"Good one," Eddie said.

On the green, Eddie putted to within two feet. Auberlain conceded the par, then sank his ten-footer for a birdie.

"Nice hole," Eddie said. "So tell me again what the problem is?"

"Shit, Eddie. It's easy here, just two guys bullshittin for a few bucks. Like bein on the driving range. Who hits bad on the driving range?"

Eddie nodded but didn't answer as they headed for the second hole, a 530-yard par-five. Auberlain missed a fifty-foot eagle putt but tapped in for birdie. He birdied again on number three, parred four and five, and birdied six. They didn't talk much, just played, and Auberlain won the front nine by four strokes.

"Sure you don't want any strokes on the back?" he asked. "No problem, you can have a couple. On accounta this here's like stealing."

It's for such sentiments that the phrase "dumb-ass" was invented. Feeling sorry for Eddie Caminetti halfway through a round of golf because he's down is like feeling sorry for a used car salesman because you think you got too good a price.

"Got a better idea," Eddie said. "Why don't we just double the stakes for the back nine?"

Auberlain laughed. "You got some shit up your sleeve! Don't bullshit me!"

"Like what?"

"Like what? Like the time you bet Al Bellamy you could hit five hundred yards and then teed up on a goddamn *glacier!*"

Eddie held up his hands in a defensive posture. "Straight golf, no funny stuff."

"This is bullshit. I can feel it."

Eddie let his hands drop. "Then don't worry about it. Let's just finish out the round, have some fun." He turned away and headed for the tenth.

"Hold it," Auberlain said as he jogged to catch up. "Lemme get this straight. You wanna double the bet on the back, no strokes, no bullshit?"

"No."

"I knew it! No, what?"

"No, let's just play. Come on."

"Okay. But..."

"But what?"

They were approaching the tenth, a deceptively difficult par-three of only 140 yards. The area in front of the green dropped off steeply, and anything falling short would roll backwards into a depression about fifteen feet down and twenty yards back. Bunkers guarded the left and right sides, and behind the green the ground angled sharply upward.

"No bullshit?"

"Fat Albert," Eddie said in exasperation, "tee up and hit the goddamned ball. You're getting too nervous."

Auberlain teed up, took his stance, addressed the ball, then turned around. "Okay, you're on."

"Forget it."

"You chicken? It was your idea!"

"You're gonna lose."

"Oh, Christ, don't start this shit, Eddie."

"Albert, in all the years you've ever known me, when did I ever tell someone they were going to lose and they didn't?"

The answer, of course, was never. "But lemme ask you this," Auberlain said. "You still on with that wild-ass guarantee of yours?"

"Which is...?"

"If I think you were bullshittin me, I don't gotta pay?"

"Absolutely."

"Then you're on."

"Don't do it."

"Why not?"

"You're gonna lose."

"Cut that shit out! Bet's doubled, so pipe down." Auberlain turned back to his ball and got ready to hit, then turned around once again. "Hey."

"What now?"

"I came here to get some help with my game, remember?"

"In the middle of a money match?" When Auberlain didn't respond, Eddie sighed, folded his arms and scratched at his chin with his thumb. "Okay. Lemme see that swing."

Auberlain set up with his back to the ball and took a few practice swings.

"Whadda you got there, a wedge?"

"Yeah."

"Hmm. Looks pretty good. Go ahead and hit."

Auberlain turned back to the tee box, eyed the green and took a few more practice swings, then got set up over his ball. He settled the club head down so it barely touched the ground, then went still as death.

"Hang on a second," Eddie said.

Auberlain straightened up and turned around.

"Lemme see that swing again."

He took a few more practice swings as he faced Eddie, who frowned in concentration.

"What?" Auberlain asked. "Same way I was swingin two minutes ago."

"Yeah..."

"So?"

Eddie gestured for Auberlain to keep swinging, watching as he did so. After a minute or so, he said, "Albert, lemme ask you something."

Auberlain stopped, set the club down and leaned on it. "Yeah?"

Eddie mimed a swing with his empty hands, stopping at the top of the arc for a few seconds before coming back down. "When you take a shot," he said thoughtfully, "do you inhale or exhale on the backswing?"

Auberlain stood there, blinked a few times, but otherwise did nothing.

"What I mean..." Eddie brought his hands up again, taking a deep breath as he did so. He held his hands and his breath, then blew out air as he let his hands drop. Then he took another deep breath, and this time let it out as he brought his hands up, and instead drew in a fresh lungful as he swung down. "Which parts of the swing are you breathing in and out on, or are you doing just one through the whole shot, or holding your breath, or what?"

Auberlain did nothing again for a few moments, then bent his knees and took a slow backswing, monitoring his breathing as he did so. He took a few quick breaths with the club at the top, then brought it back down with exaggerated slowness, breathing in a little, then out, then in again until the club brushed the ground. Back up with the club, his mouth open, down with it closed. Then the opposite. Frowning in concentration, he took a breath and held it for the duration of the swing. Then he took a really deep breath and let it out slowly as he mimed a shot, then breathed in during another shot.

He looked baffled. "I don't know what I do. Never thought about it."

"Really?" Eddie said with some surprise. "Huh." He abruptly flapped his hands toward Auberlain and took a few steps back. "Then forget I mentioned it. If you hadn't thought about it before, then it makes no difference. No sense confusing things more than they need to be. Go on and shoot."

Auberlain nodded uncertainly and stepped back to his ball. Setting up over it for the third or fourth time since they'd gotten to the tee box, he took a few slow practice swings. Eddie could hear his breath—inhale, exhale, a quick in and out, no breath, another inhale.

"Hey, toldja to quit worryin about it, Albert," he called out. "Just do what you been doin all along. Hell, you were four under on the front, so just do what you been doin, kay?"

"Okay," Auberlain replied. He set the club head behind the ball, picked it up and lowered it a few times, opened and closed his hands a few times, breathed in and out a few times, then hit the ball so far into the hydrangea bushes seventy yards off the fairway that the next person to see it would probably be an archaeologist three thousand years in the future.

Two hours later he wrote Eddie a check for $4,000.

They sat together in the lanai off the Swithen Bairn dining room. The mild night air was a riot of exotic aromas from the tropical plants that formed a necklace stretching from just off the deck to the ocean just a three-iron away. Even the smell of their cigars couldn't completely mask the fragrance. A cribbage board lay on the table between them.

"After all that dough you made offa me at golf today," Auberlain said, "least you coulda done is let me win some back playin crib."

"Not my style," Eddie said. "Another game?"

"Bite me." With an upturned hand Auberlain cupped the bottom of an oversized goblet that The Piper had set down in front of him a few minutes before, and swirled the bright yellow liquid within so it sheeted the inside of the glass. The sudden expansion of surface area released a burst of vapors that invaded his nostrils as he brought the glass up for a deep sniff. "Strega," he said. "You remembered."

Eddie grunted as he blew out a bluish cloud of smoke from his Macanudo. "You run a place like this, you remember what people drink."

"Even when you comp their entire trip?"

"It's a habit, what can I tell you?" Eddie held the cigar over an abalone shell and tapped off some ash. "You can serve em shitty food, give em lumpy beds or whatever, but if the owner comes by for thirty seconds to say hello and remembers their drink?"

"They give it four stars. People sure are funny."

"Do tell," Eddie said meaningfully, but it was lost on Auberlain.

The troubled pro took a deep, shuddering breath and slowly let it out. "I told you my game was in the toilet."

"You did that."

"Kicked my ass on the back nine. Burned-out old fart like you, and me on the tour."

Eddie didn't reply, but only stared at the glum kid and took his cigar back up. The Piper appeared in the doorway of the dining room, but made no move to enter. After another few seconds in which Auberlain didn't respond to Eddie's lack of response at so naked a plea, he looked up. "You gotta help me."

Eddie grunted softly.

"Don't get me wrong, Eddie. I know you helped me ten times more'n I can ever repay. Hell, my whole damned life——"

"You're not gonna get sloppy on me now, are you, Albert?"

Auberlain saw that The Piper had something in his hands. "No. But I'm about to piss it all away. And it's not just me. My family..."

Auberlain had moved his mother, sister and two brothers from East L.A. to Florida, where he'd bought them a house. He'd moved cousins, aunts and uncles up from Louisiana. He'd set them all up in various ways, and was spending a lot of money month by month still helping them. Now the well from which he'd been drawing was threatening to dry up, and he was in danger of leaving them all high and dry, stranded in a strange city.

He couldn't understand why Eddie was staying quiet. This Olympic-caliber loner who'd picked up a fat ghetto kid, taken him out of California, loved him like a son, albeit in his own way...how come he seemed all of a sudden not to give a shit about him? Something was very wrong here. Eddie Caminetti was inherently unfathomable but Auberlain figured he knew him better than anybody else alive did. He may have been the greatest hustler who'd ever lived, may have been the kind of sly-minded devil who was always thinking three moves ahead—hadn't he completely snookered the entire golf world when he'd played for the U.S. Ryder Cup team three years ago?—but above all else he was almost pathologically honest, reliable and trustworthy. His victims may have thought completely different, but after the inevitable fleecing every last one of them had to admit that, looked at coldly, Eddie had never lied to them. Instead, it was always their own human nature, and Eddie's uncanny understanding of it, that had led to their undoing. It wasn't just theory, either, because his long-standing, ironclad guarantee accompanied every bet he ever made: "You think I lied, you don't have to pay." The only ones who didn't cough up at the end were the chronic welshers, weasels and human parasites that seemed to infect all fields of endeavor, and, without exception, Eddie had known in advance they wouldn't make good on their losses.

So it was unthinkable to Auberlain that Eddie would suddenly turn his back on the only person to whom he'd ever played mentor. It made no sense, and if there was one thing the supremely rational enigma known as Eddie Caminetti made all the time, no exceptions, it was sense.

Unthinkable.

And he had invited Auberlain to the island, all expenses paid. So he had to still like him.

What The Piper was holding was a small box, and he was still standing in the doorway.

Auberlain looked over at his old friend and savior, who was staring right back. Eddie took in some smoke, let it settle in his mouth, then made a *moue* and puffed out a single, perfect smoke ring. Auberlain's eyes were drawn to it, but he quickly snapped his attention back to Eddie. Was that the first, faint trace of a... *smile* playing about his lips?

Eddie blew out another ring.

And he did spend the whole day with me.

Yeah, that was a smile all right. Or was it?

The O floated out over the low table between them.

"Eddie."

Another ring followed in its wake.

"Eddie...?"

The Piper had the box, although small, in both hands. Cicadas *karrupped* in the hydrangeas outside. The only other noise in the near-empty lanai and dining room was the soft *swish-swish-swish* of the ceiling fans.

"Eddie, you sonofabitch goddamned green-dick bastard... *What!*"

"What what?" Eddie said, the picture of innocence.

"Don't fuck with me!" Auberlain, grinning now, slammed his brandy goblet down so hard he almost broke it. "You're fuckin with me! I ain't askin you, Eddie, I *know* you're fuckin with me, I *always* know when you're fuckin with me and for holy goddamned sure you're fuckin with me now!"

"Am I?" Eddie answered easily as he brought the cigar back up.

"I'm gonna take that cigar"—Auberlain rose half out of his chair—"I'm gonna shove it so far down your throat you'll be blowin smoke rings out your ass. Now are you gonna tell me or do I have to—"

"Uhhrightuhrready," Eddie said, flapping his hands at Auberlain until the kid started to sink back down onto the chair. "Don't gotta get so temperamental about it." He turned and gave a half-wave toward the dining room.

Now The Piper moved, still holding the little box in two hands as he passed through the dining room and into the lanai. "Good evening, Albert," he said easily, with the practiced insouciance of one long accustomed to service but who had no illusions about any inferiority to those served.

"Whaddaya say, Piper?" Albert couldn't take his eyes off the box.

"What I say, Albert, is that we dropped a penny or two on you at the golfing contest last week."

"Yeah. Sorry about that." Who the hell else had he hurt with that pitiful performance?

"Not half as sorry as I was for you, young man. Had you the power to spontaneously evaporate yourself, I daresay you would have elected to exercise it at that point, hmm?" The Piper seemed to have noticed at that moment that he was carrying something. "Ah. Apologies. Edward?"

"Just put it down there," Eddie said, pointing to the low table.

The Piper did so. "Need anything else, gentlemen?"

"Fill Fat Albert's glass, Piper, then bring us around a cart, okay?"

"Very good, sir."

A cart? Auberlain wondered as The Piper moved off. But it lasted only a second as his mind went back to the box. "What's in it?"

"A golf ball."

"A golf ball?"

"Uh huh."

Auberlain nodded, and kept nodding.

Eddie watched him, wondering if he'd keep it up all night unless diverted. "You can open it."

"Open it." Auberlain's head was still going up and down.

"Yeah. It's closed now, and if you lift the lid, it opens. Damnedest thing you ever saw."

"Damnedest thing, yeah." Up and down, up and down... "So what's in it?"

Eddie sighed noisily. "Your career, Albert."

The nodding finally stopped. "Can I open it?"

"Chrissakes." Eddie started to reach forward but a steam shovel clamped its jaws around his forearm and threatened to crush it into jelly.

"No!" Auberlain shouted, not letting go of Eddie's arm until he was sure its forward motion had been fully arrested. By the time he did, its *circulation* had been fully arrested, as well as a good deal of its cellular activity.

Albert reached for the box as though it might disappear when he actually touched it, but it didn't, and with his other hand he gingerly lifted the lid. A ball sat in the middle of a crush of dark blue velvet. It was white. Kind of white. It glistened a little, but... only sometimes. Depended on how you looked at it. Sort of.

The logo was facing straight up, a busty she-devil, with bright red stockings and arm-length gloves. In one hand she held a golf ball, and across one upraised leg was a banner with letters on it. Auberlain held it closer and read the single word written there: SCRATCH.

"Damn." He picked the ball up with his fingertips, twisted his wrist and let it fall into his cupped hand. Like a dog maneuvering for the most comfortable position on an old blanket, the ball seemed to hunt around Auberlain's palm for a few seconds before rocking to a stop as though it had spent its entire happy childhood right there in that perfect spot. "Damn..."

"Pretty little thing, is it not?" The Piper asked.

Startled, Auberlain snapped his head up. He hadn't heard The Piper return. "Whuh?"

"The ball. Scratch. Quite the comely little bugger, wot?"

Auberlain's head started going up and down.

"Christ," Eddie said, "not again."

Auberlain stopped. "Where'd it come from?"

"A factory," Eddie answered.

"What factory?" Auberlain hadn't recovered enough of his wits to riposte with a suitable barb to that inane answer.

"My factory."

For the first time since The Piper had originally come into the room, Auberlain moved his eyes toward something other than the box or its contents. "You have a golf ball factory?"

"Yep."

"Since when?"

"Since recently."

Auberlain turned back to the ball. "Damn."

Sensing Eddie was about to deck the befuddled Auberlain, The Piper stepped in smoothly. "I say, Albert: As satisfying as it might be to stare at the Scratch, would it not be ever so much more gratifying to actually, how do you gentlemen put it, *whack it one* with a golf club?"

"Whack it—"

The cart!

Auberlain nearly flipped the coffee table over as he shot up out of his seat. "Let's go!"

"I don't know." Eddie stayed seated. "A little dark out there..."

"Don't torture the lad, Edward," The Piper admonished. "You had me bring the cart around."

"Yeah, I guess I did at that." Making a great show of painfully moving his aging joints, he got up slowly, and by the time he was fully upright Auberlain was out at the golf cart, barely taking notice of the fact that his bag had already been loaded onto it.

"Have a good time, boys," The Piper sang out as Auberlain hopped into the driver's seat. "Don't stay out too late."

As Eddie got into the passenger seat, Auberlain jumped out. "Where're the rest of them?" he asked, looking in the rear basket.

"Resta what?"

"Resta the balls."

"Don't worry about it," Eddie said as he patted the driver's seat. "You're only gonna need one."

The full moon was so bright Auberlain could still make out the little devil on the ball. He could also see the fairway of the first hole with remarkable clarity, although whether that was at least partially due to his intimate familiarity with it, he couldn't tell. He could see every square inch of this hole from tee to green with his eyes closed.

He looked at Eddie and got a consenting half-nod, then bent down and teed up the ball.

"Hang on," Eddie said, pointing downward. "Tee it with her facing the target."

"Whyzzat?" Auberlain asked as he bent to comply.

"Just do it."

Auberlain did as instructed then straightened up. He took a few easy practice swings, hesitated a second and then stepped up to the ball. He took his customary stance and his customary grip, but there was nothing customary about the faint electric thrill that raced down his spine and momentarily halted his breath. Looking down at the ball he could see bits of moonlight glinting off random atoms on its surface. He placed the head of his driver behind the ball about half an inch, and held it just high enough above the grass so it touched only two or three blades. He took one last look down the fairway and then turned back to the ball, and then thought about absolutely nothing at all as he willed himself to complete calm and stood there, motionless, as though sculpted out of granite. For several seconds he maintained that preternatural stillness, a surprisingly difficult feat attainable only by superior athletes and professional mimes, but every muscle Auberlain owned was now utterly dedicated to what he knew with profound certainty was going to occur, and he wasn't about to squander a single quantum of energy in any activity not utterly devoted to achieving that goal.

Then he backed away.

"What?" Eddie said.

Auberlain pointed toward the ball with the driver. "Eddie..."

"Whatsa matter?"

"Tell me that ball is USGA certified."

"Don't worry about it."

Auberlain shook his head, and did so definitively. He was back in charge now. "Tell me I can use that ball in tournament play."

"I said, don't worry about it."

Not good enough.

He turned around and leaned on the club. "What the hell's going on, Eddie?"

The owner of Swithen Bairn and the Scratch Golf Ball Company shrugged. "No big deal. We shipped the USGA a buncha balls last week and they've been testing them."

"When do you hear?"

"Spoza be tomorrow morning. But it's no big deal. I'm telling you, it'll be certified by lunchtime. Now get on up there and whack it one."

Auberlain stood there for a few seconds, then turned back and looked longingly at the ball sitting up on the tee. He could practically see the little devil beckoning to him, begging for him to step on up and smash the living shit out of the ball, sending her on a ride that he knew, as sure as he knew his own name, would launch her so high and so fast she wouldn't start back down until that moon looked to her twice as big as it did now.

"No." Auberlain walked back to the cart and plunged the driver into his bag, then turned and retrieved the golf ball. It pained him horribly to do it, but not as much as it would if he were to smack that ball to kingdom come only to find out the next day that he couldn't play with it because the U.S. Golf Association, the governing body of the sport in North America, reported back that it had failed their stringent series of tests.

They drove back to the main building in silence. At the front entrance they got out, and Auberlain reluctantly handed the ball back to Eddie.

Who refused it. "Keep it overnight," he said. "I got more."

The next morning Auberlain took his coffee next to the fax machine, brushed his teeth in the private bathroom right next door to the office, did his hour's worth of morning exercises next to it and had his breakfast there as well. All of that and it was only six a.m.

"How the hell long you been here?" Eddie asked when he found him there half an hour later.

"Couple minutes."

"Uh huh. What are you doing?"

"Waiting for the fax from the USGA."

"Ah. They're in New Jersey, Albert."

"Yeah, so?"

"So, it's midnight there."

Auberlain stared at Eddie for a minute, then said, "I knew that."

He ate lunch by the fax machine, too, and an early dinner, almost throwing it all up when the phone rang, once, then stopped when the fax machine answered it.

Just before six o'clock he and Eddie were back on the first tee of Swithen Bairn. Auberlain teed up the Scratch, with the little devil facing down the fairway. He didn't need to waste any time, because he'd hit this shot over three thousand times since last night, and even though this was the first time he was actually going to do it with a real club and a real ball, it hardly mattered. He knew exactly what it was going to feel like, exactly how it would travel through the air, precisely where it would touch down and precisely how far it would roll. In his mind there was a bright, shiny penny sitting out on the fairway at the exact point the Scratch was going to end up, and by his estimate he was within five feet of that spot when the real ball finally came to a stop less than sixty seconds after he'd stepped on the brake in the golf cart that had brought him to the tee.

And that five feet was past the imaginary penny, not before it.

"Nice ball," he said casually to Eddie as he handed him the club, stripped off all his clothes, ran the 320 yards down the fairway to pick up the ball, and kept on running until he crossed the green and the crushed coral sand trap and the sliver of beach, then ran into the ocean, where he swam and swam until his arms ached so bad he could barely hold on to the ball deep within his fist.

He was lying on the beach, stark naked, staring up at the moon and smiling serenely when Eddie found him about twenty minutes later. Totally spent from the mad swim but at peace for the first time in weeks, he could hardly lift his arm in greeting, or even get out of the way when Eddie threw his clothes at him. He did manage to peel his boxer shorts off his face as Eddie sat down beside him, but he hadn't yet let go of the ball.

Eddie reached over and pried it out of his hand. The Jaws of Life couldn't have pried it out of Auberlain's hand against his will, but he figured Eddie must have a reason. "'S'matter?"

"You can't have this one," Eddie said.

"How come?"

"You gotta buy your own."

Auberlain laughed as he got himself up to a sitting position. "Very funny."

"I'm not kidding."

"What the hell are you talking about?"

"We don't do sponsorships. Anybody asks you, you gotta be able to tell em honestly, the company didn't sponsor you. You bought your own."

"How come?"

"That's the way we want it." Eddie turned to him. "You cleared, what...two, three million last season? You figure you can afford to buy a couple dozen golf balls?"

"Gee, I don't know. Look like pretty expensive balls, those."

"Yeah, well." Eddie turned back toward the sea. "Try not to lose too many."

"I'll do that. You are one crazy sumbitch, though."

"Nice way to talk to a guy just pulled your bony ass out the fire."

They watched together as moonlight danced off the tops of tiny waves. Several miles away a large ship of some sort was passing by, and by shielding their eyes from the direct glare of the moon they thought they could detect a faint trail of phosphorescence in its wake, but they weren't sure. After a few more minutes the ship's running lights winked out and it was gone over the horizon.

"There *is* one slight problem," Eddie said.

CHAPTER EIGHT

"There are one or two things we can't tell you about this ball, Albert."
Auberlain nodded as Professor Norman Standish spoke. He couldn't
do much more than that other than grunt, because his mouth was full and
his Aunt Roberta—or was it his Uncle Robert?—told him never to speak
with his mouth full.

He'd nearly choked Eddie to death the night before upon hearing there
was a "slight problem" with the Scratch. With his nerves already frazzled
almost to the breaking point, it had sounded to him like the *Titanic* having a
slight problem with an iceberg. Eddie had quickly assured him, though, that
the problem was indeed slight, would not affect his ability to use it in tournament play and would be explained to him in the morning. 'Why not now?'
he demanded, and Eddie answered, 'I might as well try to explain to you
the theory of relativity.' 'You don't know the theory of relativity,' Auberlain countered. 'My point exactly,' Eddie replied, followed by 'Don't worry
about it' and capped off with 'Trust me, Albert. I've never led you wrong.'

Which was true, and after a month in which he'd lost ten pounds because
he was too upset to eat, "Fat Albert" seemed in danger of resuming his
former rotundosity in one sitting. The Piper had barely raised an eyebrow
when the young lad had started off with four fresh eggs over easy, a side of
bacon, hash browns and toasted French bread, all washed down with half
a carafe of orange juice and two cups of dark roast coffee. The Piper *had*
raised an eyebrow when he'd gone on to a stack of buttermilk pancakes
smothered in butter and maple syrup along with a chocolate malted, and
he'd had chief financial officer Oscar Petanque go phone up Eddie when
Auberlain had started in on eggs Benedict, a large bowl of oatmeal and
a peanut butter and raspberry jelly sandwich. It was the last half of the
sandwich on which he'd been munching when Standish told him there were
things they couldn't tell him about the ball.

Auberlain nodded, accelerated his chewing and swallowed. "Why not?" he said, then took another bite of the sandwich. The Piper shuddered at the sight and moved off.

"For your own protection," Eddie said from behind him.

Auberlain turned around halfway. "Huddm hay, hayee?"

"What?"

Auberlain swallowed, this time before he was finished chewing. "Whaddaya say, Eddie?"

"Nothin. They givin you enough to eat?"

"You bet. But I'm still waiting to hear what's the problem. They're supposed to explain it to me but all they keep saying is there's things they can't tell me." Auberlain scooped up a huge spoonful of oatmeal and slurped it down. "So when do they get to the parts they *can* tell me?"

"That's what I've been trying to do," Standish said, "but it's hard because I can't—"

Auberlain stopped eating and turned to him. "Professor, I'm getting ready to kill you."

"You're safe, Normie," Petanque said. "He'd have to stand up to do that."

Standish sighed. "The problem with the ball, Albert, is what materials scientists refer to as momentary gradient-compression failure."

"Ah." Auberlain dug in for some more oatmeal. "Well, that explains it all. Yo, Piper! Got any more bread over there?"

"Dear God," the others heard The Piper groan, as he moved, slowly, to comply.

"MGF, for short. You see, there are circumstances under which, ah, the elastic properties of a substance seem to weaken."

"Elastic. You mean like in my underwear? There's elastic in the ball, is that it? And it goes slack like my underwear?"

"Would you like it toasted?" The Piper asked from across the dining room.

"Nah, just the way it is."

"No, Albert, not like that at all. By 'elastic' we mean that something is capable of regaining its shape after being deformed."

"Uh huh. Any strawberry jam handy?"

"Gallons," The Piper said as he went to fetch it.

"It's how a golf ball works," Standish explained. "When you strike it with a club, you compress the face of the ball, much like you would if you'd struck a marshmallow."

"Uh huh."

"The difference is that a golf ball, which has remarkable elastic properties, will spring back to shape very quickly, and that's why it flies away from the club face."

"I thought it was the momentum of the club head," Auberlain said.

Standish brightened immediately at this bit of evidence that Auberlain was actually paying attention. "Yes, that's true, but only partially."

"You sure?"

"Am I—" Standish drew up in imminent indignation, then thought better of it. "Imagine you have a football, and you kick it. How far will it go?"

Auberlain shrugged. "Give it a good wallop, maybe sixty, seventy yards."

"Fine. Now imagine kicking with the same force, except that this time the football is slightly deflated. Now how far?"

"I dunno. Forty or fifty yards?"

"Splendid. Now imagine it's completely out of air. How far?"

"Huh."

"So you see, Albert, it's not just the force of your foot. It's the fact that you deform the ball, compress the air within, and the force of the air pushing back out snaps the ball back into shape, and it flies away at great speed."

"Huh. You telling me that's how it is with a golf ball?"

"Precisely."

"But a golf ball doesn't get compressed."

"Oh, indeed it does. If you were to see the ball at the exact moment the club head strikes it, you would see it squashed quite flat. From the side it would look as if half of it had disappeared."

"Bullshit!"

"Beg pardon?"

"He's right," Eddie said. "I've seen high-speed photographs. Damnedest thing you ever saw."

"Hello?" Petanque, ever the pragmatist, interjected. "Does any of this make a difference?"

"My word, of course it does!" Standish took off his glasses and began polishing them with the edge of the tablecloth, in preparation for delivering a lecture. "Why, it's the whole—"

"To our boy, here," Petanque said, pointing to Auberlain. "Do you think he gives a tinker's cuss about cylinder compression failure?"

"Gradient-compression failure," Standish corrected. "And only momentarily, at that."

Petanque shook his head and exhaled loudly. "Albert, what he's trying to tell you is that, once in a while—"

"A rare while," Standish inserted.

"Once in a rare while, the Scratch, well...it screws up."

"Screws up." Auberlain sniffled and, to The Piper's immense relief, set the rest of his sandwich down. "Screws up how?"

"On rare occasion," Standish explained, "the ball will fail to timely resume its normal shape after being struck."

"Uh huh. And this says to me...?"

"It'll be like hitting a turd," Eddie offered.

"A hard turd," Petanque added.

"In a nutshell," Standish agreed.

"A turd in a nutshell?"

"No, no, I meant—never mind."

"A turd, okay," Auberlain said. "So what happens?"

"Depends on the angle of attack of the club," Standish said, "and the attitude of the ball at the moment of impact."

"The ball's got an attitude?"

"I was referring to how it's lying. Which side is facing your club is a function of where the momentary failure occurs."

Eddie finally sat down, directly across from Auberlain. "Look, kid: Once in a while, the ball is going to go flat on you, but you won't be able to see it coming because it won't look any different."

"How often?"

"Not often. Like, at the most, once, maybe twice a round, or it might not happen at all for half a dozen rounds."

Auberlain looked crestfallen. "Damn…"

"Doesn't seem so awful," Standish said, a slight peevishness inflecting his voice. "After all, one or two less-than-stellar shots per round doesn't strike one, statistically, I mean, doesn't strike one as overly—"

"Eddie, I can't change balls in the middle of a round. You know that."

The other three stumbled over each other to respond, until Eddie raised a hand and won the floor. "Albert, when it happens, it's over. The ball is normal after that."

"Which is why it's called momentary," Standish said. "The *M* in MGF, you see?"

Auberlain brightened instantly. "And that's it? That's the problem?"

"That's it." Eddie motioned for a busboy to come and clear the table. "It's certainly possible that it could cost you a stroke at a crucial time. Not saying it won't. But it's also going to give you back half a dozen, so, bottom line…"

"Doesn't sound so bad. MGF, huh?"

"Here's the thing, though," Eddie said. "When it happens—if it happens—you gotta shake your head and make out like you fucked up the shot. Nobody, and I mean *nobody*, can know that it had anything to do with the ball. You get me?"

"Yeah, sure, I get you. How many people know?"

"You're lookin at em, Albert. Us and The Piper and now you."

Auberlain thought it over for a few seconds, and the others let him have his time. "You tryin to fix it, Norman?" he said after a while.

"Frankly," the physicist answered, "no."

"You're kidding. How come?"

"Difficult to explain, especially"—Standish gazed reprovingly around the table—"since these philistines seem to have no interest in the underlying physics. But, essentially, this one deficiency is inherent in the design. It's a necessary function of why the ball behaves as it does. Were we to correct this problem, the ball's desirable properties would cease to exist."

"I don't get it."

Standish thought it over. "It would be like telling your waiter the water tastes fine but could you get it less wet."

"Ah."

The Piper walked over when he sensed a lull in the conversation. "Well, Albert?"

Auberlain took a deep breath and patted his stomach as he let it out. "So what time's lunch?"

On the way out, Petanque grabbed Eddie's elbow and steered him toward the office. "Can't put this off any longer," he said. "Printer called this morning, and if we want those boxes ready to go right after the Verizon Aetna tournament, we've got to give them the go-ahead. You still want a suggested price right on the package?"

"What do you think?"

"I think it's a good idea."

"Me, too."

"Okay, then. What is it?"

When they reached the office, they went in and closed the door behind them. Eddie sat on the sofa and Petanque went around behind Eddie's desk and sat in his chair, setting his attaché on the floor beside him.

"As it happens," Eddie said, "I got a number in mind. What about you?"

"I've got one, too."

"You show me yours and I'll show you mine."

"Fair enough. A hundred bucks."

If Petanque expected Eddie to be shocked, he wasn't disappointed. "For a dozen golf balls? You gotta be kidding."

"I'm not." Petanque kept his features even to let Eddie know he was dead serious.

"That'll make them twice what any other ball ever cost."

"And that's what they're worth. What was your number?"

"I'd tell you but you won't believe me."

"Sure I will."

"A hundred bucks."

"Bullshit!"

Eddie stood, leaned toward his desk and picked up the phone, then hit two digits on the speed dial. He waited a moment, then said, "Piper? Eddie. I'd like you to tell Oscar the price I was considering for the Scratch ball. Here." He handed the phone to Petanque.

"Hey, Piper. So, what's the number?" Petanque listened for a second, then straightened up in the chair. "Uh huh. Okay, thanks." He hung up. "Guess that pretty much settles that," he said to Eddie.

"How soon is the printer ready to go?"

"Tonight." Petanque reached down to his attaché case and opened it, shoved aside a newspaper and withdrew a manila folder. He took a mechanical pencil from his shirt pocket, opened the folder and began making some markings on the layout sheet inside. "This is all they were waiting for and it's a second pass through the presses, so the rest is done. Here you go." He finished his notations and flipped the sheet around, then held it up for Eddie to see. Neatly lettered inside a circle along one edge flap, he'd written "$99.99."

Eddie leaned forward to see better. "It says ninety-nine, ninety-nine."

"Yeah, so?"

"So, we said a hundred bucks."

Petanque shrugged and started to place the sheet back inside the folder. "Same difference."

"No, it isn't," Eddie said, taking the sheet back.

"Eddie..."

"Oscar, listen. You go into a grocery store, they got fourteen thousand different items on the shelves. How many of em you figure got a price ends in a nine?"

"Let's see." Petanque looked up and pretended to do some calculations in the air. "All of them?"

"All of em, exactly." Eddie stood, reached to the far end of his desk and dragged over a stack of catalogs. One by one he lifted them from the stack and dropped them in front of Petanque. "Radio Shack, Sears, Lands' End... find me one price in there doesn't end in nine."

"I already know there aren't any."

"Why do you suppose that is, Oscar?"

"It's because twenty-nine ninety-nine sounds cheaper than thirty dollars. This isn't new news, Eddie."

"Oh, yeah?" He spotted the newspaper in Petanque's attaché and motioned toward it. Petanque took it out and handed it over.

Eddie flipped it open to the classifieds, searched for a few seconds, then turned the paper around and pointed to an ad. "So how come a Mercedes—which is *supposed* to be expensive because that's half the point of buying one, isn't it?—how'd they come up with that price?"

Petanque followed Eddie's finger to a discreetly sized price box reading "$89,999" and shrugged. "Damned if I know. Force of habit, I guess."

"Exactly. So let's break the damned habit and print a hundred bucks on the nose, so this box looks like something you should be buying in Tiffany insteada Kmart."

Petanque didn't agree right away.

"A guy at the Little Storping-on-the-Swuff Golf and Lawn Tennis Club," Eddie said, "isn't gonna give a shit about a penny one way or the other, but he is gonna give a shit, his buddies see a hundred-dollar box of golf balls in the backseat of his ninety-thousand-dollar Mercedes."

Petanque visualized it, nodded his agreement, then leaned back and looked up at the ceiling. "Man! Who's going to stock a hundred-dollar box of golf balls on his shelves?"

"Simple," Eddie said, handing back the layout sheet. "Anybody who only pays us eighty for em."

"You've got a point there." Petanque tapped his pencil on the sheet. "Now I've got a question for you."

"Shoot."

"What the heck is it about this game that makes people so crazy?"

"What do you think?"

"My friends say it's because it's played on the most unstandardized arena in the entire world of sports. You never really know what kind of shot you're going to be facing until the ball finally lands somewhere. They tell me it makes things exciting, and every round's a new deal, even on a course you played a million times."

"The element of chance? Sounds good."

"You think?"

"No. It's bullshit. You think golfers really like that random element? What happens when they land in a divot or get bounced off the course by a rock, or hit a bit of wet grass and don't get enough roll? What do you think, they smile and say, Well, let's go see what we can do with that bit of hap-penstance? Fuck no! They get royally pissed off and think it's unfair."

"Never thought of that."

"Golfers like to talk about how they find the element of chance enchant-ing, but they don't really, because you know what they're really doing?"

"What's that?"

"Removing the uncertainty every chance they get. Hell, Oscar...what do you think keeps equipment makers in business?"

"So that doesn't explain it, huh?"

"Nope."

CHAPTER NINE

THE VERIZON AETNA HAIRSTYLES-BY-GERALDO BOB'S-QUICKIE-LUBE (FORMERLY THE ENRON WORLDCOM AOL UNITED AIRLINES) CLASSIC KONA COUNTRY CLUB OCEAN COURSE, KAILUA-KONA, HAWAII

"**S**o what do you think, Bill?" Steve Farley asked. "Are we witnessing a comeback here?"

Hard to have a comeback when you've hardly been anywhere yet. "Sure is possible," Bill Winters answered amiably. "After that horrible meltdown at the Valley View, Auberlain missed the Chrysler, the Compaq, the John Deere and the MasterCard, but here at the—"

Winters paused for a split second to read the frantically scribbled sign a production assistant was holding up against the control room glass: *Not the Vly View, goddamnit! (Trevor made me write goddamnit) The "Nisn Prudntl Frt-of-Lm Texco Wste Mgmt!" And this is the "Vrzn Etna Hrstyl by Grldo Bob's Qky Lub!"*

"—here at the Kona Country Club," Winters continued, "he started off splendidly, with a birdie on the par-four first, another on the second, par on the third and fourth, and he got off a beautiful tee shot here on the par-three fifth hole."

"He certainly seems to have gotten his head together, Bill. Of course, the big question is how he'll react if he duffs one like he did at the Nissan Prudential Fruit of the Loom Texaco Waste Management Open."

Ass-kisser. "Not *if*, viewers. *When*."

"Good point, Bill."

"Nobody can hit them all perfect, and it will indeed be interesting to see what happens when Auberlain falters."

"Sure is a mental game, Bill."

"They all are."

"I understand some twenty-two million people are tuning in to this tournament. You think that's just to see if Auberlain cracks up?"

Well, let's see: Considering the largest audience we've ever had for this gig is four million, and Grotesque Industrial Amputations Caught on Tape *is Fox's highest rated show ever? Nah...they're all watching for the golf.*

Auberlain *had* **hit a beautiful tee shot** on the par-three fifth hole, but the twelve-foot putt was very tricky. Golfers on the Big Island of Hawaii liked to say that putts break toward the ocean, but Auberlain knew that what they were really doing was breaking *away* from the volcano, the long-dormant Hualalai that loomed above everything along the central Kona Coast. Problem was, since the ground everywhere in the vicinity was similarly sloped, there was little perspective against which to gauge the greens. They all looked level, because the ground around them tilted the same way, so if you couldn't see any slope, that meant it was really there and your ball was going to break.

On the other hand, if a green looked like it was angled away from the ocean, that meant it would be more level. Unless it angled too sharply, in which case the ball would actually break away from the ocean and *toward* the volcano. Exactly how much break was difficult to gauge, which was why local knowledge on island courses was worth about six strokes per round.

The green on the fifth hole looked like it angled toward the volcano and sideways at the same time. Auberlain plumb-bobbed his putter from four different directions to try to get a handle on what the net effect would be, and decided that his putt would not only break away from the water but would accelerate slightly as it approached the hole. He had to hit it harder than he would have liked in order to make sure the ball reached the hole before it turned away, but if it didn't go in it would shoot past it and he'd be left with at least a six-footer coming back. Maybe he could hit it up higher and let the slope do the work of carrying it all the way down, but if that didn't work he'd be short. Short, there's no chance it'll go in. Long, you might have a toughie coming back, but at least there's a chance it will go in. At two under through four holes and feeling really good, Auberlain could have afforded to settle for a par, but that just wasn't his style.

He lined up and gave the ball a sharp tap. It skittered for a few feet before grabbing the turf and rolling, at which point it felt the full effect of the break and started veering toward the hole. He'd gauged it well, and the trajectory looked very promising, but at the speed it was going it would have to hit the hole dead center in order to drop. An anticipatory moan rose from the crowd, and, as the ball kept moving, grew in intensity, then reached a peak as the line held. It was transmuted into a collective gasp as the ball caught an edge, whipped around and popped back out in the opposite direction and came to rest six inches away.

It was a wonderful putt regardless, and Auberlain smiled in appreciation of the crowd's admiration and sympathy as he walked forward and tapped in for his par.

His playing partner, Robert Carmichael, had it much easier. He was only eight feet away and his ball was aligned with the cup directly along the con-fluence of both of the competing breaks, which made it a dead straight shot for the hole. He sank it, and didn't bother to acknowledge the lackluster, purely perfunctory clapping from the spectators as he picked the ball up out of the hole. That halfhearted applause didn't have anything to do with it being an easy putt; they just couldn't stand Carmichael. Nobody could. He seemed to go through life resentful of ever having been born, and hardly a day went by that he didn't reaffirm his contempt for all things organic in some fashion or other. He was the only pro on tour who charged for his au-tograph, a commercial endeavor at which, understandably, he profited little. That was fine by him, because he didn't charge to make money; he did it so he wouldn't have to sign anything.

On the way off the green Carmichael held out his Rodney Cabazon put-ter to Auberlain. "Y'oughta get yourself one-a these," he said, not helpfully but contemptuously. "Nickel sole plate, barzunium peripheral weights, stressed copper facing..."

Auberlain made no move to take it. "Think I would've made that putt with it?"

"I made mine," Carmichael replied.

"Daffy Duck coulda made yours."

"Two and a half thousand dollars at Walter Craven's," Carmichael said.

Auberlain held up his Ping B-6. "Twenty bucks on eBay. Another six to have it re-gripped."

Carmichael snorted.

"Yeah, you're right," Auberlain said. "I got hosed on the re-gripping, but the guy did it while I waited, so what the heck."

Auberlain remembered well what he'd been taught during that auspicious first lesson in the searing heat of the desert just a few years ago. 'Only thing a putter can do,' Eddie Caminetti said, 'is hit the ball straight. If yours already does that, you don't need a new one.'

'What if mine dudn't?' Fat Albert Auberlain asked with a sneer.

'Then a new one won't help.'

Auberlain picked up Eddie's putter, an extremely ordinary club with a beat-up finger of brownish metal at the end of a metal shaft. 'How long you had this piece-a shit?'

'More'n thirty years,' came the reply.

Auberlain smiled a *gotcha* smile. 'So how come you held onna it so long, it don't make no difference?'

'I didn't say it doesn't make a difference. What I'm tryin to tell you is that there's no such thing as a good putter. Man comes along and tells you this here's gonna change your game? He's right.'

'He is?'

'Yeah. It'll change your game, all right. It'll fuck it up, is what it'll do.'

Auberlain held up Eddie's putter again. 'So I'm askin you, what the hell—'

Eddie took it, set the head on the ground and swung it back and forth a few times. 'The only thing that matters about a putter is that you're used to it. With this here, I know how to hit it straight and how hard to hit it. I might misread the green, but I'll never hit the putt different than I want to. Know why?'

'Cause you're used to it.'

'Right. Over the years I know how it'll behave. I hadda get used to a new one, it'd take me forever.'

'So howdja pick that one in the first place?'

'I found it.'

'Giddoudatown!'

'In a trash barrel at a local muni. Some dumbbell missed a putt, blamed it on the stick and threw it away.'

'So if you lose it, your whole game goes down the shitter?'

'Nah. I got plenty of em. And I know where to get more if they all get lost.'

'Wherezat?'

'Wal-Mart.'

'Giddoudatown!'

Auberlain himself had chosen the B-6 because he could use it to pick a ball up without bending over, which was as good a reason as any for selecting a putter.

He'd seen an infomercial for a putter once where the owner of the company had a little machine that held two putters side by side and swung them simultaneously. They each hit a ball toward a hole some six feet away. The putter they were trying to sell was fixed in place, and the guy could put any other putter in the second position. Then he'd flip a lever and both would hit a ball.

The one he was trying to sell sank the ball every time. The other one always missed by an inch, and always on the same side of the hole. Over and over he'd pull the lever, and the results were the same every time. He'd switch out the competing putter and put in a new one. It, too, would miss the hole by an inch, on the same side, while the advertised product never failed to put it in the hole. After about twenty minutes of this, even as the paid television audience clapped and cheered in complete astonishment, Auberlain and his friends were howling in laughter.

Finally, one of them volunteered to call the phone number flashing on the screen and ask the sales guy if he'd ever actually managed to find someone who'd fallen for this pitch. Tried for over half an hour but never got through because the lines were jammed.

On the 556-yard par-five sixth, Auberlain felt the ball give way at impact and he sent a vicious hook careening into the shrubbery separating the fairway from a condo development. Only a beneficent St. Andrew saved it from being a complete disaster, placing a metal fence post in just the right spot to bounce the ball back into play, albeit still a full 470 yards from the green.

Auberlain pursed his lips, made a fist and banged it into his thigh. His caddy backed away, worried that his man's driver might come flying at him with more precision than the shot he'd just witnessed, but no such histrionics occurred. Around the tee box, and around the country, pulses raced, as did speculation about what would happen next.

"Oh, boy, here it is!" Steve Farley said over the airwaves with barely disguised glee. In the control room the producer, director and staff were pumping their fists and high-fiving each other, and technicians hurried to queue the commercials that had been sold at double the normal rates under contracts that called for them to be aired at just this moment.

The monitors suddenly switched over to images of floor wax being applied by a smiling dad, two Stepford kids and a mom who was clearly still a virgin.

Winters was speechless for only a second. He jumped up out of his seat and slammed his hand onto the intercom button. "What the hell are you doing!" he screamed.

"Relax," the director called back. "It's just a ten-second spot."

By that time there was nothing much to be done about it, so Winters adjusted his headset and had prepared to take his seat again, when the happily waxing family was replaced by a crawl reading "It's as individual as you are" below a picture of a car that the manufacturer had recently announced had just sold its ten millionth unit.

Winters, electing to seethe in silence owing to the slim thread by which he was hanging based on a string of similarly indignant and equally futile protests to his network, signaled the booth to put the sixth hole feed on his monitor. The director pointed to his eyes, stuck a thumb in the air, pointed to his ears and slid a finger across his throat: *Video only, no sound.*

Carmichael shook his head as they walked off the tee, then signaled to his caddy to come over. He pulled his driver out of the bag and held it out toward Auberlain. It had a bright orange, fluorescent drawing of a snake on the back of the club head, indicating it was a Python. By purest coincidence, Carmichael had angled the logo so that the crowd and the television cameras could get a good look at it.

"That's what you need right there, sonny."

Auberlain made no move to take it. A soundman with wires and several boxes dangling from his neck came running up, microphone stuck out in front of him. Carmichael saw him from the corner of his eye.

"Yep, a Python's what you need. Won't be duck-hooking them like that last one, I can tell you."

Auberlain hadn't yet seen the sound guy. "I hit three thousand shots straight as an arrow and screw one up, and you're telling me that club is going to fix my problem?"

"Absolutely! This here's—"

"So what you're saying, it'll straighten out my hook."

"You bet! It's got a sintered face plate, mongoleum inserts, three layers of glutenized Kevlar and—"

"So if I hit the ball straight"—Auberlain grabbed the club and held it up—"this thing is going to slice it right into the ocean, right?"

Carmichael's step faltered slightly. "No!" He looked around, a tenuous smile plastered on his face. "No, it won't do that at all."

Auberlain stopped walking, forcing Carmichael to do the same. "I don't get it. If this thing takes a hook and straightens it out, then it's going to take a straight shot and spin it off to the right. Right?"

"No!"

"I mean, if I hit three thousand good shots in a row and then screw one up, with this thing I'm going to hit only one good shot every three thousand tries. I'm getting this right, aren't I?"

"No way!" Carmichael choked.

Up in the broadcast booth Winters had just gotten the audio feed and threatened to put a chair through the glass separating him from the control room if they didn't get this on the air immediately.

"Then I apologize," Auberlain was saying. "Explain it to me."

Carmichael tried to take the club back but Auberlain wasn't letting it go. "This...this club straightens out your shots!"

"So if I'm about to hook it?"

"It'll go straight."

"And if I'm about to slice it?"

"It'll go straight!"

"What if I'm about to hit it straight?"

"Then...then..."

Auberlain whirled around and looked over the crowd. He walked over to a man of about thirty, six-foot-something and moderately athletic-looking. "What's your handicap?" he asked.

"Huh?"

"Your handicap. You play golf, don'tcha?"

"Yeah, I...um...I'm a nineteen."

"Perfect. C'mere."

Auberlain lifted the rope barrier and pulled the guy through. He signaled to his caddy for a ball, teed it up, handed the driver to the guy and said, "Hit it."

"Huh?"

"Go on. Just hit one down the fairway. Hey folks! Clear a little space down there, wouldja?"

The guy looked like he'd just swallowed a whole peach without chewing. "Can I take a couple practice swings?"

"Whadda you normally do?" Auberlain asked.

"I take a couple practice swings."

"Then you go right on ahead."

"For the love of God, Trevor!" Winters called out to the director. "Are you getting this out on the—"

Trevor pointed to the main monitor. They were getting it out.

The guy took a couple of stiff, terribly uncomfortable-looking swings, then glanced at Auberlain, who waved his approval to proceed. He lined up, took a breath, tried not to think about whether he was on the air with twenty-two million people staring at him, and swung.

Considering the pressure he was under, it wasn't all that terrible. Contact was fairly solid but he'd swung outside in and the ball was slicing sharply away.

"Well, so much for that," Auberlain said as he started walking away.

"Hold on a goddamned second!" Carmichael shouted after him. "That's not a fair test!"

"Of what?" Auberlain called back. "It either straightens the shot out or it doesn't."

"I said, hold it!"

Auberlain stopped and turned around.

"It can't fix everything," Carmichael said defiantly. The Python Golf Club Company, or at least its parent, was paying him two million a year and under no circumstances could he fail to at least make an attempt at defending it. "It's science, not black magic. The guy duffed one, so how can you reasonably expect—"

"I thought he hit it pretty good."

"Bullshit! He almost missed it completely!"

"Hey, wait just a damned minute!" the guy said.

But Auberlain was already on his way back. He grabbed the club and called over his caddy.

"Is he going nuts or what?" Steve Farley asked, but not on the air.

"Not sure," Winters replied.

In the control room a phone rang. A production assistant answered it, then held it out for Trevor. "It's Tommy Trevillian."

"Oh, fuck," the director muttered. Trevillian was the president and CEO of the Medalist Golf Corporation, owner of the Python Golf Club Company.

Two seconds later Winters tore off his headset and punched the intercom button. "Now what!" he demanded, having seen the feed from the golf course replaced by a brightly smiling woman discussing her husband's diarrhea.

"Trevillian called," Trevor answered. "Said if I didn't kill the feed, he'd kill me."

"Trevor, goddamnit, you can't—"

"Bill," Trevor came back calmly, "when you start signing my checks, you can start directing my show. Now, this has got something to do with Trevillian's deal to sell a couple million balls to some Chinese company—"

"But this is about a club, not a ball!"

"Same company, and they sure as hell don't need this shit on television making them look like idiots."

Down on number six, Auberlain had stuffed half a dozen balls in his pocket and teed one more up. "Stand back a little, pal," he said to the guy he'd pulled through the ropes. By now a whole platoon of security guards had shown up to hold back the surging crowd. Spectators were pulling out video cameras they weren't supposed to have brought onto the course, and were jostling each other to get a shot of Auberlain, despite having no idea what he was up to but knowing for damned sure he was up to *something*.

Auberlain waggled the club a few times, then stepped to the ball and set up in his stance. He took the club back and, at the top of his backswing, yelled, "Left!" and swung.

The ball drew beautifully to the left.

He teed up another one, and this time yelled, "Right!" a half second before bringing the club down.

A pretty fade to the right.

"Right!" he called again, and it was so.

He turned to the guy. "Now you call it, but not before the top of my backswing. Wait until the last second, get me?"

"Yeah!"

Auberlain set up once again and brought the club back.

"Left!"

"Left!"

"Right!"

"Left!"

And then he was out of balls. "Thanks," he said to the guy, shaking his hand. "Fuck you," he said to Carmichael, handing back his club. Auberlain winked at his caddy, walked the remaining eighty yards to his ball, took out a three-wood and found Carmichael standing right next to him.

"You and I both know that was bullshit."

Auberlain nodded. "Yeah. But you started it."

"Now I'm gonna finish it."

Rather than step away and give Auberlain room to consider his shot, Carmichael waited until the security people had formed a perimeter and the crowd was once more gathered around.

"Why bother hitting it, Albert?" Carmichael said. "You know you're just going to screw it up. Why don't you just go on out to the parking lot and slam your trunk without going through the humiliation?" He'd leaned in close as though whispering intimately, but had spoken loud enough for everyone within fifty feet to hear.

"Yeah, you're probably right," Auberlain answered, hanging his head in abject misery. "Tell you what."

"Anything I can do, Albert."

"What are you so far today...two under?"

"I am. Same as you."

"Right. Well, a hundred grand says I beat you."

Carmichael blanched.

"Okay," Auberlain added, "I'll give you three strokes."

"You must be out of your mind! After that tee shot?" Carmichael looked around to make sure everyone within earshot was in on the fun. "Everybody here knows you're toast, Auberlain!"

"And you're chicken."

The spectators, sensing an imminent calamity of some sort, subconsciously began inching away.

"You can't possibly win."

"Hundred large says you're wrong."

Carmichael, trapped in the headlights, was no longer holding his own. "I believe that's against PGA Tour rules."

Auberlain turned and looked around. "Hey!" he yelled out to a man wearing a red jacket.

The tour official came over. "What's the hang-up here, boys?"

"There any rule says me and Carmichael here can't make a little side bet?"

"You each betting on only yourselves?"

"Yeah."

The red jacket shrugged. "Be my guest. Don't even want to hear about it."

Auberlain turned back to Carmichael who, when you got right down to it, really didn't have much of a choice. Croaking hoarsely through parched lips, he said, "You're on."

The crowd broke out into wild applause. On the air, the husband's case of diarrhea miraculously cleared up at the exact moment Auberlain swung his three-wood and hit his ball 255 yards smack down the center of the fairway.

Word of the side bet had raced through the crowd at nearly the speed of light. In a startling setback to traditional communications theory, groups of spectators five holes away, who had no discernible means of contact with any of the fans following Auberlain and Carmichael, somehow got wind of what was going on and broke ranks with their former favorites to hurry over and be part of the action.

Up in the network control booth a bit later, Trevor radioed down to Jorge "Zaps" Dominguez, bearer of the only portable camera that could roam freely all over the course. "Get the hell on over to number fourteen," Trevor ordered.

"Fourteen?" Zaps radioed back. "Who the hell is on—"

"Auberlain and Carmichael. Don't ask any questions, just get on over there. We don't have another unit to catch em until fourteen."

The broadcast-quality camera Zaps carried on his shoulder weighed twenty-seven pounds, including the double helix antenna sticking up above the directional microphone. The batteries arrayed around his middle like a diver's weight belt added another twenty-four pounds, and then there were the spare tapes, lens cleaning kit, two-way radio with extra batteries, his oversized headset and an emergency tool kit, all of which, when added to Zaps' own 240-pound bulk, made him look like Jabba the Suicide Bomber as he tried with limited success to jog the three-quarters of a mile to the fourteenth hole.

When he finally arrived, heaving and gasping, sweat was squirting so profusely from every pore on his body that he seemed in imminent danger of shorting out some of his gear and electrocuting himself. Just about the time he managed to stop wheezing and have a look around at what he was supposed to be shooting, Trevor, back in the control booth, having failed to accurately incorporate into his calculations the distance, the cameraman's physical condition and all the additional weight he was lugging, keyed his mike and said, "Sorry, Zaps. They're at fifteen now."

"We're getting a camera over there now," Steve Farley was saying over the air. In a remarkable display of dual processing, he was able to get those words out coherently even as he was mouthing *I will kill all of your children!* at Trevor, who mouthed back *We're trying!* and radioed Zaps to get the lead out and step on it, as though those were two different concepts.

Meanwhile, a communications major from the local college who was interning for the summer had taken it upon himself to quickly slap together a superimposed title on a side monitor. He waved at Trevor and pointed to the screen, which read: Through 14: Auberlain (-5), Carmichael (-1).

The standard way to display a score during a tournament was to post the current standings of the golfers who were being shown on camera at the time. Glancing over at the "hot" screen, Trevor saw that it was Derek Anouilh and Mack Merriwell who were now going out over the air, getting ready for their second shots on the eighteenth. But Trevor was also on the line with network headquarters in New York, where the computerized phone system was threatening to crash under the weight of calls streaming in from viewers demanding to see Auberlain and Carmichael.

He queued the live audio feed into his headset and heard Bill Winters: "...more that Carmichael seems to be spouting steam from his ears, the more Auberlain grows calm, even serene."

The voice switched to Farley. "True enough, Bill. Even when Auberlain blew an easy chip on twelve, it didn't seem to faze him a bit. How does a guy acquire that kind of maturity in the span of a few months?"

Winters: "Not just maturity...we're talking nerves of steel. Remember, he's got a hundred thousand of his own dough on the line, and this isn't some NBA-type fine the team is going to pick up. One of those boys is going to be writing a large check in about an hour."

Farley: "I think we should be getting that camera over there pretty soon. Do we know where they stand?" Farley was on his feet miming a Depression-era gangster firing a Thompson submachine gun into a rival mob's liquor truck, except he was aiming at Trevor.

The director turned to his head technician and pointed to the intern's computer display. "Queue it!" he yelled, then punched the button that would patch him into Winters' headset. "Auberlain's minus five, Carmichael minus one, through fourteen!"

Winters, adept at speaking even as he was listening, began doing so when Trevor was barely past the word *five*. "Getting word here that they're just starting the fifteenth hole, with Auberlain at five under par and Carmichael one under."

It was a cardinal rule at the network that on-air anchors never learn something at the same time the viewers do. They always had to be a step ahead, had to appear solidly clicked in and on top of things, as though deigning to dribble out bits of intelligence they'd really known all along and had just now chosen to share with their audience. Only after Winters finished speaking did Trevor punch a fist toward his technician to get the title the intern had typed up superimposed on the outgoing feed.

"Right you are, Bill," Farley said smoothly, complimenting Winters on his psychic abilities.

Zaps finally made it to the Auberlain-Carmichael pairing. By the time it was nearly all over an hour later, the network had broken an audience-share record for the first day of a minor PGA Tour stop. The three-stroke advantage Auberlain had given Carmichael did the hapless curmudgeon no good at all. He shot a 73 against Auberlain's 67.

Carmichael watched Auberlain sink his final putt, a curving fourteen-footer that hung on the lip for a second and then dropped in, to the delirious delight of the enormous crowd of spectators. As Auberlain turned to them and raised his arms in victory, Carmichael, who was standing nearer the hole, walked over and bent to retrieve the ball, fully intending to feign a show of good sportsmanship by throwing it back to Auberlain, but a few feet short, which would force the grinning winner to stumble awkwardly forward to snare it.

But when he picked up the ball he didn't turn to throw it.

"What the hell's going on?" Trevor called out to no one in particular.

"Carmichael's not tossing the ball back to Auberlain," Farley observed, as some twenty-five million people observed right along with him.

But this time it didn't occur to Winters to chastise him for uttering the blindingly obvious, because it was worth directing people's attention to in case they didn't realize something unusual was going on. "He seems to be staring at it."

Trevor punched a button on his control console. "Stay with him, Zaps!" he yelled.

Winters saw the video feed shake slightly as Trevor's shouted order hit the cameraman's eardrum. Zaps, who had both hands on his camera, was powerless to adjust the volume in his headset, and Trevor couldn't shift to one of the fixed-position units because none of them had the proper angle on Carmichael.

Auberlain was clowning around with the crowd and didn't notice Carmichael staring at his ball until a guttural, raspy shout headed his way from over by the flagstick.

Trevor heard it, too, and realized that if he heard it, the television audience could hear it as well, and he barely got his finger on the kill switch as Carmichael's exclamation hit the on-green microphones, but because of the excellent bead Zaps had on him, twenty-two million people could read his lips as clearly as if he'd tattooed the words on his forehead:

"What the fuck is this!" Carmichael had yelled, holding Auberlain's ball up over his head.

Auberlain, startled, turned around and slowly let his arms drop. Seeing that Carmichael had picked up his ball, he wiggled his fingers at him: *Toss it here.*

But Carmichael brought the ball back to eye level and took another look at it, then called out, "What the hell have you been playing with!"

As though a blanket had descended on them, the spectators ceased their wild cheering and strained to hear what was going on.

"Give me the ball," Auberlain said.

Carmichael made no move to comply. "You cheated."

A ripple ran through the crowd, an energetic one but of indeterminate focus, because nobody quite knew what to make of this. Were they supposed to be shocked? Surprised, maybe, or just indifferent? Were they seeing history, or just a forgettable display of sophomoric petulance? Was Robert Carmichael on the verge of a long-coming and well-deserved public humiliation, or was Albert Auberlain, the hero of the moment, going to be exposed as something worse in the world of golf than a child molester: a cheater?

"Cheated," Auberlain echoed.

"You heard me."

"You just lost a hundred thousand bucks fair and square and you're going to welsh in front of millions of witnesses?"

"What's the problem here, gentlemen?"

The voice had come from off to the side, and both men turned to see the reddest jacket of all, that of head tournament referee Desmond Grant, an upper-crust Brit, one of the grand old men of the game and probably its foremost rules authority as well.

"It's a private matter," Auberlain answered.

"Concerning your wager, I presume," Grant said.

"Right. Nothing to do with the tournament."

"I quite agree."

"The hell it doesn't." Carmichael marched forward and held the ball out to Grant. "*This* makes it a tournament matter."

"And this is...?"

"An illegal golf ball."

"Oh, dear." Grant pulled a pair of reading glasses out of his jacket pocket, perched them on his nose and peered down at the ball. A female devil in vamp clothing stared back up at him. "My word." He looked up and around, head tilted down so he could look out over the top of his glasses. "And whose might this be?"

Carmichael pointed at Auberlain. "His."

"Then why do you have it, Mr. Carmichael?"

"I fished it out of the hole. It's not sanctioned for—"

"Did you give him permission, Mr. Auberlain?"

"Permission?" Carmichael cried. "What are you talking about?"

"Most discourteous, sir. You have no right to handle another player's ball. I say, Mr. Auberlain...do you wish to file a protest?"

"What the hell are you talking about? The guy was playing with an illegal ball! He should be disqualified!"

Grant looked around. "Would you be so good as to keep your voice down?"

"Goddamnit, Grant!" Trevor snarled in the control booth. "Speak up!"

Security guards were spaced out around the perimeter of the green, trying to hold back crowds that threatened to overrun the pristine playing surface.

"Well then, Mr. Auberlain," Grant said. "Do you wish to protest?"

"Listen," Carmichael said, "the round was already over. He sank his final putt, so you can't disqualify me. But that's an illegal ball so—"

"What makes you say that?" Grant asked.

"Well, look at the goddamned thing! No brand name, no nothing! Here." Carmichael took his own ball out of his pocket, a Medalist Nobidium-clad Terminator 417, and tossed it to Grant. "Standard ball, right off the shelf."

"Yeah," Auberlain muttered to himself, but made sure Grant could hear it. "Right off the shelf of the Medalist research lab."

"But that thing?" Carmichael said, pointing to the Scratch. "I have no idea where he got it!"

Grant frowned in concern, and said to Auberlain, "Did you not show your opponent your ball on the first tee?"

"Sure did."

"Mr. Carmichael?"

"Well..."

"Did he or didn't he?"

"Who the hell really looks at those things! It's just a custom, anyway. And besides, I'm not the one responsible for making those calls. You are. So do your job and—"

"That's a Scratch ball, isn't it?"

"Sure is," Auberlain answered.

"Straight off the shelf?"

"Yep."

"What the hell is a Scratch ball?" Carmichael demanded.

"Doesn't matter," Grant answered. "It's legal for play, and—" His radio began beeping insistently. He held it up and keyed the mike. "Hello? Yes, hello?"

A loud whistle sounded from down the fairway. In the distance, Joel Fleckheimer was holding up two fingers.

"Oh, dear," Grant said as he switched to channel two. "Hello?"

"Chrissakes, Desmond," Fleckheimer's crackly voice said. "You guys planning a baby shower up there or what?"

"Heavens! Frightfully sorry, old man. We'll clear out directly."

As he herded the two players off the green and the security guards began pushing the spectators back, Grant fiddled with the ball. "I say, Mr. Auberlain...would you mind terribly... what I mean to say is..."

"Sure, Desmond. Keep it."

"Splendid! Thank you, Albert!"

"Listen..." Carmichael started to say.

"Oh, blow it out your ass," the head referee shot back.

CHAPTER TEN

Jerome Traumerai, puffing a little from the effort of four-putting the ninth on the North course at the Indian Wells Country Club, pushed open the door to the pro shop, stepped inside and fanned himself for a few seconds in air frigid enough to solidify nitrogen.

"Hey, Mr. Traumerai," assistant pro Jenny Dannon called out gaily. "Hot enough for you?"

"Lord have mercy," Traumerai panted back. "Wish I could play in here."

Dannon laughed in appreciation. It may have been the hundredth time she'd heard the line that week but, gosh darn it, it sure was a pip, and, by golly, Traumerai was a member.

Traumerai waited until Pete Betts, the other pro working the desk with Dannon, stepped away to answer a phone, then walked up and rested his elbows on the counter. "Say," he said, "you get in any of those Scratch balls yet?" He didn't need to keep his voice low because Betts was completely deaf in one ear and wore a hearing aid in the other.

"Got em in," Dannon said, "and they were gone in twenty minutes."

"You're kidding. How many did you have?"

"Fifty boxes. We ordered three hundred but that's all they gave us, and that was only because Ricky knew this guy who once played golf with the distributor's brother-in-law."

"Got any more on order?"

"Sure do. As many as they'll give us."

"What are you selling them for?"

"Hundred-and-a-quarter a duz." By now Dannon had almost gotten over the embarrassment of quoting that absurd figure.

Traumerai nodded. "Good price. Listen, you get some..." He reached into his pocket where he'd secreted a twenty-dollar bill before walking into the pro shop. Waiting until he was sure Betts wasn't looking, he took

Dannon's right hand in his left and pressed the bill into her palm. "...you set aside a box for your old buddy Jerome, okay?" Then he winked.

Dannon winked back. "You got it, Mr. Traumerai. Soon as they come in I'll give you a call."

"There you go! You're the best, Jenny!"

"You too. Take it easy out in that heat."

Betts hung up the phone and walked over. Dannon handed him the twenty. He opened a small door below the counter and pulled out a large cigar box. The top was ajar, owing to the large number of tens, twenties and a few fifties that were stuffed inside. He added the latest contribution, let the lid flop down without trying to shut it, and put it back. "What's Traumerai's handicap?" he asked Dannon.

"Thirty-four."

"Thirty-four." Betts shook his head and sighed. "Guy couldn't tell a Scratch from a pig's testicle."

"This from a guy with an eight thousand dollar stereo system?"

"What?" Betts turned his half-working ear toward Dannon. "Whud you say?"

"I said, handle the desk, okay? Gotta go give a lesson."

"No problem."

Traumerai watched with mounting jealousy on the twelfth tee as his brother-in-law teed up a Scratch and, a half-smile on his face, rammed it 230 down the middle. Traumerai clamped his jaws together, set down his Medalist Nobidium-clad Terminator 417 and sliced it into a rhododendron bush 140 yards away. The bush being in the backyard of a private home, he had to hit a provisional, which he managed to keep in play by bouncing it off a hummingbird feeder hanging from the roof gutter of a toolshed.

The twosome they were playing with, a father and his twelve-year-old son, teed off and hit fairly good shots onto the fairway. The father was using a Scratch as well.

As they drove up the fairway, the brother-in-law said, "I feel in control with this ball, you know what I'm saying? I step up and just *know* I'm going to put it exactly where I want."

He had 160 yards remaining to the green, which was protected in front by a lake. He fished a Medalist Apex out of his bag. "Confidence is everything, Jerome. The best way to ensure you hit a ball well is to believe, deep down, that you will." He picked up the Scratch and replaced it with the Medalist.

"What're you doing?" Traumerai asked

The brother-in-law pointed toward the lake with his six-iron. "Think I'm going to chance putting a nine-dollar ball in the water?"

On the fourteenth, the father hit a pretty three-wood shot 220 yards and slightly left. "That there ball will change your game," he said to his son. "You can hit it farther, straighter and stop it on a dime."

"So how come I don't get to hit one, Pop?" the kid asked.

The father tousled his son's hair and smiled indulgently. "You're not good enough yet."

On the seventeenth, the brother-in-law's driver made an awful, clunking sound as it glanced ineffectively off his ball, sending it clattering away toward a stand of trees.

"It true what they say?" the father asked. "Heard a rumor it caves on you once in a while, this ball."

"It's no rumor," the brother-in-law called over the sound of the carts as they started down the fairway. "Every so often, it feels just like hitting a dead rat."

"So what do you do?"

They pulled up to the brother-in-law's ball. "Not a damned thing," he said, taking out his three-wood. Radiating confidence like an odor, he took up his stance, threw a look down the fairway toward the pin and whacked a monster, straight as an arrow, to a landing less than ten yards in front of the green.

Grinning, he said, "You just step up and hit it again."

"Damn," muttered Traumerai. "Wonder if I should've given Jenny a fifty."

"What's that, Jerry?"

"Nothing."

It never even occurred to Traumerai to ask his brother-in-law if he could buy a few Scratch balls from him in the interim. Nobody would do it, nobody would blame you for refusing, and it would just make for an awkward moment best avoided.

The gradual, subtle, unadvertised introduction of the Scratch into the general marketplace was a phenomenon not witnessed in retail circles since Cabbage Patch dolls and Tickle Me Elmo. But whereas sales of those two items, like Pokémon cards, were fueled largely by the Idiopathic Pacifier rationale—the product has no conceivable use but you have to buy it or your kids will drive you psychotic—adults were buying the golf ball for themselves, justifying the seemingly outrageous cost on the basis of demonstrable utility.

While spouses in middle class households groused about the unnecessary expense, and children in some families a bit lower on the socio-economic scale went a few weeks longer without new shoes, nobody in the golf game—not network commentators or magazine columnists or golf school instructors or club pros—nobody of any note dared criticize the new ball. They'd all seen too many of their friends and colleagues suffer withering humiliation after they'd loudly derided those morons who would shell out that kind of money for a golf ball and then shown up one morning with a couple of the devil-bedecked sleeves in their bags.

The wholesale price to distributors was $80 for a box of twelve, and even though "$100" was printed plainly on the box as the retail price, it had become common practice for pro shops and specialty stores to mark the balls up to $125 and even $135 per dozen. Thus, when a golf shop in Myrtle Beach, South Carolina, ran an ad in the local Shopper's Guide proclaiming "We charge only $100 for Scratch golf balls!" the resultant stampede nearly overtaxed the city's small police department, which might have been able to deal with the matter had the golf shop stocked more than just fifty boxes. The near-riot that took place when that little piece of information leaked out, which was fully an hour before the doors actually opened for business, necessitated reinforcements from the county sheriff's office and a nearby state militia unit undergoing semiannual training exercises. The commander of the unit, a crafty old veteran who'd seen enough of actual combat to know he never wanted to see any more, and sure as hell not from a group of unorganized and undisciplined civilians with no respect for the rules of engagement, convinced the store's owners to break the boxes down and offer for sale sleeves of three balls each. The 196 customers who each got a sleeve (one box of a full dozen went to the militia commander) were so elated that none bothered to complain that they'd each paid $30 for three balls, and even took pains to point out to potential troublemakers who hadn't gotten any at all that they shouldn't act like such whiny babies over something as trivial as a golf ball. The militia unit was long gone when a few of the less-than-civil among the whiny "have-nots" took a notion to relieve some of the more vocal "haves" of their trivial sleeves of golf balls, only to find the owners resolved to defend their newly acquired possessions even to the death, if it came to that.

Retailers and golf club pro shop managers learned to keep the balls in locked cabinets behind the counter, ostensibly to prevent theft but in actuality to keep customers from knowing the status of their inventory. That way they could tell unfamiliar walk-ins that they were out of stock and still be able to supply their loyal regulars.

A surprising number of young children, the homeless, semi-coherent winos and elderly people in walkers or wheelchairs tried to buy Scratch balls. It didn't take long for sellers to glom onto the fact that, like professional ticket scalpers who paid college students and the unemployed to spend three days and nights waiting in line for Rolling Stones tickets, obsessed golfers could pay nonplayers to buy golf balls when sales were strictly limited to one box per customer. At a Fairway Dreams discount store in New Rochelle, New York, a clerk refused to sell a box of Scratch balls to a blind man, claiming that he'd seen another customer, who'd just purchased a dozen, pay the man to come in and buy him some more. The blind man was so incensed he filed a lawsuit against the conglomerate that owned the discount chain, claiming that the store was in gross violation of the Americans with Disabilities Act. The suit claimed actual loss of $20, which the golfer had demanded back because he'd not gotten his golf balls, consequential damages of $50,000 for tortious interference with the blind man's right to make a living based on his expectation of purchasing, over his working lifetime, another 2,500 boxes of golf balls for other people, and punitive damages in the amount of $8 million because of the irreparable psychological trauma the humiliating experience had inflicted on him. The store owners, despite having put up a vigorous fight even after getting torn apart in the press for basing their defense strategy on the fact that the victim couldn't even know for certain, much less prove, that he'd ever actually *been* in the store, decided to settle after the ACLU stepped in and filed a brief with the court stating that the blind man was a bona fide customer by every reasonable and customary definition, and what he intended to do with his purchase once he left the premises was his own business and not that of the Fairway Dreams discount chain. (The chain's attorney had rolled up his sleeves and prepared to make the store clerk's business judgment the key issue, but gave it up after a young ACLU attorney, out of court and off the record, asked if the company also wished to accept responsibility for the clerk's business judgment the time he'd sold a five-iron to a movie producer who'd used it a few seconds later to bash in the windshield of a car whose owner had just muscled him out of a parking spot, right in front of Fairway Dreams and in full view of the clerk.)

Inevitably, a black market in the balls developed. In Southern California word quickly spread that a lemonade stand on the corner of Washington Street and Highway 111 in Indian Wells, an intersection that was within four miles of seventeen spectacular and spectacularly expensive golf courses, was selling Scratch balls out of the trunk of a Chevrolet Camaro with an umbrella mounted on the roof. That this lemonade stand didn't have any lemonade was curious enough in itself, but it was also the only such establishment that was manned by three grown men, took credit cards and could make change for a five-hundred-dollar bill. That one of the men was armed was simply a rumor.

Eddie Caminetti and Professor Standish weren't at all put off by the burgeoning black market. The presence of operations such as the lemonade stand only added to the mystique and consequent desirability of their product, which was why they'd earmarked several thousand boxes to help perpetuate the image. Scratch delivery truck drivers were instructed to take detours through poor neighborhoods, search out senior centers and free clinics and hand out a few boxes here and there to kids working as volunteers. The deserving youngsters would either head for the local muni to sell the balls themselves, or get together, pool their treasures and lay the balls off to middlemen who'd gotten wise to the company's good-neighbor policy. It was a classic win-win situation.

The two principles of the Scratch Golf Ball Company weren't bothered by the reactions from their competitors, either. In fact they were delighted at every fresh advertising assault.

Eddie told *Golf Magazine* that it looked to him like Medalist, the five-hundred-pound gorilla of the golf equipment world, was panicking. "We're just a little mom-and-pop," he said in a phone interview. "We don't sell enough golf balls to fill half a Medalist delivery truck. Not that we're complaining, because that's the way we want it."

"It is?" the interviewer said. "Why would businessmen want a thing like that?"

"It's simple," Eddie said. "None of the owners of Scratch need any more money. We just love the game. Our goal was to sell a golf ball unlike any other on earth and target it to the most discriminating players who were concerned only about their golf games and not their wallets. We never let cost considerations even get mentioned when discussing how to construct the Scratch ball. We figured, let's get to market the very best ball it's humanly possible to make and still be USGA legal, and only *then* look at what it cost us. At that point we set the price to the customer and that was it."

"How do you market to such a narrow band of serious golfers? Where do you advertise?"

"We don't."

"I don't understand. What do you mean, you don't advertise?"

"We don't advertise."

"I don't understand."

"People know the ball exists. They know where to get it. If they want it, fine. If they don't want it, that's fine, too. But if we advertised, we'd have to roll that cost into the price of the ball. Now how do I look a customer in the eye and tell him I had to raise the price of the ball in order to convince him to buy it, when he didn't need any convincing in the first place? Doesn't make any sense."

That kind of logic was lost on the Medalist Corporation, which very much did care about whether people bought their products or not. Medalist, or at least the publicly traded parent company, had 450,000 owners, not two. Virtually none of those owners cared about anything having to do with anything other than whether the price of the shares they'd bought went up or down. They hadn't invested because they liked golf any more than they'd bought pork bellies because they liked bacon. Most of them couldn't think beyond the next quarterly earnings report, either, and the company's long-range plans were of no interest to them whatsoever. They wanted to know what Medalist was going to do *now*.

"Nipping this one in the bud" was the watch-phrase of the day around the executive suite, which technically resided on the thirty-fifth floor of a high-rise in downtown Atlanta but in more practical terms was situated on the Medalist "Test Course" in nearby Gresham Park. It was on the fifteenth green of that course that company advertising people had come up with such attention-getters as the full-pager that ran in twenty-two national magazines and proclaimed, above a photomontage of Medalist golf balls, "If you want to pay a hundred bucks for a dozen of these balls, we'd be happy to charge you that," and in smaller letters below, "...but you don't have to spend such a ridiculous sum for the best golf ball in the world." Conveniently absent from the ad was any clue as to which Medalist ball was actually *the* best, since nine different ones were pictured in the ad.

The biggest perceived threat was to the Medalist KY 9000, the crown jewel in the Medalist pantheon of golf balls, advertised as "The Ball That Brought Derek Back," referring to Derek Anouilh's return to golf after a surprise hiatus. It had caused a sensation when it first hit the market, selling for an unprecedented fifty dollars per dozen. The competition laughed it off, then sobered up quickly when it became one of the most sought-after balls in the business. Limited production and scarce availability only increased its cachet in the marketplace, and soon everyone was scrambling to come up with an expensive superball. However, Medalist's preeminence in the marketplace, coupled with endorsements for the KY 9000 from some of the biggest names on the PGA Tour, made it very difficult for anyone to break into the market, and Medalist barely reacted to the upstarts. That it had felt compelled to react to the Scratch, though, was immensely gratifying to Eddie and Professor Standish, and they welcomed the company's attention.

What did get Eddie and the professor torqued, however, was discovering that they weren't the only players in the Scratch golf ball market.

CHAPTER ELEVEN

If Wayne Chemincouver expended half as much energy in honest work as he did in trying to avoid it, he'd be a millionaire instead of a scruffy, perpetually ill-kempt no-goodnik who lacked the wherewithal even to create trouble properly. Forty years of studied lack of ambition, coupled with a self-loathing so innate he had no awareness of its existence, had carved Wayne's face into a mask that told each new acquaintance, however fleeting, that the next few minutes were going to be a dismal, teeth-grinding, monumentally annoying experience. He'd practically made a career out of pissing people off so thoroughly and so quickly that they caved in to his demands just to get him the hell away. His was the kind of personality that could faze even a discount store refund clerk.

Inspiration for one's direction in life can come in a variety of ways, most of them unexpected. When Wayne was in high school a student in his shop class had gotten some chocolate cupcakes out of a vending machine. Opening the package, the student noticed that the "squiggle," a helical loop of icing that normally sat atop the cupcake, was missing. Wayne had demonstrated his usual sympathy ('Big fucking deal, you faggot'), but the kid said he was going to write to the company and complain.

Two weeks later he showed up with an entire case of cupcakes the company had sent him as compensation for his missing squiggles and for his loyalty in writing to the company to point out a manufacturing flaw. Thus inspired, Wayne wrote a letter to the Cracker Jack company complaining that he'd bought a box of their product (he'd done no such thing) and had been devastated to discover that there was no prize inside. Several days later he received a profuse letter of apology along with a cardboard box crammed with some five hundred Cracker Jack prizes. It was a heart-stirring moment of revelation for young Wayne, and kicked off a lifetime of equally rewarding experiences, each one further reinforcing his complete willingness to shamelessly debase himself. As long as he got what he wanted, his attitude was that he'd been the better man, that he'd bested the other guy because he was smarter and more persistent. This delusion was possible because Wayne cared not a whit that nearly everyone with whom he came into contact thought him a loser, a despicable excuse for a human being and a total jerk.

That went for the guy behind the counter at the Colonel Edgar B. Lewis Municipal Golf Course in McMinnville, Oregon, too.

"Afternoon, gentlemen. How can I help you?" asked Bobby J. Troper, the pro manning the desk, as Wayne walked in with a friend.

"Chemincouver and Blodgett. Got a twelve-fifteen tee time," Wayne said. It was already 12:20.

"You're a little late," Troper said, walking over to his scheduling book.

"Five minutes," Wayne answered.

"Yeah, well, we're kind of booked up. Let me see what we can do here."

"Somebody take our tee time?"

"Uh huh," Troper said as he ran his finger down the page.

"Fine. Give us theirs."

"They were walk-ins. Didn't have a tee time."

"Okay, we're walk-ins, too."

Troper looked up from the book. "Sir, I said I was going to see what we could do for you."

"Well, we drove here, we want to play."

"I realize that, but you had a tee time and didn't show."

"Yeah, we showed! We're here, right in front of you!"

"You showed up late."

"You said you were gonna find us something, right? So..." Wayne waved at the book.

"I'm trying, sir."

"There's always a way to squeeze a couple guys in. You know that, well as I do."

"Like I said," Troper replied, returning his gaze to the sheet, "we're pretty booked up."

"Nobody'll notice if you send us out."

"The guys with the next tee time will."

"Don't worry about it." As Troper continued to try to find a slot, Wayne waved him over. "Come on, let's just write us up a ticket and we'll head on out."

"Sir—"

"Come on," Wayne said again. He had his head down and was still waving, as though he didn't need to look up to know that his wishes were being complied with. "Come on."

"Sir—"

Wayne reached over the counter and pulled a tee ticket out of a box.

"Hey!" Troper said as he turned away from the sheet and began walking back to the counter.

Wayne pulled a pencil from the top of the cash register drawer and held it out toward Troper. "You take your little pencil here, you scratch down our names, we give you some money and we go tee off. Come on, now."

Troper turned once more to the scheduling book. Jaw muscle pulsing, he said, "I can get you out at twelve-fifty."

"Yeah. You can get us out before that. Just write your little ticket." He waggled the pencil again. "Come on."

"Sir, unless there's a cancellation—"

"There's always a cancellation. You'll get us out sooner than that."

"I can't promise—"

"You'll get us out. Come on, let's write the ticket so we can get our clubs in the cart."

Anxious to be rid of this obnoxious pain in the ass, Troper complied. Filling in the two names he'd read off the 12:15 tee time, he said, "Forty bucks for the two of you. How do you want to pay?"

"It's only thirty," Wayne said.

"It's forty."

"I got a coupon." Wayne started to fish for his wallet.

"Coupons expired last week."

Wayne smiled indulgently. "Yeah, right. Who ever looks at those dates? Here it is," he said, producing a few threads of curled newsprint that might once have been a coupon but now looked like a large hair ball that had been coughed up by a dyspeptic cat.

"I told you, sir...it's expired."

"Hey, come on, come on..."

"I can't—"

"Look. You put it in the paper because you wanted business, right? Well, here's business, me and my buddy here. So just write down thirty bucks and off we go." Wayne tapped two fingers on the tee ticket. "Go ahead, write down thirty bucks. Take my coupon, write down thirty bucks...all there is to it. Here—" He reached for his wallet and motioned for his friend to do the same.

"I gotta charge you—"

"Here." Wayne reached into his too-slow friend's wallet and pulled out a twenty, then took a ten from his own and slapped them down on the counter. "Thirty bucks. Come on, let's get it done."

When Troper, his pencil still poised over the tee ticket, still didn't move, Wayne reached out and moved his hand, as though trying to write for him.

"Keep your hands off me," warned Troper, who was thirty pounds and eight thousand hours of physical conditioning beyond Wayne.

"Yeah, yeah, okay," Wayne replied, utterly undeterred. He tapped the tee ticket a few more times and shoved the money forward. "Come on. Money's right here, you got my coupon, it's business...let's get the ticket filled out and let's go."

He turned his head and pointed out the window. "Tee's open, see? Nobody on it, so just take the money, gimme the ticket and we're off."

Behind them a group of men walked in. "Hi, Mr. Galvin," Troper called out. "You guys ready to tee off?"

Wayne whirled around and said, "We're just a twosome; you mind if we go ahead of you? Be out of your way in less'n five minutes."

"I just told—" Troper started, but he was too late.

"Sure, go ahead," Mr. Galvin said.

Wayne turned back to the counter and spread his hands. "See? Like I said, no problem. Sign us up and we're outta here."

On their way out a minute later, Wayne said to his friend, "Just stick with your ol' buddy here, Franky. I know how to get stuff done."

They'd each just gotten a box of Scratch balls, Franky from a pro shop in Portland, Wayne from some underprivileged kid who'd wanted seventy-five bucks but settled for fifty after a half-hour conversation in which Wayne had come at him so relentlessly and addled him so badly the kid was sure he'd be arrested if he took more than the money Wayne was offering.

After four holes, Wayne, a twenty-nine handicap, declared that the balls sucked. That was about the time he'd lost his fourth one, this time in a lake. The other three had gone over fences and disappeared.

Franky didn't think they were too bad, but several holes later he noticed that the logo on his—he'd only used one since they'd begun—had gotten so rubbed out the little devil was barely recognizable. Wayne's, which he'd unaccountably managed to retain for five holes in a row, looked pristine, despite having been subjected to considerable friction and erosion from contact with several asphalt cart paths, a large number of tree trunks, an electrical junction box and some two dozen violent attempts to exit from sand traps.

"I don't get it," Franky said on the tenth tee. "How the hell come your little what's-her-face looks brand new and mine's all wore out?"

Wayne compared both balls side by side. "Huh."

"Don't seem right."

"Don't worry about it."

"How come?"

"Cuz I'm gonna mail this back to those fuckers, tell em it's a piece-a shit."

"But it isn't a piece-a shit. Just the picture's a piece-a shit."

Wayne shook his head and sighed. "You don't get it, Franky. You tell a company something they make's a piece-a shit, they send you a whole bunch free."

Franky scrunched up his face in confusion. "Why the hell would they think you want more of what you think's a piece-a shit?"

"Beats me," Wayne replied, "but they do. They all do. You go into an IHOP, they got a sign right in the menu: You don't like the food, you get a free meal."

"Bullshit!"

"Swear to God."

"You don't like the food, they give you *more?* That's supposed to make you happy?"

"Hey, don't lookit me. Guess it works, what can I tell you?" He held up the ball. "But this here, this is what you call a *quality control problem.* One box is good, the other's shit?" He put the scuffed one in a pocket of his golf bag. "Ain't nothin companies hate more'n a quality control problem. Gives em fits, that kinda shit gets out, so believe you me, they're gonna send us a whole fuckin truck fulla new balls. Come to think of it..." Wayne reached into the golf cart and pulled a new ball out of Franky's box.

"Here," he said, tossing it to his friend. "Fuck another one up."

CHAPTER TWELVE

THE FIRST TEE, AUGUSTA NATIONAL GOLF CLUB

Recently installed FBI director Bradford MacArthur Baffington watched Eddie as the notorious hustler took in the surroundings of the course supposedly designed by Bobby Jones and Alister MacKenzie.

That design, however, had just been the first cut of a protean layout that over the years had been worked over by such famous designers as Perry Maxwell, Robert Trent Jones, Jack Nicklaus and Tom Fazio. So exclusive that the club didn't even publish a list of its members, Augusta National had become, so the cliché went, a *shrine* to golf, but it was actually more of a high-class hooker, the kind who only did business with the very upper crust of clientele who could be trusted to report on the experience with nothing short of religious rapture in order that they themselves didn't appear the lesser for not having appreciated her virtues.

Augusta had almost as many symbolic references as Arlington National Cemetery. There was the Eisenhower Tree, the three-acre Ike's Pond, bridges dedicated to different famous golfers, a multiple-user drinking fountain commemorating a progression of course records, the Arnold Palmer Plaque, the Jack Nicklaus Plaque...the place dripped with history, tradition and good ol' boy exclusivity.

Baffington enjoyed the sight of Eddie taking in the Butler Cabin, and could practically look inside his head to see him visualizing the string of champions donning the famous Green Jacket within.

Baffington leaned on his club. "So," he said to Eddie with a sly grin, "what do you think?"

Eddie turned around and faced the tee box. "How the hell should I know?" he answered, taking a ball and tee out of his pocket. "Haven't even played it yet. So what's this here...four hundred something yards?"

Baffington's grin vanished as the two caddies politely turned away. "Um, four thirty-five," he stammered slightly. "Bit of a dogleg right. It's called 'Olive.'"

"Oh yeah? Whyzzat?"

"Each hole is named for a prominent plant that grows on it."

"How come?"

"Tradition. Say, Eddie, we haven't even decided on the terms of the bet."

"You know your end: You beat me, you're my guest for a weekend at Swithen Bairn."

"And if you win?"

"I need a favor."

Baffington turned and flicked a finger. His caddy pulled a driver from his bag and handed it over. "So you said. Except you wouldn't tell me what the favor was."

"No sense getting into it until we're finished."

"And suppose I can't oblige for some reason?"

"Then you don't have to. I told you. If you think it's unfair, just say no and we part friends."

Baffington pursed his already nearly nonexistent lips and shook his head once. "Doesn't seem like the Eddie Caminetti I've heard about."

"It's exactly like him. Don't worry about it."

"If you say so. Of course, you know I won't do anything illegal."

"Wouldn't dream of asking you to. Matter of fact, I want you to investigate a crime."

Baffington held out a hand, offering Eddie the tee. "You don't need to beat me at golf for that. It's my job."

Eddie bent to tee up his ball, aligning the little devil so she faced down the fairway. "Yeah, well, this may be a little on the small side for the Bureau to worry about. That's why it's a favor."

"I understand." Baffington also understood that Eddie was savvy enough not to try to blatantly trade the director of the FBI a weekend on the fabled island for a Bureau-related accommodation, which would be tantamount to selling a government service for personal gain.

Betting for the same service, however, was different. Sort of. "But I also like to play fair," the director added. "And you should be taking two strokes a side from me."

Eddie didn't respond right away, but stepped up to take his shot, which he hit 250 yards down the middle and slightly left in order to clear the dog-leg and also avoid the fairway bunker on the right. "Tell you the truth, Mr. Director, I'm feeling particularly good today."

"Suit yourself. And nice shot."

"Thanks."

Baffington stepped to the box and teed up his ball, also a Scratch. He turned toward Eddie and pointed to the ball. "Thanks for these, by the way. Very nice of you."

"Don't mention it. By the way, you might want to turn it so the little gal is facing the fairway."

Baffington continued to look at Eddie. The caddies turned to face him as well. "Why is that?"

Eddie shrugged and looked down the fairway. "Tradition."

A slow smile spread over the director's face. He did as suggested, then took a few steps back and held his club straight out in front of him, sighting over the ball and down the fairway, then returned and took his stance. Proud of his tip-top physical conditioning and a history of competent athleticism, it wasn't his style to hold back and he didn't, leaning into his shot with everything he had, crushing the ball with a fully extended, well-balanced swing.

The shot was perfectly straight and he'd aimed it well. It was still a good way into the air when it passed above Eddie's ball, and came to rest less than 170 yards from the green. As he bent to retrieve his tee, Baffington looked at Eddie from the corner of his eye, pleased to see the famed hustler lick his suddenly dry lips.

"Damn," Eddie muttered. Then louder, "Helluva shot."

"Thanks." Baffington turned and winked at his caddy, who grinned as he took the driver back, wiped it with a damp cloth and returned it to the bag.

"Jeez, Mr. Director," the caddy whispered. "That was about ten yards farther than you usually hit it."

"Fifteen," Baffington whispered back.

"Not sure I've seen too many people hit a ball that far but perfectly straight," Eddie called out.

Baffington came over and clapped him on the back as they walked off the tee together, the caddies following a respectful ten yards behind. "What's important is a bit of backspin," he said, "which is what makes it rise like that. Opening the club face just a drop is what gives that to you."

"I'll be damned."

"Of course, it's a bit tricky." Baffington pushed the sleeves of his sweater up, revealing sinewy forearms with well-defined muscles. "You have to practice so all the spin is backwards and not sideways. You hit it that hard with any sidespin," he said, making an arc in the air with his hand, "it's into the trees and gone."

"I see what you're saying." Eddie thought it over. "Now with the club face open like that, you have to make real sure you roll your wrists through the shot, right?"

"Yes, *but*." Baffington held a cautionary finger up in the air. "If you overdo it, you end up closing the face and losing the effect. That's where the trickiness comes in."

"Yes!" Eddie was nodding more vigorously now. "Yes, I see what you're saying!"

"Well, there you go."

They continued down the fairway, Baffington swaggering slightly, Eddie with his head down and his shoulders slightly hunched, bent with the weight of this novel insight.

"Can I ask you something now, Eddie?"

"Shoot."

"I was just wondering, maybe you had some insight..." Baffington waved his hand around, as though indicating not only the Augusta course but the entire sport. "Why do we love this game so much? Ever thought about that?"

"I don't know; what do you think?"

Baffington put his hands in his pockets. "I believe it has to do with learning about one's self. I believe you were once quoted similarly, Eddie. Didn't you say you can learn more about a person in one round of golf than you can by living next door to him for six months?"

"Believe I did."

"So that's what you think is the reason for our preoccupation with the game?"

"Nope."

"Really. And what makes you say that?"

"Ask a teaching pro the last time somebody came for lessons because he wanted to get in touch with his inner child." As they neared his ball Eddie said, "One more thing about that shot, Mr. Director. You mind?"

"Not at all, Eddie! Ask away."

"Thanks. I was just curious." They stopped. Eddie held up three fingers and the caddy brought him his three-iron.

"About what?"

Eddie took a few slow practice swings and turned to Baffington. "In your backswing," he said, "do you inhale or exhale?"

THREE DAYS LATER

Dawn dawned, but Wayne Chemincouver was nowhere near it.

He awoke much later than that, bleary-eyed and furry-tongued from a night of unsuccessfully trying to get women to go home with him. Finely tuned as he was in the art of Olympic-class denial, Wayne did not let some four thousand nights in a row of similar results disabuse him of his firmly held, near religious conviction that the drunker he got, the more attractive he became.

He rolled over and scratched for the remote. Flicking on the television, which was always set to an all-sports station because that's the only one that came through on the illegal cable box he'd bought over the Internet to skirt the monthly service fee, he rolled to the other side of the bed, opened the door of the mini-fridge that doubled as his nightstand and pulled out a beer. By the time he got a cigarette lit the on-air co-anchors were already gleefully trumpeting the latest scandal in the world of elite athletes.

"...tour veteran Robert Carmichael," Steffen O'Dougherty was saying. "How much you figure he's gonna be able to charge for his autograph now, Preston?"

"If you ask me, Steff—"

"I did ask you, Pres."

They laughed hysterically at their witty repartee for a few seconds. "I think he's gonna be able to double his fee," Preston Lamprey said, "cuz this one's gonna make him famous. Well, even more famous than he is now."

"What do you figure the PGA Tour's gonna do about it, though?"

"Do about it? Heck, Steffen, there's nothing they can do about it. Carmichael didn't break any rules, didn't do anything illegal..."

"Heck, Pres. He violated a contract between him and his sponsor!"

"Yeah, but that's between him and his sponsor."

"For those of you just tuning in...ah, heck, I just wanna see it again myself. Can we queue up the shot?"

The camera stayed on the two anchors. They held their glowing smiles. And held them. Soon the smiles became strained masks devoid of any mirth.

"Can we get that shot, Eric?" O'Dougherty said. "We need to see that—okay, here we go."

"I still can't get over this," Lamprey said as the scene shifted to a golf course, shot from a blimp high overhead. Moderately sized crowds milled about on either side of a long fairway, in the middle of which stood two golfers, their caddies, a tour official and cameraman Jorge "Zaps" Dominguez. Clearly visible on the grass were two golf balls about fifteen feet apart.

"This was yesterday, the last round of the Air Canada English Leather Classic," O'Dougherty said in voice-over. "Seventeenth hole, Carmichael and Mack Merriwell."

"Merriwell is in a tie for third place and Carmichael has sole possession of second at this point. We can hear..."

As the director brought up the recorded sound from the tournament, Lamprey's voice faded and was replaced by that of Steve Farley, who'd been the on-air announcer.

"A fairly straightforward two-twenty to the green, Bill. Pin's in the back and slightly left, so Carmichael's probably going to try a gentle draw to lay it in there close."

"I agree," Bill Winters said. "He seems to have a pretty good lie, ball sitting up nice and high on the grass. Can we get close on that, see just how that ball is sitting?"

The picture jiggled slightly as the feed was switched from the blimp to Dominguez's handheld. Carmichael and Merriwell appeared on the left and right sides of the frame, with Carmichael's ball on the grass between them and about ten feet further up the fairway. The image blurred momentarily as Dominguez zoomed in on the ball, then clarified as the auto-focus system caught up. He kept zooming in slowly as Farley spoke.

"Sure is a good lie, Bill. Sitting up just as high as you could ever expect to get on fairway grass."

The camera continued to zoom in. Soon the two golfers disappeared off to the sides.

"Like it was teed up," Winters agreed.

Only the ball and the surrounding grass were in view now. The ball grew larger.

"All Carmichael has to do now is—" Farley suddenly stopped speaking.

"What the heck is that?" Winters said. The rate of zoom had decreased, and the ball filled about ten percent of the available screen image. Despite three separate and sophisticated stabilization systems built into the camera, the picture still jiggled slightly because of the extreme telephoto setting. There was obviously a graphic of some sort on the ball but it was too blurry and indistinct to make out.

"I don't know," Winters said, "but—hey!"

The image on the screen had suddenly snapped sideways, then large swaths of green and white had chaotically flashed by, and now there was only a shot of some trees growing out of the right side of the screen and extending toward the sky on the left.

Within a second the feed was switched back to the blimp camera. From directly overhead, the handheld camera could be seen lying on the grass on its side, and Jorge "Zaps" Dominguez could be seen lying next to it.

Robert Carmichael was standing over both of them.

"Gimme audio on Zaps!" Trevor had yelled so loudly in the control booth Winters and Farley heard it through the soundproof glass.

"...stupid sonofabitch!" Carmichael was saying to Zaps. But while yesterday's audience had heard it live, there'd been plenty of time since then to edit the tape and in today's recap it was bleeped out.

"Fuck," Wayne Chemincouver muttered between slugs of his beer as he watched.

"Okay now, folks," Lamprey was saying in voice-over. "At this point Carmichael's giving the cameraman all kinds of grief about upsetting his concentration, getting into his eye line..."

"Yadda yadda yadda," O'Dougherty added as the sound from the video clip came up slightly. Carmichael's heated imprecations, which necessitated a regular symphony of bleepage, were nevertheless interpretable as a stream of accusations at Zaps for deliberately trying to sabotage his chance at taking the lead. "But all this time," O'Dougherty continued, "old Carmichael has a little something different he's worried about, because—"

"Okay, here it comes!" Winters interrupted. "While the cameraman's absorbing all of this, he's turning his handheld, trying to make it look to Carmichael like he's just trying to stand up, but what he's really doing is aiming at the golf ball, because...okay, okay, here it is..."

The scene switched back to the handheld just as the ball came back into view. There was grass on the right and sky on the left because the camera was still on its side, but since Zaps was no longer holding it the image was steady as a rock. He somehow got his finger to the zoom button and pressed it lightly, and as the ball began to fill the entire screen, an upraised leg clad in a red stocking became visible, as did an elegant little hand holding a golf ball and the letters ATCH stretched across a banner.

"And there it is!" Lamprey chortled deliriously. "Robert Carmichael—"

"Recipient of two million bucks a year from his sponsor, the Medalist Golf Company—"

"Is playing with a Scratch golf ball!"

The image of the ball was frozen on the screen, and as the two anchors laughed themselves silly it faded into a full-frame stock photo of the now-famous she-devil logo.

"Fuck," Wayne mumbled again. He hadn't yet gotten a reply to his angry letter to the Scratch company complaining about their lack of quality control, but he was sure a UPS van was going to pull up any day now and deliver him an entire case.

"Talk about your classic horns of a dilemma," Lamprey was saying on-screen. "Here's Carmichael, still a top player, but he's slipped back to about fifteenth on the tour. He's got to do something to elevate his game so his sponsorships get renewed..."

"...but the only way he can do it," O'Dougherty continued, "is to use another company's ball!"

"So even if he gets back into the top ten, Medalist is going to tell him to take a hike. And if he continues to use a Medalist and his game doesn't improve..."

"They'll drop him anyway!"

"That's tough enough, folks, but—and I'm just guessing here, Steff—but if you were the Medalist Company wouldn't you sue the heck out of Carmichael for breach of contract?"

"I'd sue him for a lot more than breach, Pres. I mean, what effect do you think this little stunt had on Medalist's image? You got huge consequential damages here—"

"Now, viewers, neither of us is suggesting that Medalist actually sue Carmichael—"

"No! No way, Pres!"

"But you were saying?"

"You got huge consequential damages here. Negligent indifference to likely harm, half a dozen different tort claims..."

"Dumb bastard," Wayne mumbled. As he reached for another cigarette there was a knock at his door.

Couldn't be Charlene. She didn't work Saturday mornings and he hadn't called for her anyway. Franky? Wayne glanced at the watch sitting on top of the mini-fridge next to his cigarettes. Eleven a.m. Too early for Franky Blodgett.

The knock sounded again.

"Yeah, yeah, yeah..."

Then it hit him: the UPS van!

Wayne swung his legs over the side, grabbed a pair of jeans out of a pile of dirty clothes on the floor, slipped them over his feet, then stood up and pulled them all the way on. Rubbing his eyes he made his way to the door, unlocked it and swung it open.

Light from the midmorning sun lanced painfully into his eyes and made him draw back.

"Wayne Chemincouver?" an authoritative voice asked.

"Who wants to know?" Wayne had difficulty keeping his eyes open, but even through the awful glare he could tell there was more than one person standing there. And UPS guys don't come in twos.

He tried to see into the street. It wasn't easy but he sure didn't see anything that looked like a van. Then something suddenly blocked the sun. Unable to focus clearly, Wayne saw that it was rectangular. Stepping to the side to take a look from another angle, he realized it was a piece of leather with a badge pinned to it.

"Special Agent Lars Niilsen," the voice said. "And this is Special Agent John Reilly. FBI. May we come in?"

"You got a warrant?"

"Matter of fact, we do." Niilsen handed it over, then he and Reilly pushed their way past Wayne.

"Hey, I ain't read the warrant yet!"

"So what?" Niilsen said. "It's valid whether you read it or not."

"Christ Almighty!" The latter exclamation was Reilly's response to the state of the two-room converted garage Wayne rented by the month. Reilly had a perpetual constipation problem and when he was all bound up like he was now, strange odors could upset his delicate intestinal balance.

"Wasn't expecting company."

"Or you'da done what?" Reilly asked. "Shoveled it out and replaced the straw?"

"Warrant look okay to you?" Niilsen asked.

Wayne read for a few more seconds. "Seems all right."

"The judge's clerk will be so relieved," Niilsen said as he took it back.

"What do you guys want? I haven't done anything."

"You wrote a letter to the Scratch Golf Ball Company," Reilly said.

Wayne wasn't sure he'd heard that right. "Huh?"

"You sent them back a ball you said was defective."

Wayne rubbed the side of his face and sat down on the side of the bed. The special agents elected to remain standing, reluctant to let anything other than the soles of their shoes touch anything. And it had nothing to do with preserving evidence. "What of it?"

"In fact, you sent them half a dozen balls," Reilly said. "Using half a dozen different names, but all with the same return address."

"So?"

"So, they weren't defective."

"The hell they weren't. The little devil rubbed off."

"All logos rub off," Reilly said. He could really have used about twenty minutes of quiet bathroom time and his patience was threatening to wear thin.

"Not from Scratch balls, they don't," Wayne insisted.

"What makes you say that?"

"On accounta I got others that don't."

"Yeah?" Reilly felt a gas bubble beginning to form. "Let's see em."

"Sure. No problem."

Wayne got off the bed and went to the corner where his golf bag rested against the wall. He zipped open a pocket and pulled out a ball, then held it up. "Played a round with this one, and the devil's still on it." He reached back into the pocket and took out two fresh sleeves. "And these came from the same box."

Niilsen held out his hand and Wayne dropped the ball into it.

"What's your handicap?" Niilsen asked as he examined the ball.

"Well..."

"I figure, what...fourteen, fifteen?"

"Little higher."

"And you played an entire round with one ball? Eighteen holes and you never lost one?"

Wayne shifted uncomfortably from one foot to the other. "Didn't say it was a whole round."

"You're right. My mistake. So where are the other defective ones?"

"Huh?"

"Hey, Wayne," Reilly spat. "You got a hearing problem?"

Niilsen waved his partner to patience. "You sent six to the company, they come in boxes of twelve. Where are the rest?"

"There aren't any more."

"Really?"

"Uh huh."

"So if we were to search this place—and believe me when I tell you we don't want to do that—we're not going to find any more defective balls?"

"Be my guest," Wayne said amiably.

"And we're not going to find anything else that you don't want federal law-enforcement officers to be finding?" Reilly added.

"Okay, look guys." Wayne set his beer down. "I been nothin but cooperative here, right? Let you in, answered your questions. So why don't we end it now, okay? You got what you want, I cooperated, so how about you guys just leave, okay?"

He walked over and opened the door, then stepped aside, his hand still on the knob. "Come on. I ain't done nothin you're gonna care about. Yeah, I sent some balls back to the company, I used different names, figured maybe I'd get them to send me some freebies. Well, that ain't no federal crime, on accounta they *were* defective, and don't tell me the freakin FB-freakin-I gives a shit about stuff like that, okay? Okay? Come on, enough fun and games for one day. Come on, just go, everything's cool. Come on." He looked down at the floor and waggled his fingers at the special agents, then put his hand on his hip, the other still on the knob.

Nothing happened.

He held out his hands and waggled his fingers again. "Come on."

Niilsen rose and walked to the door, lifted Wayne's hand off the knob and closed it.

"Hey!"

"Where are the rest of the defective balls, Wayne?"

"Not here."

"What's funny," Reilly said, "is that you still have a couple sleeves of good ones, and none of the defective ones."

"Maybe he lost them," Niilsen offered. "Hit them into the woods before he realized something was wrong with them."

"Yeah," Reilly agreed. Then he said, "Nah. Makes no sense. Why would he have bought new ones afterward?"

"So, Wayne...?"

"They weren't mine."

"Whose were they?"

"Another guy's. Look, what's this all about?"

"You volunteered to send them back for this other guy?"

"Yeah. What about it?"

"Who is he?"

"I asked you, what's this about!"

"It's about those balls being counterfeit."

"Huh?"

"Not genuine Scratch balls."

"Big problem in this country," Reilly said. "Ripping off legitimate merchandise by making cheap copies." He heaved a great breath and held it, trying to keep his bowels from acting up. "Wreaks havoc on the economy."

"I knew it!" Wayne exclaimed.

"Knew what?"

"Why I played liked shit! I told Fr— I told this guy it was the damned balls, and whaddaya know, they're fakes! I knew it!"

Niilsen frowned and said, "I thought the fakes were the other guy's balls."

"Huh?"

"You said the counterfeit balls were the other guy's. That's what you said, right? Said they weren't yours."

"Huh?"

"Wayne..." Reilly felt himself beginning to lose it. In several ways.

"Oh, yeah. Yeah, I did."

"That's what I thought. So you're just a shitty golfer and he's in possession of counterfeit balls."

"Hey, hang on a second, Lars," Reilly said. "Wayne here's in possession too, right? We got envelopes with his address and handwriting on them that he used to send the balls."

"Hmm. By God, you're right, John. Sent them across state lines too, he did."

"Hold it a second," Wayne said.

"Just tell us whose they were, Wayne." Niilsen shrugged helplessly. "You don't tell us, we've got to assume it was just you, and not this mystery buddy."

"No way I'm ratting out a friend!"

"Damn, I admire that!" Reilly said. "Nothing I appreciate more than loyalty."

"Me, too," Niilsen agreed readily. "Turn around, Wayne."

"Huh?"

"Turn around. Face the wall. You're under—"

"Hold it!"

TWENTY-TWO MINUTES LATER

"Ebay! Swear to God!"

"Happen to have a receipt?" Special Agent John Reilly asked.

"A receipt?" Franky Blodgett replied. "A receipt? I don't—I bought it on eBay, they don't—"

"How'd you pay for it?"

"How'd I pay for it?"

Special agent Lars Niilsen sighed. "Franky, how come you keep repeating our questions? You wouldn't by any chance be trying to buy some time to make up the answers would you?"

Franky shook his head forcefully. "No. Huh uh. It's just that, I mean, Christ..."

"You're nervous." Reilly nodded sympathetically. "Sure, I understand. Not every day that two federal agents with the power to completely ruin your life come around asking questions, am I right?"

"Ruin my—what're you talking about, ruin my—listen, I don't get...golf balls? We're talking about golf balls?"

"Yeah." Niilsen sat down on a chair and motioned Franky to sit opposite him on the sofa. "And we're not trying to jack you up here, Franky. But we gotta know where those balls came from, and if we have to take you down to do that, we will."

"How'd you guys find me, anyway?"

"We have people, Franky. People who know people, who know what's going on. One guy does a thing, another guy comes around the side door and makes his own deal...before you know it, a lot of stuff goes down and one hand washes the other. Kind of like Hamlet and that business with the Pancreatics. You can understand that, can't you?"

A battalion of Talmudic scholars wouldn't understand what Reilly had said.

"Yeah, course I do. Sure." Franky swallowed dryly and started to push some stray hairs out of his eyes, then suddenly stopped, his hand hanging in front of his nose. "Holy shit."

"What?" Reilly asked.

"Holy shit!" Franky cried again, and started to rise up off the sofa until Reilly pressed him back down. "This is a terrorist thing, isn't it! Holy shit! Those balls, they got like, what... *anthrax* in em? Oh, shit, they had anthrax! Now you guys're here askin me...tellin me...oh, shit! I'm gonna die, right? I'm gonna die, that's why you're here, and before I die you gotta know where I got the balls! That's it, isn't it! Holy shit!"

Franky tried to grab hold of himself and grew grim in the process. "Well you can fuckin forget it. Forget it! You bastards better save my fuckin life or I ain't tellin you *dick,* you hear me? I don't care if you beat me to a goddamn pulp, no fuckin way I'm sayin a goddamned thing unless you get me some-a that, what is it, that *Sipowitz* shit, and get it to me *right fuckin now!*"

Niilsen had let him go on because there was no sense stopping him until Reilly, off to the side and slightly behind the sofa, quit laughing. Reilly was doing his best to bury his face in the crook of his arm, but Franky was too stirred up to pay much attention to the muffled sounds anyway.

"Cipro," Niilsen said, trying desperately to keep a straight face.

"What?" Franky said.

"The antibiotic you need. It's called Cipro."

"Yeah, that's what I said! And you damned well better get me some!"

Reilly had turned away to dab at his eyes. As practiced an interrogator as he was, this situation had stretched his limits, but he somehow managed to compose himself quickly enough to meet Niilsen's inquiring eyes. "I don't know..." he said, slowly, painfully, conveying the gravity of the situation.

"Best tell us where you got the balls, Franky," Niilsen said soothingly.

Franky blinked a few times, and looked from Niilsen to Reilly and back again. "You said you weren't here to jack me up."

"We're not."

"And I figure, what with you guys tryin to catch terrorists, you ain't innerested in no little piece-a shit score I might know about, right?"

"Franky," Reilly said, "are you really going to sit there and tell me you're willing to risk a horrible, excruciating death, turning blue and suffocating slowly over two or three days, just so you don't get jacked up for some little piece-a shit score? Is that what you're trying to tell me?"

"Because if that's the case, Franky," Niilsen said gently, "you got rights. Constitution says you have the right not to incriminate yourself."

"Damned right..."

"And we," Reilly said, "have the right to walk right the fuck out that door and leave you here to spend the next few days thinking about what the end is gonna be like."

"I've seen it, Franky," Niilsen said, genuine pain creeping into his eyes as he slowly shook his head. "Oh, I've seen it, and...goddamn..." Unable to go on, he looked away and became lost in some private memory.

"Yeah," Franky said between gasps that had suddenly overtaken his breathing. "Yeah, okay, but you gotta promise me I get some-a that Sipowitz."

Reilly reached into his jacket pocket and took out an orange plastic vial. He held it next to his ear and shook it.

Franky looked at it and licked his lips, like a hardcore drunk spotting a bottle of Jack Daniel's after having gone all day without a drink. "There's this guy..." he began.

"Attaboy, Franky," Niilsen said. "What guy?"

"Owns a chop shop over on Corbett in Portland."

"What's his name?"

"Ah, come on guys...you tryna get me—"

Reilly shook the pill bottle again.

"Orlecky," Franky said. "Armando Orlecky."

"And...?"

"He's one'a those guys steals cars to order. You know? Like you tell him you want an eighty-nine Lincoln with—"

"We know what it is, Franky. What about it?"

Franky eyed the bottle again. "Couple weeks ago some guy comes in and says he knows about a shipment of golf balls, they're comin into town in a U-Haul, and can Orlecky get together a couple guys and hit it for him. Orlecky asks him if he's nuts, what the hell does he want golf balls for, and this guy says to him, none-a your fuckin business but you get five grand for an hour's work so do you want it or not?"

"So Orlecky took the job?"

"Yeah. Only when his guys hit the truck, one-a them, he's a golfer, he sees they're all Scratch balls and he says to Orlecky, hey, those balls are Scratch balls, and Orlecky says to him to go scratch his own balls, what the fuck does he care what kinda—"

"Yo," Reilly called out from his side of the room. "You wanna get to the point here?"

"Yeah. Anyways, Orlecky keeps all the balls."

"How many?"

"There was like eighty cases altogether. Fifty dozen to a case."

"And?"

"And, this guy I know, the guy works for Orlecky—just as a mechanic, you know—he sold me a box."

"And the rest?"

"Orlecky's gonna sell em to golf shops all over town."

Reilly came around and pulled over a chair. He put it next to Niilsen's and sat down. "But golf shops buy their stuff from distributors. Why would they do business with some guy who comes along out of the blue like that?"

Franky looked at Reilly in disbelief. "You're kiddin me, right? Some store's payin eighty a dozen from the company, a guy walks in and says you want a hundred boxes at fifty per?"

"Good point."

"Yeah. Okay. So you got what you need, right? You asked me, I told you. I don't know anything else, I swear to God!"

Reilly and Niilsen exchanged glances. As Franky threatened to explode out of his own chest, Niilsen finally nodded slightly, then stood up and walked away.

Reilly opened the bottle and shook out some pills. He counted them carefully, then added another two and set them all down on the coffee table in front of the sofa. "Listen, Franky, because this is important. You listening?"

Franky nodded, unable to take his eyes off the pills.

"Okay. You take two right now, with a lot of water. Two more tonight before you go to bed, then one every morning and evening for five days in a row. Understand?"

"Yeah."

"And whatever you do, don't skip a dose."

"I won't, don't worry. You kidding me? Miss a dose? Fuck, no!"

"There you go, Franky. Trust me, you'll be just fine."

"Thanks, man. Thanks a lot!"

"You bet."

Once back in their car, Niilsen and Reilly called for backup on the radio and then headed to SW Corbett Avenue in Portland, detouring only long enough to get Reilly's laxative prescription refilled.

The robbery of a truck full of golf balls had been a nonviolent event. Armando Orlecky's men followed the rig for a few hours, and when the driver pulled into a fast food joint, one of them followed him in, picked his pocket and left. When the driver got frantic looking for it at the checkout register, Orlecky's man walked back in and said, "Hey, I found a wallet in the parking lot," and asked if it belonged to anyone. The grateful driver insisted on buying him dinner, which Orlecky's guy protested over and over wasn't necessary, and in the meantime his partner was stealing the truck.

"You not having hurt anybody, Armando," Niilsen said as five of his colleagues milled around outside the tiny storefront office, "we're inclined to maybe help you out on this a little."

Orlecky, in full view of some of his guys, couldn't look weak. "I need help from you, Sergeant Preston, it'll be to clean out the toilets down the hall." He smiled at the reaction from his boys.

"That's Niilsen."

"Whawazzat?"

"My name. It's Niilsen. Sergeant Preston is from the Yukon."

"Oh, yeah, right. Well, Yu-kon go fuck yourself."

More gratifying chortling.

Niilsen grinned appreciatively. "That's a good one, Armando. Really. Here's another good one." He pulled a folded piece of paper from his inside jacket pocket and handed it to Orlecky.

"Whoa!" Orlecky put his hands up in his air. "What's that?"

"It's a warrant."

"Warrant? Hell, you don't need no warrant, Sergeant Preston." He waved around the tiny office. "Search all you want. Be my guest."

"It's not a warrant for here, Armando."

"Oh, yeah. Where's it for?"

Niilsen reached for one of Orlecky's hands and pressed the paper into it, then pointed off to the right. "There."

There was a massive garage with a thick metal sliding door, up to which one of Niilsen's men was driving a portable battering ram.

Orlecky, throat suddenly gone dry, swallowed and said, "That's not my place."

"Good," Niilsen responded. "Then you and your clerks can just go on back to your work here in the office and not worry about anything. Unless you want to get in on the betting?"

"What betting?" Orlecky asked, unable to take his eyes off the vehicle with what looked like a small submarine mounted in its nose.

"On how many shots it's going to take to get through that—"

The office shook nearly off its foundations as the ram crashed into the metal door and then disappeared through it.

"Oh, well," Niilsen said. "Too late. Oh, do me a favor and stick around while we have a look inside, will you? You and the office staff?"

Six pairs of eyes darted toward the window just in time to see several agents draw shotguns from the trunk of a sedan. Niilsen, his back to the window, didn't look.

"Okay, hold on a minute here," Orlecky said. "What makes you think I stole some damned truck?"

"Armando, let me ask you something." Niilsen put one foot up on a wastebasket and rested his forearms on his knee. "How much bullshit do you want to feed me while my men are hunting around next door in that garage you don't have anything to do with? Now the guys you paid to hit the truck, one of whom has his face on a surveillance camera at a Choke 'n Puke about two hundred and forty miles from here, is this guy like a brother or a cousin or something? You know, somebody who's going to stand up? Because how long you figure it's going to take him to cop a plea to an interstate felony when—"

"Innerstate? What the—"

"He crossed a state line to pull the job. How long you figure it's going to take him to give you up in exchange for a walk?"

Niilsen couldn't believe that Orlecky wouldn't be scrambling to see what kind of a deal he could get at this point. Then he realized why.

"Reilly!" Niilsen called out to the street. When his partner came up to the door he said, "Take these fellas outside, cuff em and make em comfortable. Remember, there's probably some citizen with a video camera out there so don't hurt em yet."

"Roger that," Reilly replied, then began herding the others out.

When they were gone, and no longer witnesses to the negotiating, Niilsen said, "I can help you out on federal charges of soliciting to commit a felony, possession of stolen goods, et cetera, et cetera, but I've got to know a couple of things."

"Such as?" Despite his sudden acquiescence, Orlecky folded his arms across his chest and lifted his chin in the air so his boys would think he was hanging tough.

"Such as, you tell me the guy who put you up to the truck. The guy who knew what was in it and where it was going to be."

"What about those guys?" Orlecky pointed to four agents standing expectantly on top of the metal door now lying flat on the ground.

"Those guys?" Niilsen thought it over for a few seconds. "They leave. But there's one other thing."

"That figures. What?"

"You have to give me the rest of the golf balls."

"There aren't any left. Sold em all."

"Damn, that's too bad. So if my guys go into the garage, they won't find any, right?"

"Bullshit!" Orlecky grew angry and took a step back. "You said you wouldn't—"

"Hey, relax, Armando. Just give me a few boxes, okay? I've got to have some evidence."

Orlecky's angry expression soon gave way to a sly smile. "You fuckin Mounties're all the same." Then he laughed. "Evidence! Yeah, right."

Orlecky walked over to the battered desk sitting against the far wall, opened a drawer and took out two boxes of Scratch golf balls. He brought them back to Niilsen and handed them over. "Here's your *evidence*, Sergeant Preston. Try not to hit too many into the water."

Niilsen smiled, going along with the gag as though he'd been busted and was embarrassed. "Now write down the guy who tipped you off. Everything, including address and phone number."

As Orlecky went back to the desk to consult his Rolodex, Niilsen said, "You got what...four thousand boxes of these babies? Fifty a box to golf shops that don't give a shit where they really came from at that price?"

Smart enough not to answer, Orlecky held out his hands in a helpless, *What can I tell you?* gesture, then handed over the slip of paper. His smug expression hung in as he watched Niilsen pocket the paper and then open one of the boxes. "What're you gonna do, Preston...count em?"

"Nah." Niilsen reached into his pants pocket and pulled out a penknife. "I trust you, Armando. You and me, we're doing honest business together." He unfolded a file from the penknife. "In fact, I'm gonna keep you from getting your head busted."

"Oh, yeah? How you gonna do that?"

Niilsen opened a sleeve of balls and let one drop into his hand. A couple of quick swipes with the file and then he tossed the ball to Orlecky.

"Hey, whud you scrape the little bitch off for?"

Niilsen folded back the file and dropped the penknife into his pocket. "You can't do that with a real Scratch, Armando."

"A real Scratch? What the hell are you talking about?"

"You stole a truck full of fakes."

"Bullshit!"

Niilsen shrugged. "Suit yourself." He turned and walked out onto the street. "But nobody's going to buy any of those balls from you without testing to see if they're genuine." *At least not after word about this gets out,* he said to himself.

Niilsen waved his men away from the garage. They got back into their vehicles and drove away. About two hours later, at almost exactly the moment Orlecky and his boys finally got the big metal door repaired, a portable battering ram from the Portland police department, which had been tipped off by an anonymous phone call, knocked it down again.

CHAPTER THIRTEEN

FBI Special Agent Denny Deloyne and three of his men showed up at four in the morning at the warehouse on the corner of West M Street and Highway 81. There was some grumbling about how this was a waste of resources given everything else that was going on in the world, and why were they running around trying to bust some local goombahs who'd knocked off a few dozen golf balls?

"It's a favor for some guy," Deloyne told them for the thirtieth time. "He's a friend of the boss."

Grumpy and needing coffee, the men dutifully got out, weapons drawn, and headed for the warehouse, which was completely dark. They jumped a little when some motion-activated lights snapped on, but the warehouse had no guards. Deloyne's radio crackled. He picked it up and was told by his office dispatcher that the monitoring company had just deactivated the alarms, as per a court order delivered the night before.

They tried to use bolt cutters to snip several padlocks from one of the loading bay doors, and when that didn't work they brought out a handheld diamond saw they'd bought at the local Home Depot for $79.95, a model favored by professional bicycle thieves, and sliced through the brass hasps in less than five minutes. Lifting the counterweighted sliding metal door was easy, as was finding the switches for the overhead lights. Deloyne flipped them on.

"Holy shit," one of his men breathed as they took their first look around.

FBI Special Agent Lars Niilsen picked up the phone before the first ring had finished. "Tell me," he said into the handset without preamble.

"Think you hit the jackpot here, Larry," replied Denny Deloyne. "You sitting down?"

"Let's hear it."

"McCool Junction, Nebraska. And don't laugh, because I'm serious."

"Where is it?"

"Six miles from Lushton."

"Denny..."

"Okay, an hour west of Lincoln. Made up of fourteen streets and a ware-house. And in the warehouse?"

"Phony Scratches. How many?"

"About two hundred cases."

Ten thousand dozen. Niilsen gave a low whistle. "Wow."

"Yeah, but that's not the jackpot."

"It isn't?"

"Uh uh."

"Denny..."

"The jackpot, Larry, is the thirty-two hundred cases of other phonies."

Niilsen did a quick mental calculation: It was well in excess of two million golf balls. "What kind?"

"Name a brand."

Every top-selling ball was represented, over forty brands and models. Niilsen tried to take notes as Deloyne rattled off the quick inventory his men had done. When he finished, Niilsen said, "Guess I'd better start making some phone calls."

"Yeah. Lot of executives are going to wake up with a headache. Talk to you later."

Niilsen handed the list to an office assistant and told him to get the phone numbers of all the presidents of the companies that manufactured the real versions of the counterfeit balls. He also asked for a rough estimate of the haul's worth.

Less than an hour later the assistant returned and handed him a list of five names.

"That's it?" Niilsen said with some irritation. "How the hell hard could it be to get all the names?"

"These are all the names, sir."

"What are you talking about?"

The assistant handed over a scratch pad with the forty brands and models organized into five columns. The first column contained the names of twenty-two balls, the second had twelve, and the remaining sixteen were spread about evenly over the last three columns.

The assistant pointed to the first column. "All of these are made by one company."

Niilsen's eye ran to the top of the column, which was headed Medalist. "You telling me one company makes all these balls?"

"They make two dozen others also, but those are low-end. Probably doesn't pay to knock them off." He tapped the list with a pencil. "These are the ones found in the warehouse."

"What about an estimate on what the stuff's worth?"

"Sally called some people and did a quickie SWAG. Cost to manufacture would be about a million and a half."

"And the retail value?"

"Two and a half million."

Niilsen looked up from the paper, his eyebrows raised high. "That's some profit margin."

"Very lucrative business, golf balls. And depending on how often the counterfeiters turn over inventory, they could be selling, I don't know...couple million boxes a year?"

Niilsen considered the implications, along with the attractiveness of the enterprise. "Better than dope," he concluded. "Maybe not as much money, but nicer customers, nobody gets killed, and you can always claim you got misled by whoever you're buying them from."

The assistant nodded his agreement. "And prosecutors don't get zealous about what a threat to society you are."

"Right. But one thing I don't get."

"What's that?"

Niilsen, an eight handicap, looked over the list again. "All of these balls are different."

"Yeah. I don't play, but I looked a few up on the 'Net and they sure are different: distance, durability, feel, spin, compression, dimple pattern...lot of different construction types, too, like wound, three-piece, multilayer, and materials I've never heard of. Must be pretty exotic stuff, at the prices they charge."

Niilsen scratched at the back of his head. "Exactly. So it's hard to imagine how counterfeiters could reproduce all of that."

"Probably done overseas," the assistant guessed. "If we caught one distributor, there must be others, and all over the world. Cheaper materials, cheaper labor, less quality control... they could be making a couple hundred percent profit."

Everything the assistant was saying made sense, which led Niilsen to an obvious next step. "We need to find out how they're getting them into this country."

Having formally launched an investigation, there was no way for the FBI to keep the news of the counterfeit golf balls from going public.

Initially, there was some consternation in the Bureau. The nation's security status was bouncing around the color chart like a psychedelic dream, and since hardly anybody could remember what each part of the multihued coding meant ('Why the hell didn't they just call it one through five?' Eddie had asked Bradford MacArthur Baffington just before the FBI director had gone to pieces on the back nine at Augusta), every time it flipped from orange to yellow or blue to green, anxiety levels rose because of the difficulty people had figuring out if they were supposed to breathe a little easier or buy more Lockheed stock. So how would it look if it got out that the Bureau had diverted resources toward cracking a golf ball counterfeiting ring?

Baffington, being new in the job and therefore an X-factor in the realm of public relations, couldn't blame his people for their early unease. Little did they know that, in his earlier incarnation as the CEO of a $30 billion dot-com whose only real output was press releases, it was said by insiders that if Baffington had been White House chief of staff in 1974, Richard Nixon's face would now be on Mount Rushmore.

He knew he was in a good starting position. The president, five cabinet secretaries, four Supreme Court justices, all of the joint chiefs and the publishers and editors of the *New York Times* and the *Washington Post* were all avid golfers. Furthermore, he knew that more than 25 million

Americans played at least four rounds a year, and while his fellow citizens were more than happy to throw away money on state lotteries and heartless psychics who claimed they could communicate with departed loved ones, they hated like hell to get ripped off by foreigners taking advantage of their trusting nature.

And it was the foreign aspect that Baffington concentrated on the hardest. "Third world countries exploit their people horribly," he intoned somberly in his prepared remarks for the press conference. "They're paid a pittance, if anything, made to work in conditions not fit for a dog, and the exploiters ship the inferior product of their bitter labors to our shores in an attempt not just to suck money from the pockets of hardworking Americans, but to put those hardworking Americans out of work! Onto the street! This is not a victimless crime....a day's labor for pittance wages overseas is a day's honest labor that some American will not be called upon to perform for a living wage!"

A day later, at a supposedly private speech given to a trade association in Seattle, it leaked out somehow that Baffington had labeled as "commercial terrorism" the theft of U.S. intellectual property. 'When they steal our trademarks,' he'd said, 'when they violate the patents and copyrights that American corporations have struggled to develop and bring to market, they undermine the very fabric of what makes our country great, which is the immense reward that comes with innovative success. They undermine the very fabric!' he'd thundered, and, mixed metaphor notwithstanding, the impact was significant.

Indignation swept the land. "How dare they," trumpeted a *New York Times* editorial. "What's next?" asked a *Washington Post* op-ed essay written by J. Spalding Horton, senior vice president of the nation's fifth largest retailer, answering his own question in the body of the text: "Pharmaceuticals? If federal law enforcement is lax in its investigation and prosecution of this egregious infringement of a respected trademark, might we see the day when substandard prescription drugs are unleashed on an unsuspecting public? Worse yet, might we be inviting a terrorist cell, emboldened by a limp-wristed response to the seemingly innocuous ersatz golf balls, to slip a slow-acting poison into ten million counterfeit doses of

Prozac?" Horton had written the piece at the behest of Tommy Trevillian, president and CEO of the Medalist Golf Corporation, whose corporate auditors had always thought it somewhat odd that the nation's fifth largest retailer had sold over two hundred thousand more boxes of Medalist golf balls than they'd purchased, and had done it three years running. Anticipating the filing of a lawsuit whose claimed dollar amount would pale in comparison to the damage it would cause the retailer, Trevillian had sat down with Horton, come to an out-of-court settlement whose details and even existence went undisclosed, and not signed the papers until the op-ed essay had appeared in the *Post*.

Two midlevel Medalist vice presidents, competing with each other for promotion to head of the Athlete Relations division, had wracked their brains to try to come up with some radical strategy for how the company could turn the whole situation to its advantage. One of them had suggested the terrorist link, the other the blackmail of J. Spalding Horton, and it was Trevillian himself who'd put the two together.

But it was a bookish accountant from the receivables department who ended up in Trevillian's office after dropping a slip of paper in the suggestion box near the condiments counter in the company cafeteria. Rather than be cowed by his first ever face-to-face with the single most powerful man in the world of golf, the accountant decided that this was his one chance to shine.

"Just you and me, Mr. Trevillian," he said, waving to the legion of corporate vassals barnacled to the conference table.

Trevillian hesitated a moment, trying to decide between clearing the office or having the accountant beheaded. Then he waved everyone else out and said, "I like the cut of your jib, young man. I hope you're not going to waste my time."

"Only time will tell, Mr. Trevillian. And I only need five minutes."

Trevillian sat back on his custom-crafted chair, which was made from leather salvaged from the ruins of a fifteenth-century Spanish castle. "Your suggestion had something to do with our cash reserves and corporate malfeasance. I already know about the cash, so what's this about wrongdoing." Not a question, but a command to speak.

"Not our wrongdoing, sir. Everybody else's." The accountant leaned forward, put his elbows on the table and gestured with his hands as he spoke. "The Medalist Corporation has more cash on hand than all but two dozen countries on the planet. And you know as well as I do that if we don't do something with it, you'll have to divvy it up among the shareholders in the form of dividends, which is about as useful as setting it on fire."

Trevillian shuddered inwardly at the mention of his shareholders, four hundred institutions and a thousand times that many individuals, maybe three or four of whom actually cared about the company and its business, the rest of whom thought of it as a roulette wheel, or would if you could complain to a roulette wheel.

"On top of that," the young man continued, "those same shareholders are making noises about this Scratch business, wanting to know why we're not responding to an obvious threat to our market share. And, sir"—he lowered his voice to a conspiratorial whisper—"it can't be a secret to you that Medalist employees, who get as many of our golf balls as they want for free, have been buying Scratch balls with their own money."

No, it wasn't a secret. At a company outing a six-handicapper from the shipping department had hit a ball over a fence and into a swimming pool and nearly freaked when an advertising vice president had gone to fish it out. The shipping clerk had screamed at him to leave it alone, that it was on private property, he didn't care about the ball and so on, but the ad guy had twisted open a seventeen-foot retriever and fished it out. Noticing that it was completely devoid of any logo, he yelled out to the shipping guy sixty yards away, "Hey, you using somebody else's ball?" He'd laughed, because it was meant as a joke, but someone from publicity had overheard and come by and asked to see the ball. The shipping clerk's excuse that the logo had worn off hadn't cut much mustard, the ball looking otherwise pristine, and a tearful confession had followed that it was in fact a Scratch ball whose logo he'd removed with some alcohol. That you weren't supposed to be able to remove a Scratch logo even if you dragged the ball along a concrete runway from the tail of an F-16 was lost amid the resulting brouhaha, which included an examination of every player's ball followed by the signing of hastily drawn-up legal documents between the company and seventeen of the employee players stating that they could keep their jobs if they never spoke of this day again.

"At the same time," the accountant went on, "we're in a business environment where nearly three-quarters of the American citizenry believes that large corporations have fallen into the hands of greedy executives who'd kill their own mothers for a bigger jet or courtside seats at Lakers games. CEOs who used to snuggle up to the press and have their pictures taken with the president, they're now hiding in their offices, afraid to use their limos or even eat at a fancy restaurant in case some slob from East Jesus who owns a single share of stock comes by and demands to know if it's going on an expense report. Now"—he paused to catch his breath—"if you could spend a hundred million of the company's money to turn it overnight into the most caring, concerned, benevolent and enlightened organization since the ASPCA, would you do it?"

Would I do it? Trevillian scratched the side of his nose and tried to look like he was still unimpressed and waiting for some payoff. *I'd write the goddamned check out of my personal bank account.* He also noticed that the accountant was savvy enough not to have mentioned the beneficial impact on the CEO's public persona. "Depends. What's your proposal?"

"Simple, really." The accountant took his elbows off the table and folded his hands in his lap. "Actually kind of surprised no one else thought of it." A sickening thought occurred to him at that very moment: What if somebody already *had* suggested it and been tossed out on his kiester?

But there was no going back now.

CHAPTER FOURTEEN

"**C**an't thank you enough for agreeing to come on the show, Tommy."

Randolph Fitztipton, late of the BBC and fast becoming the number one talk show jockey in the United States, made it sound like Tommy Trevillian was doing the network a big favor by deigning to appear. That was one of Fitztipton's gifts, a style so relentlessly ingratiating that anybody watching would feel guilty for even thinking anything negative about television's number one Nice Guy. His slight British accent didn't hurt the image either, as Americans were almost genetically incapable of disliking anyone whose diction smacked of Whitehall, Soho or Sussex.

"It's my pleasure, Fitz," Trevillian replied with the subtle but unmistakable humility he'd been taught by some of the best spinmeisters in the business. Having come from the steel business, where executives are generally not known to the public, he'd been interviewed to death by the Medalist Corporation's board of directors, who'd then turned him over to the marketing department for "public image review." After two full days photographing him, videotaping him, attacking him with mock reporters and running him by five different focus groups, the company flaks had declared him "too short, too fat and too ugly" to properly represent a company in the consumer sporting goods arena. Shoe lifts, hair transplants, thrice-daily tanning sessions, cosmetic surgery, a physical conditioning regime that would have killed an Ironman athlete and a Ph.D.-equivalent education in public relations had transformed him into the ideal CEO to represent a company that prided itself on projecting health and quality to its customers.

"Your office corrected us," Fitztipton was saying. "I guess one of our people called you the president and CEO of Medalist, and that, uh..."

Trevillian smiled, the kind of smile that could blow fuses, all white teeth and good-humored, sun-carved crow's feet that completely dominated any room he walked into. "Not all that important, really. The parent outfit is called MedalCorp, but since Medalist is our most visible and popular brand division, people have just generally taken to calling the whole ball of wax by that name. It's fine."

"But you own other things as well."

"Oh, sure. Golf is our life at MedalCorp, and we're a part of various aspects of the game." Trevillian didn't mention that, among those other things were the Pericles, Ace, Zenith, ProAm, Stroker, PinHigh, Slammer, SpinJockey, Whammer and TotalFeel brands of golf balls, nor the Python, AccuBlast, St. Andrews, RamRod and CompetiTrue brands of golf clubs, nor the FootCocoon, StableStance, TruGrip and TractionPro brands of golf shoes, nor any of the other divisions that made gloves, shirts, shorts, socks, replacement grips, head covers, distance finders and over two hundred types of training devices. Two *thousand,* if you counted instructional videotapes.

"Okay, so let's get to it, Tommy," Fitztipton said, frowning as though he were about to lob a cruise missile at his guest and pound him into quivering jelly. "By now the counterfeit ball scandal has exploded across the American consciousness, and I think you'll agree that its importance goes well beyond damage to just a recreational endeavor."

Reeling from the crushing blow, Trevillian said, "You're absolutely right there, Fitz. Anything that undermines the fabric of legitimate American business is a grave threat to us all. We have over eleven thousand associates, and whenever one of these counterfeiters steals a trademark or a patent we struggled to create, it literally takes food out of the mouths of hardworking Americans."

Fitztipton, his mind like a steel trap, immediately latched on to the logical flaws, subtle racism, baseless assumptions and self-serving, xenophobic paranoia in that statement. "Couldn't agree with you more, Tommy. They used to say, what's good for General Motors is good for America, and while that phrase has fallen into a bit of disfavor of late, you and I both know there's more than a grain of truth in that sentiment, wouldn't you agree?"

"Absolutely." One lesson Trevillian had learned well from the spinmeisters: Americans don't trust "yes." If you want to appear weak, indecisive and barely in control, you say "yes." But if you really want them to know you mean "yes," you drive it home with a battering ram. "Absolutely" doesn't mean just "yes," it means "you're goddamned right, yes, and if you doubt me, you're either a lunatic or a traitor."

"But this has to have hurt your business, Tommy," Fitztipton said with genuine pain in his eyes. "You and your employees."

"Associates, Fitz. Not employees. At Medalist we're all equals. More like a family than a corporation."

"Ah. I should have guessed. And your associates must have been affected, yes?"

"To a limited extent."

"Well, all those balls people bought from unscrupulous criminals. By rights those sales should have gone to Medalist, right?"

"Absolutely."

"So what are we talking about in terms of losses?"

Trevillian held up his hands and let them drop to the table. "We don't know yet. All we know about is what's been found so far. We don't know the extent of the entire conspiracy, or what's going to turn up tomorrow or next week."

Fitztipton bit his lip and shook his head sympathetically. "What steps are you taking to counter this threat and protect the company?"

"You know, Fitz..." Trevillian furrowed his brow and hunched his shoulders slightly. "I've gotta tell you, at this point, protecting the company isn't our main concern."

"Really? What is?"

The CEO tapped two fingers on the table. "I'll tell you what is: protecting our customers. That's our number one priority at this point."

"Good show, Tommy. How are you going to do that?" Fitztipton's timing was perfect. After hours of consultation among the network brass, the show's producers and Medalist's marketing and PR departments, it had been decided that seven minutes into the show was the time to plant the bomb. Twice as many people tuned in to the beginning of *The Randolph Fitztipton Show* as ended up still watching at the end. Whether they stayed or switched to *Senior Mud Wrestling* was determined in the eight minutes prior to the first commercial break, so seven minutes was the ideal place to grab viewers by the throat and keep their hands off their remotes for at least one long set of ads.

"Well, we're going to do something unprecedented, Fitz. We think you'll be amazed."

"Very little doubt in my mind, Tommy. Most anxious to hear about it, so let's cut away for a little business and we'll be right back, folks."

When the live feed monitor went blank, Fitztipton picked up a phone from underneath his side of the table and punched a single button. "What's on the meters?" he said after a moment. "Ah hah...ah hah...ah hah...good. Lemme know in the earpiece which way it's trending." He hung up, then said to Trevillian, "Retention's projected at over eighty percent, but that'll dip by four or five by the time we're back live."

Trevillian nodded. "Sports demographic will be higher than that but the Knicks pregame comes on at six-thirty."

"I think we need to hit this hard in the next segment."

"Agreed. But let's save some ammo for just before we cut out at six twenty-seven, tide em over the break."

"Yeah. We'll hold the bit about, you know, that thing with the do-they-know-if-they're-bullshit-or-not."

"Good idea."

Fitztipton listened to something in his earpiece, then pointed toward a production assistant, who said, "In five...four...three..." as he held up that many fingers, then mouthed *two, one* and stepped away.

"We're back with Tommy Trevillian, president and CEO of...now, that's MedalCorp, right, Tommy?" Big smiles back and forth.

"You got it, Fitz."

"You were just about to reveal, right here on *The Randolph Fitztipton Show* for the very first time, how your company is going to protect the loyal customers who've depended on you for so long."

"That's right, Fitz. Candidly, we finished putting together this plan just hours before I came on the show, so this is about as good a forum as I can imagine to announce it."

"I'm flattered, Tommy. Truly. And our viewers are excited to be a part of this as well. So let's have it."

"Well, Fitz, after all the discussion and planning and figuring and what-if scenarios, what I did, I just sat our top guys down in my office and I said to them, I said, Guys, this is no time to be pinching pennies and worrying about what's possible. We've always had a can-do attitude, and after eighty years of making—and I'll be truthful as hell here, Fitz—I said, after eighty years of making one hell of a profit from all those millions of people who've come to depend on Medalist products as the very best, very finest quality equipment available at any price, we just gotta do something to show how much that means to us."

"I'll tell you," Fitztipton said, his face serious, "it's that kind of thinking, that kind of attitude that separates the real captains of industry from the wannabes. It's what made this country great."

"Thank you, Fitz. Kind words indeed. So I said, cost be damned—heh, heh, I can say that on television, can't I?—I said, never mind the cost." Here he paused and looked his host right in the eye. "What's the right thing to do?"

"Bully for you, Tommy. No wonder you're so admired among the business elite."

"Thank you, Fitz."

"Why don't we take a break, and when we come back we'll hear what Tommy Trevillian, president and CEO of MedalCorp—I get that right, Tommy?"

"You bet, Fitz."

"We'll hear what Tommy Trevillian is doing to support his loyal customers."

The live feed monitor went blank.

"Hope I didn't catch you off guard there, Tommy. I know we said we'd get into it in this segment, but—"

"No, no, are you kidding? That was beautiful, how we played off each other there. I think we jacked the tension—"

"The suspense. It's—"

"The suspense, yeah. It's off the scale. So now we give em the basics, talk about that for a—"

"I got you. Hear you loud and clear. Then they stick through the Knicks pregame to—"

"To get the details. Beautiful. Perfect."

"Okay. I'm going to—hang on...hang on...okay, retention's way, way up there. I'm going to walk you through this, so just follow my lead."

"With you all the way, Fitz. Let's set some records."

"Now you're—okay, watch the P.A....Back with you here on *The Randolph Fitztipton Show,* with Tommy Trevillian, president and CEO of, uh, *MedalCorp*."

Trevillian genially nodded his approval of the correct name of his company.

"Tommy, lay it on us. What's your plan for standing by those customers who have stood by you for so long?"

"Well, Fitz, as I said, we just want to—you know, let me make something clear here. None of this is our fault."

"Nobody ever implied that it was."

"What I'm saying, when you get right down to it, we could simply sit by and do nothing and nobody would blame us. After all, we're the ones who got hosed."

"Good point. Excellent point. Which only makes it all the more extraordinary the lengths to which you're prepared to go to put things right. Now, of course I don't know what those lengths are, but we're about to hear them and it's clear you're not obligated to do any of them."

"You know, Fitz, maybe I ought to just go on ahead and give you the basics. Just in its most simple form, without dressing it up with a lot of detail."

"Great idea, Tommy. Let's have it."

"Okay, here it is." Trevillian frowned again, and took his time, counting on Fitztipton, with whom he seemed to be in almost telepathic contact, to groove along with him and not say anything. Fitztipton played it perfectly and stayed quiet. AC Nielsen meters were pegging all across the country.

"Fitz," Trevillian said at last, relaxing his features to show that all was about to be set right with the universe, "the Medalist Golf company is prepared to replace every single counterfeit golf ball with a genuine Medalist ball, at absolutely no cost to the customer whatsoever."

Fitztipton's mouth fell open. "You're kidding."

"I am not kidding."

"You. Are. Kidding. Me!"

"I most certainly am not."

"Okay, okay, hold it a minute here, let me make sure I understand: Are you telling me that Medalist is prepared to replace every single counterfeit golf ball with a genuine Medalist ball, at absolutely no cost to the customer whatsoever?"

Trevillian spread his hands. "You got it exactly right."

"I don't believe it."

Trevillian held up his right hand, the middle three fingers together and straight up. "God's honest truth."

"That is unbelievable."

"It's the least we can do to protect our customers."

"That's going to cost you, what...hundreds of millions of dollars?"

"Whatever it costs."

"And your board of directors is going along with this?"

"Fitz...I haven't even told them."

"You're kidding!"

"They're finding out about it at the same time you are."

That, at least, was true. In a manner of speaking, anyway. Fitztipton and the board both found out two days ago, Fitztipton when the guest shot was arranged, the board when they'd approved the plan. That approval was really authorization for Trevillian to proceed if he chose to, so, technically, the board didn't really *know* that it was going to happen. They just said it was okay if it did.

"Tommy, a million questions just popped into my head."

Trevillian smiled a knowing smile. "I'll bet they did."

"I'm guessing this isn't anywhere as easy as it sounded at first blush." Fitzgerald turned to the camera. "Don't go away, and we'll find out all about it."

He turned back to his guest and, as the breakaway crawls and logos splattered across the screen, was heard to mutter "unbelievable" several times before he was finally overwhelmed by his theme music.

Eddie aimed the remote at the television in his office at the Scratch plant in Hallettsville, Texas, and pressed the mute button. "Unbelievable."

"It really is unbelievable," said CFO Oscar Petanque.

"I meant it. I tell you this, no shit, Oscar," Eddie said, nodding slowly at the television. "That is one smart sonofabitch."

"You think so?"

"Don't you?"

"Yeah. But that doesn't mean he can't be outsmarted." Petanque was lounging on the sofa facing the television.

Eddie sat quietly for a few seconds, then said. "You got something in mind?"

"Why? Do you?"

"Bet I know what you're thinking."

"I'm thinking, we need to hear more about how this works first."

"You're right."

Eddie unmuted the set and they listened to Trevillian outline his plan which, while a blindingly obvious PR stunt, was nevertheless an extraordinary move by a corporation that had committed no wrongdoing. While it had become *de rigueur* for companies caught with their pants down to stage a full-scale Swaggart, trumpeting all their sins in public and throwing themselves on their swords in order to be redeemed by the Christian charity of a forgiving public, for a totally innocent company to step forward and atone for the sins of *others*, and to do so at considerable expense, was unprecedented. It was magnanimous, visionary, history-making...

"This is the most brilliant piece of pure bullshit I've ever heard of," Petanque said. "I wish that slippery fucker was running this place insteada you."

"Makes two of us," Eddie agreed. "Especially since I'm the major stockholder."

"How can people tell if they're counterfeit?" Fitztipton was asking on-screen.

"Several ways," Trevillian said, "all based on their inferior construction. Dab a little alcohol on the logo. If it rubs off, it's a fake. On the box of a dozen, the little printed rays coming out of the Medalist logo will be smudged instead of standing out in sharp relief. But Fitz, let me make one thing absolutely clear before we get into unnecessary detail."

"Hang on a second. What if a customer isn't sure it's a fake? What if he has trouble telling?"

"Good question, because that's exactly what I wanted to talk about!"

"What's that, Tommy?"

"I want to emphasize this because it's important."

"As opposed to emphasize it because nobody gives a shit," Petanque said.

"You're talking to a television, Oscar," Eddie said. "Shut up so we can hear the emphasis."

"...to drive home," Trevillian was saying, "is that it doesn't matter. You don't have to know for sure. Heck, you don't even have to check. Bring em back and you get a new box, a new sleeve, whatever. We'll check them out at the factory. All we ask is that you bring a receipt for the original purchase. That's a firm requirement."

"Do they have to be new?" Fitztipton asked.

"Absolutely not! And if you don't have a dealer close by, send them to us by mail. We'll send your new ones out within twenty-four hours."

"But they have to have a receipt."

"Fitz, it's because we need to find out what retailers have been buying phony balls and ripping off their customers, and also help law enforcement officials get to the heart of who the counterfeiters are."

Eddie aimed the remote again and this time clicked the off switch. "I can't find a hole in this."

"Me neither," Petanque said. "This is going to cost Medalist a fortune."

"But they'll get a rep as the most customer-service-oriented company since Murder, Inc. Even if it costs them a hundred million out of pocket it'll be like a billion in advertising."

"Won't cost them anywhere near that, Eddie. It'll only seem that way, when they report on the results using retail numbers instead of manufacturing costs. The more I think about this, the more I see the pure genius of it."

"So you said you had an idea."

Petanque finally sat up on the office sofa. "So did you."

"I'll show you mine if you show me yours."

"Okay. We make the same offer as Medalist."

Eddie opened a drawer, took out a pad of paper and dropped it on the desktop. "My sentiments exactly."

"It's going to make them very angry."

"They're the competition. We're supposed to piss em off."

"I mean, we're *really* going to get them mad."

Eddie started making notes on the pad. "Yeah, whatever."

CHAPTER FIFTEEN

THE SWANSON CHIPPED BEEF SOS CLASSIC
PINEHURST NO. 2, NORTH CAROLINA

"Tommy," Steve Farley said, one arm planted familiarly over the shoulder of his on-air guest, "can't tell you what your gesture means to the whole golf world."

"Why, thank you, Steve," Tommy Trevillian said in pleased surprise. "Means a lot coming from a veteran such as yourself."

The president and CEO of MedalCorp sat crunched between Farley and Bill Winters at the tiny table that served as the only set decoration for the announcers. Behind them, the lush green rolling hills of the tournament golf course, just one of eight courses on the Pinehurst property, formed the only backdrop they needed.

"Do you have any estimate yet of what it's going to cost the company?" Farley asked.

"A lot," Trevillian answered, then smiled as he waited for the laughter from his delirious quip to die down. "The final figures aren't in yet, so we don't know where we're going to end up by the time this is all over. But I can tell you that the extent of this thing has surprised even the most jaded among us, and its deleterious effect on American golfers has us all pretty steamed, believe me."

"Boy, I'll bet."

"Think this offer from Scratch is going to hurt you at all, Tommy?" Winters said.

Trevillian turned away from Farley to address the other co-host. "What offer is that, Bill?"

"I'm talking about their own buy-back offer."

Trevillian shook his head. "The number of counterfeit Scratch balls was very minor. Since there's not much of a market for them, I guess the conspirators didn't see much point in bothering—"

"I think he was talking about their offer to buy back Medalist balls."

Trevillian, well practiced in the art, kept his shiny smile solidly in place as he turned back to Farley. "What?"

"Sorry, Tommy. Would've thought sure you'd heard."

Trevillian whipped back to Winters. "Heard what, Bill?"

Then back to Farley.

"Scratch is offering twenty bucks off a dozen of their balls for any box of fake Medalists turned in."

This time Trevillian turned face forward instead of looking from one announcer to the other. "Really."

"Oh, yeah." Winters pointed toward the monitor. "Our crew caught up with some people right here at the Pinehurst pro shop this morning."

The live feed showed a line of people stretching from the pro shop door to the putting green. They were all clutching boxes of Medalist golf balls. Before Trevillian could try to make the case that they were all participating in the Medalist exchange program, a tape came on of Winters buttonholing someone as he was leaving the shop.

"Looks like you got yourself a box of Scratch balls," Winters said.

"You betcha," the happy shopper answered.

"Turn in some Medalists for those, did you?"

The man grinned sheepishly. "Tell you the truth, I bought a boxa Medalist Apex balls down at the Kmart for eleven bucks, then turned em in for twenty off on these babies." He held up the now-familiar Scratch box, then used it to gesture toward the line of people behind him. "Heck, whatcha suppose alla these boys're doin!"

The scene switched back to the live feed. "Bet that's one development you hadn't anticipated, Tommy," Winters said.

Trevillian laughed good-naturedly. "Can't say as we did, but I'll tell you, Bill, you just can't beat a creative American golfer, can you? Wonder if the people at Scratch know that all those balls from Kmart are genuine Medalists and not counterfeits."

"Beats me, Tommy. Well, looks like we've got to get back to the tournament. Hey..." He held out his hand and Trevillian took it. "Good to have you here, guy." Winters tried not to wince as Trevillian sought to crush his fingers into talcum powder.

"A pleasure, Bill," Trevillian hissed through clenched teeth.

"How the fuck could you let this happen, Whiff!" Trevillian screamed into his cell phone.

"Whoa, whoa, take it easy, Tommy." Network sports director Compton Whiffington gestured frantically for the assistant who had put the call through to listen in and stand by for instructions. "What the heck's going on down there?"

"What's going—" Trevillian took the phone from his ear, made a fist and bit it, then put the phone back. "I'll tell you what's going on here, you fried green sonofabitch. I'm at the Swanson and those two fuckin fruitcakes you call on-air commentators just cut my balls off on national television, that's what's going on here!" Inside of the three minutes it had taken Trevillian to get from the broadcast desk to a spot where he was reasonably certain he couldn't be overheard, six months of intensive public and media relations training had evaporated and left behind the steel-making executive from East McKeesport, Pennsylvania.

Whiffington put his hand over the phone and said to his assistant, "I want the last three segments on my office monitor in less than two minutes. Go!" He uncovered the mouthpiece. "Tommy, calm yourself, you're gonna blow an artery. Now tell me—"

"That pencil-dick fuckhead from Scratch is stomping on our buy-back deal!"

"You mean Eddie Caminetti?"

"Of *course* I mean Caminetti, you dumb geek! You tellin me you didn't know what he was up to?"

"You mean offering twenty bucks off if you turn in bogus Medalists?"

Trevillian took a deep breath, then bit his fist again, this time drawing blood. "Yes. Yes, Whiff, that's what I'm talking about."

"What about it?"

"What about it is that your two hired dickwads blindsided me with it, that's what! Here I am as a guest on your piece-a shit coverage and they stick one up my ass! With no fucking warning!"

"Chrissakes, Tommy"—the assistant returned, and flipped the monitor on—"what the hell's the big deal here? The guy's a two-bit flash-in-the-pan hustler."

"Oh, yeah? That's what you said about Paddington, that numb-nuts with the golf ball that was *really*, *really round*. Remember *that* little two-bit flash in the pan?"

Whiffington winced at the memory. After Trevillian had gone on the record on dozens of talk shows denouncing the idiocy of a golf ball that was rounder than others, MedalCorp had been forced to buy the Circolo Golf Ball Company at four times its true worth just to be able to put it out of business.

"Caminetti," Trevillian growled into the phone. "That sonofabitch's been busting our balls ever since he came out with that piece-a shit Scratch! Every time I turn around some disloyal bastard's got a dozen of those things comin right out his ass! That slimy prick Carmichael, that fucking hosebag, using a Scratch on national television...you swore to me that was the last fuck-up!"

"Hang on, Tommy...I'm getting it now but I mean, gimme a goddamned break. What asshole is gonna think twenty bucks off a hundred-dollar box of balls is any kind of a..."

"Whiff? Hey, Whiff! Goddamnit, are you there?"

The image of a long line of golfers holding boxes of Medalist balls snaking its way out of the Pinehurst pro shop had just come on the monitor. "Yeah...yeah, I'm here. Holy shit." He'd just seen two smiling customers walk out with Scratch boxes.

"Yeah, holy shit. Glad you finally got around to getting your head outta your ass. Do those two pansy mooks know you're on my board of directors?"

"Don't know. But that smart-mouth shithead Winters has always been a pain in my ass."

"What the hell are we gonna do?"

"Can't put this one back in the bottle, Tommy, him makin you look like an asshole."

"I don't give a rat's ass about how I looked. What I'm asking, how the hell are we gonna make this Caminetti fucker go away?"

"Won't be easy. I think we need to get the board together."

"All of em?"

"Don't be stupid. None-a those institutional horse's butts from the pension funds. Let's get the hardcore guys who know how to put the screws to a troublemaker."

"Good idea."

"And one other thing, Tommy: We need a lawyer."

"I got a whole staffa lawyers."

"Not tax and corporate guys. A gunslinger."

"Now you're talkin! Who?"

Whiffington thought it over. "There's this guy, he's done some work for the network. I'll give him a call."

"Fine. One thing, Whiff."

"What's that?"

"I'm gonna want the network all over this. I'm talkin every one-a your talking heads gets the word on what their opinion's gonna be so they get it right."

"Forget it."

"What the hell do you mean, forget it! It was easy enough, that schmuck chumping me on television. Now you make it right!"

"I said, no. This isn't a race riot or a war, Tommy. It's just golf balls, for God's sake! Try to remember that before you go havin a stroke."

"I'll do that. Whiff. And *you* remember how many shares of MedalCorp you own and what's gonna happen to your little bungalow in Fiji if we tank."

DESERT CANYON GOLF RESORT
ORONDO, WASHINGTON
A WEEK LATER

"I'm driving through apple farms."

Tommy Trevillian sat in the rear seat of the ten-year-old station wagon staring straight ahead. "I'm in Orondo-freakin-Washington and I'm driving through apple farms."

"Orchards," said the driver.

"What?"

"Apple orchards. Not farms. Orchards."

"What the hell's the difference?"

"Orchards, you grow fruit. Farms, you grow sorghum."

"What the hell is sorghum?"

"How should I know? I'm an apple farmer."

The bespectacled man in the front passenger seat, the only one of the five people in the car wearing a suit, turned to face Trevillian. "Just a few more minutes, Mr. T."

"Tell me again why we're here?"

The suit, whose name was Horace Nickton, sighed. "I told you two dozen times already."

"Well, I'm paying you four grand a day, Horace, so tell me again."

Out the right side of the car, the Columbia River was in full view in all its majestic splendor. Nearly sheer rock walls rose from its western shore, and on the east side, neatly trimmed orchards stretched the entire length of the broad bank. For all Trevillian cared at the moment, though, he might as well have been driving through New Jersey.

"For this to be truly objective," Nickton explained, "as well as defensible against future challenges, we need to be free of outside attention. If we did this at a course in Myrtle Beach or Palm Springs, reporters would be swarming all over the place and make the subjects nervous."

"But why in the middle of farming country?" Trevillian asked as a pickup truck shot past them. "Why this course?"

"Because," Nickton said patiently, "Desert Canyon has five sets of tees that make it look like five completely different courses. Nearly two hundred people are going to play it today, and we'll have every kind of player you could ever hope to get together in one place on one day, everything from eighty-year-old ladies who only use three-woods and putters to young guys who are only two strokes away from being on the tour."

"Did you tell him how beautiful it is?" the apple farmer driver asked.

"I've never seen it," Nickton replied, as a beat-up Bronco flashed its lights and roared past them. "People sure are in a hurry around here."

"Not normally. Damnedest layout you ever saw. Heck, they got a par-five sits up on a—"

"Yeah, thanks." Trevillian took out a cell phone and dialed a number, then put the phone to his ear. "What the hell's going on?"

"Can't hardly get no signal here, Mr. Trevillian. Terrain's too rugged."

"Beautiful."

"Here we go." The driver slowed and turned left, directly away from the river, and began a gentle climb up a two-lane road that wound through the middle of a series of orchards. In the few minutes they were on that road, another pickup and a Cadillac Eldorado shot past them. Then they turned, this time into the landscaped entrance of the club itself.

"Hey, look at that," one of Trevillian's junior executives said, pointing first out the left window, then the right.

On either side of the car, bright green swatches of carpetlike grass snaked their way through desert scrub and sandy washes. The fairways looked as though they'd been poured in liquid form and frozen in place as they coursed their way down natural arroyos and ancient tributaries. Sand traps, like blots of brilliant white ink dropped from some celestial fountain pen, splotched their way around the landscape. Two flags were visible from the entrance road, inviting, beckoning, alluring. Jackrabbits bounded away from the car, stopped, then turned to keep a careful eye on the intruders.

"Damn," Trevillian said. "Anybody bring my clubs?"

The parking lot was jammed. "Never seen it this crowded," the driver said.

"Head for the clubhouse," Nickton directed.

They were greeted at the entrance by the head pro, the general manager and the superintendent of groundskeeping. Trevillian, locked into autopilot, was gracious and charming, but couldn't keep his eyes off the course. "That the first hole?" he said, pointing.

"Sure is," the general manager answered. "C'mon and have a look."

Trevillian tried not to gulp as they approached the tee box. The fairway dropped steeply downward, and gave the impression of a jade glacier meandering slowly in and around stands of cactus, exotic desert plants and jagged rock formations. The sand traps toyed with perspective, such that you couldn't tell if you were looking at bunkers or dunes.

Trevillian was entranced, so Nickton took over. "Everything going smoothly?"

"Far's I can tell," the GM said. "Your people were here even earlier than we were this morning."

"How many golfers have you gotten out so far?"

"About two hundred," the head pro said, nodding at the bag drop behind them. "And they're still coming." Trevillian turned to see the Cadillac and pickup truck that had passed them on the way in. Bag boys were unloading clubs from the back of each, and the occupants were walking rapidly toward the clubhouse.

"Two hundred?" Nickton exclaimed. "Why, that's terrific! I thought you said you were only expecting about two hundred *all day,* and it's barely ten o'clock."

"I did. But when people showed up and found out they were playing for free today, a lot of them called their friends to get on over."

"How many took us up on our offer?"

The GM turned to the head pro, who said, "I only know of four guys who didn't."

"Wouldn't mind playing a few holes myself," Trevillian said with a self-conscious chuckle. He was supposed to be here on business.

"Suit yourself," the GM said. "Hell, you bought the whole course for the day, so do whatever you want."

They walked into the clubhouse and headed for the pro shop. Trevillian had difficulty keeping his eyes off the parts of the course visible through the large bay windows. The UV coating on the glass enhanced the contrast between the green of the grass and the soft reddish and purplish hues that suffused the dramatic rock formations. Even a string of power lines running across the tops of massive steel towers was more dramatic than intrusive. As the lines disappeared into the distance they added to the almost other-worldly beauty of the place.

A special desk manned by several of Nickton's people had been set up in the pro shop. Trevillian and his entourage got there just as the men from the pickup truck were walking away and the Cadillac group stepped up.

"Morning, gentlemen," a staffer said cheerily. "You heard it right. If you help us out with a little test, today's round is on Medalist."

"Carts too?" one of the players asked.

"You bet. And there's a beverage cart running around the course and that's on us as well."

"So what's the catch?"

"Not much of a catch. We just want you to use our balls." From behind the desk he picked up two plain boxes with no markings other than a big *A* on one and *B* on the other. Setting them down, he opened the lids of each. "As you can see, each ball is labeled with an A or a B. We'd like you to use both kinds during your round, and at the end, just come on back and tell us which one you liked better."

"That's it?"

"That's it."

"Hang on a second," one of the players said. "These aren't, like, trick balls or anything, are they? Or some experimental whatchacallit that's gonna ruin my game?"

"No, sir, these—"

"Cause I play these jokers here for money, see, and I don't want to get blindsided."

"Sir, I can assure you that—"

"Not used to these, could blow my whole game."

Three more groups had come in and were waiting behind the Cadillac bunch, listening in.

"Both of these balls are currently on the market, both very popular. Used by millions of people. All we did was remove the logos."

"I use damned good balls, sonny. Best on the market. We got some money on the line here."

"I'm sure you do. Shouldn't be a problem. Just use some of each and—"

"Don't want to see my game get—hey!"

The staffer, smiling and nodding in understanding, had pulled back the two boxes of balls. "You make a good point, sir. So if you've got some big bets going"—he pointed to his right—"you're probably a whole lot better off just using your own balls. The club people will take care of you right over here."

"Huh?"

"Just pay your green fee and we're sorry we bothered you."

There was some impatient grumbling from the two dozen people now stacked up in front of the desk.

"Well, wait just a second." The player turned to one of his friends. "I mean, seeing as how all of us'll be using these same balls..."

"Yeah, that's right. What the heck, let's help em out."

"Good idea," said another one of the bunch.

The first guy shrugged and said to the staffer, "Okay, we'll help you out."

"Wonderful!" said the staffer, without a trace of sarcasm. "We sure do appreciate it." He closed the lids and handed over both boxes. "If you need any more, the beverage lady will have some."

"We get to keep these?" one of the players asked.

"Ah, fraid not. We need them all back at the end...except what you leave in the canyon, of course."

They all had a good laugh, then the staffer said, "But as a token of our appreciation for agreeing to help us out, you'll each get a box of brand new Medalists after you check back in and give us your opinion."

"Good deal!" they agreed, then headed out to the course as the next group stepped up to the desk. The staffer spread his arms and gestured for them to move in closer so he could explain what was going on to all of them at once.

Trevillian pulled Nickton aside. "How'd we get all those logos off the Scratch balls? Thought you couldn't do that."

"You can't," Nickton replied. "We covered them up."

"How?"

"Wasn't easy."

The GM walked up and clapped Trevillian on the back like they were old buddies. "So what exactly are you testing?" he asked.

"Which one's better," Horace answered. "Mr. Trevillian, why don't you go on ahead and play? We've got things under control here."

"Don't want to jump ahead of anybody," Trevillian answered. He made it sound almost as though he really meant it.

"Don't worry," the GM said to his new pal. "Nearly all of these people are walk-ins so we'll just fill in a tee time for you."

"You don't think that's unfair, do you?"

"Unfair?" The GM laughed. "You're about the only one's paid a green fee, remember?"

About ninety minutes later Trevillian stood on the tee box of the par-five sixth hole, a jaw-dropping monster that plunged 150 feet by the time it arrived at the green 679 yards away. In the far distance a rocky bluff slashed across the sky, and to the left of the fairway, visible through the maw of a narrow canyon, was the gleaming ribbon of the Columbia River.

"It's called Lake Entiat here," the pro said.

"Sorry, what?" Trevillian asked.

"This section of the Columbia. It's so slow above the Rocky Reach Dam, it's like a lake. Pretty view, isn't it?"

Trevillian nodded as the sound of an approaching golf cart made itself apparent. The gasoline-powered engines of the carts were the only break in the silence of the eerily stark landscape, an unfortunate necessity because nothing with an electric motor could make it up the many steep hills of the course.

Trevillian was glad of the interruption, because it gave him time to savor his upcoming tee shot, which was likely to be one of the more memorable of his life.

"How's it going?" the pro asked the cart's occupant when it pulled up.

"Very well," came Nickton's voice in reply.

Trevillian forced himself to tear away and turn to the cart. "You know, Horace," he said, "we really need to make absolutely certain we do this right. I don't think these good people would mind if we bought the course for another day."

The pro smiled. "Hell, no. I mean, let's face it: Not much of a downside for us, is there?"

"There you go."

"No need for that," Nickton assured Trevillian. "Looks like we're going to get nearly three hundred subjects, so—"

"But the more we have, the better we are right?"

"Well, yes, certainly, but—"

"Just strengthens our position, doesn't it?"

"Couldn't get much stronger than it already is, sir. And a single day was a pretty expensive undertaking to start with."

Trevillian turned back toward the hole. The tee shot wasn't just a simple matter of gripping it and ripping it. The fairway was shaped like an hour-glass, narrowing to a small gap with a rock outcropping in the middle and scrubland on either side before widening back out again. If you didn't lay up, you had to make sure you could clear the gap or you'd risk losing the ball. It was about 260 to the ideal landing area, but that was as the crow flies. Because of the dizzying drop in altitude, maybe 240 or even 230 would do it...

"Gonna be pretty expensive if we screw it up, Horace," Trevillian said with finality. "Go on back and set it up with the GM."

"Mr. Trevillian..."

"So what do you think," Trevillian said to the pro as he twisted the grip of his driver in his hands. "Take it a little right to left, just in case?"

"Left to right, if you can. You're better off on the left if you come up short."

Nickton, who'd only brought one change of socks and underwear and hated having his laundry done in a hotel, waited in silence for Trevillian to line up and take his shot, figuring afterward he could talk some sense into the enraptured CEO and get them all home by that night.

It was a solid strike that sent the ball out to the left and began bringing it slowly back. "That enough?" Trevillian asked anxiously, still poised in his follow-through.

From this distance and this altitude and this early, it was impossible to tell whether the ball sinking beneath them and gliding rightward was going to clear the narrow throat or hit it and bounce over or disappear into it, never to be seen again.

But as it continued to drift downward, boring its way through background strata of sky, rock, water and grass, the pro began to nod in approval. "Looks like one hell of a shot there, Mr. Trevillian."

Nickton saw the ball disappear in the vicinity of the scrub to the left of the narrow gap. Nobody in the teeing area moved. Three seconds later it rolled into view on the grass on the far side of the hourglass. Trevillian turned, a serene grin on his face, as the onlookers clapped and congratulated him.

Nickton hit the gas and turned the cart around. Maybe the GM would know of a store in the nearby town of Chelan where he could buy some socks and boxers.

CHAPTER SIXTEEN

Charlie Trilling, ace investigative reporter for the *Los Angeles Chronicle*, was nearly blind with fatigue, dehydration, road hypnosis and a budding case of the squirts owing to the four bags of potato chips made with artificial fat he'd eaten since passing through Phoenix. Charlie, proud of himself for going for the low-fat variety, didn't know that it was the potato chips that had given him the squirts, because there was no warning printed on the bag. The FDA had determined that the squirts, which they'd referred to in their reports as "anal leakage," may have been uncomfortable, may have been potentially embarrassing, but didn't rise to the level of a bona fide health problem along the lines of cancer or heart disease or bubonic plague and therefore didn't merit a mandatory warning label.

Not that it would have made a difference to Charlie had he known, because by the time he'd pulled off at a roadside mini-mart he was so exhausted from following that goddamned semi all the way from goddamned El Paso, and so hungry from not daring to stop anywhere and take his eyes off of it, that he would gladly have eaten maggot-infested garbage straight out of the can had it been available. What he would not eat, however, was whatever the hell it was that had been sitting behind an impossibly grimy display case in the mini-mart, doughnut-sized patties of what looked like a cross between squashed hamsters and the stuff that had been dripping out of the alien in the movie of the same name. So he'd grabbed the closest thing that he could be assured had been sealed somewhere other than on these premises, which were the four bags of chips, and ran back to his car, hoping that his plan of stopping quickly and then catching up with the truck wouldn't go awry because, after over a thousand miles of nearly nonstop driving from Hallettsville, Texas, if the semi turned off I-10 in the next half hour and lost him, he was liable to take out his rage on the next unsuspecting sonofabitch bastard who smiled and said, "Have a nice day."

But it didn't. Charlie caught up to it, offered his firstborn to any deity who would make them stop for a potty break, and some three hundred miles later followed as the truck took the exit for the 210 freeway, the first turn it had made in two days. It was 2:30 in the afternoon when the big rig turned off onto Sierra Madre Boulevard, turned left onto Oswego Street, pulled into the parking lot of the Pasadena City–Lamanda Park branch of the county library...and sat there. Doing nothing.

Charlie's intestines were moving toward some kind of critical go-no-go juncture—if he didn't go, they would—and since it didn't appear as though the big rig drivers were in much of a hurry to do anything, he got out of the car, ran a block north to the Comfort Inn on East Colorado Boulevard and in short order rendered the lobby bathroom uninhabitable for about the same period of time as if it had been used as a nuclear waste disposal facility.

He ran back to the library parking lot on wobbly legs and found the semi in the same place he'd left it. Those bastards driving it had probably crawled up into their comfortable over-cab bunks and nodded off, the mere thought of which nearly made him fall asleep while he was still standing. He didn't dare, though, not after all he'd gone through to track them this far, at least not without knowing if they'd be out for five minutes or five hours, or not without a way to wake up if they moved.

He got back into his car and slowly, quietly, pulled it up behind the big rig, blocking its way out, but making sure the front end of his car could be seen clearly from the truck driver's rearview mirror. He reclined his seat, threw an arm over his eyes and tried to fall asleep.

Four days ago Charlie Trilling had gotten an anonymous tip about fifty-five-foot semis that pulled into the Scratch, Inc., parking lot in Hallettsville, East Texas, three times a week, then pulled out and made their way west to someplace in California. This would normally not be terribly unusual, given that trucks had to come in and load up product before they could head out and deliver it, except that, according to the tipster, the trucks pulling in seemed to be as heavily loaded as the ones going out. And deliveries of finished product were made by different trucks.

Charlie sighed and rolled his eyes. 'Raw materials gotta come from somewhere.'

'Nuh uh,' the caller said. 'Not in these babies. Stuff from suppliers they get in a whole loada smaller vehicles.' He pronounced it 'vee-hickles.'

'So?'

'I'm just sayin, is all.'

'Saying what?'

'Well, they gotta be doin somethina them balls...'

'How do you know that?'

'Read it in one-a yer columns, cryin out loud! This Charlie Trilling or ain't it?'

'Yeah, okay, keep your shirt on.'

'An they're doin it somewheres.'

'And?'

'I'm just sayin.'

'Not a lot to go on.'

'Then jus fergit it,' the guy said before hanging up.

But Charlie couldn't fergit it. He flew to Houston, rented a car and drove a hundred miles to Hallettsville to stake out the Scratch factory. That night at nearly one a.m., observing discreetly from a stand of withered trees, he watched as a giant rig backed into one of two loading docks behind the single-story building. The truck bore no markings of any kind beyond the obligatory DOT information.

It took four men with forklifts about an hour to empty the truck of forty pallets of cardboard cartons. Through binoculars, Charlie noticed that each box bore a hastily applied stamp of some sort, a blurry, purplish insignia whose details he couldn't make out.

Almost as soon as they finished offloading, the forklift operators were back on the dock. This time they brought pallets out from inside the building and loaded them into the big rig. The cartons looked the same, but none bore the purplish stamp. By around four in the morning the loading was complete. A foreman-type stepped onto the dock, pulled down the rear door of the truck and locked it, and made a notation on his clipboard. He nodded to the driver, who was smoking a cigarette a few yards away. The driver flicked away the cigarette, waved to his partner and got inside the cab. He started the engine, and as soon as the other driver hopped aboard, they pulled out of the lot.

Charlie, who'd been counting on at least a night and a day to load up on supplies before he had to hit the road again, followed at a discreet distance.

The sound of a Saturn 5 rocket taking off less than a hundred yards away knifed its way into the center of Charlie's brain. He bolted upright, then went down again as his head slammed into the underside of his dashboard. Dazed, disoriented with respect to three-dimensional space and in considerable pain, the last thing he needed was for the rocket to fire its engines again, which is about when he realized that it was the big rig's horn he was hearing. Or, more correctly, feeling, as the maxi-decibel klaxon threatened to shake the rivets loose from the chassis of his rental car.

"Hey, move it, will ya, Mack?" was the form of the evening's good wishes that greeted him.

"Yeah, yeah," he grumbled as he swiped at his eyes, sat up straight and started the ignition. He would have committed armed robbery for half a cup of tepid coffee, and remembered the "For Guests Only" pot of free java he'd seen in the motel lobby a few hours before. Fixing his mind on it hungrily, he pulled away to let the semi out and wondered if they'd have coffee in that pot at this time of night. Which was...?

He glanced at his watch: One a.m. What the hell was it with these guys and late nights?

The big rig pulled out of the parking lot and headed away from the motel and the coffee and down to California Boulevard (*Was everything a goddamned boulevard in Pasadena?* Charlie asked himself in some irritation), where it turned right, cruised slowly for about a mile, then stopped. Charlie saw the brake lights flare brightly, then dim down again. He quickly punched at his own light switch and pulled over to the side of the road. Up ahead, the driver got out of the truck and looked around. His partner then got out and did the same. They walked all around the rig, still looking, then got back in. A few seconds later the semi pulled ahead slowly, its lights still out, then turned just as it passed a large sign. Once it was safely down what appeared to be a very long driveway, Charlie pulled ahead to the sign and looked up at it: California Institute of Technology.

Caltech? What the hell were these guys doing bringing a load of golf balls to the most prestigious science university in the world?

He saw the truck's brake lights in the distance as it slowed at a guard shack near a four-story building with TARGET STATION painted on its side in beige lettering. Deciding that following in his car wouldn't work, Charlie pulled over to the side of the road and got out, then walked among some trees lining the service road, making his way toward the truck. The driver was in conversation with a guard, who soon waved them through. As the truck maneuvered to turn itself around in a somewhat smallish ramp area, Charlie arrived at the side of the building and stayed in the shadows. Leaning against a brick wall, he heard a distinct hum and felt a vibration in the bricks but didn't have time to give it much thought because a bright light stabbed at the darkness surrounding him and almost gave him away.

He stepped back into a shadowed area and found the source of the light, a large sliding door that had just opened atop what looked like a loading bay. Narrowing his eyes against the sudden brightness, Charlie looked through the door and saw a stunning array of exotic and futuristic equipment lining the entire interior wall. There were display screens, meters, banks of switches, a wild profusion of wires running in all directions, and what appeared to be a mainframe computer dominating the center of the room. At least he thought it was a computer, except that it was round rather than rectangular, and pipes rather than wires led away from it.

All of that was beside the point, because standing in the bay with the harsh interior light streaming past them were none other than Eddie Caminetti and Professor Norman Standish. Trilling blinked in surprise and kept watching as the two began supervising the unloading of what must have been 800,000 golf balls. Then the doors were closed and the drivers got back into the truck but didn't leave.

About half an hour later the humming from the brick wall increased in pitch and intensity. Trilling, frightened for some reason he couldn't identify, pushed away from it and began looking for a doorway into the building.

Coming around to the front, he saw a brass plaque with the letters HEP but no indication as to what was inside. The double doors to the right of the plaque were locked, as were all the other doors he came upon as he circled the building. Returning to the loading bay area he eventually found a window he figured had to look in on the main floor, but it was some twelve feet above ground level. Low voices wafted out above the humming sound but he couldn't make them out.

Charlie looked around and saw a mini-Dumpster of sorts. Trying to make as little noise as possible, he managed to wheel it under the window, then clambered up onto it, pulled out his dictating machine, set it to record and held it up to the windows with its microphone facing inside. When his arm started to ache he set the machine on the windowsill and climbed down.

With nothing to do for the twenty minutes of recording capacity on the tape, he though it worthwhile to try to figure out what this place was. He lit a match and held it up over the opening to the mini-Dumpster's interior, then rooted around among some papers. He found an envelope and read the address by match light: "Caltech High-Energy Physics Laboratory." So that was what HEP stood for. It figured, Norman Standish being a physicist. But what did that have to do with golf balls?

He tried to find more papers worth reading but none told him anything worthwhile. Then he heard a rapid clicking sound and whirled around to see what it was, realizing seconds later that it was the sound his dictating machine made when it came to the end of its tape.

As Charlie scrambled to get back up on the mini-Dumpster, the voices from within the building stopped. He could hear the sound of wooden chair legs scraping on linoleum, and then saw a stream of light issue forth from the sliding loading ramp door as it opened. He got his hands on the dictating machine, jumped to the ground and ran toward the front of the building. Heart pounding, he squeezed himself between two support columns and tried to listen, but the blood pulsing through his ears was louder than anything coming in from the outside. He waited for ten minutes before daring to move, then slinked across a grassy patch and into the tree line before heading back toward the entrance to the grounds and his car. He pressed rewind on the machine, started the car engine and drove off, a bit more rapidly than good sense might have dictated.

Once safely away, he pressed play.

"Four." Standish's voice.

"Nine." That was Caminetti's.

"Seventeen."

"Twenty-four."

"Thirty."

"That's a go. Eight."

"Eighteen."

And so on. It was gibberish to Charlie. He looked at his watch, calculated that it was about 7:30 a.m. in Washington, picked up his cell phone and dialed a number.

"Hello?"

"Dr. Ehrhart? Charlie Trilling."

"What a pleasure," Professor Kevin Ehrhart said without a trace of pleasure.

Charlie, in the thick-skinned way required of nosy reporters, took no notice of it. "Got a question for you." Without waiting for permission, he said, "High-energy physics building at Caltech. What's a target station?"

"In twenty-five words or less?"

"Yeah."

There was an audible sigh at the other end, followed by a pause. Then, "In high-energy physics, you use very big and powerful machines to speed up subatomic particles and then smash them into something."

"What for?"

"To find out what's inside them."

"Why not just look at them?"

"Because you can't 'look' at something that's smaller than a wavelength of light. You smash it into stuff, and the debris from the collision tells you what went on."

"How do you speed particles up?"

"Many ways. Like spinning them around in a cyclotron. On every lap you give them a little kick, which boosts their energy. Couple of billion laps later when they pack a lot of punch, you redirect them out of the cyclotron and into the stuff you want to see."

"And that stuff...?"

"Sits in a target building."

"And that's it?"

"Of course that's not it. You want a whole course in physics by phone?"

But Charlie had heard enough. He thanked the professor, then called his editor.

Los Angeles Chronicle, September 23:

THEY'RE NUCLEAR!

"SCRATCH" GOLF BALLS
GET THEIR JUICE FROM
PARTICLE BOMBARDMENT
IN ATOM SMASHER

SECRET REVEALED BY
CHRONICLE INVESTIGATIVE REPORTER
CHARLES TRILLING

The National Enquirer, September 25:

THE BALL IS A BOMB...
LITERALLY!

NOTED PHYSICIST SAYS SCRATCH
GOLF BALLS ARE
"MINIATURE ATOMIC BOMBS"

WARNS OF SEVERE RISKS TO
GOLFERS AND THE PUBLIC

MESA, ARIZONA—University of the Atlantic senior physicist Lamarr
Oppenheimer told the *National Enquirer* yesterday that Scratch golf balls,
the hottest thing to hit sports equipment in decades, are built on the same
principle as an atomic bomb.

"The A-bomb works by squeezing plutonium using conventional explosives," he said in an exclusive interview. "But in a package the size of a golf ball, you don't need dynamite or TNT."

Professor Oppenheimer told the *Enquirer* that the force of a golf club hitting the ball is enough to cause implosion of the nuclear particles scattered throughout the ball.

"When that happens," he said, "tiny atomic explosions take place, and that's what gives the ball its immense power."

And the risk? "If this were to get out of hand—for example, if a truckload of Scratch balls went over a cliff and all the balls got squeezed together when the truck hit the ground?"

The professor shuddered at that point and was unable to continue.

The Globe, September 27:

TRANSPORTATION SECURITY ADMINISTRATION TO ADD SCRATCH GOLF BALL TO LIST OF BANNED ITEMS ABOARD AIRLINES!

CHAPTER SEVENTEEN

When aliens from another galaxy invade Earth and demand one good reason why they shouldn't reduce our worthless planet to cinders, Derek Anouilh's swing should pretty much convince them to leave us alone.

"The Kid" was the number one golfer in the world—maybe in history—three years ago when he took a turn around a racetrack in an Indy car during a promotional shoot and almost broke the course record. He was so smitten with the feel of fast driving and hyper-adrenalized, head-to-head competition that he quit golf and dove headlong into auto racing.

A year ago, giving in to the ardent entreaties of both a new girlfriend, who was worried about his safety, and his business manager, who was worried about impending bankruptcy, he decided to give up racing. His agent had approached Tommy Trevillian of the Medalist Golf Company and the two had worked out an elaborate marketing scheme that would tie together Medalist's launch of a revolutionary new golf ball and Anouilh's return to professional golf.

The story, carefully stage-managed by the public relations firm of Ward/Hunsecker/Falco, was obediently picked up by every magazine and newspaper in which Medalist advertised, which was virtually all of them. The Kid was ensconced in the Plaza Hotel in New York City for three solid days, giving five-minute interviews to an endless stream of reporters, all of whom had been flown in at Medalist's expense. The company supplied a staff of photographers to take pictures of each reporter interviewing Anouilh and examining the new ball, and a complete set of prints in various sizes, along with a CD containing the images in electronic format, was handed to each of them within fifteen minutes of the interview's conclusion. Medalist also set up a suite full of personal computers, printers and communications gear so the reporters could file their stories without delay, and even retained a staff of professional copywriters to help with the crafting of the articles, assisted by a database of over 7,000 prewritten leads, headlines, paragraphs and quotes that could be called up instantaneously.

Meanwhile, on another floor of the Plaza, eight rooms were completely overhauled and turned into miniature television studios. Hundreds of on-air personalities from local stations all over the country and Europe were led into the rooms one at a time by eight separate crews and allowed to interview Anouilh, who was nowhere to be seen. Each reporter was given a menu of eighty possible questions, and asked any that he wanted, phrased any way he liked, to an empty chair that was off-camera. At the conclusion, a digitized copy of the demi-interview was piped down to the hotel's ballroom via fiber-optic cable, where a dozen teams of video technicians intercut the reporters' questions with preshot footage of Anouilh answering them. He had also spent two hours sitting in front of a camera smiling and saying, "Thanks, Doug. Thanks, Andrea. Thanks, Phil. Thanks, Vinny," from a list containing the names of every television reporter who would be shooting the virtual interviews. These closings were spliced onto the ends of the interviews to imply that each reporter had a special, intimate familiarity with the superstar.

Over a period of four days, the story of the KY 9000, "The Ball That Brought Derek Back," had so saturated the consciousness of the public that the heaviest-hitting, nationwide outlets were falling all over themselves to get some live one-on-one time. On a single Friday, Anouilh was shuttled among the morning news shows of all the major networks, did as many mid-morning, lunchtime and midafternoon talk shows as was logistically feasible, and wrapped up the week with an hour on *The Randolph Fitztipton Show*.

One week later he played in his first pro event since announcing his comeback, and won it by seven strokes.

The KY 9000 launch had cost over $16 million, not including the $7 million paid to Anouilh for his first year of sponsorship, but the ball, at $50 a box, had sold more in the next month than all other balls on the market combined.

LANDMARK GOLF CLUB AT OAK QUARRY
RIVERSIDE, CALIFORNIA

"What ball you using, Derek?" Joel Fleckheimer called out to Anouilh on the first tee. "Hope it's not that piece-a shit KY Jelly."

Anouilh grinned as he took it out of his pocket. "Ball this sweet is wasted on a *patzer* like you, Fleckminster," he said, using the Yiddish slang for an inept chess player. He and Fleckheimer had been two of the most popular players on the U.S. team at the infamous Ryder Cup three years before, referred to affectionately as "the Kid and the Yid." Their endless ribbing of each other had become legendary around the tour, and the rivalry they'd developed was one of the key factors in boosting viewership at tournaments prior to Anouilh's exit from the game.

Alan Bellamy, three-time Golfer of the Year and captain of that Ryder Cup team, gestured out toward the fairway. "Chrissakes...it's only three hundred yards, Anouilh," he scoffed. He'd pronounced the name correctly: *An-wee*. "You could reach it with a range ball."

"But I'm only using a three-wood." Anouilh was holding a driver.

As the others laughed, Eddie Caminetti said, "Tell you what, Derek."

"Tell me what." Anouilh took a tee from his pocket.

"Play you straight up for five grand."

Fleckheimer and Bellamy lost their smiles in an instant and turned to Eddie. "What's the gimmick?" Bellamy asked.

"No gimmick. Straight up, no strokes."

Fleckheimer said, "You want to play the number one golfer in the world straight up."

"For five thousand dollars." Bellamy added.

"Yep."

"You must be outta your mind."

Eddie shrugged.

Bellamy turned to the Kid. "So whaddaya say?"

"Nope." Anouilh bent down and teed up his ball.

"Nope?" Fleckheimer, incredulous, stared at Anouilh. "What are you, fuckin nuts?"

"Nope."

"I don't get it," Bellamy said.

Anouilh straightened up and stepped away from the ball. "Me neither," he said, as he took his driver from under his arm and worked the grip in his hands. "But one thing I know for goddamned sure, if I bet this crooked sonofabitch, sure as I'm standing here I'm gonna be out five large when we're done."

He looked out at the fairway, then stepped back to the ball and got set up. "I don't know how it's gonna happen, but it is, and when it does, there'll be no way in hell I can say he pulled a fast one."

"Oh, for God's sake, Derek," Fleckheimer said disdainfully. "Straight up is straight up. What could he pull?"

Anouilh straightened up from his stance and looked at Fleckheimer. "Okay, tell you what: You're number four on tour...*you* play him straight up. That okay with you, Eddie?"

"Absolutely."

As the others waited, Fleckheimer turned to Eddie, who stood there doing nothing at all except staring out over the spectacular course, which had been built in and around an old stone quarry.

"Fuck no!" Fleckheimer said at last, laughing along with the others. "You think I'm some kinda lunatic?"

Still grinning, Anouilh resumed his stance, but before he could settle down in preparation for his shot, a shout drifted up from the starter's booth down the concrete cart path. "What the hell...?"

"Somebody's on his way up!" the starter yelled. "Shop called and said for you to wait!"

"They gotta be kidding," Bellamy said. What he didn't say was that any golf course in the country would be glad to send a private jet just to have these golfers play their course, so what could possibly be important enough to hold up their round?

They looked down the path and saw the starter beckoning to a golf cart on its way up the steep drive from the clubhouse. As it came into view, they could see that it was being driven by an ordinary-looking man in a coat and tie. He had an envelope in his hands.

"Bet it's a check for Derek," Fleckheimer said.

"For what?" Anouilh asked.

"Hell difference does it make? Don't you get paid just for breathing these days?"

"No, but I'll run it past my agent."

The starter pointed up the hill and the cart turned accordingly. As it neared the tee box, the driver got his first look at who was standing there. The gasoline engine faltered and died, and the cart threatened to slip back down the hill until he caught himself and stomped on the brake.

"Come on!" Bellamy ordered impatiently, waving the man forward.

Unable to take his eyes off the foursome, the man left the cart where it was and got out. He stood there until Bellamy waved him forward again.

"What can we do for you?" Fleckheimer said as the man finally reached them and stopped.

He turned to Eddie. "Mr. Caminetti?"

"Yeah."

The man took a deep breath. Pain in his eyes, he held out the envelope. "Sorry about this, but...you're being served. Lawsuit. Sorry."

Eddie took the envelope, stared at it for just moment, then tucked it into his back pocket.

"Aren't you even gonna look at it?" Bellamy asked.

Eddie shook his head. "I know what it is. What's your name?" he asked the process server.

"My...uh...my...Franklin. My last name, I mean. Franklin."

"Well, Franklin. You play golf?"

"Do I...I, uh, yeah, I play golf. I mean, you know..." He waved a hand at the foursome, as though to indicate that he didn't *play* in the sense that this august foursome *played*.

"What's your handicap?"

"My...eleven. I play to an eleven. Yes."

"You got clubs with you?"

"Do I...what? Clubs? Jeez, Mr. Caminetti, how come...what do you mean, do I have clubs?"

"I mean, Do. You. Have. Clubs?"

"Yeah, sure. In my car. Always carry...I mean, way my day goes, you never know if...why?"

"Got any money on you?"

"Uh, no, not a lot...how come—"

"Checkbook?"

"Chrissakes, Eddie," Fleckheimer said.

"Yeah! Yeah, I gotta checkbook. But what—"

"Why don't you go get your clubs and play with us?"

Franklin's lower jaw almost came unhinged as it fell from the upper.

"Go on," Eddie urged. "We'll hit off and then wait for you."

Franklin was still staring at him in stupefaction.

"Bugs're gonna fly down your throat, you don't close your mouth," Bellamy said.

Franklin snapped his jaw shut.

"Course, we play for money," Eddie said, trying to ignore the others as they began rolling their eyes. "You know, make it interesting."

Franklin nodded.

"Tell you what," Eddie said. "I'll bet you a thousand bucks you can't beat Derek here."

Franklin slowly turned his head toward Anouilh, then quickly snapped it away, as though even to gaze on the Kid might turn the gazer into a pillar of salt.

He may have been awed, but he wasn't stupid. "Play An—" he almost said the name. "Play against *him?*"

"Yeah."

"But..." Franklin tried to clear his throat. "But he's...I'm just..."

"You're right." Eddie thought it over. "Okay. He'll give you two strokes a hole."

"Hey..." Anouilh started to say.

"Shaddap," Eddie said. "It's my dough, not yours. Whaddaya say, Franklin. You game?"

"Two strokes a hole? I mean, sure, yeah, but..."

"But, it's not fair, that's what you're thinking, right?"

Franklin nodded at Eddie.

"He should only give you, I don't know…sixteen or seventeen, right?"
Franklin nodded again.

Eddie shrugged. "Then this is gonna be the easiest thousand bucks you ever made in your whole life."

Some neuron deep within Franklin's brain that evolution had left intact over the generations and was the seat of the survival instinct fired at just that moment. "What's the catch?"

"Catch? There's no catch. Just got a feeling, that's all."

"Doesn't sound right. Are you guys toying with me?"

"No way!" Eddie insisted. "In fact, I'll tell you what, with these three guys as my witnesses. When we're done, and if you lose and think I snookered you? You don't have to pay."

"Huh?"

"No questions asked. You think I pulled a fast one, you walk away."
Franklin blinked.

"He means it," Bellamy said. "I'll back you up."

"Same here," Fleckheimer chimed in.

Anouilh, who had no idea what the play was, wisely stayed quiet.

"Well, gee…" Franklin said.

"Go on and get your clubs," Eddie said. "We'll wait."

Franklin looked from one face to the next, trying to figure out if they were making fun of him, or was he really about to play a round of golf with three of the best professionals on earth and one of the craftiest hustlers who ever lived.

"Go on," Bellamy said.

Franklin took a few steps backwards, turned, sidled a few more steps, bumped into the golf cart and inched his way around it, then sat in the driver's seat.

"We'll tee off and wait," Fleckheimer said.

Franklin turned the cart around, started down the path, and nearly flattened the starter's shack as he tried to take the turn with the gas pedal fully depressed.

"What the hell are you up to?" Bellamy demanded of Eddie.

"Way I figure it, the guy'd gladly pay a grand to play with you clowns. But it'd be pretty chintzy of me to charge him."

"You might say that," Bellamy agreed.

"So this way, all he does is lose a bet and pay the same grand, which I get to keep."

"With thirty-two strokes?" Anouilh said.

"Even if he's having a bad day," Fleckheimer agreed, "the guy's gonna win by at least twelve."

"Yeah, maybe," Eddie said. "But what I'm betting, this guy is lucky if he doesn't shit his pants by the third hole."

"What if I tank it on purpose," Anouilh asked with a wicked grin, "just to watch you get hosed?"

"Yeah, right," Eddie said. "You'd give up your left nut before you let yourself get beat. At *anything*."

Bellamy looked toward the parking lot in the distance, where Franklin was scrambling to get his gear together and dropping things one after another in his nervousness. The sounds of clubs and shoes hitting the pavement was audible in the still air. "What is it about this game that gets the blood going like that?"

"What do you think?" Eddie said.

"It's really challenging," Fleckheimer ventured.

"So's archery," Eddie countered.

"Well then, even eighty-year-olds can play it," Bellamy said.

"Yeah," Eddie came back, "but they can play lawn darts, too, and besides, that's not why *I* play it. Or you."

"Okay," Anouilh threw in. "It's got a great tradition going back hundreds of years."

Eddie shook his head. "So does curling, and tossing the caber, and when your seventy-eight-year-old Uncle Pierre down in Baton Rouge heads out to the links for the fifth time in a week, it ain't on accounta he feels a deep connection to the Scottish highlands. Now go on and hit your shot."

As Anouilh returned to the tee box, Fleckheimer said, "So who's suing you, Eddie?"

"Medalist," Bellamy guessed.

"Yeah." Eddie shook his head. "Only thing I can't figure is why they waited this long."

"**What does it allege, specifically?**"

In answer to Oscar Petanque's question, Eddie threw the summons to him. "Beats me."

Petanque made no move to pick up the document. "What are you talking about?"

"Haven't read it yet. What difference does it make?"

"Tell me you're not serious."

Eddie walked over to the sofa and sat down on it heavily, then rubbed a hand through his thinning hair. "How long you been in business with me now, Oscar?"

"Too long, that's how long. Why?"

"Because you haven't learned a damned thing. This is just a marketing ploy, Trevillian's way of striking out at some competitors because he's getting his ass kicked."

"Yeah?"

"He did the same thing with that dumb-ass Circolo ball, the *round* one, remember?"

"Yeah."

"So...?"

"So, of course I know it's a public relations maneuver. Don't have to be Eddie Caminetti to recognize that."

"Good. So what's the problem?"

"The problem," said Petanque as he reached for the summons and held it up in the air, "is that he's filed a lawsuit." No reaction from Eddie. "In a court of law." Still nothing. "With judges and lawyers and procedures and great big men with handcuffs if you don't show up."

Eddie leaned his head on the back of the sofa and closed his eyes. "It's still bullshit. Everybody knows it's bullshit."

"It doesn't matter! We still have to treat it seriously!"

"I plan to. Just not gonna get all exercised about it."

"Good." Petanque opened the thick envelope and pulled out the tri-folded document. "Hey, guess where they filed it."

"No idea."

"The United States District Court for the Southern District of Georgia"—

he paused for a second—"Augusta Division."

Eddie's eyes flicked open. "Augusta?"

"Yep."

"*That* Augusta?"

"Uh huh."

Eddie laughed and closed his eyes again. "Well, I'll be damned."

"Pretty poetic touch."

"Poetic, hell. Trevillian's a member at Augusta National. Bet the sonofagun plays every day we're down there."

"Gee, do you think he'll invite you?"

"Sure, why not? Hell, I'll just play him for the case."

"What?"

"Whoever wins, wins."

"Very funny. Maybe *you* could do that, but Medalist is a publicly traded company. Win or lose, he'd go to jail."

"He wouldn't go if he won."

"Good point. So. We need to get us a lawyer and figure out how we negotiate a settlement."

"No settlement. We're going to trial."

"Are you crazy?" Petanque slammed the document down on the desktop. "*Nobody* goes to trial!"

"We're gonna."

Petanque took off his glasses and laid his head on the desk. "Why me, Lord?"

Eddie opened his eyes and sat up. "Come on...it'll be fun."

"Fun?" Petanque picked his head up. "You think a federal trial is gonna be *fun?*"

"Sure. What could Trevillian possibly have on us?"

"You keep saying Trevillian. It's not like one guy suing you because he doesn't like the way you mow your lawn. These guys have more lawyers than we have employees."

"Doesn't matter how many they have, Oscar. You get more lawyers, you don't get more law on your side, do you?"

"No, but you get more guys figuring out how to *use* the law. Okay, look."

Petanque pumped a palm at Eddie and picked up the summons. "Let's see what they're suing us for before we get all excited."

"Wasn't me getting excited. But go ahead."

Petanque put his glasses back on, flipped to the second page of the document and ran his eye down the bill of particulars. "Holy Moses. Makes it sound like we're terrorists or something. I don't even understand half of this...how the heck could we have done it!"

"Like what?"

Petanque put his finger on the page. "Profited illegally by engaging in criminal activity for commercial advantage...tortious interference with Plaintiff's relationships with its customers and dealers...predatory pricing for the sole purpose of stealing market share..."

"Whoa!" Eddie turned toward the desk, frowning. "Predatory pricing? What the hell is that?"

"It's when you purposely lose money on something in order to gain more market share."

"By charging less, right? Get people to buy yours insteada the other guy's?"

"Yeah."

Eddie stood up. "We're charging eighty bucks a box, wholesale!"

Petanque looked back at the document. "Good point. What do you suppose—hey, wait a minute..."

"What?"

Petanque read through some more of the claims. "Here, listen to this: 'an inferior product that is wildly overpriced.'"

He took off his glasses and looked at Eddie. "Do you suppose these guys are going to claim that we stole market share by *over*pricing the balls? That we misled people into thinking they're special when they're not?"

"Has anybody ever done that before?"

"Not since yesterday. Boy, you've got to give these guys credit for creativity! See what a boatload of lawyers will get you?"

"You got a point."

"Good." Petanque dropped the papers and folded his hands. "Any ideas for lawyers?"

"Yeah."

"Who?"

"Me."

"Yeah, who're you thinking of?"

"I just told you: me."

"You."

"Right."

Eddie heard about color draining out of someone's face but never thought it was possible until this moment. "You okay, bud?"

Petanque gulped and picked up the phone.

"Who you calling?"

"First, the professor. Then Jack McGrange."

"McGrange? We already paid him back. Double, just like I said. What's he got to—"

"I'm going to have him kill you, that's why I'm calling him. You— Norm? Oscar. I'm in Eddie's office. You need to get down here right...huh? Norm, I don't care if the other half of this building just got up and started walking down Front Street! Get over here right now!"

The public relations firm of Ward/Hunsecker/Falco prided itself on its ability to leap into action with all cylinders pounding at virtually a moment's notice. Oil spills, chemical disasters, announcements of investigations and impending indictments... they'd seen it all and they were ready. Having a full three weeks to prepare for Medalist's lawsuit against the Scratch company was pure luxury for them, and they took advantage of the lead time to—as senior partner Beetrix (that's how she spelled it) Ward had put it—"get this mother tried, decided and executed before the goddamned trial even starts."

The first step was an impromptu interview with Tommy Trevillian at a charity event in Van Cortlandt Park, the oldest continually operating public course in the country, located smack in the middle of the Bronx. Ward/Hunsecker/Falco had hastily arranged for a group of club pros from the Greater New York area to come to the course and give lessons and pointers to several dozen inner-city kids from a local school. The principal of the school had originally asked if "you people are completely nuts," but a sizable donation to the extracurricular activities fund quieted him down in a hurry.

As Trevillian himself took on a small group of kids and tried to show them the finer points of not breaking your shins when swinging, Billy Winters and a camera crew wandered by and stopped in absolute amazement, just as they'd been instructed by memo direct from network sports director Compton Whiffington.

Winters waited until the crew got set up, did a sound and color balance check, then walked over to the driving range. "Is that...Tommy Trevillian? Can't be! Hey, boys, get a shot here, will ya? Tommy!"

Trevillian didn't look up at first, but grabbed the nearest kid and stuck a five-iron in his hand, then quickly got behind him and began swinging the club back and forth.

"Git yo raggedy-damn ass offa my neck!" the kid said, scowling, and then stomped on Trevillian's instep.

The president and CEO of MedalCorp gritted his teeth and tried not to wince as he backed away and said, "There you go, son! You're getting the hang of it now!"

"Hang this up yo three-piece ass, bitch," the kid muttered as he turned away.

"Tommy!" Winters called again.

Trevillian, turning every which way to try to locate the source of the shout, finally spotted Winters, a cameraman, a sound technician and two production assistants, all of whom he'd inexplicably failed to notice until now, walking toward him across a grassy area. "Billy Winters?"

"Come on, guys," Winters said as the camera rolled. "Let's see if we can get a few minutes with him!"

Astoundingly, they could. And after establishing that one of the most powerful men in the entire sports business world had taken time to personally coach some needy kids, Winters got down to business.

"I know your lawyers have probably forbidden you from talking about the lawsuit, Tommy—"

"Never a good idea, Billy."

"But, just generally, without going into legal specifics, what's really going on here?"

Trevillian scratched his head and grimaced, fighting with himself, obviously dying to get something important off his chest but bound by his responsibility as a Titan of Industry to protect his company by not blowing whatever strategy his legal team was probably still working on. "You know, Billy," he finally said with great reluctance, "nobody wants to go to court, least of all me, but, gosh darn it, you know? Sometimes you gotta do things you don't like just because it's the right thing to do."

"Sure do, Tommy, and I—"

"What I mean is, there's more at stake here than just golf balls and market share and all that blather that just gets heads and tongues wagging."

"Couldn't agree more with—"

"What this lawsuit is really about," Trevillian said, cupping his hands as though they encompassed a single ball of truth and he had the best handle on it of anybody, "is that the Scratch company has got golfers everywhere completely snookered, and they're doing it with an inferior product that is poorly manufactured and wildly overpriced"—here, the cupped hands pulled apart, to be replaced by one index finger pointed directly at the heart of what was right and proper—"and, by God, we can prove it!"

"Now, when you say—"

"It's an inferior ball, we *will* prove it, and we'll do it in a way people can understand! *That's* why we want our day in court!"

Winters was starting to get steamed at being railroaded by this overbearing windbag, but held his tongue...

"The Medalist company has built up a relationship of trust and confidence with its customers that goes back decades," Trevillian rolled on, "and for us to stand idly by while people who care nothing for the great game of golf yank the rug out from under it would be to betray that great store of trust and confidence!"

...until he could hold it no longer. "There's also the question of the Scratch ball having severely cut into your market, right? Isn't it costing you sales?"

Trevillian, who'd forgotten that this was a live television interview and not a stage play, was momentarily disoriented, not so much by the incisive question he hadn't been expecting, but by the fact that he'd gotten so carried away he'd lost track of what it was Winters was supposed to have asked next.

Then he remembered the question Winters did ask. "The problem with this country," he said, eyes narrowing, "is that every thing that happens in business, people assume it's about money. Nobody wants to believe that a corporate executive could do something just because it's right."

"But aren't your shareholders—"

"The media are largely to blame in that regard, always looking for the cheap shot rather than the real heart of the matter. There's more here, a lot more, than just creating shareholder value. There's international relations at stake, too."

What the hell…? "What?"

"Sure! We recently made a deal with a Chinese company to supply them with millions of balls for the burgeoning Asian market. We have an obligation to protect them as well, to do everything we can to prevent fraudulent interlopers from stealing market share by deceiving the golfing public."

"Ah. I see. Very noble. Well, I'm afraid that's all the time we have, Tommy. Really want to thank you for stepping aside to speak with us. Looks like your little buddy there is anxious to get back to his lesson."

Winters wiggled his foot for the cameraman to aim at the hitting mat, where Trevillian's little buddy was peeing into a still-half-full bucket of range balls.

"Inferior product?" Eddie said as he clicked off the television. "Fraudulent interlopers? Man's got a lotta goddamned nerve."

"He's also got a lot of goddamned money," Jack McGrange said. "And a lot of goddamned lawyers."

"We've got *one*," Oscar Petanque said. "Perry Mason his own damned self here."

McGrange, who hadn't yet introduced the man he'd brought with him, went behind Eddie's desk and sat down. "Eddie," he said, folding his hands in front of him, "somebody once told me that any man who acts as his own attorney has a shithead for a lawyer and an asshole for a client."

Eddie reached into his shirt pocket, but it was empty. "Been called worse."

"And you gonna *get* called worse, believe me." McGrange opened a drawer in the desk, fished around and found a pack of cigarettes and tossed them to Eddie. "Now me, I'm no longer part of this company."

"I meant to mention that." Eddie flicked the cellophane open with a fingernail.

"But I still got a lotta affection for it, well as for y'all." He nodded at Petanque and Professor Norman Standish. "And Lord knows you made me a lotta dough. 'S'why I'm helping you out."

"And don't think we don't appreciate it, Jack." Eddie lit a cigarette and exhaled a cloud of blue smoke toward the ceiling. "Now why don't you tell us who your friend over here is and why you brought him."

"Okay." McGrange leaned back on the chair and put his hands on the armrest. "I already know you're gonna ignore good advice and act as your own attorney, stubborn cuss such as you are."

"What the—" Petanque, who'd been pleased thus far, suddenly wasn't. "You're giving in just like that?"

"Ain't mine to give in," McGrange said. "It's his company, he can do whatever the hell he wants."

"It's mine, too," Standish said.

"I know. And that's why, what I'm suggesting, Eddie, is that you let my good friend over here help you out."

"And he is...?"

The stranger rose and stuck out his hand. "Leif Hoogenband. Glad to meet you."

"Likewise," Eddie said, taking the proffered hand. "You're a lawyer."

"That he is," McGrange said. "And a damned good one, too. Been in fronta circuit courts his whole adult life."

"And I need him why?"

"Because," Hoogenband said, "you don't know jack shit about the law. You walk into a federal court and try to wing your way past the procedures and the rules and the etiquette, they'll toss you out so fast you won't even get your briefcase unsnapped."

"Handle the case any way you want," McGrange said, "but let Hoogenband here help you to do it right. He knows what papers to file, how to subpoena witnesses, alla that stuff. Without him, you're dead."

Eddie turned to Hoogenband. "You play golf?"

"Yeah, I do. Play like shit but I play anyway."

Eddie shrugged. "Okay."

The others looked at each other. "What do you mean, okay?" Petanque asked.

"I mean, okay. I'd like him to help me. It's a good idea."

"I don't get it," Petanque said.

"Me neither," Standish added.

"Done deal," McGrange said. "Now, Eddie. What's your case strategy?"

"How the hell should I know?" Eddie took another hit off the cigarette. "No idea how they're gonna come at me," he said as he blew the smoke out. "See what happens, then I'll decide how to handle it."

"Have you done any discovery yet?" Hoogenband asked.

"Discovery? Discover what?"

"You are shitting me, right? Just pulling my leg?"

"Don't know what you're talking about."

McGrange stood up and walked around to the front of the desk, then leaned back on it. "Discovery is when you ask the other side for everything they're going to use as evidence," he explained, "and for everything you need from them to use as *your* evidence."

For the first time since the meeting had started, Eddie was the one to be dumbfounded. "Now you're putting *me* on."

"Nuh uh."

"I get to ask them to give me what they have?"

"Yep."

"And they have to give it to me?"

"Yep."

Eddie looked around the room, then exclaimed, "Bullshit!"

"It's true," Hoogenband said. "Just wait until you get their discovery request. They're going to want to know your mother's grades in junior high, and you have to tell them."

Eddie was having difficulty grasping the concept. Showing your hand in advance did not come easy to a man who was a genetically predetermined hustler. "Damn, what a crock! Sure glad I didn't become a lawyer."

"And I'm sure the profession returns the sentiment," Petanque remarked.

"That's why you need Hoogenband," McGrange said, slapping Eddie's shoulder.

"And damned glad to have him, too," Eddie said with sincerity. "But we do the strategy my way, understood? That's nonnegotiable."

Hoogenband put his hands in the air. "Hear you loud and clear, Eddie."

"Okay, good," McGrange said. "Now, first thing we gotta do is issue a press release, to counter some of the garbage Trevillian's been spreading."

"I've got about five hundred requests for a statement on my desk," Petanque said.

"Fine." Eddie grabbed a piece of paper and scrawled the entire statement on a single line: *The Medalist corporate strategy: If you can't fight em in the market, fight em in the courts.*

It was the lead item on every major wire service the next morning.

CHAPTER EIGHTEEN

THE CHAMBERS OF JUDGE FENWICK C. HOWELL

"Mr. Caminetti," Judge Howell began, "I may be jus a dumb-shit judge from southa the Mason-Dixon Line—"

Tyrell Bardswith, chief counsel for the Medalist Golf Corporation, smiled indulgently. "Why, I'm quite sure your honor is in reality just as sly as an old—"

"No, I really am a dumb shit. Trust me. Ask anybody."

"He's right," said Eddie's co-counsel, Leif Hoogenband.

"You hush up now, Soderberg. Mr. Caminetti, I'm of the opinion that anybody who acts as his own attorney has an asshole for a client and a shithead for a lawyer."

"I thought it was the other way around."

"Long's you unnerstan the concept. But the law does allow it."

"Thank you, your honor."

"For what? Callin you an asshole and a shithead? Nah'm a judge, and I do demand respect, but don't be blowin smoke up my ass and we'll get along fine. At least you got some help from a real attorney. Mr. Bardahl, you know alla our procedures dahn here?"

Bardswith tapped his briefcase. "I believe I'm quite familiar with—"

"Good. So what the hell's the problem, we gotta have this little confab here?"

Bardswith shifted in his seat, pulled some papers from his briefcase and cleared his throat.

"This int gonna take all day, is it, Bardsmith?"

Tyrell Bardswith's claim to fame was that he'd sued a major long distance carrier on behalf of nearly sixty million customers who were overcharged due to a computer billing error. In a massive victory for the rights of consumers, he negotiated a settlement in the class-action suit, for which he and his law partners received a fee of $17 million and were selected as the American Bar Association's "Consumer Champions of the Year." According to the terms of the landmark deal, every customer who filled out a six-page, notarized form and supplied copies of the relevant bills from the time of the infraction some eight years prior would receive a $2.37 credit on the purchase of a new satellite telephone (not to be combined with any discount offers).

"Not at all, your honor," Bardswith replied. "The problem is that we informed the defendant that we intended to call Professor Norman Standish to the stand, and they informed us that he wouldn't do so."

"Huh." Howell frowned and turned to Eddie. "In't he a named defendant in this suit?"

"Yeah, but just cause *those* guys named him doesn't mean he's gotta say anything, does it?"

Hoogenband jumped in quickly to put it in the proper wording. "We're making a motion that he not be compelled to testify."

"What kinda basis you got?"

"His right not to incriminate himself," Eddie said, taking over again. "Says so in the Constitution."

"No shit. Cept there ain't no incriminatin goin on here. Hoopleburg, din't you explain this to your client?"

"He's not my client. He's my—"

"Whatever. If you're assistin him, least you could do is explain the difference tween a civil and criminal case."

"I have, your honor. But we've got kind of an unusual situation here."

"Nonsense," Bardswith interjected. "There's nothing unusual about it."

"Barker," Howell said, "how the hell can you know it ain't unusual, the man ain't even explained hisself yet?"

"This is a very straightforward case, judge." Bardswith put down his papers to show that he didn't need any notes to explain such a simple situation. "We're contending that—"

"Hold on a second." Howell waited for him to stop speaking. "I know what y'all are contending. What I want to know is, what's your specific objection to the defendant's contention that there's an unusual situation here?"

"Simple. It's not unusual at all."

"What isn't?"

"Whatever he says is."

"Which is…?"

Bardswith, trapped by his own rhetoric, had no answer. At least not a good one. "Whatever counsel says is unusual, we maintain that it isn't."

"Even though you don't know what it is."

"Doesn't matter."

"I see. Well, given that you've presented no specific argument to counter defendant's motion, I find for the defendant. So if there ain't any more issues, let's get this—"

"Just a moment, your honor! You can't do that!"

"Do what?"

"Find in favor of the defendant's motion! We haven't even been allowed to argue against it!"

Howell looked genuinely crestfallen, and sank back in his chair. "You know, you're right."

"Thank you."

"So go ahead."

"Go ahead and what?"

"Argue against defendant's motion. I'm listenin, so please proceed." Howell put a finger to his chin and waited.

"Uh…"

"Take your time, son. We don wanna hurry justice here. Go on, now."

Bardswith nodded miserably. "Plaintiff contends that there is no unusual situation here of sufficiently compelling moment to prevent Professor Standish from taking the stand." Then he fell silent.

"That it?" Howell asked.

"Yes, sir."

Howell let Bardswith wallow for a few seconds, but wasn't about to subvert justice just to prove a point. "Bainsworth, I'm gonna give you a choice. I can rule right now, or you can pipe yourself down for the couple three minutes it's gonna take for the defendant here"—Howell leaned forward, slammed a hand on his desk and shouted—"to tell me what the hell is on his mind! Now you got some kinda goddamned problem with that!"

"No, sir," Bardswith answered meekly.

"Well, thank you very much!" Howell turned to Eddie. "Now why don't you go on and tell us why the good professor oughtn to have to testify."

"I'll do that, your honor. Thing is, what happens if, in the course of him being on the stand, the professor, on accounta his being under oath and all, what happens if he has to reveal something that, well, some law enforcement authority might look on as, uh, not entirely kosher?"

Howell thought it over carefully. "You mean like, say, he stole something somewhere along the line."

"Yeah. Not that he did or anything. I'm just sayin, is all."

"Course not."

"Tell you the honest truth, your honor, we really don't know if the professor broke any laws. We just don't want to take any chances."

"Wait a minute," Bardswith said. "Unless you're saying that he *did* do something illegal, you're just trying to snooker me. The way you just put it, that would give blanket permission for anybody in any civil suit to escape having to testify!"

"Man's got a point," the judge said. "He's got a right to more'n that."

"And Standish has a right not to incriminate himself," Hoogenband added. "Look, can we go off the record here?"

"No, we cannot!" Bardswith shot back instantly. He wasn't about to let the Scratch corporation win the point and get away with murder, and do it off the record.

"Tell you what," Howell said. "How's about you gimme a hypothetical regardin what the professor might be gettin into that could cause him some troubles with respect to the criminal statutes. That all right with you, Boardman?"

"For the nonce," Bardswith replied. "We'll see how it goes, where it leads us."

"The nonce?" Howell looked over and scrunched up his face. "What the fuck is a *nonce?*"

"For the moment, your honor."

"Well, jeez...why the hell don't you just say so. Caminetti?"

"Okay. Just a hypothetical, right?"

"Absolutely."

Eddie scratched the bottom of his chin for a few seconds before speaking. "Supposin—and I mean just that—supposin Professor Standish had to get his hands on some materials, some special stuff, in order to make his golf ball."

"What kind of special stuff?" Bardswith asked.

"Really none of your business," Eddie replied. "We still have the right to hang on to our trade secrets, don't we, your honor?"

"True enough."

"All right then. But let's say it was the kind of materials that, well, it isn't always exactly clear who's allowed to have what."

Howell frowned. "You're losin me here."

"Yeah. Okay, here's an example. Let's say you're trying to mix up some special paint for the bottom of your boat."

"What's that got to do with golf balls?" Bardswith demanded.

Eddie turned to him with undisguised impatience. "Not a damned thing, Bardswith. It's an analogy, you know what that is? It means, it's *like* the thing you're talking about, but it's—"

"I know what an analogy is, Caminetti."

"If you know," Howell said, "then what the hell you botherin him for?"

"As I was saying," Eddie went on, "while you were mixing up this paint, experimenting with various kinds of chemicals, somewhere along the way you accidentally whipped yourself up a bunch of, say, uh, a bunch of Prozac."

Howell blinked at him a few times as Bardswith's face went all wrinkly in befuddlement. "Prozac?" the judge said. "What in the hell are you—"

"Prozac's a prescription drug, your honor," Eddie explained. "You're not supposed to have it unless you got a prescription for it, and then you have to get it from a licensed pharmacist."

"Okay..."

"Except here you were just tryin to make some *paint*, and you ended up with Prozac. Now: Suppose you were being sued for violating somebody's patent on boat paint, and you were called to testify, except that it was pretty likely that during the course of testifying you were eventually gonna have to admit that you'd manufactured a controlled substance. Well sir, that'd mean you were being forced to incriminate yourself and that is by God unconstitutional!" Eddie turned to Hoogenband. "Isn't it?"

Howell and Bardswith both thought it over. Howell said, "And you're sayin a situation akin to this Prozac bit pertains to your case?"

"Akin, yeah. Well, it might be."

"Might ain't good enough," Howell replied, before Bardswith could protest. "How bout annutha hypothetical? You know, one that's more, uh..."

"Relevant?" Hoogenband ventured. "But still purely hypothetical?"

"Zackly!" Howell said happily.

Eddie nodded and gave it a few seconds' thought. "The professor works at Caltech. He's a physicist, you all know that. Over there at Caltech they got all sorts of exotic stuff, what with their experimental guys all the time bombarding atoms with other atoms and making stuff that maybe never even *existed* before. Now..."

Eddie leaned forward, whether because he was warming to the subject or because he was buying time to be careful, no one could say. "The professor experimented with all kinds of things. Hundreds, maybe thousands of different kinds of molecules and whatnot. I'm not saying what ended up in our golf ball, and I'm not saying that any of it is classified stuff or radioactive or weapons-grade or—"

Bardswith's jaw dropped so far down he looked like Marley's ghost in Scrooge's living room, but unlike that loquacious specter, Bardswith seemed totally incapable of mounting coherent speech. So Eddie just continued.

"—whatever. But the point is, we can't be sure if the professor followed every single last protocol or paperwork requirement, and in this day and age someone's liable to come crashin down an anybody who was anywhere near—"

"*I knew it!*" Bardswith finally managed to thunder, leaping to his feet and pointing accusingly at Eddie. "I just knew it!"

"Hey, Blackberry, calm the hell—"

"You're using nuclear stuff on that ball!" Bardswith continued, heedless of the judge's admonition. "All along you've been zapping it with—"

Eddie stayed calm and let him finish. The judge, more amused than angry, did the same. When Bardswith finally ran out of air and had to stop to draw breath, Eddie said, "We didn't bombard it with anything. I'm just saying, is all."

"Bullshit!" roared the normally more civil attorney. "You just admitted that—"

"Dint admit nothin," Howell said. "Was all hypothetical, like the man said."

"Your honor," Bardswith said, getting hold of himself with admirable aplomb, "plaintiff objects most strenuously to this blatant attempt to obstruct justice! We demand that the court deny their motion to prevent us from calling Professor Standish to the stand!"

Howell, facing a genuine dilemma, wasn't about to be rushed into anything. "Mr. Caminetti, are you averrin to this court, under penalty-a perjury, that there is a reasonable likelihood that Professor Standish might incriminate himself should he take the stand in this case?"

"Your honor, you're not seriously considering—"

"Hush up, Bardot! Let the man answer! Caminetti, you need a word with your co-counsel?"

"No. Tell you what: If we agree in advance to limit the professor's testimony, I'll withdraw my motion."

"Sounds fair," Howell agreed, nodding vigorously.

"Limit it how?" Bardswith asked skeptically.

"You don't ask him anything about how the ball is made."

"Horsepucky," Bardswith spat. "Why else would I call him?"

"He's got a point," Howell said.

"No, he doesn't," Eddie countered. "Your honor, this trial has nothing to do with how this golf ball is made. It only has to do with how it *performs*. Nothing else matters, so why get into the details of its construction?"

"Nonsense," Bardswith said, laughing derisively. "How it's made has everything to do with how it performs."

"Never said it didn't," Eddie replied. "It just doesn't make any difference." He turned to Howell. "Your honor, you know all those car ads that tell you about aerodynamic efficiency, dual overhead what-the-hell-evers, fuel injection, and so on and so on?"

"I do."

"Well, none of that's relevant. It's designed to mislead people. Just tell me how fast it goes and what kind of mileage it gets, and that's all I need to know. Everything else is besides the point."

He pulled a golf ball out of his pocket and threw it to Bardswith, who scrambled to catch it. "Same thing with that ball there. All that matters is how it behaves. If your client thinks we've been deceiving anybody about how this ball performs, then base your case on how it performs. And for that"—he wiggled for Bardswith to throw it back, which he did—"you don't need Norman Standish."

"Hell," Hoogenband tossed in, "the man can barely hit a golf ball, much less testify about how it does on a golf course."

"Your claims about its performance," Bardswith said, "are based on its construction."

"Whadda you think about that, Caminetti?" Howell asked. He seemed to be enjoying himself.

Eddie grew sober and took his time answering, which seemed to gratify Bardswith no end. "Well," he said at last, "I'll make an offer to counsel right now."

Bardswith, who'd forgotten that he'd been standing all this time, resumed his seat. "I'm listening."

"Simple, really." Eddie drummed his fingers on his knee, then stopped. "You produce any evidence, from any source, from any time, that the Scratch Golf Ball Corporation ever made any claim at all about its ball other than that a box of a dozen was guaranteed to have twelve balls in it, you can have the company."

Into the stunned silence he added, "And if you can't, your side doesn't get to bring up how the ball is made."

Bardswith gasped for a few seconds, in remarkable similarity to a flounder just tossed up onto a dock. "I have to consult with my client," he managed at last, "to see if he's willing to accept such a proposition."

"No, you don't," Howell said smoothly. "He just did."

CHAPTER NINETEEN

The United States District Court
for the Southern District of Georgia
Augusta Division

Transcript of Proceedings

In the matter of:

MedalCorp Golf Equipment Company
Thomas J. Trevillian
Plaintiff
Rep: Tyrell W. Bardswith,
Higgenbotham, Bardswith and Chichester

v.

Scratch Golf Ball Company
Eddie (sic) Caminetti
Defendant
Rep: Eddie (sic) Caminetti
Leif T.F. Hoogenband

Justice of the Circuit Court Fenwick C. Howell, presiding.
Heard in Courtroom D, 501 E. Ford St., Augusta, GA

Transcript

Mr. Bardswith:
If it please the court. Plaintiff intends to demonstrate, inter alia,
that the golf balls produced by Plaintiff are superior in every...

Mr. Caminetti:
Objection, your honor.

Justice Howell:
Goddamnit.

Whereupon the proceeding was suspended upon relocation of all parties to chambers.

CHAPTER TWENTY

THE CHAMBERS OF JUDGE FENWICK C. HOWELL

"Why," snarled Judge Fenwick C. Howell, "in the name of all that's holy are we back in my chambers, Hoagieboy?"

"Because," Hoogenband answered, "we'd like to know why counsel decided somewhere along the way that he needs to deal with the quality of his client's golf ball relative to ours."

"It's really quite simple, your honor," said Bardswith. "We wish to demonstrate, in a court of law and under oath, that our golf balls are superior. That they're all my client claims them to be."

His client, Tommy Trevillian, nodded enthusiastically.

"And why, zackly, do we give a shit?" the judge responded.

Bardswith picked at some nonexistent lint on his pants. "Goes to the very heart of our case, judge. We're claiming that the Scratch Corporation has put forth their golf ball as superior to ours, and is therefore guilty of false advertising and perpetrating a fraud upon the public. Now—"

"But them's criminal matters," the judge interjected. "Or at least some kinda reg-yoo-latory folderol. This here's a civil trial we got goin."

"It's all of a piece, sir. The fraud involved is a public concern at the criminal level, but what we're concerned about here is the effect on our sales."

"I thought it was the effect on all those loyal customers you were tryin to protect," Eddie said.

"If I might be allowed to continue?" Bardswith said frostily. "If we can demonstrate fraud, then our case is made."

"I don't know..." Howell said uncertainly.

"Is that what your first twenty-odd witnesses are really all about?" Hoogenband asked Bardswith. "Are you planning to troop them up to the stand like this was some kind of revival meeting and they're all going to start speaking in tongues about how terrific your—"

Eddie leaned over to Hoogenband and whispered something in his ear. The attorney frowned, then whispered something in Eddie's ear.

"You two wanna be alone?" the judge asked.

"A moment, sir," the attorney said. More whispering, then the attorney cleared his throat. "I want no mistake here. As corporate counsel I have advised my client against the course of action he wishes me to convey to you and opposing counsel. I want it perfectly clear that—"

"Oh, hush up and just tell us what the hell's going on!"

"Yes. Very well. But as I said, this is not coming from me. In fact, I wish to execute a codicil and enter it into the record to the effect that the stipulation I'm about to convey is by no means—"

"I'm gonna execute *you* if you don't—"

"Your honor." Eddie touched his lawyer's arm and gestured for him to back off. "What this brave and loyal stalwart of the legal profession is trying to say is that we'll stipulate that the Medalist golf ball is superior."

"And...?" Bardswith prompted.

"And, nothing. We'll—that's the word, isn't it? Stipulate? We'll stipulate that their ball is superior."

Howell and Bardswith stared at Eddie. Hoogenband stared at the ceiling. Howell and Bardswith looked at each other, then at Trevillian, then back at Eddie.

"I don't get it," Bardswith finally said.

"Me neither," said the judge.

"Which part?" Eddie asked.

"Any of it," Bardswith answered.

"Yeah," the judge agreed.

Eddie thought about it, then nodded. "I guess I used that word wrong. Sorry. Me not being a lawyer, I should stay away from the lingo, am I right?"

Howell and Bardswith nodded.

"Okay. So let me put this in my own words: We'll agree that the Medalist ball is superior."

Howell and Bardswith looked at each other, then back at Eddie.

"I don't get it," Bardswith finally said.

"Me neither," said the judge.

"Which part?" Eddie asked.

"Any of it," Bardswith answered.

"Yeah," the judge agreed.

"Well, gee whiz, fellas...I don't know how to put it any plainer."

"Let me make sure I understand this." Bardswith stood up, crossed his arms and leaned forward imperiously. "Are you saying that you're willing to stipulate that the Medalist golf ball is superior to the Scratch?"

Eddie remained motionless for a second, then turned to his attorney. "I tell you, it's downright amazing how fast this guy catches on. Why, just like that, he went right to the very heart of—"

"Very funny, Caminetti," Bardswith said crossly. "What the hell are you trying to pull?"

"Pull? Your honor, these guys want to take two or three days of the court's time to trot out a load of witnesses who'll sing hosannas to their product. All I'm saying, there's no need to do that. We'll agree to it."

"So what you're saying," Howell said, "is that you're willing to go back into court and agree that the Medalist golf ball is superior to yours?"

Eddie knew whom he could throw jabs at and who was off limits. "That's exactly right."

"What are you trying to pull?"

"Your honor—"

"Hold on here, just hold on," Trevillian said. "I don't want them stipulating to anything."

"Tommy..." Bardswith began.

"Give me just a minute here, Tyrell. Now look: Him just going into court and saying, Yeah, yeah, okay, Medalist balls are better, and rolling his eyes and then we move on? Not good enough. We've got a right to present our side in a way that makes an impression on the jury, and him stipulating isn't going to do it."

"Man's got a point," the judge agreed.

"The hell he does!" Hoogenband ejaculated. "This is a court of law, not a Movie of the Week! We're after truth, we're after facts, not bashing jurors over the head and impressing them."

Judge Howell chuckled softly. "Criminy, counselor. Where the hell *you* been the last hunnerd years?"

"Your honor, if they want to establish the superiority of their product and my client—their very adversary!—is willing to admit that in open court, what is the need for the extended charade they're proposing?"

"Jeez, Leif. Three minutes ago you were all about per-tectin your pecker and now you're gettin all huffy about what your client wants to do?"

"I'm still his advocate," Hoogenband sniffed.

"Actually," Eddie corrected, "you're my co-counsel. But look here, all I want to do is move this along. Tommy, you don't want to trot out all those witnesses."

"Says who?"

"Says me. It's a mistake. Trust me."

"Trust you!" Trevillian snorted. "If I trusted you, why would we be in court at all?"

"Good question, but it's too late for that. Just listen to me when I tell you, take the stipulation and don't call all those witnesses."

"You must be out of your mind if you think—"

"Hold it a second," Bardswith said. "Mr. Caminetti, do I take it that you won't object to our calling these witnesses if we so choose?"

"Mr. Bardswith, what I'm trying to tell you, you really don't need to—"

"I'm not in the habit of taking case strategy advice from the opposition, sir, so if you'll kindly answer the question: Will you object to our calling witnesses who will testify to the superiority of the Medalist golf ball or not?"

Eddie could feel Trevillian holding his breath. He waited a few seconds, then said, "No, I won't object."

He waited a few more seconds, feeling the exultation building in the opposition camp, then said, "Just one thing."

"Bet I already know what it is, Mr. Cami...sorry. *Counselor*." Howell tilted his head back and sighted down his nose. "You're gonna want a delay so's you can prepare. Depositions and all that bushwah."

"Well, obviously," Hoogenband retorted. "You don't spring two dozen witnesses right out of your hat and expect us to—"

"Stuff and nonsense," Bardswith said. "They've been on our witness list all along."

"But we didn't know why they—"

"Hey!" Eddie said, and waited for quiet. "We don't need to depose anybody, your honor." He began waving Hoogenband down without bothering to wait for him to start bouncing off the walls.

"What, then?" Bardswith asked suspiciously.

"Just give us the right to recall them," Eddie said. "That's the correct phrase, right? So we don't have to cross-examine them right away?"

"So what you're saying," Bardswith said, "you're going to let us do our direct examination of all these witnesses, uninterrupted, and then you're going to bring them back later for cross? All at once?"

"Yeah."

Bardswith rocked his head back and forth a few times. "Well, then, I'd say that pretty much settles things as far as—"

"Hold it," Trevillian said. "*When* will you recall them, Caminetti?"

"When?"

"Yeah. These people will be coming from all different places, some from far away. How long are you going to make them stick around before you get around to cross-examining them?"

Bardswith, suddenly caught short at his failure to latch on to a possible trick from the renowned hustler, jumped in right away. "Exactly! See here, Caminetti, don't expect to—"

"Right away."

"Right away whut?" Howell asked.

Eddie turned to Bardswith. "The day after you finish with your last witness—I mean, your last witness on this topic—we'll do our cross."

"You will?"

"Yep." Eddie looked at the judge. "And we'll finish all of them the same day."

The others were all staring at him again.

"What are you trying to pull, Caminetti?" Bardswith demanded.

"Okay, that's it!" Judge Howell slapped his thighs and rose to his feet.

"Swear to God, Bordenstein, ain't never seen a man so gol-durned unhappy to git zackly what he asked for!"

"But he's got something up—"

"Git the hell outta my chambers, Birdbath! Alla you...git!"

"Unbelievable how this game gets the passions up," Hoogenband said as they walked into the lobby of the court building. "Even if you're not playing it but just fighting about it."

"I'd rather play it," Eddie said.

"Me, too. Couple of guys in my office would rather lose a case than a tee time."

"What do you think it is?" Eddie asked.

"I know what it is. It's the incredible mix of different skills you have to use. Driving, putting, chipping, sand shots...don't you agree?"

"Nope."

"Nope? What other sport calls on you to do so many different things?"

"Good question," Eddie said as he pushed open the outer door. "Next time I run into Bruce Jenner I'll ask him."

CHAPTER TWENTY-ONE

"**Good morning, Mr. Johnson.** And thanks very much for agreeing to come here today."

Tyrell Bardswith dripped sincerity, bonhomie and confidence as he addressed the first of his long list of witnesses who would testify to the virtues of the Medalist KY 9000 Double-Wound Super-Precision Long-Flight Soft-Feel Control-Spin golf ball, affectionately known as the K-9.

"Certainly. Glad to be here."

"I don't doubt it. Now Mr. Johnson, you've been playing golf for how long now?"

"Forty years, roughly. Started when I was nineteen. Father took me to the local driving range."

"Excellent. Mine did the same when I was fifteen."

Leif Hoogenband started to rise in protest at this unctuous oozing of irrelevant camaraderie, but Eddie pulled him back down.

"But it's bullshit!" Hoogenband whispered.

"It's harmless bullshit," Eddie replied. "Let it go."

"And you've had the opportunity to try many different golf balls in your career, is that correct?"

"Now he's leading the witness!" Hoogenband hissed.

"Let him lead," Eddie whispered back.

"You bet," Johnson was saying. "Pretty much tried most of them, I'd guess."

"And, more specifically, you've played both the Medalist KY 9000 Double-Wound and the Scratch, correct?"

"Yes, sir, I have."

"And what is your opinion?"

This time Hoogenband didn't consult with Eddie, but jumped up on his own. "This witness hasn't been qualified as an expert, your honor! In fact, he hasn't been qualified as anything! What is counsel's foundation for relying on his opinion?"

"He's a golfer, counselor. Just an ordinary, weekend golfer. Which is all we said he'd be when we—"

Eddie stood up. "We take it back."

Howell glared at him. "You mean it's *withdrawn?*"

"Idn't that what I said?"

"Yes, it's withdrawn," Hoogenband said, pulling Eddie down to get him out of the judge's line of fire.

"Proceed," Judge Howell directed.

Eddie plastered a big smile on his face, jiggled his shoulders as though laughing at some private joke and turned toward his attorney. "One more objection," he said under his breath, "and I'll kick your ass clear across the room. Now laugh!"

Hoogenband put his head back and laughed. Eddie clapped his shoulder, then turned back toward the front of the room.

"Mr. Johnson?" Bardswith prompted.

"Yes, well...I started using the K-9 about a year ago, and I was amazed at what a terrific ball it was. It was very precise, it flew a much longer distance than any other ball I'd ever used, it had a nice, soft feel and excellent spin characteristics."

"I see. So what you're saying, it made you a better golfer?"

"Let me be very accurate here, Mr. Bardswith. I was the same golfer as I was before. The ball didn't make me better. It let me *play* better. That's an important distinction, see?"

"A-*ha!* I do see!" The attorney's astonishment at this revelation was a palpable thing, and he made sure to let it wash over the jurors as well as observers in the gallery. "So it improved your game, is that it?"

"Exactly! I had more precision, I hit the ball farther, I had better feel and the controlled spin was a great help."

"I understand. And you said you also tried the Scratch ball. How did it compare?"

"Well..." Mr. Johnson rubbed the back of his neck and smiled sheepishly, as though reluctant to speak ill of anything or anybody. "I'm kind of, uh, sorry to say this, but, well...it just didn't measure up."

"Didn't measure up in what way?"

"Well, sir, it simply wasn't as precise, it didn't fly as long, it didn't have that nice, soft feel, and the spin characteristics, well...not even close. Didn't putt so good, either. Hate to say it, but I'm under oath, so there it is."

"And we appreciate your candor. We truly do. No further questions, your honor."

"Witness is ex—"

"Your honor?"

"Mr. Caminetti? Thought you were going to—"

"Judge, if counsel has no objection, might I ask a quick question without giving up my right to recall this witness?"

"Well..."

"For information purposes only. I promise I'm not out to mess him up."

"We have no objection, your honor," Bardswith announced expansively.

"Very well. Go ahead."

"Thank you. Mr. Johnson, you said the Medalist ball was more precise, flew farther, had better feel and better spin and putted better than the Scratch, is that correct?"

"That's about the size of it."

"Okay. I just wanted to make sure. By the way, what's your handicap?"

"I'm a thirty-four."

"And so, Mr. Chadwick, as a corporate CEO such as yourself might put it: Bottom line, how would you say the Scratch ball measures up to the Medalist KY 9000?"

"Doesn't."

"Meaning?"

"Meaning, it doesn't. No comparison. The K-9 is more precise, goes farther, has a softer feel and spins better. All there is to it."

Bardswith preened visibly. "Thank you, sir. That will be all."

Corporate titan and captain of industry John Chadwick stood up, all steely-gray-haired, square-jawed six foot three of him. "And before you ask, Mr. Caminetti...I'm a four."

"Sorry?" Eddie looked up from the papers he'd been studying. "Were you talking to me?"

"Sure was. I said, I'm a four."

Judge Howell banged his gavel. "You've been excused, Mr. Chadwick."

"A four what?" Eddie asked, confusion tripping around his face.

"What do you...a four handicap!"

"You mean in golf?"

"Of course I mean in golf! What do you suppose I mean?"

"I have no idea. I thought, you know, like maybe a four on a scale of ten when it comes to running a corporation."

"Now see here...!"

"Gentlemen!" the judge said sternly, banging his gavel once again.

Chadwick stormed off the witness stand, eyeing Eddie menacingly as he passed the defendant's table. "Four handicap, that's what I am," he whispered hoarsely.

"Good for you. Give me two a side and I'll play you for—"

"That will be quite enough, *counselor*. Call your next witness, Mr. Chapstick."

Bardswith called Denise Duckworth, a short-order cook from Fontana. Then he called Jose Lopez, an aerospace engineer. Then he called Vaughn Oscarson, a club pro from Washington state, and eighteen other witnesses, all of who testified as to the greatness of the Medalist KY 9000 and its clear superiority over the Scratch. At the end of each of Bardswith's direct examinations, Eddie asked what the witness's handicap was, then iterated his intention to recall him.

"You have one more witness on your list," Judge Howell said. "Please call him."

"With pleasure." Bardswith turned to the gallery and announced, "Plaintiff calls Gerry Agnormo."

Every head in the courtroom whipped around to catch a glimpse of the legendary New Zealand golf pro known as "the Kiwi" as he strode forward, his lanky limbs willowy and his hips rolling athletically. Magnetic, charismatic and supremely self-confident, he put his hand on the Bible and said "I do" proudly before dropping onto the witness chair in an untroubled half-slouch. Bardswith got right to it.

"You're a professional golfer, is that correct?"

Agnormo dropped his head and smiled slightly. "I am," he said, with discomfited modesty.

"Your honor?" Eddie interrupted.

"What is it?"

"I'd like the record to reflect that I have some personal acquaintance with this witness."

"The nature of which is?"

"I played a match against him once a few years ago."

"Huh. So you're friends?"

"Hardly. I beat him."

"The hell you did!" Agnormo snapped angrily.

"The hell I didn't."

"You screamed in my bloody ear!"

"Easy, fellas. Any objections? No? Please proceed, Mr. Backstop."

"Thank you. Mr. Agnormo, you're actually one of the best golfers in the world, so I'm led to believe."

"Well, stone the crows, that's for others to say."

"Oh, come now, Mr. Agnormo! You won the—"

Eddie got to his feet. "Defense will stipulate that the witness is one of the best pro golfers in the world."

"You will?" Bardswith said.

"Sure. Just told you, I played against him. Guy's terrific." Eddie turned to the court. "The best."

"Thought you said you beat him," Howell said.

"I did—"

"The hell you did!" Agnormo barked.

"—but he's a better golfer."

"Yes, he is. Thank you." Bardswith threw the jury a deeply meaningful glance and went on. "What is your opinion of the Medalist KY 9000 golf ball?"

"Best in the world, no doubta that," Agnormo said, with obvious pride.

"And why is that?"

"It's precise, has great distance, a soft feel and excellent spin control. Wonderful for putting, too."

"I see. And tell me, have you played at all with the Scratch ball?"

"God's truth? No, I haven't. Hit a few on the range, though."

"And?"

"Didn't much care fer em."

"Oh, really?"

Agnormo dropped his head again, then smiled, painfully, seemingly to mitigate the harshness of what he had to say. "Bloody awful, frankly."

"I see. Now, the Medalist Corporation is a sponsor of yours, isn't that correct?"

"They are."

"And so one might reasonably assume that your testimony is somewhat, ah, shall we say, somewhat *skewed* by that relationship?"

"One might, but they'd be too bloody wrong."

"And that's because…?"

"I could have been sponsored by any golf ball manufacturer in the world, but I chose Medalist because I thought they made the best ball."

"Thank you for your candor, Mr. Agnormo. No more questions."

"Witness may step"—Howell saw Eddie's hand in the air—"Mr. Caminetti?"

"Just one fast one, your honor."

"Very well…and from now on just stand up, you got somethin to say."

"Okay."

"Now hold on!" Bardswith shouted indignantly. "I thought counselor reserved the right to call all these people back. So is he going to cross-examine this witness now or what?"

"Din't seem to bother you none with the last twenty witnesses," Howell admonished.

"I was trying to give a little leeway, your honor. In the interest of expediency. But now I think it's gone far enough!"

"With one guy left?"

Eddie stood up. "It's all right, your honor. Counselor has a point. I'll wait until it's my turn to cross."

"You sure?"

"Absolutely."

"Very well. Witness is excused. Thank you, counselor."

"No problem," Eddie said.

But Agnormo didn't step down. He sat there, then jerked a thumb to get Bardswith's attention.

"Hah?" Bardswith looked at his witness quizzically. Then his shoulders dropped. "Ah, Christ..." he muttered.

"Mr. Bandwidth?" Judge Howell prompted.

The attorney, looking as though he'd just realized he'd sat on a pizza, sighed. "Your honor, the witness has some pressing commitments related to his profession. It will be extremely difficult for him to remain in town, and the plaintiff would request that, um..." Pain creased his forehead. Some ob-servers remarked later that they thought they'd heard him say "shit" under his breath, but they couldn't be sure. "If counsel would be so kind as to put to Mr. Agnormo any questions he has at this time, rather than, ah..."

Eddie and Hoogenband remained motionless as Judge Howell seemed to draw himself higher on his seat. "Mr. Bardsdale, am I givena unnerstand that, coming on the heels of your vo-*cif*-erous objection, you're now tellin this court you *want* opposin counsel to ask his questions at this time?"

There was no graceful way out of it. "Yes, sir. Of course, we realize the defendant has reserved the right to, ah...and your honor has granted that right, but, um, seems to have slipped my...if we might beg an indulgence here...?"

Bardswith looked at the defense table with naked pleading.

"You don't hafta, Mr. Caminetti," Howell said.

Eddie let Bardswith stew for a few seconds, then said, "Ah sure, what the heck," and stood up. He wasted no time. "Mr. Agnormo, when did you switch to the KY 9000?"

"Just about a year ago."

"Exactly when?"

"I can tell you that. It was just before the U.S. Open."

"Which you won."

"I did indeed."

"Think the ball had something to do with it?"

"Sure as hell—whoops, sorry. Too bleedin right, I do. It's a great ball, and it's the reason I won that tournament."

"So it's not because you're one of the best golfers in the world, then."

"Sorry?"

"What I mean, you were the same golfer before you won the Open. Like when you placed thirty-eighth in the British."

"Hey, wait a second..."

Bardswith jumped to his feet. "Objection! Stating facts not in evidence!"

Eddie held up his hands. "Sorry, your honor. I'll rephrase."

"Very well."

"Where'd you finish at the British Open?"

Agnormo glared at Bardswith with undisguised hostility. "Thirty-eighth."

"All righty then. Glad we cleared that up. So you're the same golfer you were before, and you go from thirty-eighth to first and it was all because of the ball, right?"

"Right. No! Not just—"

"But you said, um...could we get the reporter to read back the answer?"

Howell gestured to the court reporter, who reached into the wire bin that collected the paper strip containing a coded transcript that only she could read. She leafed through the fan-folded paper until locating the relevant portion, then read it out loud with no inflection. "Question: Think the ball had something to do with it? Answer: Sure as hell—whoops, sorry. Too bleedin right, I do. It's a great ball, and it's the reason I won that tournament." She smiled prettily and dropped the folded strips back into the basket.

"Thank you," Eddie said. "So was it the ball or wasn't it?"

"It...I...my game got better!"

"It did?"

"Of course! I work hard, Mr. Caminetti. I'm on the bloody range six or eight bloody hours a day! I'm good because I work at it!"

"Understood. So it wasn't the ball after all."

"No! I mean, yes, of course it— Look, it's a great ball!"

"And it won you the Open. Because you're not really that good a golfer, right?"

"You're twisting my words!"

"Well, then, I apologize. Go ahead, use your own words. I won't interrupt."

"What?"

"Not another word from me. Go ahead, and take your time." Eddie sat down.

"What?"

Agnormo looked helplessly at Bardswith, who jumped immediately to his feet. "Objection! Counselor is badgering the witness."

The judge looked at Eddie, who was sitting quietly. "Don't look t'me like he's badgerin nobody. Witness may answer."

Agnormo tried to wipe the sweat off his lip without looking obvious. "Could you—could he repeat the question?" he asked limply.

Eddie stood back up. "I'm not trying to trick you, Mr. Agnormo, so let me say something and then you tell me if I'm right or not. Fair enough?"

"Yeah. Yes."

"Okay. Between the British and U.S. Opens, you switched balls and you practiced like crazy, right?"

Agnormo nodded.

"Speak up, son," Judge Howell said. "Court reporter can't—"

"Oh. Sorry. Yeah. Yes. Both those things."

"Fine. So then you don't really know which one was the main reason you won the U.S. Open, isn't that correct?"

Agnormo looked miserably at Tommy Trevillian, the man who was paying him $8 million a year to say it was the ball.

"In fact," Eddie went on, "you don't know if it was just a lucky day, do you? Maybe you were just in the zone, or maybe it was Joel Fleckheimer splashing his tee shot on seventeen. You have no way to know, do you?"

"Well…"

"Because if it was really the ball, then you should have won the PGA and the Masters instead of placing fortieth and fifty-fifth, right?" Eddie paused, then cocked his head slyly. "You did use the KY 9000 in those tournaments, didn't you?"

"Of course he did!" Trevillian shouted from the gallery.

Judge Howell angrily gaveled him to silence.

"Did you?" Eddie asked.

"Of course I did," Agnormo answered indignantly.

"Well then," Eddie said as he resumed his seat, "maybe I oughta send you over a couple dozen Scratches, eh? I mean, seeing as how that KY 9000 sure as hell isn't doing the job."

"Objection!" Bardswith screeched. "Objection, your honor! Counselor is making a speech, not asking a question!"

"Withdrawn," Eddie said, then looked at Howell, who flashed him a laudatory tip of his head for being such a quick study. "Gerry—sorry—Mr. Agnormo. You started the Python Golf Club Company, didn't you?"

Wary now, Agnormo took his time before answering. "Yes, I did."

"And why was that?"

"I'll tell you why. I wanted to create the best bloody golf club in the world, that's why!"

"I see. And did you?"

"You bet I did!"

"Congratulations! So how many Python clubs do you carry in your bag?"

"What?"

"Sorry, I'll speak more clearly. How many Python clubs do you carry in your bag? You know, when you're playing in a professional tournament?"

Panic seized the witness's throat. His face started to turn red and his eyeballs seemed on the verge of popping out of his head.

"Objection!" Bardswith shouted. "What could possibly be the relevance of this question?"

"Well," Eddie said, "it's got to do with what it takes to get the witness's endorsement of a product. You know…whether that endorsement can be bought."

"Listen, you slimy sonofa—"

Howell slammed his gavel down. "The witness will get control of himself!" When he'd gotten the quiet he demanded, Howell said, "Counselor, you got some kinda basis for an implied accusation like that?"

"Possibly. I've heard that—and I realize this is going to come as quite a shock—I've heard that there are athletes selling their praise to the highest bidder, and I just wanted to make sure the witness isn't one of them."

"You're damned right I'm—"

Howell gaveled Agnormo to silence.

"We got basketball players shilling for cars they don't drive," Eddie continued, "baseball players swearing to high heaven that a hair cream changed their lives, football players telling millions of fans they're going to some amusement park right after the Super Bowl when what they're really gonna do is get drunk for three days...and I just wanted to know if Mr. Agnormo here is hawking clubs he doesn't even use."

"This is outrageous, your honor!" Bardswith bellowed. "Counselor is deliberately provoking my witness!"

Howell rubbed the side of his face. "Don't know how you boys do things up north, or out west or wherever the hell y'all are, but down here, provokin a witness ain't hardly no grounds for an objection. Hell, it's half the damned *point,* in't it?" The judge was grinning broadly but lost it quickly as Bardswith retook the soapbox.

"It's accusatory, your honor! My witness isn't on trial here, and this blatant attempt to unfairly impeach—"

"Oh, take it easy, f'cryin out loud! Mr. Caminetti, I can rule here, but how intent're you on—"

Eddie waved his hand dismissively. "Forget it, judge. I'll move on."

"Thank you very much. Kindly proceed."

Agnormo, near trembling now, locked his eyes onto Eddie, who rose, put both hands on the defense table and leaned forward, deep in thought. Trevillian had his hands on the pew in front of him, trying to squeeze it into powder. Even the clerk and bailiff were holding their breaths.

"No more questions for this witness," Eddie said.

As Agnormo, stooped and beaten, descended from the chair, Eddie said,

"Judge, unless the counselor has another witness, whaddaya say we call it a day and I'll get started on my cross in the morning."

"Sounds good t'me. We'll—"

"Your honor," Bardswith said, "why not start cross right now? The witnesses are here and waiting."

Howell looked at Eddie, who said, "Nope."

"What do you mean, nope?"

"He means nope," Howell said, banging his gavel. "That was the deal you made, Birdbath. Have your witnesses here tomorrow."

As everyone rose and shuffled around preparing to leave, Bardswith called out, "All of them, your honor? Do they all need to be here? How long is cross-examination going to take?"

"How should I know?" Howell was halfway to the exit behind the bench but decided maybe he was being too harsh with Bardswith and stopped. "Mr. Caminetti, any estimate?"

"I'll have em all outta here by lunchtime, your honor."

"Lunchtime?" Bardswith asked, incredulous. "All of them?"

"Yep. At least, if you don't start jumping up and down with a lot of dumb objections."

"Now see here, Mr. Caminetti! I'm a—"

"Or, I could keep em here all week."

Bardswith glared for a few seconds, then wisely elected to keep his mouth shut and began packing up his papers as Judge Howell continued toward the exit.

But he just couldn't help himself. "Why didn't you just do them all today, if you can get them done so fast?"

"Gotta make some phone calls first," Eddie responded amiably.

"How long could that take? How many phone calls?"

"How many witnesses did you just call?"

"Twenty-two."

"Then I gotta make twenty-one calls."

"I said twenty-two witnesses."

"Yeah." Eddie picked up his briefcase, turned to swing open the low bar separating the lawyers from the gallery and stepped through. "But I'm already done with Agnormo, remember? Besides, I think we should just meet for a drink later and settle this whole thing."

"Excuse me?"

"Yeah. You know, come to think of it, that's a good— Your honor!"

Howell turned just before disappearing through the door to the rear corridor leading to his chambers. Eddie started making his way forward.

"Sumpin on yer mind, Caminetti?"

"Yessir. I think—"

Howell held up his hand. "Know yer a li'l new at this, but you and me cain't be havin no conversation lessen t'other guy's here, too."

"What the hell are you doing, Caminetti!" Bardswith demanded as he walked up.

"Judge," Eddie said, "you wouldn't mind us settling this thing before the start of court tomorrow, wouldja?"

"Are you kiddin? Hell no! Clear me a good piece-a calendar, by crikey. You think it's possible?"

"Why not? Seems to me—"

"You're out of your mind!" Bardswith spat, then spun on his heel and strode away.

"Don't worry, judge," Eddie said. "He'll come around."

"Don't look like it t'me."

"Wanna bet?"

"How much?"

"Hundred bucks?"

"Yer on. But lemme ask you sumpin." Howell leaned forward over the top of the bench and looked down at Eddie. "You really scream in Agnormo's ear?"

"Yeah, but only once," Eddie replied. "And he said I could."

CHAPTER TWENTY-TWO

THE CHAMBERS OF JUDGE FENWICK C. HOWELL
THE NEXT MORNING

" **I take it you two boys din't solve nothin.**" Tyrell Bardswith shifted uncomfortably in his chair and flashed a smile. "Well, I wouldn't say that, your honor."

"I would," Eddie said. "Why are we in chambers, judge?"

"Always like to kinda push the settlement process along, I do. See if a little persuasion can't be brought to bear on the sitchation."

"Well, forget it. Might as well go back in and get started."

"Bein a little recalcitrant, are we, Mr. Caminetti?"

Eddie stood up. "Mr. Bardswith refused to meet with me, judge. What do you want me to do?"

"Did he now. Huh."

Bardswith stood up, too. "Counsel is right, your honor. It's a waste of time."

"And whyzzat, zackly?"

"Why?" Bardswith straightened his tie and reached for his briefcase. "Because we're going to win this trial, that's why. And when we do, my client will get everything he deserves instead of half."

"Sound pretty sure of yerself there, feller."

"All due respect, sir, that's a matter for my client to determine."

"But you haven't even heard the other side's offer!"

"Doesn't matter. Unless they agree to everything we would have gotten when the jury decision goes our way, there's nothing to discuss."

"And what is it you want?"

"We want the Scratch Golf Ball Company to remit to us every dime they ever made on the sale of their balls, and then we want them to dissolve the corporation, and we want the principles to promise they'll never go into the business again for the rest of their lives."

"Sounds pretty reasonable to me. Whaddaya say, Mr. Caminetti?"

"Very funny. Shall we?"

Bardswith, smiling smugly, exited first. Judge Howell tugged at Eddie's sleeve, holding him back. "Wanna take back our bet, son?"

"Wanna double it?"

"Yer nuts."

"So take the bet."

"Yer on."

"Defense calls Mr. William Johnson."

Johnson strode confidently to the witness chair, turned and raised his right hand.

"No need for that there," Howell informed him. "Yer still unner oath from yesterday. Y'unnerstand?"

"I do, your honor."

"Good. Set on down, then. Counselor?"

Eddie stood up. On the table in front of him were stacks of paper covering nearly the entire surface. He took a single sheet and walked partway to the witness stand.

"Mr. Johnson, you testified yesterday that you started using the KY 9000 a year ago, is that correct?"

"Yessir."

"What was your handicap thirteen months ago?"

"Thirteen—heck, I don't know. Can't remember month by month that far back."

"Guess you're right. That is asking a lot. Sorry."

"That's okay."

"Appreciate it. But you're a thirty-four now, right?"

"That's right."

"And you were a thirty-four last month, right?"

"Uh...yeah. Yes, that's right."

"And the month before that?"

Bardswith rose lazily. "Your honor, are we to take the witness month by month all the way back to his childhood?"

"Mr. Caminetti?"

Eddie looked at Bardswith. "No."

"Please proceed."

"Wait a minute," Bardswith said. "No, what?"

Eddie stayed silent.

"Well?"

"Mr. Bardsworth," Howell said, "the court would preciate it if you din't engage in personal conversations with opposin counsel."

"Oh, very well. Will your honor kindly inquire of counsel what he meant by no?"

"Whadja mean by no, Mr. Caminetti?"

"I meant, no, I'm not going to take the witness month by month all the way back to his childhood."

"Thanks for clarifyin. Please proceed."

"Your honor...!"

"Siddown, Barnstormer. Witness may answer."

"I forgot the question."

Eddie nodded solicitously. "If I might be permitted a little leeway, I can get through this quickly."

Howell nodded his approval.

"Mr. Johnson," Eddie said, "you're a thirty-four now, you were a thirty-four last month, you were a thirty-four the month before that—"

"No!"

"No?"

"No. I was a thirty-*three* the month before that."

"Ah. My apologies." Eddie looked at his paper. "A thirty-three point seven, mattera fact. But let's not quibble: You've been about a thirty-four for, what is it now...eight years?"

Johnson squirmed and shrugged his shoulders. "I guess."

Eddie tapped the sheet of paper he was holding. "Your handicap is kind of a tradition at the Glen Oaks Maplewood Golf and Country Club, isn't it?"

"I guess."

"So—and I'm just going out on a limb here, Mr. Johnson, so you be sure and correct me if I'm wrong—it's a pretty safe bet that you were about a thirty-four before you started playing the KY 9000 ball, and you were still about a thirty-four afterwards. That about right? Give or take."

Johnson gulped audibly. "Give or take."

"Fine. Thanks very much. So what exactly did you mean when you said your game got better after you started using that ball?"

"Like I said, I had more precision, I hit farther, I could—"

"Oh, yeah. Sorry, I remember now. My apologies."

Tommy Trevillian grabbed his lawyer's arm and squeezed. Hard. "What the hell is he doing!" he hissed through clenched teeth.

Bardswith, too upset even to feel his blood circulation being cut off, was also too upset to answer his client. It wasn't clear he'd even heard his question.

"Goddamnit!" Trevillian insisted, his hoarse whisper growing louder. "You gotta stop this!"

Still Bardswith didn't respond.

"He's gonna kick the shit outta every one of our witnesses! Do something! Object! For cryin out loud, Bardswith, you gotta—"

"I can't," Bardswith finally managed to croak.

"Why the fuck not? We're gonna get murdered out there!"

"Because," Bardswith said, while trying to twist his arm away from Trevillian's grasp, "we agreed to let him do his cross all at once, that's why!"

"But we didn't know he was gonna pull this crap!"

"No shit," Bardswith said, as he finally managed to rescue his arm and pull it away.

"Can't you stop it?"

Bardswith shook his head. "The jury has already heard our side. There's no way on earth the defense gets stopped from cross-examining them."

"How come?" Trevillian was practically whining now.

"Because," Bardswith said, turning slowly to his client, "it's in the goddamned Constitution, that's how come."

Howell banged his gavel. "Some kina problem, gennamen?"

"N—" Bardswith rose, on shaky legs. "No, your honor. No problem."

Howell nodded at Eddie to continue.

"Witness is excused," Eddie said. "Defense calls John Chadwick."

When corporate titan and captain of industry John Chadwick was seated in the witness chair and the judge had reminded him he was still under oath, Eddie asked, "What's your handicap?"

"I told you yesterday."

"You'd already been excused and weren't on the record. So if you don't mind..."

"I'm a four."

Eddie looked at his piece of paper. "You mean a four point three, right?"

"Didn't know you wanted it so precise," Chadwick sniffed.

"No problem. Just wanted it clear for the record. When did you start using the KY 9000 ball?"

"Six months ago."

"Okaaayyy..." Eddie consulted his paper again. "What was your handicap seven months ago?"

Chadwick stretched his neck against his collar. "A four. About a four, I mean."

Eddie stayed silent and stared at him.

"Actually, uh, about...I think it may have been four point two."

"Could it have been, maybe, four point one?"

"Objection," Bardswith called out. "Asked and answered."

"Withdrawn," Eddie said easily. "We'll let the witness's answer under oath stay on the record."

"Wait a minute, wait a minute...let me think." Chadwick put his hand to his forehead and creased his brow. "It's quite possible it was four point one."

"You sure?"

"Quite possible. Yes."

"Okey-doke. Witness is excused."

And so it went for nineteen more witnesses. By lunchtime it was over.

Bardswith stepped over to the defense table. "Nice job, Caminetti."

"Thank you."

"And good move, too." Bardswith was enough of a sport to pay a compliment when he'd been outmaneuvered.

"Don't know what you mean, but thanks. I guess. Ready to talk now?"

"Not really. You may think this looks bad for us, but it didn't really go to the heart of our case. Embarrassing, perhaps, but not fatal."

"How you gonna worm your way out of it, Bardswith? To the public, I mean, the fact that your client's ball didn't improve the game of a single one of your witnesses."

Bardswith waved it away. "There are too many factors that enter into it. These were purely anecdotal stories from satisfied customers."

"Twenty-one out of twenty-one?" Neither Eddie nor Barnsworth thought the testimony of the twenty-second witness, Gerry Agnormo, worth commenting upon.

Bardswith laughed. "Statistics, counselor! One out of forty-nine million doesn't seem to bother the average joe buying a lottery ticket. You think he's going to understand the meaning of this testimony?"

"You got a point there."

"First-timers always get a little overconfident when they think they pulled off some damaging cross-examination. Think they won it right there on the spot."

"Guess I did get a little excited."

"Don't worry about it." Bardswith stifled a laugh and said, "You'll do better on your next case."

Eddie smiled amiably. "You're sure you don't want to talk settlement."

"I'm sure."

"Suit yourself."

CHAPTER TWENTY-THREE

In the afternoon, Bardswith called Tommy Trevillian to the stand and took him through his direct, which occupied the rest of the day.

The CEO gave a detailed account of the long and distinguished history of MedalCorp. As planned, he showed not a trace of personal animosity toward the Scratch Company or Eddie Caminetti, and only got emotional when discussing his unwavering appreciation and loyalty to the customers who had made his company what it was.

"We stood by as the Scratch golf ball, a product of inferior quality, made inroads into the marketplace by deceiving those loyal customers," he said. "We watched, helpless, as hardworking Americans dipped into their savings and paid exorbitant amounts of money for that inferior ball. There wasn't much we could do except step up our advertising in an attempt to let people know how they were being shamelessly manipulated by unscrupulous marketing practices."

Bardswith nodded in sympathy, at times looking like he was about to cry.

At around four o'clock the attorney intoned somberly, "And then, did something occur to make you take more drastic action?"

"Yes," Trevillian answered softly, his voice trembling. "At just the moment my company was sacrificing a fortune to protect customers who'd been duped by criminal counterfeiters..." He paused, barely able to keep a grip on himself, and looked down at the floor. "At just that moment when we and our loyal customers were most vulnerable, the Scratch Company crossed the line." He looked up, fire and defiance in his eyes. "They took advantage of a tragic situation, and we no longer had a choice."

By informal count of the court reporter when she processed her transcript that evening, Trevillian had referred to the Scratch as "inferior" fifty-two times, but never once referred to any evidence to back that accusation up.

"It's a clear trap," Hoogenband said to Eddie at dinner that evening. "He wants you to take him on, to challenge his assertion that the Scratch is an inferior ball."

"Whadda you figure he's got in mind?"

"I don't know." Hoogenband made sure he had Eddie's full attention, then said, "You have to let it go, Eddie. You understand? Don't go any-where near it."

"Got it."

THE NEXT DAY

"Mornin, evuhbody," Justice Howell said. "Y'all can begin yer cross-examination now, Mr. Caminetti."

Bardswith stood up. "If it please the court..."

"What?" Howell said in annoyance.

"Might I inquire of counsel how long he intends to keep the witness? Mr. Trevillian is a very busy man."

Howell looked down at him over the tops of his reading glasses. "Y'all gotta be kidding."

"Your honor?"

"Mr. Caminetti didn't call this witness; you did. Alls he's doing, he's cross-examining him. Your client was so damned busy, maybe you should-na called him in the first place."

"Your honor, with all due respect—"

"Evuh time I hear you say that, I know somethin disrespeckful's comin."

"Not at all, sir. Please don't misunderstand. I'm not trying to limit counsel's right to cross. I'm just trying to get some notion of the time so my client can plan his schedule accordingly. Just as a courtesy."

"Yeah, well, counsel's under no obligation to—"

"Not a problem, judge," Eddie said as he stood up. "I'm happy to give him an estimate."

"You don't hafta," Howell said.

"I know that. But, like he said, he's just asking for a courtesy, and I'm a courteous guy."

"Very well."

As Trevillian, betraying his anxiety, leaned forward in his chair, Eddie turned to Bardswith. "If Mr. Trevillian answers me truthfully and in a straightforward manner, I'll be done in fifteen or twenty minutes."

Trevillian, relieved, dropped back and exhaled audibly. Bardswith's mouth opened in surprise, then he recovered and tried to look nonplussed as he said, "I see. So, realistically, no more than a half hour, then?"

"Realistically," Eddie replied, "I figure we're gonna be here all day."

Howell tried to gavel down the laughter rolling around the courtroom, but wasn't terribly effective owing to his own ineptly suppressed guffaw. Too late—much too late—Bardswith forced himself to laugh as well, and Trevillian managed a weak smile, but nobody bought it for a minute.

As Eddie sat down, Trevillian, still forcing himself to smile, said to his lawyer, "Why don't you object to that slanderous characterization!"

"That's what they're hoping I'll do," Bardswith replied, "so we look like bigger horse's asses than we do now." He leaned toward Hoogenband and said, "Why don't you get a grip on your co-counsel, counselor?"

"The man's a rank amateur," Hoogenband responded. "What can I tell you? No manners, no courtroom etiquette. By the way..." He leaned toward Bardswith. "Next time you got a 'courtesy' question, ask him in the hall, not open court."

"And why is that?"

"Because rank amateurs have a funny way of seeing right to the heart of professional bullshit, that's why." Hoogenband straightened up. "And next time you got any professional advice for me, file a fucking affidavit."

"Now see here...!"

"Y'all set, Mr. Caminetti?"

"Yes, sir." Eddie stood once again, and waited patiently as Trevillian retook the stand.

Eddie wasted little time getting to it. If anybody was going to be responsible for this taking all day, it wasn't going to be him.

"Good morning," he said cheerily.

"Good morning," Trevillian responded icily.

"With millions of counterfeit Medalist balls flooding the market, did you ever once, *ever*, get a letter from anybody complaining that one of those balls didn't perform the way a Medalist usually does?"

Trevillian's team of attorneys, with whom he'd been locked away for weeks, had prepared him for every eventuality. They'd so thoroughly rehearsed Trevillian that Bardswith had to bring in a media consultant to help him appear more spontaneous instead of sounding like he was reading scripted lines. They'd warned him of every cross-examination tactic, including getting lulled into false confidence by an opening series of innocuous, even flattering questions delivered in a friendly manner.

What they hadn't prepared him for was getting hit so hard so early. But all that rehearsal time was about to pay off, because even though Trevillian had been somewhat thrown by the suddenness of the pointed question, the question itself wasn't a surprise, and he was able to shift into his prepared speech smoothly.

"Of course we got complaints."

"Really. Such as?"

"The logo running if certain liquids got spilled on it, the poor quality of the printing on the box—"

"Perhaps I wasn't clear about—"

Trevillian turned to Howell. "I'm sorry...your honor, might I be allowed to finish my answer?"

Howell nodded. "He's entitled to complete his answer, counselor."

"Not if he's answering a different question than I asked."

"I *was* answering your question."

"No, you weren't."

"Hey, fellas...remember me?" Howell waited to make sure he had their attention, then said, "Court'd preciate it greatly if y'all would talk to me rather than each other in the event we got a dispute, all righty? Now: Why's it you figger this witness in't answerin your question?"

Hoogenband stood up. "Could we have the reporter read it back?"

"Good idea." Howell waved at her to do so.

The court reporter fished around in the catch basket of her steno machine, pulled on a section of folding strip, adjusted her glasses and read out loud,

"Mr. Caminetti said: With millions of counterfeit Medalist balls flooding the market, did you ever once, ever, get a letter from anybody complaining that one of those balls didn't perform the way a Medalist usually does?" She waited for acknowledgment from the judge, then dropped the paper back into the bin.

"Okay," Howell said. "You were askin about complaints regardin the performance of the ball, zat it?"

"That's it exactly."

"And he was answerin about how it looked."

"Correct."

"Got it. Witness'll answer the question that was asked."

Trevillian clenched his jaws, a pulsation visible in his cheek, as though he'd been found out and was angry about it and trying to recover. In truth, he knew exactly what Eddie had meant. "No. We never got any complaints about performance."

"That didn't strike you as a little strange?"

"Not at all." And then the zinger he'd set up perfectly. "In fact, it was *not* getting any complaints that worried us the most, and which mobilized us into action."

"Please explain."

Trevillian got comfortable, shifting around in the chair and folding one leg over the other so that he was looking straight at the jury and seemed to turn a dismissive shoulder to Eddie.

"Golfers always assume it's their own fault when they hit a bad shot," he said easily. "As it happens, only ten percent of all golfers regularly break a hundred. Now, if someone is a twenty handicap and he hits a bad shot, he assumes it's his fault, not the ball's, because he hits bad shots all the time. Let's be realistic." He unfolded his legs, put his elbows on his thighs and held his hands with the palms together as he spoke. "The difference between an ordinary golf ball and a superior one is not two-fifty straight down the fairway versus a duck hook into the azaleas." The jurors smiled and several of them chuckled. Trevillian smiled back at them. "The difference, like the difference between two brands of beer or cigarettes, is not that profound and it surfaces over many shots, not just one. Few golfers, with the possible exception of some professionals, are so consistent that they can take one shot with a new ball and notice the difference immediately. And since the vast majority of golfers are high handicappers, they hit more bad shots than good. So when one of these fake balls goes hooking into the azaleas"—he looked for more smiles and chuckles, but he'd already worn the line out so he hurried on—"when a fake ball doesn't go as planned, the golfer naturally assumes it was his fault, not the ball's. And *that*—"

He sat up straight and slapped his knees loudly. "*That* is why these fakes are so insidious! They obscure the golfer's true abilities and lead him to need-lessly doubt himself. And, to be perfectly crass about it, for the better golfer, rather than complain to us, they'll simply assume we don't make a good golf ball." He shook his head and looked down. "And that is simply not fair."

The impact on the jury was self-evident. Several of them nodded slightly.

Eddie thought about it for a long time. "So what you're saying, one indi-vidual high-handicapper might not have noticed a difference, because it's a little on the, whadja call it there, a little on the *subtle* side, that right?"

Trevillian looked up. "Exactly."

"Tough for one lone guy to spot."

"Correct."

"But over a lot of guys, the effect pops up, that it?"

"Absolutely."

"Okay, so: If there's a boatload of phony Medalist balls out there, there should have been a whopping impact on the national average handicap, wouldn't you say?"

Trevillian looked up. "What?"

Eddie lifted a shoulder and let it drop. "What I'm saying, if millions of people are using phony Medalist balls of inferior quality, then we should have seen a big uptick in their scores, if you add em all up. Millions of people using a crummy ball... national handicap shoulda shot up like the mercury in a New York August, wouldn't you say?"

"Well..."

"Well, what?"

Trevillian thought of something, and seized on it. "We're not the only balls on the market, you know." He looked at the jury again and smiled. "Hate to say it, but there are others." Appreciative smiles were returned to him.

"Good point. So what percentage of golf balls out there are yours?"

"What?"

"You want it read back?"

"No. Sorry, no. Just got distracted for a second. Our share of the market, well. That depends on many factors, such as whether you include—"

"Hold on a second." Eddie jerked a thumb toward Bardswith without turning to look at him. "This is one-a those deals, how long we're here depends on you. One way or the other, we're gonna come to the right number, so you figure out how much time you want to spend gettin there."

Trevillian waited for his lawyer to make an objection, and when he didn't, looked at him to find out why. Bardswith lifted his chin, and Trevillian caught the signal.

"We have fifty-one percent."

"Fifty-one percent. What you're sayin is, fifty-one percent of the balls on the market are one-a the brands owned by your company."

"That's the general definition of market share, Mr. Caminetti," Trevillian sneered.

"I didn't ask you about market share."

"But—"

"What I asked you was, what percentage of golf balls out there are yours?"

Trevillian looked genuinely puzzled. "Not sure I follow."

"That's okay, I'll explain. You said fifty-one percent of the balls on the market are one-a the brands owned by your company."

"And that figure is correct."

"Not saying it isn't. But what about the balls you make that aren't sold under one-a your brands?"

Trevillian stared at Eddie, not moving a muscle.

"I mean, you guys make golf balls that other people sell under their own names, isn't that right? Like that deal you made to sell millions of balls to a Chinese outfit? Or am I all wet here?"

"Those balls are intended specifically for sale overseas."

"But you sell others to American companies for sale right here, right?"

"Yes. We do."

"Okay, there you go. And those are the same balls, same quality and everything except for the logo, same as the ones you sell under your own brand names, isn't that right?"

"Right."

"Okay. I apologize for any confusion, so let's rewind and start all over. What percentage of the balls on the market are made by one of the Medal-Corp companies?"

"No, I apologize. I misunderstood your question."

"No problem at all. What's the answer?"

"Can we stick to just the U.S. market?"

"Good point. Let's do that."

"Sixty-two percent."

"Wow! Oh...sorry, judge. Didn't mean to...sixty-two percent! Okay, then, back to my original question, which is what got us started off on alla this: If you guys have sixty-two percent of the market, shouldn't there have been a huge rise in the national average handicap on accounta all those fake Medalist balls?"

There was no way out, except for Trevillian to look unworried, which was impossible, so he tried to answer without appearing to hedge. "Makes sense. Offhand, I mean, without having had a chance to think about it. It makes sense."

"Yeah. Do you happena know how the national average handicap has changed?"

"No, I don't."

"Really?"

"Objection!" shouted Bardswith. "Asked and answered."

"Huh?"

"Means you already asked it and he already answered it," Howell said to Eddie. "No need to make him go repeatin hisself."

"Oh. I get it." Eddie began walking back to the defense table.

"Ahm so pleased. And you're welcome for the lesson."

"Thank you. Guess I was just tryin to make sure Mr. Trevillian didn't know, but, well, I guess he doesn't."

"There you go."

"So Mr. Trevillian," Eddie continued. "What other evidence you got that your company's balls are better?"

"Plenty. Over forty of the top pros on tour endorse our ball!"

"And why is that?"

"Because it's better, that's why."

"The two or three million each you pay those guys to endorse your ball doesn't enter into it?"

Trevillian had been itching to get that question. "I'll tell you something, Mr. Caminetti, and you can take this to the bank." He jabbed a finger into the air. "There isn't a single professional golfer on tour who would endorse a golf ball for a *hundred* million dollars if he thought there was any chance it would hurt his game!"

"I believe you," Eddie said with sincerity.

"Okay, then."

"But if they thought one ball was as good as the next, then they'd say yours was the best if you paid them more than the other guy did. That about right?"

"Maybe. But one ball isn't as good as the next. Which is kind of why we're here, isn't it?"

"Beats me. You're the one who put us here, not me."

"Ob—!"

"Overruled," Howell said to Bardswith. "Your guy asked the question. Counsel merely answered it. Please proceed, Mr. Caminetti."

"Okay. As I understand it, Derek Anouilh endorses the KY 9000, Mack Merriwell pitches the Pericles, Joel Fleckheimer goes for the SpinJockey, Robert Carmichael swears by the TotalFeel...those are all Medalist balls, aren't they?"

"I'm proud to say they are."

"So which one's the best?"

"What?"

"Well, you said a pro wouldn't use anything but the best. So which one is it? Cause it seems to me that three of the guys I just mentioned are shilling for balls they know are junk compared to the one they'd really like to be using. Come on, tell us the secret: Which ball's the real deal?"

"You misunderstand."

"Straighten me out."

"It's not just a question of which one is better. It has to be of a construction that's appropriate for your particular style of play."

"Ahhh...I see. So is there any chance some pro out there might find the Scratch ball appropriate for his style of play?"

"I doubt it. The ball first has to be of top-quality construction, and only then do you worry about specific characteristics."

"What about Albert Auberlain?"

"What about him?"

"Uses a Scratch. Does pretty well."

Trevillian *harrumphed* noisily. "And what are you paying him to use it?"

"Nothing."

"Yeah, right."

"We don't sponsor anybody."

"Sure. Auberlain buys his balls in a pro shop, right?"

"I don't know for sure where he gets em. But for damned sure he doesn't get em from us. No golfer does."

Trevillian's squirming was evidence enough that the point had been made, but Eddie couldn't resist one last jab as he returned to the defense table. "Didn't give any to Robert Carmichael, either. Wonder where *he* got em."

"Great," Hoogenband whispered as pandemonium broke out in the court, Bardswith objecting his heart out, Trevillian fuming and demanding an apology, reporters scribbling like mad and the jurors, who weren't supposed to be considering anything that wasn't presented as part of the trial, laughing nevertheless because they knew all about Carmichael's use of the Scratch.

Eddie shuffled through some papers. "Great, what?"

"You got sidetracked and forgot that you started off talking about the counterfeit balls, that's what."

"You think the jury remembers?"

"Doesn't matter, because Bardswith will remind them in his closing, and if you don't do something about it, the record will stand as is."

"Come to think of it, I don't remember myself."

"Then I'll remind you. For all you know," Hoogenband said, "the counterfeit balls really did make people play worse, and you can't prove otherwise because you don't know, and now the jury thinks Medalist balls are better."

"Oh, yeah."

"Told you a hundred times, Eddie: Never ask a witness a question you don't already know the answer to."

"How about one the *witness* doesn't know the answer to?"

"What?"

Eddie stopped fiddling with the papers. By that time the commotion had quieted down, and he looked at Trevillian. "You have absolutely no idea at all whether people's games have suffered because of the counterfeit balls, is that right?"

"Sorry?"

"I'm back to those lousy, inferior knockoffs flooding the market. You don't know whether they're making any difference at all."

"Well...it's a surmise. Because they're not genuine Medalists."

"A surmise."

"Correct."

"You mean you're guessing."

"Asked and answered," Bardswith called out.

"Your honor," Eddie said crossly, "I don't know what the hell a surmise is. If the man's just taking a guess, let him say so in plain English."

"Sounds good to me. Mr. Trevillian, you guessin or do you know?"

"I'm assuming."

"Assuming," Eddie repeated. "Okay, let me put this another way. You have any evidence at all that people are playing better with the real Medalists than with the fakes?"

"Absolutely. We have anecdotal evidence from customers. Plenty of customers."

"Anecdotal. What's that mean?"

"That means they told us."

"You mean, without any scientific basis? Without being under oath, that kind of thing?"

"That's absolutely correct. In our judgment, the spontaneous and heart-felt opinions of our customers who have direct experience with the ball is a thousand times more valuable than all the scientific tests in the world put together."

"Fair enough. So how'd they tell you?"

"What?"

"Your customers. How'd they tell you the real balls are better? I'm askin because they sure as hell didn't write any letters. You said so yourself."

"I said they didn't write any letters of complaint. I believe the transcript will bear me out."

"You know, you're right. I forgot. So the letters you did get..."

"Customers telling us how much they liked our brands of balls."

"I see. And nobody wrote to tell you how much they liked the counterfeits."

Trevillian was starting to look a little pale. "Something like that."

"Except that, with millions of phony balls out there, you really don't know if any of those letters were actually telling you how good the *fakes* were, right?"

Now Trevillian was definitely pale. He swallowed, but didn't answer.

"Hey, you know, come to think of it?" Eddie snapped his fingers and looked like he'd just had a revelation. "I betcha mosta those customers, they been playin Medalists for years, then they accidentally bought a box of fakes and they were so much better, why, they sat themselves down and wrote you a letter about it!"

"That's nonsense!" Trevillian shot back.

"No, it isn't! That's exactly what happened! They got a box of fakes and thought you'd improved the ball!"

"How could you possibly know that, Mr. Caminetti!"

"Well," Eddie responded, "it's a surmise."

Bardswith tried futilely to shout over Judge Howell's ineffectual attempts to quiet down the courtroom, but Howell did what the red-faced attorney was going to ask him to do anyway.

"Recess!" Howell called out as he banged his gavel repeatedly. "This court'll be in recess for one hour!"

"Let's get to the matter of Medalist balls versus the Scratch."

"Thank God," Trevillian muttered.

Eddie looked up from some papers on the defense table. "'Scuse me?"

"I'm just saying, it's about time."

Eddie lifted a piece of paper and took a step away from the table. "What, you don't like how I'm conducting myself here?"

"I don't like anything about you, Mr. Caminetti."

Eddie stopped, the piece of paper in his hand fluttering slightly from the breeze of a ceiling fan. "What?"

"You heard me."

Eddie didn't move, but just stood there, his mouth slightly agape. If Trevillian was expecting some snappy comeback he was disappointed, because Eddie looked genuinely distressed by the comment.

"Mr. Caminetti?" Howell prompted him.

Eddie turned his head toward the sound of the judge's voice. He looked at the paper in his hand to remind himself of where he was and what he was supposed to be doing. Everybody in the room could tell he'd been thrown by Trevillian's glib cruelty, and there was much shuffling of feet and muffled coughing in an attempt to mitigate the discomfort that seemed to have seized the very air.

Eddie looked up and scratched his forehead, looked down at his paper, said, "Um..." and exchanged the paper for another one. He seemed disoriented and unable to look the witness in the eye.

The jurors, on the other hand, glared daggers at Trevillian.

Eddie took a deep breath and stepped back behind the defense table. "Mr. Trevillian, did you do anything to determine that the Scratch ball is inferior to the Medalist?"

"We sure did."

"Really? Oh, sorry. Asked and answered, yeah. I take it back."

"The preferred phraseology—" Howell began.

"Withdrawn, got it. All righty, then, Mr. Trevillian. When we asked your company for certain documents, we didn't get any reports of engineering tests."

"That's because there weren't any."

"Huh. So whud you do?"

Trevillian, who'd been dying to get this question since he'd first taken the stand, warmed to it immediately. "What we did was go right to the heart of the matter. We asked golfers."

"How'd you do that?"

"We went to a golf course in Washington and gave about three hundred golfers both balls to play. When they were done, we asked em which one they preferred. It's as simple and straightforward and easy to understand as you can get. And they liked ours one whole hell of a lot better than they liked yours, *counselor*." His last word was laced with all the derision he could muster, which was considerable.

Eddie swallowed and creased his brow. "Did they know you guys were from Medalist?"

"Yep."

"Did you give them anything for doing the test?"

"We paid for their round and gave them some free balls."

Eddie looked around the room, the beginnings of a smile playing on his lips. "Don't you think that might've biased them just a little?"

Trevillian smiled as well, but without any warmth. It was the smile of a rattlesnake that had just lured a mouse into a bush. "No, I don't. None of them had any idea which ball was which. We made sure of that."

"Oh."

Trevillian, grinning openly now, folded his arms and winked at his attorney.

"Couldn't tell em apart?"

"Not in a million years."

"Huh. So you changed the balls?"

"Just cosmetically."

"Huh."

"I can assure you that the characteristics of the balls were utterly unchanged."

Trevillian kept smirking as Eddie squirmed. Anxious glances were exchanged around the audience section of the courtroom. Eddie scratched at the back of his head and frowned, then he looked up, bewilderment radiating from his face. "How'd you do that?"

"Do what?"

"How'd you make it so people couldn't tell the two balls apart?"

"We disguised em, that's how."

"What I'm asking, how did you disguise them?"

Bardswith said, "Irrelevant, your honor. Do we really want to get into a technical discussion here?"

"Mr. Caminetti?" Howell said.

"Yes, we do."

"Overruled. Witness may answer the question."

Some of Trevillian's smirk faded, but just slightly. "We made both balls look the same."

"Yeah. Look, I hear from your lawyer that you're a busy man with a busy schedule. Me, I got nothin to do for the rest of my life. So I'm perfectly happy to stand here for the next fifty years until you decide to get around to answering the question."

"Badgering the witness," Bardswith protested.

"I'm gonna badger him my own damned self, he don't answer the question," Howell shot back. "Mr. Trevillian, don't you be playing games with this court or I'll hold you in contempt, you hear me?"

All traces of swagger in the witness vanished. "Yes, your honor. Certainly. But I'm not sure of exactly what—"

"Givin you the benefit of the doubt," Eddie said, "let me be specific. For example, the Scratch ball has a different color to it than the Medalist, kind of a, whatchacallit, shiny sort of surface." He waited for some reaction from Trevillian but got none. "Are you following me so far?"

"Yes. I'm just waiting for a question."

"What'd you do about the shiny surface? Because that'd be a dead giveaway, wouldn't it?"

"We took away the shine," Trevillian answered.

"How?"

"I don't know. Why don't you ask my engineers?"

"It took engineers to do this?"

"We wanted it done right. But look, we did the same thing to both balls, so what difference would it make!"

"I have no idea."

"Damned right."

"And neither do you. Now as to the details of exactly how it was done—"

"I told you: Ask my engineers."

Eddie thought it over for a minute. "Okay," he said, then turned toward the judge. "Can we get a Medalist engineer in here?"

"So ordered. Mr. Trevillian, have one-a your—"

"Hold it a second!" Bardswith rose to his feet. "There's no engineer on any witness list. If counsel wanted an engineer he should've thought of that sooner."

Eddie remained facing the judge. "I didn't know their chief witness wouldn't be able to answer some simple questions. Heck, your honor..." Eddie pointed to the witness box. "*He's* the one told me to ask one-a his engineers." Then he jerked a thumb over his shoulder, toward Bardswith. "So what's he grousing about?"

"Beats me." Howell once again addressed Trevillian. "I want your head guy in here tomorrow morning."

Bardswith started to protest again but Trevillian waved him down. "Not a problem, judge. I'm more than happy to have my chief engineer testify. But at least give me a day."

"Fine. Day after tomorrow then. Anything else, Caminetti?"

"Yes. Mr. Trevillian, did you ever hear that a Scratch should be teed up with the logo facing forward?"

"Yeah, I heard it, and that's baloney, too."

"How do you know that?"

"Because I do. It's a gimmick. And I'm not biased here." Trevillian turned toward the jury. "I also heard the Scratch goes as soft as a limp— goes as soft as a marshmallow once in a while." Then back to Eddie. "But you don't see me running around claiming it's true. And that business about facing your logo forward when you tee up is baloney, too."

"Maybe it is, but none of the people in your test group were able to do it anyway because they couldn't see the logo, could they?"

"No. But they could see where it'd been covered over. And if they'd wanted to they could have faced that part forward, and before you ask, it didn't make any difference that they didn't know which ball was which, because all they had to do was do the same thing with both of them, since we covered both logos!" The face radiated a full-wattage beam of triumph now.

"So they knew one of the balls was a Scratch."

Somebody hit the dimmer switch on the beam of triumph. "What?"

"Your test subjects. They knew it was Medalist against Scratch, which is how they coulda faced the logo forward if they'd wanted to."

And then killed the power altogether. "No. I...I just forgot for a second."

"Ah, don't worry about it. I do it all the time. All I was getting at was that this test you did, it was between two balls that had been doctored until you couldn't tell em apart, that's all."

Trevillian didn't get where he was by backing down from a fight. 'No mariner ever distinguished himself on calm seas,' he liked to tell his people, without bothering to tell them where he'd picked up the pithy platitude. "None of that made any difference, Mr. Caminetti. I—"

Eddie hadn't been paying much attention to the autonomic denial but his ears pricked up when Trevillian suddenly stopped speaking. "Sorry. What were you saying?"

"Nothing."

"You sure."

"Yes."

Eddie's sensors were on full alert now. He quickly replayed the last half hour of Trevillian's testimony in his head and stopped the tapes when something got stuck. "Earlier in your testimony you said, let's see, you said you could assure me that the characteristics of the balls were utterly unchanged. I get that right?"

"Something along those lines."

"Because we can have it read back."

"No. That was it."

"So what makes you so certain?"

Trevillian looked down and fiddled with his fingernails. "Engineers told me."

"Did they. And how'd they know?"

Trevillian shrugged. "Not real sure."

The witness might as well have had I'm hiding something tattooed in fluorescent letters across his chin.

Eddie stopped concentrating and let his instincts take over. "You by any chance have any scientific tests done you're maybe not telling us about?"

Trevillian shrugged again. "Well...when you say *scientific*..."

"I mean guys in white coats sitting in a room somewhere instead of a bunch of randomly chosen hackers out on a public golf course."

"When you say *tests*..."

"Don't try this court's patience, Mr. Trevillian," Howell warned. "Answer the man's question!"

Trevillian, trying to look defiant and unafraid, looked up at Eddie. "There were no tests we could report on. Some of the guys had started to run a few studies, but they were inconclusive and I knew right away that if we finished them and tried to present those results in a court of law, they'd be so difficult to understand, and to explain, that we'd look like we were trying to put something over on somebody."

He was in a groove now, and seized the moment. "So I said, let's cut through all the bu—let's cut through the baloney and just take this one straight to the people. And, by God, that's what we did!"

It was powerful, effective and dramatic.

"What do you mean, 'inconclusive'?" Eddie asked.

"I mean...you couldn't draw any conclusions from them."

"You mean, there were no differences between the two balls?"

"I didn't say that."

"Well, were there? Differences, I mean."

"The tests were never finished."

"But you had preliminary results."

"None to speak of."

"Then how did you know they were inconclusive?"

"Because that's what my people told me. And I believed them."

Bardswith stood up. "Your honor, think we might have a recess at this point?"

"I'm almost done," Eddie said. "If we keep going, I can wrap this up pretty quick."

"Proceed."

"Mr. Trevillian, the KY 9000: That's the one you call 'The Ball That Brought Derek Back,' isn't it?"

"You're damned—yes, it is."

"And it's the one Derek Anouilh uses on tour?"

"Yep."

"Same ball any customer buys when he goes into a store?"

Trevillian relaxed, relieved to be back on safe ground. "Sure is."

"Exactly the same?"

"Absolutely. Except for a couple of purely cosmetic differences, of course."

"Oh, you mean, like, I don't know...same kind of thing you did to those balls when you ran your real-world test with real live golfers?"

"Objection!" Bardswith shouted. "Badgering and argumentative!"

"Overruled."

"Yes, that kind of thing," Trevillian conceded. "I already told you: It makes no difference."

Eddie turned and walked toward the jury box. "The ball that Derek Anouilh uses, those cosmetic differences?"

"I told you. They make no difference whatsoever in performance."

"And you're sure of that."

"Hundred percent positive."

"Got it. So why make them?"

"Huh?"

"Why the differences, if they make no difference?"

Trevillian looked away, and then said, "You know what? That's a really good question."

"So you don't know?"

"Actually, no. He asked for them, and we did them for him."

"So you don't know why the number one golfer on the planet Earth insisted on those changes but you're prepared to swear they make no difference."

Trevillian had no choice at this point. "I am."

"Because your engineers told you."

"That's right."

And Eddie had no place to go with it. Sort of. "One last question, then."

Trevillian nodded, relief washing over him in visible waves.

"How come Derek Anouilh never throws a ball to the crowd?"

The waves crashed up onto the shore and broke apart. "What are you talking about?"

"You know, like if he makes a great shot, or toward the end of a tournament if he's ahead, which is almost always? Pros are always throwing balls to the fans. Gives em a heck of a thrill. How come Derek never does that?"

"How should I know?"

"I don't know. I'm just asking. Do you know or not?"

"No!"

"Then just say so."

"I just did! I don't know!"

"Well there you go! No more questions for this witness. Oh, wait, sorry. I do have one more."

"Very well," Howell said.

"Any of your engineers ever cut open a Scratch to see what makes it tick?"

Trevillian didn't answer at first. A smile started to appear on his face, and even though he suppressed it quickly, he still looked like a lion licking his lips before biting into a nice, juicy gazelle. "No."

"That's interesting. How come?"

"Because," Trevillian said, dragging it out, "I wouldn't let them."

"You wouldn't let them? Why the heck not?"

"In my personal opinion, it might've posed a health risk."

Eddie snickered. "A *health* risk?" he said with a smile. "What are you talking about?"

"I'd heard rumors..."

"What kind of rumors?"

"That there might have been some nuclear radiation used in making the balls."

The smile left Eddie's face, and he stood there, silent and motionless.

Back at the defense table, Hoogenband cleared his throat. Then he did it again, loudly. When Eddie still didn't respond, Hoogenband stood and said, "A word with my co-counsel, your honor?"

"Make it quick."

At the sound of Judge Howell's voice, Eddie shook himself out of his trance and went back to the defense table. Hoogenband dragged him down into his chair and leaned in toward him covering his mouth with his hand.

"Eddie, listen! You listening?"

Eddie nodded.

"Before when you asked him about the logo facing forward, he said it was bullshit, and just a rumor. Remember?"

Eddie nodded again.

"So ask him why he didn't believe *that* rumor but he believes *this* one, which sounds like ten times more bullshit! Ask him does he only believe rumors that help his case! You get it?"

Eddie nodded again.

"Okay...go get him!" Hoogenband slapped Eddie on the shoulder and sat back, a shit-eating grin on his face that he could see was worrying Trevillian.

Eddie stood up and said, "No further questions for this witness."

CHAPTER TWENTY-FOUR

Reporter Muffy Berkowitz of KXQR-South Dakota stopped the first customer she saw leaving the Drive-In Golf Shop in Plankinton with a box of Scratch golf balls clutched in his hands, and stuck a microphone in his face. The customer barely got his cigarette out of the way in time.

"Hi! What's your name?" she asked.

"Grady," he said, smiling widely as the camera crew moved in and got a good shot of all three of his teeth. "Grady Dean Kreuzer."

"I see you got yourself a box of Scratch balls there, Grady."

"Grady Dean. Folks call me Grady Dean."

"Okay, Grady Dean. So about those Scratch balls...aren't you worried about them?"

"Worried? Bout whut?"

"Well, there was some testimony in the Medalist trial that seemed to indicate that there might be some radiation in those balls."

"Huh? Oh, yeah. I heard that." He was still grinning directly at the camera.

"But you're not worried?"

As Grady Dean drew in an enormous lungful of his Marlboro, the camera zoomed out, revealing a potbelly hanging over the belt he was presumably wearing. Then he exhaled a cloud of smoke so thick his face was completely hidden behind it. "Do I look worried?" he said as smoke continued to boil out of his mouth.

"I guess not. But doesn't it bother you that—"

"Lady," Grady Dean said as his face began to reappear on camera, "it takes balls to play golf, you know what I'm sayin?"

Later in the day it was reported that whatever Scratch balls had still been in stock as of the day before were now completely gone, and the company had hired armed guards to accompany their delivery trucks on their rounds because of phoned-in tips to police departments around the country warning of imminent hijackings.

Horace Nickton, having been in far hotter seats than this many times, exuded confidence and even faint arrogance as Bardswith took him through his credentials. Nickton, a graduate of MIT, had been a professional market researcher and political pollster for over twenty years, and had conducted some of the best-known studies in both of those fields of endeavor.

"I'm also led to believe," Bardswith said coyly, "that you were the brains behind the Sawmill Challenge, hmm? The landmark study that pitted two of the world's most popular soft drinks against each other in a head-to-head, nationwide taste test?"

Nickton shyly picked at some nonexistent lint on his trousers. "I was responsible for those tests, yes," he said modestly.

"Thank you. So let's move to the present, shall we?"

Led expertly along by Bardswith, Nickton went on to describe the study he and his team had conducted some weeks before. "It was as fair as it was possible to design a test," he averred definitively when he finished giving an overview.

"Indeed," Bardswith said. "And how was it conducted?"

Nickton cleared his throat. "It was actually quite simple. The two balls, the Medalist KY 9000 and the Scratch, were absolutely indistinguishable visually. Except for the coded markings, of course."

"The coded markings..." Bardswith prompted him.

"Yes. They were each labeled A or B. But none of the golfers to whom we gave the balls had any notion of which was which."

"I see." Bardswith cupped his chin in his hand, and for a moment was lost in thought. "But your people knew which was which."

"No, sir, they did not!"

Bardswith let his hand drop and raised his eyebrows in surprise. "They *didn't?*"

"No," Nickton said, with a half smile. "That's why we call it a double-blind study, Mr. Bardswith. Neither the subjects nor the testers had any idea which was which."

"And the reason for this was...?"

"To make absolutely certain that no cues of any kind, conscious or inadvertent, were given to the subjects that might hint at which ball was which."

"And this makes the test more fair?"

Nickton shook his head. "No, sir."

Bardswith's expression turned to one of dismay. The jurors leaned forward in their seats. The entire court seemed to hold its breath.

"It makes it absolutely foolproof," Nickton finished.

"Ahhh..." Bardswith sighed, as did dozens of others, and then he looked at the jury box. "Foolproof!"

"That's correct."

"Meaning no one could tamper with it. It couldn't be falsified."

"Exactly."

Bardswith nodded. Vigorously. Several times.

Hoogenband stood up. "Is counsel finished with this witness?" he asked. "May we begin our cross-examination?"

Bardswith turned and glared at him. "I am not finished."

"Okay. Sorry." Hoogenband sat down. "My apologies."

The spell broken, Bardswith turned back to Nickton. "And at the conclusion of each round you asked the golfers for their opinion."

Hoogenband started to get up again but Eddie grabbed his arm and held him down.

"He's leading the witness!" Hoogenband whispered.

"Who gives a shit?" Eddie said. "Gonna come out anyway and this just saves some time."

"But that's not—"

Eddie waved him off. "Pick your battles carefully, counselor. This one's not worth fighting."

"Yes," Nickton replied. "And it was as simple as can be. We asked each golfer which ball he liked better. That was it. Nothing fancy."

"And they had no idea which was which."

"None whatsoever."

"And you didn't question them about spin characteristics or distance or anything of that nature?"

Nickton shook his head emphatically. "Absolutely not."

"And why was that?"

"Two reasons. First, we didn't want to get them anxious or apprehensive. Had they known that we'd be asking them to report on such specifics, they would have been fearful, lest they not report knowledgeably or had failed to notice such things. It would have felt to them more like a final exam than a simple preference test. This way, we said, Which did you like better, A or B? And they said one or the other and we thanked them for their participation."

"I see! Most clever!"

Hoogenband started to rise again, and again Eddie held him down.

"But you said there were two reasons," Bardswith went on. "For keeping it so simple, I mean."

"The other reason was to avoid obscuring our results."

"Obscuring, how?"

"Well, quite frankly..." Nickton looked uncomfortable for the first time. It was well practiced, designed to make the jury think he was in a ticklish spot so things looked that much better when it turned out he really wasn't. "We knew this test was being conducted for purposes of this trial. The client—Mr. Trevillian—the client insisted that the results be crystal clear and unambiguous, and not laden with so much scientific baggage that it would confuse a jury."

"A-ha. Yes, I understand. That's good thinking."

"Objection, your honor!" This time Hoogenband jumped up before Eddie could stop him. "Is counsel prepared to be cross-examined on the opinions he's expressing as to his own witness's testimony?"

"Sustained," Howell ruled without hesitation. "Mr. Barndoor, ask questions and keep the opinionatin to yourself, y'hear?"

"Yes, sir. Mr. Nickton, let's cut to the chase here." Bardswith turned to the jury and looked at them as he asked his next question. "What were the findings of your team?"

Nickton adjusted himself and folded his hands in his lap. "Seventy-two percent of the respondents indicated a preference for the Medalist KY 9000 over the Scratch ball."

Bardswith whirled toward the witness stand so fast his eyeglasses almost flew off. "Seventy-two percent!" he said in astonishment.

"That's correct."

"Almost three times as many people liked the Medalist better?"

"Mr. Bardswith." Nickton held up an admonitory hand before Hoogenband could object. "I'd prefer not to characterize my testimony, especially using words like 'almost.' I can't answer any better than with the actual number. It was seventy-two to twenty-eight in favor of the Medalist."

"I appreciate your desire to keep it scientific," Bardswith said apologetically, "but I'm afraid I must ask you for an opinion, based on your expertise in conducting studies of this kind. Okay?"

"I'll do my best to comply."

"Thank you. In your opinion, based on your experience in conducting polls and surveys, would you consider that margin of preference to be significant?"

Nickton thought it over for a second, then seemed to decide that the question was legitimate. "In my opinion," he said carefully, "that margin is nothing short of staggering."

"Really!"

"Yes. In our planning, we determined that anything wider than fifty-four to forty-six was statistically significant, anything approaching sixty-forty was definitive, and anything greater than that was, well...to be honest, it's almost unprecedented."

Bardswith stayed quiet, and let Nickton's final statement sink in to the jurors and observers. There was nothing he could possibly do to get a stronger statement, and anything further would only risk blunting the powerful point that had already been made.

So he waited, and listened, and when he thought he'd detected the faintest rustling of the fabric on Hoogenband's suit as the defense attorney got ready to stand up, he slapped his hand on the bar that stretched in front of the jury box, said, "Thank you, Mr. Nickton," and proclaimed to the judge, "No further questions for this witness, your honor!"

"Counsel may cross-examine," Howell said to Eddie.

"So you ran the Sawmill taste test, did you?"

Nickton, too experienced at this sort of thing to let himself get suckered into complacency by a skillful interrogator feigning friendliness, made sure to stay on his guard. "Yes, I did."

"Well, whaddaya know about that." Eddie was still behind the defense table. "Which side were you working for, Sawmill Cola or Mom's?"

"Well, Sawmill's, obviously. They're the ones who commissioned the study, which is why it was called the Sawmill Challenge."

Eddie slapped the side of his head lightly. "Sorry. Stupid question. Uh, withdrawn?"

Howell looked up at the ceiling. "You can't withdraw it if he's already answered it, Mr. Caminetti."

"Oh. Yeah. Sorry." He cleared his throat. "Well, anyway... so who won?"

"Pardon?"

"Who won the Sawmill Challenge?"

Nickton straightened up slightly. Proudly, perhaps. "Sawmill Cola won."

"Did they."

"Yes, sir."

"Your client."

"Yes." Some may have noticed a slight hesitation in Nickton's reply. Others hadn't.

"And Medalist won the Medalist challenge."

"We didn't call it that."

"Call it what you want...Medalist won, right?"

"Most clearly."

"Also your client."

"Yes."

"Thank you." Eddie wandered slowly from behind the table, and paused a few feet to the side of it. "Where did you get the Scratch golf balls?"

"Mr. Trevillian supplied them."

Eddie looked at Trevillian, with mild surprise. "Really? Where'd he get them?"

"I have no idea."

"You don't? Then how do you know they were really Scratch balls?"

"To tell you the truth," Nickton said easily, "I can't tell you whether they were or weren't. And that wasn't my job."

"It wasn't? I'm a little confused."

"Then I'll explain. I was given two shipping crates of golf balls. One was identified as containing Medalists, the other Scratches. My job was simply to find out which crate held the balls golfers liked better. That was it."

"Okay, now I get it. So *you* knew which was which."

"Yes." Now the hesitation was unambiguous. "But I had absolutely no part in the conduct of the actual test. I simply had the balls code-marked and gave my team their instructions. That was it."

"But you were at the golf course."

"I was there for part of the day. I had no interaction with golfers, or with anyone else on my team who was involved with the study."

Eddie thought it over for a second, then nodded agreeably. "Okay. I get it. When you did the Sawmill Challenge, was it done the same way?"

"Meaning?"

"Some cups of cola were marked A, some B, people tasted them, they told you which they liked better. That about sum it up?"

"Yes, I'd say it does."

"And Sawmill won, right?"

"They did."

"Same strict double-blind whatever, that sort of thing?"

"Absolutely."

"Good. What was the winning margin?"

Nickton blinked several times. "What?"

"How much did Sawmill beat Mom's Cola by? What was the percentage?"

Bardswith, who had stayed quiet until now because he knew better than to try to kill an attorney who was already in the process of committing suicide, saw his witness's hesitancy and stood up. "Objection, your honor. What could possibly be the relevance of this line of questioning?"

"A little leeway and I'll get right to it," Eddie said.

"See that you do," Howell said. "Overruled."

"Mr. Nickton?"

The witness swallowed, trying not to let it show. "Seventy-two percent versus twenty-eight percent."

Eddie froze. Then he seemed to realize something and shook himself out of it. "Oh, gee, I'm sorry, Mr. Nickton. I didn't make myself clear. I was referring to the Sawmill Challenge, not the Medalist test. What was the final outcome of the Sawmill Cola test?"

Nickton took a breath and held it. "That *was* the Sawmill Challenge."

Eddie straightened up and blinked a few times, trying to get himself oriented. Then he frowned in puzzlement. "The Sawmill Challenge came out seventy-two to twenty-eight in favor of your client?"

"Yes." It came out as a hiss more than a word.

"The same exact margin as in the Medalist Challenge?"

"We didn't call it that."

"I don't give a rat's—I'm not concerned with what you called it. The result was exactly the same. Right?"

"Yes."

"Well, now! That's what I call one hell of a coincidence!"

Bardswith jumped to his feet. "Objection! Counsel is—"

"Yeah, yeah." Howell waved him back down. "Mr. Caminetti—"

"Sorry, your honor. I apologize. It's just that..." He shook his head. "I'm sorry. But I mean, Mr. Nickton, didn't that strike you as downright eerie?"

"Not at all. There aren't that many integers between about twenty-five and seventy-five, and, with as much work as I've done, you're bound to get duplicate results all the time."

"Yeah." Eddie nodded, forced to admit that this was a truism of statistics. "Which cup was the Sawmill Cola in?"

Nickton couldn't hide his reaction to Eddie's sudden non sequitur. "Wh-what?"

"A or B. Which cup was the Sawmill in?"

Nickton began to blink rapidly, looking from Eddie to Bardswith and back again.

Bardswith didn't miss the signal, and got to his feet immediately. "Your honor, how long does counsel plan to meander endlessly? This is beginning to smell like a pathetic fishing expedition."

"Mr. Caminetti?" Howell said.

"What's a fishing expedition?" Eddie asked.

"It's when you ask a lotta pointless questions on accounta you ain't got a point and hope you kin find one accidentally," Howell responded.

"Ah. You mean a fishing trip. I've never been on a fishing 'expedition.' That's why I didn't under—"

"Yeah, very innerestin. So how much longer you planna be wanderin about?"

"I think I'm there." Eddie pointed to Bardswith. "And he knows I'm there, which is why he keeps—"

"Your honor!" Bardswith howled.

"Ask your question, counselor."

"Right." Eddie turned back to Nickton. "Which cup was the Sawmill in?"

"It was in the cup marked A."

"All the time?"

"Yes."

"And why was that?"

"Made the data easier to track. My people didn't have to do extensive record keeping to know how to interpret the results of each sampling. It was less error-prone."

"Got it. Makes sense. So which golf balls were marked A?"

Again Bardswith rose, but this time Howell waved him down before he could even open his mouth.

"Mr. Nickton?" Eddie prompted.

"The Medalists."

"I see. All of them, right? For the reasons you already mentioned for the cola test."

"That's correct."

"Okay. That's all I really wanted the jury to know."

Nickton heaved a huge sigh of relief and put his hands on the arms of his chair in preparation for leaving the witness box.

"So I've just got one more question and that'll be it."

Nickton grimaced, then slowly sank back onto the chair.

"In your entire career," Eddie said, "have you ever come up with a result that wasn't favorable to your client?"

Nickton gaped at him, but didn't answer.

"Yo." Howell looked down at the witness. "Mr. Nickton, you with us here?"

"I...what?"

"In your entire career," Eddie repeated slowly, "have you ever, even once, come up with a result that your client didn't like?"

Nickton looked to the side, then back at Eddie. "Yes," he said defiantly.

"Really?" This time Bardswith didn't offer the asked-and-answered objection. No reason to, when it was working in favor of his own side.

"I sure did."

"How many times?"

"Well, uh...kind of hard to remember..."

"I can understand that, as many years as you've been in the business."

"Right."

"So let me help you out." Eddie returned to the defense table and picked up a piece of paper. "How does *once* sound? Once in your entire career, you delivered bad news to the client. Coming back to you now?"

"Sort of."

"Sort of. And how long ago did that happen?"

Nickton, unable to take his eyes off the paper in Eddie's hands, licked his lips. "About nineteen years ago."

"'About' meaning closer to twenty. That fair to say?"

"I guess so."

"And what happened?"

"What?"

"What happened after you delivered news your client didn't want to hear?"

Nickton waited, then remembered that he was supposed to breathe. He inhaled with a shudder, held it, then blew it out. His whole body sagged as though it were the exhaled air that had been holding it up. "I got fired."

"Never made that mistake again, did you," Eddie said, but withdrew the remark after Bardswith nearly blew an artery objecting.

CHAPTER TWENTY-FIVE

"**P**laintiff rests, your honor."

"Good. Mr. Caminetti, call your first witness."

"I only got one."

"A blessing. Call him."

"Defense calls Professor Ivgeny Hochweiss."

"Objection to this witness," Bardswith said.

"Shit," Howell muttered.

"Nooooo..." Howell squeezed out at Bardswith through clenched teeth shortly after he'd waved the attorneys up to the bar. "We will *not* go inta chambers. Now what in the hell is your problem!"

"My problem," Bardswith said, remaining exasperatingly calm and level-headed in light of the judge's wrath, "is that the defense is calling a witness whose specific purpose is to call into question my client's marketing methods."

"Now how do you know what they're gonna do?"

Bardswith held out a hand toward Eddie. "Ask him."

"Well, Mr. Caminetti? What do you plan to do with this witness?"

"Call into question his client's marketing methods."

"See?" Bardswith said. "I told you."

"Fine. So you're the Amazin-frickin-Kreskin. What's the objection?"

"The objection," Bardswith said, turning and cocking his head toward Tommy Trevillian, "is that my client isn't the one on trial here. His marketing methods are irrelevant."

Howell turned to Eddie and lifted his shoulders in inquiry, but it was Hoogenband who answered. "It is not our intention to implicate Medalist in any way, nor do we mean to imply that anything they do or might have done is in any way improper. However, since they're suing us for fraudulent and deceitful practices, and since fraud and deceit are at least partially determined by what is reasonable and customary within a business segment, and since Medalist is the company who is bringing this suit, and since they sell over sixty percent of all the golf balls used in this country...well, your honor, it seems only reasonable to use their own business practices as a preliminary, de facto standard against which to judge those of my client."

The other lawyers and the judge stared at Hoogenband, who stood his ground for a few seconds and then wondered if perhaps he hadn't been clear. "What I mean—"

"In other words, judge," Eddie volunteered, "if Medalist is doing what they're accusing *us* of doing, well then, they don't have much of a case, do they?"

Bardswith sneered and put his hands up on the bench. "Is there some case law on—" He pulled his hands away just as Howell's gavel slammed down on the same spot.

"You were sayin?"

Bardswith swallowed and put his hands in his pockets. "Is there some case law on counsel's assertion? Some *legal* precedent?"

"Yeah," Eddie responded. "It's known as the Pot Calling the Kettle Black Theory."

"Yep," Howell agreed. "Hearda that one. Objection is overruled. Step back."

"Your honor—"

"Bluenose, what the hell could you possibly want now!"

"Just alerting the court that I plan to renew my objection on the record."

"Thank you for the heads-up. Now step the hell back."

When everyone was back in place, Eddie said, "Defense calls Professor Ivgeny Hochweiss."

"Objection!"

"Overruled."

"...undergraduate degree in economics from MIT, master's in statistical science from Oxford, and a Ph.D. in analytic methods from Stanford."

"And you are currently...?" Eddie prompted.

"Professor of statistical methods at the Harvard Business School," Dr. Ivgeny Hochweiss responded.

"I see. Now, professor—"

"Your honor..." Bardswith drawled as he stood up slowly. He looked bored, unimpressed and uninterested. "Plaintiff will stipulate that the witness is an expert, and so on and so forth, so we can just get on with it."

Judge Howell looked at Eddie to see if there was any objection, since he had a right to trot out his witness's credentials for the jury.

"Fine with us, your honor." Before Bardswith had fully resumed his seat, Eddie said, "Professor, you've had a gander at the test that Medalist conducted of their balls against ours, right? The one where they gave some-a each to a few hundred golfers?"

"Yes. I've looked at it in detail."

"Pretty impressive piece-a work, was it?"

"Oh my, yes. Most impressive indeed."

"Double-blind, that sort of thing? Nobody knew which ball was which?"

"First class all the way. The client got his money's worth."

"Did he."

"Yes, sir."

Eddie looked crestfallen. But this was his own witness so Bardswith had all his antennae on full alert.

"So from that test," Eddie went on, "why, we'd have to conclude that the Medalist is the superior ball, right? At least in the opinion of actual golfers. Isn't that right?"

Hochweiss shook his head. "No, it's absolutely wrong."

Eddie, startled, cocked his head quizzically. "It's *wrong?* How could it be wrong? You just said it was a first-class piece of work!" Eddie looked over at the jury, as if pleading for help in trying to understand what was going on here. "That the client got his money's worth!"

"It was, and he did. Because it was a first-class piece of deception."

Eddie threw up his hands and let them drop. "Professor, I'm confused. What's going on?"

"Pretty simple, really, and the oldest trick in the book." He turned to face the jury. "Let's say you're testing two things against one another, except that they're not different, they're both exactly the same, like the same soda in both cups, or the same golf ball in both boxes, and you label one with an A and the other with a B?" Hochweiss waited until he was sure the jurors had grasped the setup. "More people are going to say they liked A better than B."

The jurors, with stunned expressions on their faces, turned as one to look at Trevillian, who kept his eyes toward the front of the room, and Bardswith, who was writing on his legal pad and pretending not be interested in anything this snotty witness had to say.

"You gotta be kidding me!" Eddie exclaimed.

"I don't kid around under oath," Hochweiss said.

"What you're saying," Eddie echoed, "is that, if there's no difference whatsoever, people are gonna pick what's labeled A just because it's labeled A?"

"Yep. 'B' has a bad connotation in our society. B movies, the B-side of a record, getting a B on your math test instead of an A. 'A' is first class, top shelf, first quality. 'B' is the also-ran. Just the way it is in people's minds."

"And is this generally known to people who do surveys and studies and such?"

"It's as basic as breathing. In my Marketing 101 course I have the students do a demonstration study over at the student union. I call it the Sawmill Bamboozle. Same soda in both cups, one labeled A, the other B."

"And...?"

"A always wins. That's why, when you do comparative studies, you give things labels like '65TL982' versus '65GP137.' You never use A and B." Hochweiss turned to the jury again. "Unless you're trying to snooker somebody."

"Objection!" Bardswith called out. "Calls for speculation."

"The witness is an expert," Eddie responded. "Mr. Bardswith said so himself. As an expert certified before this court, he can speculate as much as he wants about anything he wants. Isn't that right?"

Howell nodded in approval. "Very good, Mr. Caminetti. You been readin up. Objection is overruled."

"Exception!" Bardswith declared.

"Noted," Howell said. "Now hush up."

"You were saying, professor?"

"Anybody with Horace Nickton's experience and expertise who pulls the A-B trick—that's what it's called in professional circles, the A-B trick—anybody who does that is doing it to deceive someone. Can't be any other explanation."

"Ob-*jec*-tion!" Bardswith shouted again. "This witness can't possibly know what Horace Nickton knew and what he didn't know!"

"The hell I can't," Hochweiss said calmly.

"Huh? What?"

"I know exactly what Horace knew."

Howell was too startled to point out that it was not proper for witnesses to answer attorney objections. "Now how in heck can you know that?"

"Because," Hochweiss replied. "Horace Nickton was my student. He was even in my Marketing 101 class."

Bardswith didn't so much sink back onto his seat as drip down into it.

"Every time you pull the A-B trick," Hochweiss continued, "and if you use at least a couple hundred subjects, the numbers come out the same way, give or take a few percentage points."

"And what numbers are those?" Eddie asked.

"About seventy-thirty in favor of whatever was labeled A." He put a hand into the air, palm down, and rocked it back and forth. "Give or take."

"No kidding?"

"No kidding."

"And the Sawmill Challenge? Mr. Nickton has sworn on numerous occasions that people liked Sawmill better. What do you think?"

"What's the relevance here?" Bardswith demanded. "We're supposed to be talking about golf balls!"

"Mr. Nickton testified as an expert that Medalist balls are better than Scratch," Eddie responded. "Plaintiff brought up the taste test to verify his expertise. I have the right to call his expertise into question."

"Overruled. Proceed."

"Professor? What's your opinion of the Sawmill Challenge results?"

"After years of repeating it with my students?" Hochweiss smiled and scratched his ear. "There are maybe five people in the western hemisphere who can actually tell the difference between Sawmill Cola and Mom's, and they need a mass spectrometer to do it."

"And Mr. Nickton's conclusion that people like Sawmill better...?"

"Junk science that gives us all a bad name."

"So when you look at the results of the golf ball test Mr. Nickton conducted on behalf of his client, Medalist, are there any firm conclusions you can draw at all?" Eddie paused for a second. "Other than that it was rigged?"

"Objection!" Bardswith nearly screamed as he came to his feet.

"On what grounds?" Howell asked him.

Bardswith's mouth worked silently, but no words came out at first. "Casting spurious aspersions!" he finally managed to sputter.

"Yeah, right. Now seddown and hush up. Mr. Caminetti, you were sayin..."

"Just asked the witness if we can draw any conclusions from the rigged test."

Howell pointed a warning finger at Bardswith before the attorney could object.

"Yes, actually," Hochweiss answered. "There is one solid conclusion you can count on to be statistically valid."

"And what might that be?"

"That there was no difference whatsoever between those two balls that the golfers were able to detect."

"No difference."

"Nope. If you'd switched the labels on the balls, seventy-two percent of them would have liked the Scratch ball better."

"So what you're saying, the seventy-two percent Mr. Nickton testified to...?"

"What the golfers liked better was the letter A, not the Medalist ball."

"Well whaddaya know about that. Your honor, how about a quick recess?"

"Twenty minutes."

After Howell banged his gavel, Eddie went back to the defense table.

"Beautiful," Hoogenband said.

"Thanks."

"You just proved the Scratch ball is no better than a Medalist."

"Yeah, I know. Don't worry about it."

"Me? Worry? Not a chance."

"Soon as we get that engineer in here I'll take care of it."

"Witness understands he's still unner oath?"

"I do," Hochweiss answered the judge.

"Proceed, counselor."

"Thanks." Eddie rose, but stayed behind the defense table. "Your honor, we asked for the court reporter to bring with her a draft transcript of Mr. Trevillian's testimony."

The court reporter nodded at Eddie and held up a sheaf of papers, then turned and showed them to the judge.

"Thanks very much," Eddie said. "Dr. Hochweiss, you heard the testimony of Mr. Trevillian here, is that right?"

"I did."

"Do you remember the part where I asked him, and I'm just doing this off the top of my head here, I said, With millions of counterfeit Medalist balls flooding the market, did you ever once, ever, get a letter from anybody complaining that one of those balls didn't perform the way a Medalist usually does?"

"Yes, I remember that."

"Okay, and do you remember where he said, No, because golfers always assume it's their own fault? He said something about over ninety percent of golfers being very high handicappers, and then said that if someone is a twenty and he hits a bad shot, he assumes it's his fault, not the ball's, because he hits bad shots all the time. Do you recall that?"

"Yes, I—"

"Objection!" Bardswith came to his feet. "I'm not going to have my client's testimony potentially misrepresented or mischaracterized based on the memory of opposing counsel!"

"You want to have it read back from the transcript, is that it?" Howell asked.

"I do, sir!"

"Very well." Howell motioned for the reporter to comply.

She leafed through the sheaf of papers and found the relevant passage, then read it out loud: "Mr. Caminetti said: With millions of counterfeit Medalist balls flooding the market, did you ever once, ever, get a letter from anybody complaining that one of those balls didn't perform the way a Medalist usually does? Mr. Trevillian said: Golfers always assume it's their own fault when they hit a bad shot. As it happens, only ten percent of all golfers regularly break a hundred. Now, if someone is a twenty handicap and he hits a bad shot, he assumes it's his fault, not the ball's, because he hits bad shots all the time." She looked up, received approving nods from Eddie and the judge, and set the papers back down.

"That about do it for you there, Barnstable?" Howell asked.

Bardswith mumbled something and sat down.

"I said, does that—"

"Yes, your honor," Bardswith replied.

"Glad we got that settled," Eddie said. "Professor, you remember all of that?"

"I do."

"Fine. So whaddaya think?"

"Objection," Bardswith said yet again, but stayed in his seat. "Overly broad."

Before Howell could rule, Eddie said, "I'll rephrase it, your honor, and make it more specific. Doctor, was Mr. Trevillian lying through his teeth?"

"Your honor...!" Bardswith bellowed. This time he stood up.

"What?" Howell asked calmly.

"What? You ask me *what?*" Bardswith pointed at Eddie with a trembling finger. "He...he called my client a liar!"

"Did you call his client a liar, Mr. Caminetti?"

"No way, your honor. I asked my witness if *he* wanted to call him a liar."

"That's what I thought. Overruled."

"Your honor!"

"Shaddap, Barnaby! Proceed, counselor."

"Thank you. Doctor?"

"I can't say one way or another whether Mr. Trevillian was lying or not. I don't know for sure what he knows versus what he testified to. But I can tell you one thing for sure."

"And what's that?"

"I can tell you that his company sure as hell doesn't treat golfers like they think it's their own fault. They treat them like they don't think *anything* is ever their own fault."

"And what makes you so sure of that?"

"Because they spend over four hundred million a year on advertising, and every single dime of it is designed to drive home to golfers only one point: *Nothing* is your fault."

"Now what would make you say a thing like that?"

"Well..." Hochweiss reached down to the side of the witness chair and brought up a thick attaché case. "May I?" he asked the judge.

"Certainly."

Hochweiss opened his case and withdrew a manila folder about a quarter-inch thick. Holding it up he said, "Last night I asked the desk clerk at my hotel to go and buy a few golf magazines and then tear out all the Medalist advertisements."

"Why didn't you do it yourself?" Eddie asked.

"So no one would think I was loading the dice. Now if you look at those ads—"

"Enter as exhibits, your honor?" Hoogenband called out from the defense table. The clerk of the court took the folder from Hochweiss and made the appropriate entries, then handed it to the first juror and asked her to pass the contents around.

"If you look through those ads," Hochweiss continued, "you'll begin to see that the underlying message is the same in all of them: Everything that's wrong with your game is because of your equipment. It's your ball or your shaft or your glasses or your shoes or your tees or your clothes. Every magazine ad, every television commercial, every athlete's endorsement... they all say the same thing: Buy this club or that ball and your game will improve. Shave strokes! Take fewer putts! If everything they say is to be believed, it would cost a twenty handicapper less than two thousand dollars in equipment to qualify for the PGA Tour."

"I see," said Eddie. "Now, are you saying that this is not true? That the ads are deceptive?"

"You didn't ask me to consider that."

"Oh, yeah. What did I ask you?"

"You asked me about Mr. Trevillian's testimony, the part where he said that Medalist got no complaints about the counterfeit balls because golfers always assume it's their own fault. And I testified that Medalist spends upwards of a half billion dollars a year based on exactly the opposite assumption. That's all."

"But you said an interesting thing, Doctor. You said the Medalist company's attitude is that golfers believe that nothing is their own fault."

"Yes, I did."

"You didn't say that Medalist itself actually believes that, only that they think golfers do. Is that right?"

"Yes."

"And why is that? Don't you think Medalist believes it? After all, half a billion in advertising..."

"Because," Hochweiss answered, "every year they spend another half billion trying to convince you that everything they sold you the year before is such crap that its continued use would not only be detrimental to your game but quite possibly dangerous to your health as well. Now if all that stuff is so terrific"—he held up a finger—"how come your game didn't get any better last year, and"—he held up a second finger—"why would Medalist think that with this year's gear, it will?"

"Not sure I follow."

"I'll make it simpler. Look at a guy who's been playing for fifty years and still spends thousands of dollars on the latest and greatest golf equipment. Nothing he's ever bought has helped his game, but does he learn? Does he stop buying new stuff and maybe take some lessons?" Hochweiss shook his head. "No. What he does instead, he spends *more!*"

Eddie folded his arms and cupped his chin with one hand. He stood that way for some moments, as though mulling over the implications of the testimony he'd just heard.

Finally, he said, "Professor, I think I understand what you're saying, but there's still one thing I don't get."

Hochweiss, not having been asked a question, waited patiently.

"The issue was why Medalist never got a complaint about ball performance despite the millions of counterfeit balls flooding the market. Remember?"

"Yes."

"And Mr. Trevillian said it was because golfers always assume bad shots are their own fault, which you've now demonstrated is malarkey, or at least demonstrated that Mr. Trevillian's own company thinks it's malarkey. Am I stating that correctly?"

"You are."

"So here's my question: What's the real reason nobody ever complained about the counterfeit Medalist balls?"

Hochweiss shrugged, and seemed surprised by the question. "Kind of obvious, isn't it?"

"How so?"

"Well, Mr. Caminetti...it's because nobody could tell the difference."

CHAPTER TWENTY-SIX

"Tell me something, doctor," Hoogenband said.

"Sure," Hochweiss said. "But don't call me that unless I'm on the meter."

"So what should I—"

"Professor." Hochweiss waved a fork in the air. "Ahh, just kidding. It's Gene."

Eddie looked around the restaurant. "Just keep your voices down, will ya? Our case isn't over yet and—"

"Yeah, sorry." Hoogenband leaned forward. "All Eddie really did in there was prove that the Medalist balls are no better than the Scratches."

"I didn't hear everything," Hochweiss said, "but you're probably right. So?"

"Well, he said that *you* said it won't make any difference. That people will still shell out a hundred bucks a box."

"I guarantee it."

Hoogenband sat back and dropped his hands on the table. "Now how is that possible!"

His eyes narrowing in mirth, Hochweiss took a sip of wine and said, "Leif, how many sets of golf clubs have you bought in the last ten years?"

"Well..."

"Come on, don't be embarrassed. You're no different than twenty million other people."

"That's what embarrasses me. Been through four sets."

"Okay. Any of em ever make a difference?"

"As a matter of fact, yes. I played a whole lot better and—"

"Any of that improvement ever last more than two, three rounds?"

Hoogenband fiddled with his fork as he thought it over. "Not that I can remember, to be honest with you."

"Okay. So you bought new clubs three times, none of them made any difference in your game, and then you went out and bought a fourth set."

Hoogenband set the fork down. "You put it like that, I kind of look like a schmuck."

"You kind of look *human*." Hochweiss sawed eagerly through his steak. "Same thing, really. Now, you know why you did that?" He popped the piece of steak into his mouth.

Hoogenband thought about it. "I'm not sure."

"It's because you had *faith*, that's why," Hochweiss said around the steak. "Faith fashioned by very clever advertising. Aren't you going to eat?"

"Not hungry. What are you talking about?"

"Order some more wine and I'll tell you."

Eddie waved at the waiter and made a pouring motion with his hand. The waiter nodded and disappeared into the kitchen. "Listen to the professor, Leif," Eddie said to Hoogenband. "He knows what he's talking about."

"As well do you, Eddie," Hochweiss said.

"Yeah, but you explain it better than me."

"Ah." Hochweiss gestured modestly with his knife and swallowed. "It's so damned simple nobody realizes it. Leif, listen. Some time ago these guys did a study of this religious group. A cult. That's what you call it when they believe in something you don't and they have less than fifty million members. A cult."

"What study?"

"This cult, they believed the end of the world was coming. They even knew the specific day and time, about two years out. So these guys, the ones doing the study? They hung out with the cult because they wanted to see what would happen to their beliefs when it didn't happen."

"What if it did happen?" Hoogenband asked with a smile. "Then the guys doing the study would have looked pretty foolish."

"To whom?"

The smile vanished. "Oh, yeah. So what happened when the world didn't end?"

"What would you guess?"

"Well, I guess the cult disbanded. Because their core belief was shown to be false."

"Good guess."

"Thanks."

"But wrong." Hochweiss set down his knife and fork. "What happened was, their belief got *stronger*. Much, much stronger. They became more fierce in their convictions, and more strident in their insistence. They just said they made a mistake in the date, and they calculated another one."

"But that doesn't make any sense!"

"I didn't say it did. I just said it happened. And happens all the time."

Hoogenband wasn't buying it. "You're telling me, if I sat one of those guys down, looked him right in the eye and pointed out that their prediction had been dead wrong, he'd give me an argument?"

"That's the very nature of faith! When people believe in something strongly enough, nothing can shake their faith, not mathematics or science or tidal waves of evidence. Trying to prove them wrong will always backfire on you, because all it will do is strengthen their conviction."

"Yeah, well, religion. I mean, you can't prove anything one way or the other, so that's hardly a fair—"

"Forget religion, Leif. That's too easy. Just look at golfers!"

"Golfers?"

"Why, certainly! You think golfers spending billions on products with no discernible benefit, and doing so over and over and over despite proof—absolute proof!—that they're wasting money...you think that's different from those guys pushing back the date when the world is going to end?"

The waiter arrived with the wine, and they suffered through the elaborate bottle-opening ceremony. Hochweiss said to the waiter, "Did you know that four out of five wine experts can't even tell the difference between red and white if they're both served warm and the experts are blindfolded?"

The waiter smiled and poured a small bit for Eddie to taste. "Very funny."

Eddie told the waiter to go ahead and pour. "If it's sour, we'll tell you later."

"That's not really true, is it?" Hoogenband asked when the waiter had gone. "About telling red from white?"

"Oh, yes. Quite true." Hochweiss took a sip of wine and smacked his lips appreciatively. "Never spend more on wine than you can taste unless you're trying to impress somebody." He picked up his knife and fork again. "Eddie here, he's going to rake some engineer over the coals tomorrow, to try to make a case that his golf balls really don't perform just the same as the opposition's. Apparently at your urging."

"Of course. He has to rehabilitate his product in the public's eyes."

"No, he doesn't."

"You can't be serious."

"Oh, but I am. The Scratch ball has passed into that rarefied realm called *cult status*. It no longer matters what you prove or don't prove about it, any more than it matters that my ten-dollar watch from Radio Shack"—he held up his arm and pulled back his sleeve—"keeps better time and is more rugged than a ten-thousand-dollar Rolex. Medalist could trot out a hundred engineers and a roomful of test results proving beyond any doubt that the Scratch performs no better than a worn-out range ball, and people will still buy it."

"Pretty cynical attitude, don't you think?"

"Cynical? The government convincing its own citizens that odds of forty-nine million to one is a real good reason to buy a lottery ticket? *That's* cynical."

"Leif," Eddie said, "you remember me asking Trevillian about the national average handicap?"

"Yeah. What was the deal there?"

"Wouldn't believe me if I told you."

"Try me."

"Okay. We spend more dough on plutonium-shafted, kryptonite, chrono-synclastic what-the-fuck-evers than it would take to send a manned mission to Mars, and the average handicap hasn't changed squat in decades."

"Bullshit!"

"See? Told you you wouldn't—"

"But what about when all those counterfeit balls came on the market?"
Eddie tilted his head away and just stared at him.

"You telling me there was no change at all?" the lawyer said.

"That's what I'm telling you."

Hoogenband sighed and rubbed the side of his head. "I still find it so hard to believe that the public would ignore such overwhelming evidence."

"I know you do," Hochweiss said with good humor. "And that"—he reached over to pat Hoogenband's arm—"is why my dear friend Eddie here is a multimillionaire."

"I'm the chief engineer for MedalCorp's golf ball division," Farnsworth Rafaelson said defiantly. There wasn't much reason to be defiant, since Eddie had only asked him one question so far, which was to identify himself, but he'd been following the case, didn't like the way his company was being treated, and he was pissed off.

"Which one?"

"What do you mean, which one?"

"Which ball are you the engineer for?" Eddie said.

Rafaelson, not quite sure where the question was going, said, "For all of them."

Eddie, who had been pacing, stopped. "*All* of them?"

"Yes."

"You mean you're the head engineer for Pericles, Ace, Zenith, ProAm, Stroker, PinHigh, Slammer, SpinJockey, Whammer and TotalFeel golf balls?"

"I sure am."

"Wow." Eddie gave a soft whistle. "How do you keep all those different design specs sorted out?"

"I don't memorize them. We write them down."

"Oh, yeah, right. You happena know anything about how the Scratch ball is constructed?"

"No."

"Really? Didn't even cut it open to have a look?"

"Cut it open? Hell, no, I didn't cut it open!"

"How come? You must've been curious."

"Hah! You must be kidding. That ball's not even allowed on airplanes, you think I'm going to stand over it and open it up? No way!"

Eddie didn't say anything for a few moments, and then spoke slowly. "Not allowed on airplanes? Where on earth did you hear that?"

Rafaelson gave a lopsided grin. "I read about it, that's where."

"Read it where?"

"Newspaper. Where else?"

"Which newspaper?"

Rafaelson flipped up a hand. "I don't know. Some newspaper."

"You read it in a newspaper and that's why you believe it."

"Of course."

"But you don't remember which one."

"Might've been any of a number."

"Well, which ones do you read regularly?"

Bardswith stood up. "Your honor, of what possible relevance is any of this?"

Eddie turned to face him. "Are you serious?"

"Address the court, Mr. Caminetti," Howell said. "But my guess is, he's serious. Where's the relevance?"

Eddie turned back to the bench and pointed to Rafaelson. "He just testified in open court that he's afraid to cut open a Scratch golf ball. He says it's because you're not even allowed to carry them on airplanes. Now I got two problems here."

He turned slightly and tilted his head toward the gallery. "One is that there are a dozen reporters back there who're gonna print what this guy said."

"Already been reported," Howell said. "Been on TV."

"Nothin I can do about that, judge, but TV people aren't under oath."

"That's for damned sure," the judge agreed.

"And this guy is," Eddie said, turning back to the witness box.

"I gitcher point. What's t'other reason?"

"The witness is saying some pretty nasty things about my golf ball. Don't I got a right to find out if he's, you know...?"

"Credible? Yeah, you do. Objection's overruled. But let's step it up a bit, whaddaya say?"

"Hell, I can floor it, you gimme a little leeway."

"Go ahead."

"Okay. Mr. Rafaelson. Still trying to find out where you read about this, seeing as how you don't remember. What newspapers do you read regularly?"

"Oh, let's see..." Rafaelson looked up at the ceiling and tapped his chin. "*New York Times, Washington Post, Economist...*"

"Was it one-a them?"

Rafaelson looked back down. "Really can't remember."

"But probably one-a those, you figure."

"I'm guessing. Would have to have been, really."

"Yeah. I imagine you're right. Except..." Eddie lifted his briefcase from the floor and set it on the defense table. "Far's I know, that story was only reported in one newspaper, and it wasn't any-a those you mentioned. Lessee here."

He fumbled around inside the bag without finding what he was looking for. "It's called the *Globe*. Heard of it?"

Rafaelson shifted in his chair. "Yeah, I've heard of it."

"But not one you read regularly."

"Of course not!"

"Huh." Eddie snapped the fingers of his free hand, the other still being inside his bag. "I know! I bet your wife brings it home from the grocery store! That possible?"

"I suppose it is."

"Well, there you go. Now what I'm betting, she brought it home the day this story came out. What do you think?"

"It's possible."

"So which issue was it?"

"What?"

"The date. Just trying to narrow down what your source was."

Rafaelson, feeling trapped and toyed with, saw a chance to strike back. "How should I know! You remember the date of every newspaper you read?"

"No way!" Eddie said with a good-natured grin. "Hell, I never remember!"

Then he seemed to finally latch on to something in the bag. When he pulled his hand out, he was holding a tabloid-sized newspaper folded in half. "But what I sometimes *do* remember is other stuff that mighta caught my eye, knowmsayin? Might spark my memory a little. Kinda like remembering what you were doing when Kennedy was shot or *Seinfeld* went off the air. See what I'm drivin at here?"

"Sure, I get you."

"Good. Now, regardin the paper you read when you found out the Scratch was banned on airlines"—Eddie unfolded the newspaper, looked at the front page, then held it up for all to see—"did it have a headline readin 'Aliens Ate My Baby'?"

As laughter ricocheted around the courtroom, Rafaelson's face grew red and he seemed to shrink within himself.

"Let's try page two," Eddie said, opening the newspaper. "There's this story about how it isn't really the president who's calling the shots in the White House, it's an evil brother who's growing out of his chest. That one familiar?"

Bardswith rose and tried to make himself heard above the howls coming from the gallery and the jury box. "Your honor, I must protest!"

"How about this guy who saw the Virgin Mary's face in his oatmeal?"

"Your honor...!"

Howell put a hand over his mouth to hide his laughter. "Mr. Caminetti, g'wan and make yer point."

"Sure." Eddie turned one more page of the newspaper, said "Damn!" at whatever was printed there, then put it down. "Your honor, as far as I know, that story about the Scratch ball being banned on airplanes appeared in only one place, on only one day, and it was in this newspaper." He pointed to it lying on the table. "This story is obviously baloney—"

"Citing facts not in evidence!" Bardswith objected.

Both Howell and Eddie looked at him, but didn't say anything.

"What?" Bardswith demanded.

Howell answered. "You really want him t'git somebody in here to testify you can carry Scratch balls on a airplane?"

Bardswith sniffed once or twice, said, "Plaintiff will stipulate that no such ban actually exists," and sat down.

"I'm sure we're all relieved about that," Howell said. "Mr. Caminetti, you made your point. Move on."

"Okay. Mr. Rafaelson, were you the guy who disguised the Medalist and Scratch golf balls for that test your boss conducted?"

"I devised how it was going to be done and supervised the work."

"So you're real familiar with what went on."

"Intimately."

"Good. So how did you get rid of that special shiny surface on the Scratch?"

"We didn't get rid of it. We hid it. Sprayed on a matte finish coating."

"Ah. I get you. But you'd still be able to tell it apart from the Medalist, because the Medalist has a glossy surface."

"Obviously. So we painted the Medalist balls a slightly different shade of white and that removed the gloss as well."

"Same color as the Scratch?"

"No. We had to lay another coating over the matte finish that was the same as the one we used on the Medalist."

"Interesting. How thick was the coating?"

Rafaelson knew where this was going, and stopped it in its tracks. "It was extremely thin. Barely a few atoms thick."

"And what about the logo?"

"What do you mean?"

"Well, the Scratch has a brightly colored logo, and that coating being only a few atoms thick, wouldn't it show through?"

"We banded over the logo."

"What's that mean?"

"We painted a white rectangle over the logo so it wouldn't show through."

"But you could still see that band through the coating."

"Right, so we did the same thing to the Medalists. Like Mr. Trevillian was trying to tell you, they looked identical."

"And like I was trying to tell him, I never doubted it. Do you happen to know whether the original coating on the Scratch ball—just remembered the word, by the way: it's iridescent, right?—do you know whether that iridescent coating has anything to do with how the Scratch performs?"

"That's absurd!" It was Rafaelson's first chance to strike a blow for the cause, and he made no attempt to hide his emotion on the topic.

"What is?"

"That the coating on the Scratch makes any difference!"

"Who said it did?"

Rafaelson faltered slightly. "But...you just..."

"I just asked if you knew, is all. But never mind. How much did the matte coating and the extra coat of paint weigh?"

"Next to nothing."

"How next? Or don't you know?"

"As a matter of fact, I do know. It was about eighty-nine micrograms."

"Right. And the band of paint over the logos. Did you do both sides of the ball?"

"Of course. There are logos on both sides."

"But not the top or bottom."

"No."

"So you had more weight on the sides of the ball than the top."

"I told you, it didn't—"

"Didn't make any difference, right. What about the shape of the dimples?"

"What about the dimples!"

"Did the coating and the paint change them at all?"

"Yeah. It coated them. And that didn't make any difference either."

"But—"

"Look, Mr. Caminetti, let's save a little time here."

"Okay..."

"I know everything there is to know about how the Medalist KY 9000 is constructed, so I can swear under oath that what we did makes no difference!"

"That's because you know the ball so well."

"You're damned right!"

"Everything about how it's made."

"You bet."

"Everything? Even how the component materials are made?"

"You bet."

"But you don't know anything about the Scratch."

"What?"

"You don't know anything about the Scratch. About how it's made. True?"

"Yeah. I guess."

"You *guess?*"

"No. I know. I mean, I don't know."

"Thank you. Now you said you can swear under oath that all that paint and coating you sprayed on the Medalist didn't affect its performance, on accounta you know how it's constructed, right?"

Rafaelson hesitated.

"Your exact words were: You're damned right, You bet, and You bet."

"Okay. I can swear that stuff didn't make any difference."

"Well, thank you! You know, it's a whole lot easier to just tell the truth because there's so much less you gotta remember."

"Objection!"

"Withdrawn. So given that you don't know a damned thing about how the Scratch is constructed, can you swear that what you did to disguise it didn't affect its performance?"

"I guess not."

"You're guessing again? What the hell happened to You're damned right, You bet, and You bet?"

"Objection!" Bardswith slammed his hand on the defense table. "Badgering, argumentative—"

"Overruled!"

"Well?" Eddie demanded. "Can you swear you didn't affect the Scratch ball's performance?"

Rafaelson had his fists balled and his knuckles were turning white. "No."

"So when you told Mr. Trevillian that it didn't make any difference, you didn't really know what the hell you were talking about, did you?"

Rafaelson didn't answer, but just glared at Eddie. At least when his eyes weren't pleading with Bardswith to get him out of this jam.

Eddie stepped into his sight line, cutting off his view of Bardswith. "You did tell Trevillian that, didn't you? That it made no difference?"

"Yeah." Rafaelson tried to force his hands to relax. "Yes, I did. And you know what?"

"What?"

"I believe it, too!"

"Really?"

"Absolutely! Nothing we did to that ball made any difference whatsoever!"

"I understand." Eddie tapped at his lip as he thought it over. "Matter of fact, I appreciate the depth of your conviction."

"Thank you." Rafaelson, satisfied that he'd finally scored, and scored big, unraveled his fists and sat back slightly. Bardswith, enjoying Eddie's concession to the witness's integrity, saw no reason to undercut it by making an objection about Eddie having offered an opinion when he was only supposed to be asking questions.

Eddie turned back to Rafaelson. "So what else did you assure Mr. Trevillian of when you had absolutely no idea what the hell you were talking about?"

"Objection!" Bardswith barked.

"Withdrawn. No further questions."

CHAPTER TWENTY-SEVEN

"**Y**ou ready for your closin statement, counselor?"

"I am," said Bardswith as he got to his feet.

Eddie stood up as well. "Approach, your honor?"

Howell waved them up to the bench.

"I need to talk with counsel," Eddie said when they arrived.

"Brewster?" Howell inquired.

A slow smile spread across Bardswith's face. "Why certainly. Up-stairs?"

"Sure."

"How long you boys need?"

"Ten minutes," Eddie said.

"If you're so sure-a that," Howell said, "why not settle it right here? I can move things along if y'all get hung up on details."

"Sounds good to me," Eddie said.

"I'm listening," Bardswith said.

Eddie turned to him. "I'll shut down the company, and we get to sell off existing inventory."

"Fine," Bardswith responded, still facing the judge. "What about all the money you already made?"

"We keep it."

"No way."

"Why not divvy it up somehow?" Howell offered.

"How would you suggest?" Bardswith asked.

"Don't bother," Eddie said. "I keep it all."

"Not going to happen," Bardswith insisted.

"Yeah, it is."

"Then let's do our closings and let the jury decide." Bardswith turned to face Eddie. "You hurt us, Mr. Caminetti. There's no denying that. You scored some very big points, but most of them were totally irrelevant as pertains to this specific case. We're not too worried about how the public is going to perceive us, because nobody's ever going to bother to read the details or listen past the first two sentences of any explanation. So we'll recover from that. But we'd never recover from a wimpy conclusion to this case."

He addressed Howell again. "In my closing I'll separate all the irrelevant jabs they got in from the real substance of this case, and I'm confident the jury will find in our favor. I believe in the basic intelligence and honor of juries. In my experience, they generally do the right thing."

Once more he turned to Eddie. "If you want to get out of this thing without a judgment against you blotting your record, we're happy to settle. But we need it to be definitive. You made a lot of money by embarrassing our company, and here in court you've attempted to impugn the integrity of a great man, so now—"

"Impugn the...what?" Eddie said. "Who're you talking about?"

"Mr. Trevillian, obviously. A man of enormous integrity, whose bond is his word, and you did your best to sully it. We cannot sit idly by and let that go, so now you're going to give up all the money you made unfairly. That's the price we demand for not having a jury decide against you."

Bardswith took his hands from his pockets and clasped them behind his back. "It's all or nothing, Mr. Caminetti. Anything else and you can save your breath."

Howell and Eddie, sobered by Bardswith's impassioned conviction, as well as by his total lack of fear about how the jury would rule, stayed quiet for a few seconds.

Then Eddie said to Howell, "Gimme twenty minutes upstairs with this guy."

"Won't do you any good, counselor," Bardswith assured him.

"And you can dismiss the jury," Eddie finished.

"I rather think not," Bardswith snorted.

"Go," Howell commanded. "Court'll reconvene in thutty minutes."

As the two lawyers walked out of the courtroom together, Bardswith shot Tommy Trevillian a discreet thumbs-up. *It's over!* he mouthed silently.

Trevillian made a fist and pumped it once, then rose to follow his lawyer and Eddie out of the room.

Bardswith spread himself out on a couch in the attorneys' lounge, arms thrown over the back, his body language open, receptive and unafraid. Trevillian slouched against a wall, his hands in his pockets, the very picture of confident insouciance.

Eddie stood in the middle of the room, no particular posture, no special expression, looking neither confident nor anxious, just...Eddie. But it was enough to cause a small tickle of apprehension in the other two, albeit at a sufficiently low level that neither of them recognized it as such. Maybe just a bit of free-floating unease. Maybe not.

They said nothing; it wasn't their meeting so it wasn't their move.

"I'll play you for it," Eddie said to Trevillian.

Bardswith puffed air through his nose and shifted on the couch. "Talk to *me*, counselor. Play him what, for what?"

"Play him golf. For the case."

"Right." Bardswith took his arms off the back of the couch, slapped one of the leather cushions and stood up. "Are we through here?" he said as he buttoned his jacket.

"We are if the answer's no."

"The answer's no. Come, Tommy. We've got better things to—"

"Hold it." Trevillian didn't move, but stayed pressed against the wall. "You serious, Caminetti?"

"Tommy!" Bardswith said sternly. "Don't get sucked into his game! We won by playing ours!"

"You didn't win yet," Eddie said to Trevillian, with maddening calmness.

"We will."

"Maybe." Eddie turned to the attorney. "But if you led your client into thinking the verdict is a done deal, you're guilty of—"

"I did no such thing, sir. I'm neither a fool nor a charlatan, and I—"

"Fine. So you could still lose."

"Theoretically. But I doubt it, which is the assessment I gave my client."

Eddie nodded. And waited.

"What'd you have in mind?" Trevillian asked.

"Tommy!"

"Hold it, Tyrell. What's the harm in hearing him out?"

"The harm," Bardswith answered, "is that you get hoodwinked into abandoning your case strategy and my advice."

"That assumes I'm a naïve rube from Scumbucket, Idaho, and not the CEO of the largest sporting goods company in the world. What do you think, Ty? You think Hannibal Lecter here is going to eat me alive if I listen to him?"

"Of course not. It's just that—"

"Then let the man speak. What's the harm?"

Eddie waited politely, until Bardswith shrugged and sat back down on the couch, then said, "Very simple, Tommy. I've already offered to dissolve the company, but I don't want to give you the money I made. You didn't earn it, so you don't get it."

"Not your decision, Caminetti."

"I know that. But even if I lose the case, whether or not I have to give you that money is a separate decision for the court."

"I'll grant you that."

"So the bottom line here isn't which of us wins and which loses; it's whether you and I want really want to throw our fate into the hands of twelve people who couldn't get out of jury duty or an eccentric judge who's liable to do something wacky just to make some point nobody understands."

Trevillian lifted an eyebrow and tilted his head to one side, signaling grudging agreement with what he was hearing. "But we won't get anywhere negotiating, either. We're too far apart."

"Right. So what I'm saying, two guys like us, neither of us is the kind likes to let other people call the shots for him? Let's duke it out, just you and me, the way we know best."

"You want to play a golf match to decide the case."

"Yep. That way, you're the only one responsible for how it comes out. Nobody gets to decide it for you."

Trevillian thought about it for a few seconds. "But a golf match doesn't have anything to do with who's right and who's wrong."

"Who's right and—" Eddie turned to Bardswith. "This off the record?"

"Better be," the lawyer answered. "Medalist is a publicly traded company. If shareholders knew their CEO was discussing this even in jest, they'd nail him to a cross."

"What I mean is, are we *legally* off the record."

"We are."

Eddie turned back to Trevillian. "Two world-class bullshitters like us, let's not kid each other, Tommy. You and I both know this case is a loada crap. There's no right or wrong here, just business, and business is a shark swimming around trying to eat every damned thing it comes across. It has no conscience, and it spends about as much time thinking about right and wrong when it's eating something as you do when you destroy a competitor or bring a lawsuit not because you've been wronged but because you can."

"Which is about as much thought as you gave to right or wrong when you trumped our buy-back offer." Trevillian smiled maliciously at his perfectly aimed boomerang shot.

"Well, obviously," Eddie said, spreading his hands. "You think I'm claiming to be Mother Teresa? We saw an opportunity and we went for it." He let his hands drop. "I think what pissed you off is that it's the same thing you woulda done, you'da been in my shoes."

"When I need a shrink, I'll call you." Trevillian pushed off from the wall. "What're you proposing?"

"Tommy!" Bardswith gasped. "You're not seriously considering—"

Trevillian waved him down.

Eddie stayed where he was and watched Trevillian move along the wall. "Like I said, it's simple. I already agreed to dissolve the company. We play a match for whether I get to keep my dough. Augusta's right around the corner, you're a member, so let's hop on over there and play."

Bardswith rose to his feet. "Tommy, I must impose myself here. You can't do this!"

"Why not?"

"Because you don't own Medalist, that's why! The shareholders do. You're a hired manager and there are limits to what you can do without board approval."

"I already have board approval to dispose of this case any way I see fit."

"But there was no indication that you might——"

"You're wrong there, counselor," Eddie said.

It brought the lawyer up short. "Excuse me?"

Eddie pointed to Trevillian. "If he loses the case, nobody will blame him. As a matter of fact, they'll blame *you*."

"Well, that's not necessarily——"

"So what the hell difference does it make if he lets a jury decide or decides himself? Which is essentially what he'd be doing if he played me for it."

Trevillian folded his arms across his chest. "Let's not forget that I might win."

"Well, there you go. You get all my dough and you're a big hero."

Bardswith shook his head. "If the SEC were to find out that the CEO of a Fortune 500 company gambled the fate of a major lawsuit on a——"

"They don't gotta find out," Eddie said, "unless you tell em, Bardswith. And you and I both know you can't do that."

Bardswith, momentarily nonplussed, recovered quickly. "Tommy, this is madness. I feel very strongly we'll prevail with the jury, so don't do something you'll regret."

"Your faith in my ability to win a golf match is truly touching," Trevillian said, then turned to Eddie. "My real worry is that you've got something up your sleeve. It's not like I don't know who you are. I'm not afraid to play a legitimate match, but you've never played a legitimate match in your life."

"I've never played anything *but* legitimate matches."

"Yeah, right. And I suppose you'd want strokes."

"You're at least three or four better'n me, and it's your home course. Seems only fair for you to give me strokes."

"Seems fair the way you put it, but I post every score so we know my handicap's legit. You don't even have an official one."

"Well, you got a point there," Eddie said. A small smile played around his lips, and he saw that the same was true of Trevillian, each of them acknowledging the accuracy of their respective bits of research. "But playing you straight up is nuts and you know it."

Trevillian shrugged but said nothing, leaving it to Eddie to come up with a proposed solution.

Bardswith let out a loud exhale. "I don't even want to hear this," he said, and got ready to leave.

"I think you should," Trevillian said. "Just to keep things honest. Caminetti, you have a right to a witness as well."

Eddie regarded the agitated lawyer for a second. "Nah, Bardswith's okay by me. Wrapped a little tight but I like him, and he seems trustworthy. Cept when he tells me about what integrity you have."

Trevillian smiled at the amiable jibe. Bardswith didn't. He didn't look like he'd ever be able to smile again. "If this is really what you want, Tommy," he said, "we could have done this a long time ago and saved the bother of the trial." *And not have wasted all my efforts on your behalf,* he didn't need to add.

"Not true, Tyrell. Neither of us knew how strong our case was. Had to find that out first." Trevillian turned to Eddie. "Still think we would've won, but...you never know. So, how do we want to do this?"

Eddie walked over to the window, scratching at the bottom of his chin with his thumb. "Tell you what," he said, turning to face Trevillian. "I'll play you straight up."

Trevillian, no dummy, asked, "And...?"

Eddie looked down, as though finalizing some details in his head, then looked back up. "You use a Medalist, and I use a Scratch."

"Obviously."

"We each bring only one ball."

"What?"

"You only bring one ball. Lose it, you lose the match." And he let it hang there.

"That go for both of us?"

"Yep."

A storm of implications swirled through Trevillian's mind, but every problem that he thought of disappeared when he reminded himself that they'd both be playing by the same rules.

There were, however, some details.

"What if the ball gets cut?"

"You keep playing it."

"What if it goes out of bounds?"

"Strict rules of golf. Long as you can find it, take a penalty and keep playing it."

"How much time to look?"

"Whatever you want. Five minutes okay with you?"

"Fine. What if we're even at the end of eighteen?"

"We keep playing until we're not. First guy to win a hole wins the match."

"Don't do it," Bardswith said when he sensed Trevillian had run out of questions.

"I already told you, I'm—"

Bardswith glared at his client. "It's not that, Tommy. It's him." He pointed to Eddie. "I don't trust him."

"Well, gee..." Eddie started to say.

"You said not to kid each other," Bardswith responded with great seriousness, "so let's not. You've got something in mind. Don't bother to deny it. We know a good deal about you, Mr. Caminetti, so don't try to persuade us that you're entirely on the up and up."

"Tyrell..."

Bardswith snapped his head toward Trevillian. "Tommy, don't let your ego get in the way of your judgment. Do you honestly believe that this man is going to step onto a golf course with someone of superior skill without an agenda? You may not like his business tactics but give him his due when it comes to betting on golf!"

The attorney's impassioned plea sobered Trevillian up instantly; there was no denying either the logic or the force with which it was delivered. Disappointment edged its way onto the CEO's face as the promise of some real excitement, some hand-to-hand combat—the chance to definitively *cream* this upstart sonofabitch—wafted away on the light breeze of reasoned temperance.

"Tell you what," Eddie said after Trevillian's ardor seemed all but irretrievable.

The CEO's eyebrows inched up inquisitively even as his lawyer groaned. "What?"

"Bardswith here thinks I'm an underhanded sneak." Eddie waited for some diplomatic backpedaling from the attorney, but none was forthcoming. "Thinks I got something 'up my sleeve' that you're too stupid to see coming."

"Now see here...!" Bardswith protested indignantly.

Eddie ignored him. "So if you think I pulled a fast one on you, you can call off the bet."

Trevillian waited for a follow-on that never came. "You're not serious."

"He's a witness," Eddie assured Trevillian, pointing to Bardswith, who went back into lawyer mode.

"Call it off, when?" Bardswith asked.

"Anytime he wants."

"Even if he's losing?"

"Even if he's already lost."

Now it was Bardswith's turn to be taken aback. "Pardon?"

Eddie said to Trevillian, "Anytime you think I bamboozled you, misled you in any way, anytime you think I didn't explain the bet right, or was unclear about the rules...you can call it off. No questions asked."

"Even if I already lost?"

"Yep."

"I don't get it," Bardswith said.

"Don't start that shit!" Eddie admonished crossly. "How the hell could it be any clearer? He can call it off anytime he wants!"

Bardswith was not about to be cowed by a display of anger. "And how do we know we can trust you, Caminetti? After all, you—"

"How do you know?" Eddie said, taking a step closer to Bardswith. "Because there's nothing written down and no other witnesses, that's how. There's no proof of anything, so you can always deny a bet even existed. Christ, Bardswith, you're so damned sure you're gonna win anyway, let's just go back into court and you can get your verdict."

Eddie inclined his head toward Trevillian. "Now me, on the other hand, I got nothing. Nothing except your client's integrity. I don't even have my own witness to tell my side of the story if you guys decide to fuck me, so I ask you—"

He stepped back and regarded the two of them for a moment, then held out his hands. "What the hell do you possibly have to lose?"

On the way out of the attorneys' lounge, all the way down to the court to ask Judge Howell for a one-day continuance, on the way out of the building and into the parking lot, Tyrell Bardswith tried to talk his client out of making a terrible mistake, and failed.

He'd known for a certainty he was going to fail, but gave it the old college try anyway, knowing that if the story ever came out, he'd need to be able to say he did everything in his power to dissuade Trevillian from a course of action that was not only ill advised on the face of it, regardless of whether he eventually won or lost, but was also in direct contravention of half a dozen SEC regulations and a host of state laws as well.

In fairness, though, it must be said that Bardswith argued not just to cover himself but out of the conviction that this was wrong and that Eddie had already perpetrated a swindle, albeit a subtle one, by appealing directly to Trevillian's ego and indirectly threatening his manhood. Since preservation of his manhood, or at least his perception of it, was the primary motor powering the rocket of Trevillian's success, threats to it could not be taken lightly, even if those threats were substantially meaningless.

"Listen here, Tyrell," the CEO said to Bardswith, and repeated a story he'd told countless times, in countless speaking engagements, a legendary and true tale in which the head of a then-fledgling package delivery company a day away from bankruptcy took what little corporate cash was left and hit the craps tables in Vegas, winning enough in one night to make the week's payroll.

"That's real balls, Tyrell," he concluded, aiming a remote at his Mercedes and getting the familiar *squirnch-whoop-nyurk* in reply. He liked to drive himself once in a while instead of using one of his many limos, so that everyone knew he was a man of the people. How many of those people drove a virtually priceless, original (if you didn't count the upgraded electric door locks) 1952 Mercedes SL 300 prototype was beside the point.

"One-on-one, him against the table. Guy saves the company, then goes on to build it into the biggest of its kind in the world."

"Great story, Tommy," Bardswith said as he pulled open the gull-wing door. "Only thing is, if he'd have lost that money, he'd still be in jail today."

"Well, he isn't, and he was counting on luck." Trevillian got into the driver's seat but didn't shut the door. "I'm not. I can beat this guy."

"You're going to spend more time trying not to lose your ball than scoring."

"So's he, remember? And I got a little trick up my own sleeve."

"What might that be?"

"You just get Gerry Agnormo and that prick Carmichael on the phone. Get em both over to my hotel by six."

"What for?"

"They've both played against Caminetti. Now they're going to tell me how to play him."

Bardswith had to admit it wasn't a bad idea. "But Carmichael? For heaven's sake, Tommy. You as much castrated the man after that business with him using a Scratch ball in competition. What makes you think—"

"We'll forgive him," Trevillian said as he swung his legs into the cramped cockpit of the racing legend. "We'll run a whole campaign around him coming home to Medalist after abandoning that scratchy-ass piece of shit."

"I don't—"

"Business is business." Trevillian motioned for the lawyer to take his hands away before the door came down. "You want to hold sophomoric grudges, become a prizefighter. Me, I got a corporation to run, so just get Carmichael here ASAP."

"What if he won't come?"

"Turn down an opportunity to stick it to Eddie Caminetti?" Trevillian pulled down the gull-wing door and yanked the seatbelt across his chest. "Gimme a fuckin break."

TROON McALLISTER

"**What Caminetti does,**" Gerry Agnormo said, "he doesn't so much beat you as let you beat yourself."

Robert Carmichael grunted contemptuously. "Don't go gettin all mystical, Gerry. He's a two-bit hustler with a bag fulla tricks. Plays with your head but it's not like he's a mind reader." He turned to Trevillian. "His only advantage is that he's pulled all his bullshit thousands of times, but the other guy's never seen it before and gets blindsided. You figure out in advance what he's got up his sleeve, he's dead meat."

Agnormo set down his glass of Lagavulin scotch and leaned forward on his deep leather chair. "There's always a trick," he said. "Well, maybe not a trick exactly, but there's always something about the situation he's aware of and you're not, but it's something you could have figured out if you'd just thought about it a little."

They were in the Ritz-Carlton suite at the hotel of the same name, a thirteen-hundred-square-foot plot of pure luxury with a marbled entryway, master and guest bedrooms, and a bath with an extravagant garden tub. The three of them were gathered around a coffee table in the spacious living room, opposite a baby grand piano perched elegantly in front of a huge bay window with a panoramic view of downtown Atlanta.

"I'm not worried about tricks," Trevillian said. "He said I could call off the bet if I thought he'd tricked me."

"He always does that," Agnormo said. "But it's meaningless. Whatever kind of shady tripe he's up to, one thing you can bank on with Eddie is that he's the most honest bloody swindler you'll ever meet in your life. He never lies, and I mean never."

"Don't make him out to be a saint," Carmichael said. "He's low-class scum, pure and simple, and he's always got an angle."

"But he's serious about calling off the bet?"

"Hundred percent," Agnormo assured Trevillian.

The CEO waited to hear from Carmichael, who grudgingly said, "Yeah, whatever."

Agnormo cast him a reproving glance. "Not 'whatever,' Robert. You know that good and damned well."

They both knew that Carmichael had refused to honor a losing bet with Eddie several days before the infamous Ryder Cup tournament. Eddie, a far inferior golfer to Carmichael, had nevertheless won the match, and done so in front of a handful of witnesses, all of them members of the U.S. Ryder Cup team. When they'd started up a storm of protest over Carmichael's shockingly unsportsmanlike conduct, Eddie himself had put an immediate stop to it, pointing out that his guarantee was sacred and inviolate, and if Carmichael didn't want to pay up, he didn't have to.

"So when you say he pulls tricks," Trevillian asked, "like what kind of tricks?"

"He once bet a guy he could par a hole even if he teed off from the roof of the loo at some muni in South Florida," Agnormo answered. "And he did."

"So what was the trick?"

"He'd been hitting tee shots off the top of that shithouse for three days. Hundreds of em, until he had it down cold."

Trevillian thought it over for a few seconds. "Nothing says he had to tell the guy that. All he said was that he could do it, right?"

"That's the point with this con man," Carmichael said. "He doesn't lie; he just doesn't tell you the whole truth."

"Well, let's get back to my match tomorrow morning." Trevillian signaled to the butler in the kitchenette to begin preparing dinner. "Been going over it in my head for the past hour and I'm damned if I can see a trap anywhere."

"Straight match play, nobody gets strokes?" Carmichael asked.

"And you have to make sure you're not the first to lose a ball?" Agnormo added.

"That's it. Way I see it, it's all about strategy. How do you win holes without taking too many chances? What I can't figure out is why that strategy would be any different for Caminetti than me."

"It can't be," Carmichael agreed. "You each have to play conservative as hell, hoping the other guy makes mistakes."

"And if *he* doesn't," Agnormo observed, "at some point you either gotta get aggressive or go into overtime and keep waiting it out. Only problem is..."

"What?" Trevillian prompted him.

"Eddie's the one came up with this format. Means he's got something in mind. No way Eddie Caminetti bides his time and waits for luck to decide the outcome."

"That's the thing right there!" Trevillian shook his finger at the Kiwi and rose from his chair. "I *know* that! Whatever else that weasely little prick is, he's not stupid and he doesn't take chances." He turned away and walked toward the piano. "So what the hell's up his sleeve?"

"I'll tell you what," Carmichael said. "He'll play with your head, that's what. He'll make noise, or get you thinking about something that'll upset your game, or give you bad advice you didn't ask for or shuffle his feet in your backswing or—"

"Bullshit," Agnormo declared.

"Whadda you mean, bullshit?" Carmichael demanded.

"I mean, you're full of shit, Robert. You ever seen him do any-a those things?"

"I've never seen him do a lot of things. He's pulled cons on thousands of people—including you, buddy boy—and none of them had ever seen what he did until he did it to *them*."

Agnormo looked away from Carmichael to address Trevillian directly. "It won't be that, Tommy. He's polite to a fault, and his etiquette is flawless."

"Thought you said he screamed in your ear."

"He did."

"You call that polite?"

"He had my permission."

"That's what he said in court! You mean he wasn't kidding?"

The Kiwi shook his head. "Long story. Fact is, he proposed something, I accepted it, and he kicked my bum."

"You pay him?"

"Course I paid him." Agnormo sensed some uncomfortable shifting from Carmichael, and decided he'd better get off that topic. They were here to help Trevillian, not resurface old gripes. "But you can forget about him purposely rattling you. You tell him to stay quiet, he'll not say a word for four hours."

"Then I don't get it. Are we really going to play a straight match? What's he got in mind?"

Carmichael looked down at his glass of beer, uneasy at having been summoned by a man he'd embarrassed acutely on national television and now unable to come up with anything useful.

"I'll tell you exactly what he's got in mind, Tommy," Agnormo said.

Trevillian dropped down onto the piano bench, sitting sideways facing the other two. "I'm listening."

"You're not gonna like it, mate."

"Don't fart around, Gerry. I pay you too much goddamned money for you to soft-soap me. What's the deal?"

Agnormo picked up his scotch, took a small sip and set it back down. "He's gonna bank on you tripping over your own dick when your ego gets in the way."

Trevillian kept his features even, betraying neither indignation nor offense. He was man enough to take criticism, even when he knew such criticism was utterly unwarranted and misplaced, like it was now. "Meaning what?"

"Meaning, you play golf like your manhood was at stake, except that you don't measure the size of your *schvanz* by the final score but by how many hero shots you can pull off."

Trevillian tried to relax his jaw, which was threatening to break a few of his teeth if he didn't lighten up. "Really."

In for a penny... "You like to hit em long, you like to blast your way out of tight spots instead of sacrificing a stroke and getting out safely, you like to hit over lakes Derek Anouilh wouldn't attempt. You get more satisfaction out of guys in the clubhouse talking about miracle shots you've made rather than how well you scored. Fact is, Tommy"—Agnormo picked up his drink again—"if you got a grip on your ego, you could be on the tour."

As Carmichael tried to remember which voodoo incantation would allow him to shrink to the size of an atom so he could slip down between the threads of the upholstery, Trevillian stared at one of the most popular superstars in the Medalist stable and tried to decide the best grip to use in heaving him through the bay window so he'd wind up as a jellied lump down on Peachtree Street.

The Kiwi saw no need to make Trevillian acknowledge the harsh critique he'd just delivered. The point hadn't been made to embarrass the man, but to help him. "What makes Caminetti such a good match player isn't that he's such a great golfer. Lotta guys are better, and not just tour players. But one-on-one?" Agnormo shook his head admiringly.

"Why?" Trevillian asked, when he finally thought he might be able to hold his voice steady.

"He has infinite patience and zero ego. Caminetti doesn't care if you think he's a horse's ass, a pussy or a complete fucking idiot. It doesn't matter to him."

He could tell Trevillian wasn't buying it, so he went in for the kill. "Tommy, this guy purposely blew the last putt of the Ryder Cup in front of two hundred million people on worldwide television just to pull off a hustle only he knew was even happening."

Carmichael came back to life. "He did that on *purpose?*"

"Stone the bloody crows, Robert...of course he did! And less than two years later he had enough scratch to buy an entire island and turn it into the most exclusive golf club in the solar system."

He looked back up at Trevillian. "He's as steady as the tides, Tommy. He doesn't make mistakes, he's incapable of getting rattled, and there's not a damned thing you can do to pull him out of his game. He doesn't give a rat's ass what you think of him, and that attitude makes him invulnerable. On the other hand, if *you* show even the slightest sign of weakness, give him any opening at all to tweak your ego or challenge your manhood, he'll eat you alive and spit you out before you get to the fourteenth hole. And he'll do it without saying a single word."

Trevillian absorbed what was obviously the raw truth being flung at him, then took a deep breath and let it out slowly. "So how do I play him?

Way you make it sound, I'm dead before it even starts."

Agnormo tapped his fingers on his knee. "Actually," he said, his torso rocking slightly, "if you keep your emotions out of it, Caminetti's the one who's dead before you even start."

Trevillian felt something electric wriggle its way up his spine. "How do you figure?"

"Pretty bloody simple, when you think about it." As though coming to some final determination, he stopped tapping his fingers and sat up a little straighter. "You're a better golfer than he is, Tommy. Don't fall for his bullshit and you'll beat him."

Trevillian nodded slowly, then went still again. "But I've never played like this before. Worrying about losing a ball and not quite knowing what shots to hit."

The Kiwi smiled broadly. "May be the best thing that ever happened to you, old friend. You force yourself not to play like it was the charge of the light brigade, you'll not only stomp all over Caminetti, you might even shoot the best round of your life."

Trevillian smiled for the first time that afternoon. "Believe me, if it's my company on the line and not my own wallet, I can do what I gotta do. Thing is, like I said"—he sobered up as his mind jumped ahead to the actual match—"I've never had to play a round like that. Entirely different strategy. What do I do...make it up as I go along?"

"No," Carmichael ventured. He was desperate to help Trevillian out, to get back into his good graces and recover his lucrative endorsement contract. "Just the opposite, Tommy."

"Meaning...?"

"We plan every single shot you're going to take. We anticipate every mistake you might make and exactly what you're going to do about every one."

"More than that," Agnormo added. "We also figure out what Caminetti's likely to do on every one of his shots, and what you do when it works and when it doesn't."

"I like it," Trevillian declared, relieved at the sudden lifting of the burden he'd been anticipating of playing against Eddie with no clear plan in mind.

"You know," Carmichael said, now on a roll with his new best buddy, "you're not just a better golfer than that dickwad, you'll be playing on your home course."

"Huge advantage," Agnormo agreed.

"Yeah!"

"He ever played there at all?" Carmichael asked.

"Once," Trevillian answered. "With Brad Baffington."

"The FBI director?" Carmichael said, impressed.

Trevillian nodded. "Kind of how all of this started, come to think of it."

"All of what?" Carmichael asked.

"The FBI busting up that golf ball counterfeiting ring." Trevillian got a faraway look in his eyes and his voice took on a trace of wistfulness. "You know, if it wasn't for Caminetti tipping off Baffington, it might never have gotten discovered at all."

An awkward silence settled over the little gathering, each man lost in his own thoughts.

It was broken when Agnormo slammed his hand onto the coffee table so hard the glass top rattled and Carmichael's beer fell over. The butler came running out to see what was the matter, then went back to fetch a towel.

"Goddamnit!" Agnormo barked to his flustered colleagues. "This is just the kind of shit I've been warning you about!"

He stood up as the butler came back to mop up the spilled beer. "What, you feel *sorry* for the conniving bastard now? Think he did your company a favor by getting the FBI involved?"

When he got no answer he plowed in further. "He did that to protect himself, not you. And when you tried to serve the interests of your customers, he barged in and hijacked your strategy." Agnormo stepped over and bent down, putting his face less than a foot from Trevillian's. "That's why you sued him, f'chrissakes!"

"I know that, Gerry! What're you getting so steamed about?"

"I'll tell you what!" Agnormo shot back, straightening up. "The sonofabitch isn't even *here* and you're already letting him fuck with your head!"

He sat back down and gripped Trevillian's eyes with his own. "He's the enemy, Tommy. He's trying to beat you out of God knows how many millions of dollars, he's banking on your vanity to help him do it, he'll stomp on your balls if you let him, so don't you think about a single goddamned thing except how to do it to him before he does it to you, get me? I don't care if he asks about your kids, or compliments you on a great shot or tells you how cool your fucking shoes are. It's all bullshit, every bit of it, and if you let any of it get to you, you deserve to go back to slinging steel in Pittsburgh."

Trevillian wasn't used to being spoken to like this, not by anybody. But this was no time to stand on ceremony, especially not when Agnormo was only trying to help him.

"I hear you, Gerry."

Agnormo looked skeptical.

"Tyrell Bardswith's gonna carry my bag," Trevillian added. "He'll keep me on an even keel."

Agnormo nodded in approval. "Who's carrying Eddie's?"

"Eddie is."

"Figures. Okay: Let's eat and figure out what you're gonna do."

Trevillian waved to the butler to begin serving, and as they got up to move to the dining table, he said, "We got—" and glanced at his watch.

But before he could figure out how much time they had, Carmichael interrupted him. "What time're you playing?"

"Seven. Gotta be back in court by one."

"Then we break at ten o'clock tonight, no matter what."

"But—"

"He's right," Agnormo said. "Full night's sleep is more important than anything we're gonna decide here."

"Okay," Trevillian conceded. "But we work over dinner."

For four solid hours they analyzed, discussed, debated and argued. Trevillian took notes, tore them up, took more notes, set them aside, came back to them later, kept some, revised others.

All three were intimately familiar with the layout at Augusta National, Trevillian because he was a member, Agnormo and Carmichael because they'd played in the Masters fourteen times between them and, as touring pros, had privileges to play the famed course whenever they wanted to.

If they were missing some piece of information, Trevillian used his corporate switchboard, which he'd kept on late, to put him in touch with whoever had it.

"What's the cutting schedule on number eight?" he asked the grounds superintendent at Augusta at about 6:30, then held his hand over the receiver as he said, "The fairway was done this morning, green before dawn tomorrow."

"Ask him when they're gonna water it," Carmichael instructed.

"Not until the afternoon," came the reply.

Carmichael nodded. "Fresh cut and dry. Gonna be tough to hold on a long approach."

"Yeah." Agnormo made a note as Trevillian hung up the phone. "Now, like we already said, Caminetti may never have hit a tee shot over two-fifty in his entire life, but—"

"He puts it smack down the center every time," Carmichael finished for him. "Expect it, and don't worry about it."

"Even when he makes birds," Agnormo said, "don't let him suck you into playing a different game than we planned. He's gonna win a few holes, sure, but so are you. The rest you're gonna halve, and there'll be a lot of those. Just don't worry about any of it."

"Yeah. I stick to the plan. No heroics."

"Exactly. You've never seen a more conservative player than Caminetti. Only time he makes birds is when they fall into his lap because he made a great approach or accidentally sinks a long putt. He'll never take a chance to do it, though, never hit outside the envelope of what he knows for sure he can do. He's gonna bank on you being the one to make mistakes, so no matter what..."

"I stick to the plan."

"That's the ticket."

"Say..." Carmichael pointed to Trevillian's cell phone. "Call your guy and find out where the pins are gonna be set tomorrow."

Trevillian picked up the phone but said slyly as he dialed, "You just tell me where we *want* them set."

And so it went.

At nine o'clock Carmichael tossed his pencil onto the table. "That's it," he announced. "We got one hour to review and then we're out of here."

"But we're only through the sixteenth hole," Trevillian objected.

"Doesn't matter. You're never gonna get past sixteen. You gotta get some z's and we need an hour to go back over all of this, so let's do it. Number one hole." He pulled off the first sheet in the neat stack next to him and placed it in front of Trevillian.

"I can barely reach that bunker on my best day," the CEO said, "so it's no factor. Three-wood, then five-wood to the green, anywhere. Chip or putt close for a par opportunity, settle for bogey if I have to."

"But..." Carmichael prompted.

"I'm gonna let Eddie hit first. He does his usual two-fifty- down-the-middle bullshit."

"I'd give my left nut to see his face when you hit three-wood insteada driver!" Carmichael chortled. "Poor sonofabitch is gonna shit a brick."

Agnormo smiled and nodded. "Probably won't sleep a wink thinking about the nine different ways you're gonna self-destruct. He sees you taking it easy like that, soil his bloody drawers, he will."

The three laughed in anticipation of that moment, then Carmichael suddenly sat up straight. "Damn, you know what? I got an idea."

"Little late for revisions there, Carmichael," Trevillian said.

"No, no, listen to this." Carmichael looked at Agnormo. "Let Caminetti win the first hole."

Agnormo's face became expressionless. Then the smile came back. "You slinky bastard!"

Trevillian laughed despite his puzzlement. "What the hell are you guys talking about?"

By now Agnormo was too excited to let Carmichael explain his own idea. "Listen, Tommy: Caminetti's gonna plant a safe one down the middle, then go for the green on his second shot. Odds are about ninety-five percent he's gonna make it. Then what you do?"

"You lay up," Carmichael said.

"Lay up?" Trevillian exclaimed. "I don't go for the green?"

"No!" the two pros chimed in unison.

"Even if he's four feet from the fuckin flag," Carmichael continued, heedless of his inadvertent alliteration, "you just put your second shot close, then chip up."

"But why?"

"Because right away the slimy scumbag sees you've got a plan, and he sees there isn't shit he can do to shake you off it!"

"Thinks he's got you figured, Tommy." A gleeful tone crept into Agnormo's voice as he drove home the point. "Thinks you're gonna play like Rambo while he fiddle-farts his way around the course just waiting for you to shoot yourself in the head."

"Rattle his ass good, boy," Carmichael said with undisguised malice. "*He'll* be the one scrambling for a midcourse correction."

"Fuckin A," Trevillian agreed with equal venom as he caught on. "Let's go to the second hole."

"He starts with another boring safe one down the center..." Agnormo began, reaching for the next sheet.

CHAPTER TWENTY-NINE

THE FIRST TEE, AUGUSTA NATIONAL GOLF CLUB
THE NEXT MORNING

Eddie accepted the invitation to tee off first and leaned into his shot with such violent power it seemed a wonder his back didn't snap apart, and as his ball screamed along the left side of the fairway and began fading back to the right on its way to setting down just short of the bunker that was three hundred yards away, Tommy Trevillian's bowels turned to mush and scrambled to make room for other organs about to do the same.

What was left of his brain was just enough to keep him breathing—barely—so while he thought he heard Eddie say something, he couldn't be certain, and sure as hell he had no idea what it was.

"Tommy?" Bardswith prodded him gently.

"*Fnyrklpft*," Trevillian muttered unintelligibly as Eddie picked up his tee and headed back their way.

Eddie took a towel from the side of his bag and began wiping his driver. "What I said was, just because we have a few bucks on the line doesn't mean we can't be civil. I hit a nice shot." He looked out at the fairway, then back at Trevillian. "It's okay to say so."

Trevillian tried to swallow but it was like drawing sandpaper across a piece of rubber. "Nice shot," he croaked.

"Thanks," Eddie said amiably, then held a hand out toward the tee box.

For all the good Trevillian's legs were doing him as he tried to move, they might as well have been ropes. He put a hand to his face. "Can I get a minute? Something in my eye..."

"Damn," Eddie said. "Want me to fish it out for you?"

"Huh? Oh. No, no. Just..."

Eddie dropped his club into his bag, put his hands up in the air and stepped away. "Take your time, Tommy. I'm in no rush. Hell," he said, smiling at Bardswith, "not every day a schlump like me gets to play Augusta!"

Bardswith smiled back weakly and turned to help Trevillian. "Grab your eyelid, pull it out and—"

"There's nothing wrong with my goddamned eye, you idiot!" Trevillian whispered hoarsely.

"Then what—"

"Did you see that shot he hit!"

"Looked like a good one."

"A good one?" Trevillian turned his head to see how the lawyer was enjoying his first trip to this galaxy. "A *good* one?"

Bardswith had no idea what the problem was, but he'd spoken with Agnormo and Carmichael and knew what he was supposed to do. "Come on, Tommy," he said, patting his client on the back. "Just get back to the strategy."

"What about *him!*" Trevillian jerked a thumb over his shoulder, indicating Eddie. "Tell *him* to follow the fucking strategy!"

But there was no sense taking it out on Bardswith, and no sense falling apart either, so Trevillian pretended to swipe at his eye for a few more seconds while he tried to get hold of himself.

Gerry Agnormo and Robert Carmichael had spent four hours telling him Eddie Caminetti was at heart a wimp who always played it safe and never took unnecessary chances. But on his very first shot of the day, in a match in which a lost ball meant disaster, the wimp had smashed the living daylights out of his ball and blown it nearly three hundred yards down the fairway, a shot so daring and dramatic Derek Anouilh himself wouldn't have attempted it unless he was down by ten on the last day of a major tournament and had nothing to lose.

Now what?

Trevillian forced himself to think rationally. Caminetti wasn't that good a golfer, and he wasn't stupid. What the hell could he be thinking?

Something that the Kiwi had said, something insulting. *He's gonna bank on you tripping over your own dick when your ego gets in the way.*

Which it was trying to do right now. Even as Trevillian fought to figure this situation out, he found himself thinking about taking his driver and trying to equal Eddie's shot. Two minutes into the match and already he was on the verge of abandoning the strategy mapped out for him by two of the best pro golfers in the world, both of whom had played against Caminetti themselves and had seen him in action against others.

Well, no way was he going to let this sonofabitch do that to him.

As that realization dawned Trevillian first berated himself for being such a dope, then began to relax as the familiar pieces of his world settled comfortably back into place.

Blinking rapidly as though rewatering his eyes, he turned back toward the tee box, spotted his crafty opponent standing respectfully to the side, and said, "Sorry, Eddie. Didn't even see it. You get a good one?"

"Real good one. Sorry you missed it."

"Me, too." Trevillian took out the driver he had no intention of using, and began walking toward the tee. "Where'd you end up?"

"Almost in that bunker."

Trevillian purposefully faltered, and twisted around toward Eddie. "The bunker? You gotta be shitting me!"

"Nope. Got every piece-a that one."

"Well, I'll be goddamned." Trevillian looked at his driver for a few seconds, hoping that Eddie would notice, then walked back to his bag and exchanged it for a three-wood. On the tee he waggled the club a few times, making sure Eddie saw what it was, then knocked a clean one 230 yards down the middle of the fairway. It was simple, workable and safe, a chicken-shit shot of the first order, and he was damned proud of it. And of himself.

Nothing fancy, Trevillian's whole demeanor said casually as he walked off the tee. *Just keep it in play and see what happens.*

He couldn't help but sneak a peek back at Eddie, and was delighted to be met with a look of utter bewilderment and perhaps a trace of fear. They trooped out onto the fairway in silence, Eddie with his head down and his gait stiff. Trevillian looked around, admiring the olive trees for which this hole was named, enjoying the morning sun. Brimming with confidence, he took his five-wood and, as planned, plopped his ball safely in front of the green, looking completely unconcerned as Eddie leaned into a pitching wedge, went straight for the stick, and brought his ball to a dead stop less than six feet from the flag.

"Beauty!" Trevillian said cheerfully.

"Thanks," Eddie mumbled listlessly.

Trevillian purposely chipped short, landing two feet further from the hole than Eddie. "Oh, well," he said with convivial good cheer. "Guess I'm gonna show you the line." He then two-putted for a bogey, and, as Eddie bent over his own putt, said, "Pick it up, buddy."

Eddie looked up in surprise, but Trevillian said, "No way you're gonna take more'n two putts. Why go through the motions?"

"Well...thanks, then." Eddie picked up his ball and they walked off the green, Eddie in the lead by one.

Having won, Eddie had the honors on number two, and hit a safe, wimpy, boring three-wood that confirmed in Trevillian's joyfully leaping heart his wisdom, his cool under fire and his imminent trumping of Eddie Big-Goddamned-Deal Caminetti.

At least that's what was supposed to happen. What actually did happen was that Eddie nearly came out of his shoes as he once again used his driver and smashed the crap out of the ball.

This time, Trevillian refused to worry about it at all. *Fine. Keep that shit up and see how long it takes to lose your ball*. He once again put his own shot safely in the fairway with his three-wood and then used the five to get comfortably within one-fifty of the green.

It was when Eddie hauled off with a three-wood and landed twenty yards from the green that Trevillian began to wonder if perhaps he was missing something here. Eddie chipped beautifully and sank his six-foot putt for a birdie. Trevillian missed his forty-footer and was down by two after two holes.

Number three was only 350 yards long. Nobody in his right mind would take a risky tee shot on such a short hole, which was why Trevillian had some trouble understanding why Eddie ripped into yet another drive with everything he had. He made par, but so did Trevillian, and then they went on to halve the next two holes as well.

The sixth was a dangerous par-three, the flag set nearly on the front edge of the green, just a few feet from a bunker. The only reasonable shot was to play for the center of the green, as Agnormo and Carmichael had decided the night before, but Eddie teed his ball up high and whacked it with a five-iron, an absurdly risky shot that barely cleared the sand trap, then trickled toward the hole and almost dropped in.

"I love this game," he said, looking around for his tee. Unable to find it, he gave up and cleared off to let Trevillian hit.

With a sure birdie for his opponent and no real danger of losing his ball here, Trevillian decided there was nothing to be lost by throwing caution to the wind. Anything less than a two on this hole and he'd lose anyway, so he did the same thing as Eddie: teed it up high to get some loft and just went for it.

He pulled it horribly and it disappeared into the woods left of the green.

Stunned, he stood there, not quite knowing what to do next.

"You'll find it," Eddie said encouragingly as he hoisted up his bag and began walking.

"What did you say you had?" Bardswith asked as he lifted his client's bag. "Five minutes?"

Trevillian nodded miserably.

"Then shouldn't we get moving?"

"The five minutes doesn't start until we get there," Trevillian answered, handing his lawyer the iron.

Then he saw Eddie set down his bag near the green and walk into the woods.

"Shit!" Trevillian hissed.

"What?" Bardswith asked.

"If he finds my ball first, he'll stomp on it and make it disappear!"

Bardswith sped up, alternating running and walking in an awkward half-canter that made the clubs on his back rattle noisily. He dropped the bag without standing it up and hurried into the trees, keeping his eyes on Eddie, ready to pounce in an instant if—

"Got it!" Eddie cried.

Bardswith stumbled to a normal walk. "Say again?"

"Right over here, Tommy!" Eddie yelled past him. He pointed down and grinned. "And you won't believe this but the damned thing's playable!"

The lawyer turned toward his boss and raised his eyebrows. Trevillian only shrugged in response.

"Hey, Bardswith!" Eddie said. "Hand him a seven-iron. Bet he can punch this sucker right on up to the green."

Trevillian took the club from Bardswith as he passed by him. He drew up to where Eddie was standing. Sure enough, the ball was sitting up high on some wet leaves and there was a fairly clean line to the green.

Eddie walked out of the trees and out of Trevillian's line of sight, watching as his opponent gauged the distance and the angle, got himself lined up and swung.

It was a fine shot, but when Trevillian got to the green and saw Eddie's ball only a foot from the pin, he bent down and picked up his ball, conceding the hole.

As they walked to the next tee, Trevillian reviewed in his mind what was happening. It wasn't a difficult analysis.

Caminetti wasn't sticking to the strategy Trevillian had been assured he would be following. He wasn't playing like the Eddie Caminetti everybody thought they knew.

He was playing like a goddamned lunatic. And he was getting away with it.

Trevillian, on the other hand, was adhering to his safe strategy, and was now down by three. Unless something changed, he'd safely lose the match and his lawsuit by the thirteenth or fourteenth hole.

Surely Caminetti couldn't keep this up forever. Some tough holes were coming up, and water too, which made the loss of a ball a real danger. No way he could keep it up.

Number seven was an absurdly narrow, dead-straight hole with pine trees squeezing in from both sides. After the broad expanses of the first few holes, it looked like a funnel drop in a carnival fun house. *Nobody* hit driver on this nasty, claustrophobic beast.

Eddie did, and he nailed it. Trevillian gritted his teeth and stuck gamely with his three-wood. Now, with 190 left to go, he had to contend with the five vicious sand traps guarding the green, into one of which he landed with an ignominious thud. Eddie, needing to cover a mere 130 yards, smoothed a pitching wedge to within ten feet of the hole.

Trevillian hit a brilliant sand shot and one-putted for par. Eddie two-putted and they halved the hole.

"Lovely," Eddie complimented his opponent. "One sweet touch out of the sand, that."

"Thanks" was all Trevillian, gloomy and rattled, could manage.

Eddie launched another rocket on number eight and Trevillian smacked his hand angrily on the side of his leather bag. "I'm getting murdered!" he spat through clenched teeth.

"Don't let him get to you," Bardswith said, handing him the three-wood.

"Get to me?" Trevillian said, turning on his attorney. "He's up by three goddamned holes, f'chrissakes! You want me to stay cool and calm and let him rip my balls off?"

"He can't keep this up, Tommy. Sooner or later one of those shots is going to get away from him and—"

"Maybe it will and maybe it won't! And what am I gonna do in the meantime...sit on my ass and leave it up to *him* to decide how this comes out?"

Eddie's words came back to him in a flood. He couldn't recall them exactly, but it had something to do with letting other people decide your fate while you sat around and watched. Wasn't that the very sentiment that had gotten him to agree to this match in the first place?

And yet here he was, watching helplessly as this lowlife asshole took him apart bone by bone, laughing and grinning and having a good old time as Trevillian stuck to a half-assed strategy that—

He looked around suddenly, feeling as though a light had gone on in his brain, even though he wasn't yet sure exactly what it had illuminated.

"What's wrong?" Bardswith asked. "I mean, other than the obvious."

What was wrong? Trevillian hardly knew where to begin. Or how to sort out the thoughts streaming through his head. Words, pictures and random bits of memory floated around in a chaotic mess, then suddenly receded, leaving only one concept glowing at the center of his consciousness: He was mindlessly sticking to a strategy that was based on the wrongest goddamned set of assumptions since the Bay of Pigs.

"Tommy?"

Every single thing he and his pros had discussed the night before had been based on Caminetti playing his usual, steady, conservative game, a game that bore no resemblance whatsoever to the one the hustler had been playing since his very first shot of the day.

As Trevillian liked to say to his division heads, with the kind of home-spun wisdom for which he would like to have been known, *If what you're doing isn't working, do something else.*

"Give me the driver, Tyrell."

"The driver? But I thought you were supposed to—"

"Goddamnit, Tyrell, I don't have time for this!" he barked, and took the club out of the bag himself.

Bardswith grabbed his arm. "Tommy, listen. I know what's going on here. I may not play the game but after fifteen years with Medalist I understand it well enough. So give me two damned minutes, would you?"

It was a reasonable request, and Eddie wasn't rushing them, so Trevillian stopped and faced his lawyer.

"All you have to do is wait him out," Bardswith said. "There's no way in hell Caminetti can keep this up."

"I'm down three holes, Tyrell."

"Doesn't matter if you're down thirteen! Soon as he loses a ball, he loses the match. All you have to do is wait for it to happen. *He can't keep this up!*"

Maybe Bardswith was right, that all they had to do was wait it out. The logic of it certainly seemed unassailable. After all, not even a pro could pull off what Eddie was trying to pull off, not at Augusta, and Eddie wasn't close to being a tour-class player. So the odds of his being able to keep this up had to be vanishingly small.

Trevillian eventually nodded his acquiescence and accepted a three-wood. He hit a nice shot and a few minutes later managed to halve the hole. Maybe they were on to something here.

Trevillian and Bardswith sneaked surreptitious little smiles at each other as they walked to the ninth hole, a 460-yard par four with a slight dogleg left. Trevillian started to feel a little better about the world, and shifted his shoulders around to try to ease the tension that had been building up. Bardswith jauntily tossed him his three-wood and they both jauntily tossed good wishes to Eddie, who was already on the tee box and looked up in surprise at the sudden outpouring of congenial camaraderie.

"Ah, what the hell," Trevillian said. "Beautiful day, beautiful course...what's the point, couple of guys can't have a little fun, am I right or am I right?"

"Right as rain, Tommy," Eddie replied.

Then he hit an ordinary, wimpy, boring, *safe* shot down the middle with his three-wood, and Trevillian felt his world collapse.

Bardswith soon figured it out, too, and this time he didn't need to ask his boss why he looked like he'd just swallowed a grenade as he walked grimly along the course.

Up by three holes, Eddie didn't have to take any more chances. All he was doing now was hanging on to his lead by playing a game so ultraconservative it seemed as though aliens had invaded his brain and completely reprogrammed it. Gone were the towering drives, the daredevil approach shots, the who-gives-a-shit attitude about traps and other assorted hazards. He was settling for the same pars and bogeys as Trevillian, who'd been playing that way all day long as he stubbornly refused to rise to the challenge Eddie had been flinging down at every opportunity.

After the fifteenth, Eddie was "dormie," ahead by three holes with three left to play. He could no longer lose, and Trevillian would have to win all three to force a playoff. If he lost just one, or even tied one, he'd lose the match.

The par-three sixteenth was only 170 yards over water, but Eddie picked up a six-iron, took a very easy swing and landed on the back of the green on the left side. It was the ultimate safe shot, avoiding the water and the sand traps, the goal being par and not birdie.

Trevillian didn't have that option. If they both parred, he'd lose the match. He needed a birdie to stay alive, and the real risk was playing it safe. He chose an eight-iron, needing that amount of loft to stop the ball once it struck the green, and put everything he had into his swing to get the ball far enough, hoping he could stay in control as he powered through the shot.

It worked brilliantly, and Eddie let out a low whistle when the ball came to a dead stop right where it landed, about five feet from the flag.

Eddie chipped up and one-putted, then watched as Trevillian sank his five-footer for the birdie and the win.

"Beauty," Eddie said. "Didn't think you'd make it with an eight-iron."

Trevillian didn't answer. Bardswith wasn't even sure he'd heard the compliment. On the seventeenth, Trevillian, with no real choice, leaned into his driver as hard as he ever had in his life.

The ensuing slice was horrendous. The ball struck a tree and came straight down. He got it back onto the fairway but missed the green with his next shot.

Eddie got on in two, Trevillian in four. Even if the CEO made his putt, Eddie would have to four-putt to lose, something he hadn't done since the earth cooled.

It was over.

Eddie waited on the green and offered his hand, which Trevillian took.

"Tough way to finish," Eddie said by way of condolence.

"Yeah." Trevillian let go of Eddie's hand, folded his arms and stepped back. "I think you conned me."

Eddie went stock still. Even the birds in the nearby trees seemed to have stopped moving. "What?"

"I said, you conned me."

"I conned you."

"Yeah. So I'm not paying off."

Bardswith froze in disbelief. He was about to say something but a threatening glance from Trevillian reminded him that he was still his lawyer, with obligations that transcended his client's behavior.

"Conned you how?" Eddie said. There was a subtle alteration in his voice, an undertone of menace.

"Doesn't matter," Trevillian answered, his entire posture a challenge. "No questions asked, you said. Or am I misquoting you?"

Eddie looked away, then down at the grass. "No. That's what I said."

"That's what I thought." Trevillian let his arms drop, then turned to walk away, motioning for Bardswith to follow him. "See you in court, Caminetti."

Bardswith was still in some kind of shock and didn't move. Trevillian, not sensing motion behind him, stopped and turned. "Let's go, Tyrell."

The lawyer shook his head. "I'll catch up."

Trevillian looked at him suspiciously, then let it go. "Fine," he said as he resumed walking. "Don't be late."

Eddie and Bardswith watched as Trevillian strolled away, his gait untroubled and his head held high. "Let's clear the green," Eddie said.

They picked up the bags and headed toward the clubhouse, but Bardswith stopped near a bench under a magnolia tree, unloaded his bag and sat down. "Jesus Christ," he muttered abjectly, looking as though he might begin crying any second.

Eddie set down his own bag alongside the bench and took up a seat next to the attorney. He zipped open a pocket, one of many on his bag, and withdrew a pack of cigarettes and a lighter. He held the pack out to Bardswith, who waved it away.

"I think I know what's going through your mind, Bardswith," Eddie said as he pulled a cigarette from the pack with his lips and flipped up the top of the lighter.

"Think so?"

"Uh huh." Eddie got a flame going and touched it to the tip of the cigarette, inhaling deeply. He blew out a cloud of smoke and said, "You're thinking, how could that guy I admire so much have done such a dishonorable thing."

He closed the lighter and slipped it back into the bag. "And you're feeling bad for me, because I just won the match fair and square and got stiffed, and there's nothing I can do about it. Right?"

"Something like that. And also how come you're not going ballistic."

"Yeah, well." Eddie picked a piece of tobacco from between his front teeth and flicked it away. "You want to take a guess how many times this has happened to me?"

Bardswith hadn't looked at him since they'd left the seventeenth green, and still couldn't bring himself to do so now. "A lot?"

Eddie shook his head. "Maybe two, three dozen, tops."

"Huh. Guess that makes sense."

"But you want to hear something interesting, Tyrell?"

"Sure."

Eddie looked around, absorbing the peaceful sights and breathing the fragrant air. "Not once has it ever happened that I didn't know in advance it was going to."

Now Bardswith turned to him, and regarded him full on. "You're not serious."

"I'm dead serious."

Bardswith realized his jaw was hanging open and he closed his mouth. "You knew Trevillian was going to renege on the bet?"

"Yep."

"I'm not sure I believe you."

"That's okay."

"So why'd you even bother to play him?"

"You kidding? You know how often I get to play Augusta?"

"Baloney," Bardswith said. "Now I know you're pulling my leg."

"Yeah, a little. Be honest with you, this course does nothing for me."

"So what happens now, Eddie?"

"Now?" Eddie took a last drag and got ready to flick the cigarette away before remembering where he was. As he looked around for an ashtray or a trash can, he said, "Now, we settle the case."

"I don't think so," Bardswith responded, back in lawyer mode. "We don't have any reason to do that. I won't say that I'm not embarrassed, but he's still my client, and I have an—"

"Tyrell, listena me." Eddie looked at his watch. "We gotta be back in court in about an hour, and you still needa talk to your client after we're through here, so let's not waste too much time, whaddaya say?"

Bardswith chuckled softly. "You're a real piece of work, Eddie."

"Yeah, I know. The real reason I played him this round of golf?"

Bardswith turned to look at Eddie. "Was...?"

"To see how much of a prick he really was before I told you how we're going to end this."

A startled Leif Hoogenband came into the courtroom only to find Eddie sitting alone, doing a newspaper crossword puzzle. "What the hell...?"

Eddie turned around at the sound of his voice. "Hey, Leif. 'Sup?"

"Where's Bardswith?"

"Talking to his client."

"Why?"

"That's what lawyers do. They talk to their clients."

Hoogenband made his way to the defense table and set his briefcase on it. "What's going on?"

"I told Bardswith how we're going to settle it. I guess he has to talk to Trevillian first. Not sure why."

"Because Trevillian runs the company and Bardswith's just his lawyer. It's Trevillian's call."

"Ah. That explains it. Say, what's a four-letter word meaning 'woman' that ends in u-n-t?"

Hoogenband thought about it for a second, then said, "Aunt."

"Damn. Got an eraser?"

"Caminetti...!"

Eddie grinned and put the newspaper down. "Uhrightaready. Relax, will ya? Siddown, take a load off."

There really wasn't anything else to do, so Hoogenband did as Eddie suggested. "You really agreed on something with Bardswith? You think Trevillian will go along?"

"Oh, yeah."

Clearly, Eddie wasn't planning to get into the details. And Hoogenband knew better than to press him. He opened his briefcase and began removing his papers.

"Not gonna need any-a that stuff," Eddie said.

"Maybe not, but you don't want to look cocky, like it was a foregone conclusion and you knew it all along. The idea is to win, not to rub it in the other guy's face."

Eddie thought about it for less than a second. "You're right," he said, then hauled his own briefcase up and began unloading it. The rustle of papers and the soft *whoosh-whoosh* of the ceiling fans were the only sounds in the cavernous courtroom for the next few seconds.

"What's on your mind?" Eddie asked.

"What makes you think there's anything on my—"

"You're a lawyer and you're not talking. What?"

The rear door opened and several reporters carrying notebooks came in. They took up seats in the rear row of the gallery. "Remember I asked you once why people were so obsessed with golf?" Hoogenband said.

"Sort of."

"You turned it back on me. I gave you an answer, and you said I was full of baloney."

"Did I use those words?"

"Words to that effect."

"I love that lawyer talk. 'Words to that effect.' I could get used to that."

"I think you already have." Hoogenband finished spreading out his papers and put his briefcase back on the floor. "You never gave me your own answer."

"You didn't ask."

"Now I am. And I have a guess. You think it's because of how difficult it is. The challenge. That you can never perfect your game. No such thing as rolling a three hundred or vaulting a perfect ten."

"That's sort of it. But that's not it."

"It isn't?"

"No." When Eddie had no more papers left he rubbed his hands together and sat back. "Has more to do with the fact that while the game is fiendishly difficult, it's still doable. It almost never calls on you to do something you're not capable of."

"Okaaayyy..."

"Leif, lemme ask you something." Eddie leaned forward and folded his hands on the table. "At your home club, how many of the holes have you birdied at one time or another?"

"Pretty much all of them. And a bunch of eagles to boot."

"That's what I figured. You ever run a two-thirty marathon?"

"No."

"Ever clean and jerk three hunnerd'n fifty pounds?"

"Are you crazy?"

"Ever climb Mount Everest, or broad-jump thirty-one feet, or throw a quadruple axel?"

"Eddie, what the hell are you talking about?"

"You're not too damned likely to do any of those things. None of us is likely to do anything that even remotely *approaches* any of those things."

"No shit, Eddie," Hoogenband said. "Physically impossible for all but a few."

"Exactly." As more people drifted in, Eddie lowered his voice and leaned toward his co-counsel, who subconsciously leaned forward in response. "But suppose that tomorrow morning you decide you want to go out on your home course and shoot a fifty-six. Sixteen birdies."

"Yeah, right."

"I know. Nobody's ever shot a fifty-six. And you've never even broken par."

"Well, there you go."

"But here's the thing. You're not going to do a triple-gainer or finish an Ironman, because you've never done anything like that and you know you can't. But…"

"But what?"

"If you want to go out and shoot a fifty-six tomorrow morning, you don't have to do one single thing you haven't done before. Nothing. You know you can birdie sixteen holes because you've already done it."

"Not in one round!"

"That's not the point." Eddie sat up and unfolded his hands. "The point is that you already know it's possible."

Hoogenband blinked a few times.

"Look at Oscar Petanque," Eddie said. "The guy's played about eight rounds of golf in his life. Three weeks ago we're at Shadowridge, and on the thirteenth hole, he put his second shot in the water, took a drop, hit a sand wedge eighty-five yards and put it in the hole for a par."

Hoogenband shrugged. "I believe it. Guys get lucky."

"You don't get it, Leif. If Fat Albert had made that exact same shot at the Kemper, it would have been on the nightly news all over the world. But *Oscar* made that shot. He's like a thirty-six handicap, but once in a while he can do what Fat Albert can do, or Derek Anouilh or Gerry Agnormo."

Realizing he'd tensed up a little, Eddie forced himself to relax. "When somebody's been having an absolutely crummy day, hasn't hit a single decent shot, and then on number fifteen his club, his brain, his attitude, the sky and even the grass all decide to cooperate in one phenomenal instant and he whacks the purest three-iron he's ever hit in his life, and as that ball goes rocketing off on its way to landing dead center two hundred and thirty yards away, what is it the other guys in the foursome will always say to him?"

"*That'll bring you back*," Hoogenband answered quietly.

"Exactly. That one shot *will* bring him back. Why? Because no matter how rotten a round he's having, that one perfect, blissful shot tells him that it's *possible*. If he can hit just one of those, it proves that he *can*, and there's no reason why he can't do it again. And it's that evidence, that possibility, that *hope* that springs eternal in the human heart and says to him, you know what? Tomorrow, they may *all* be like that. So every time he starts a round he's thinking, This could be the day."

"But they rarely *are* all like that."

"And people rarely win the lottery, but they still buy tickets by the billions. It's the *possibility*, see? Even if you've bought ten thousand lottery tickets and never hit the jackpot, every time you buy another one you're thinking, This could be the one. And every time you step up to the first tee, you're thinking—"

"This could be the day," Hoogenband finished for him.

"Exactly! It's not like getting underneath a four-hundred-pound barbell. That's out of the question. But on the first tee, a voice in your head is saying, You can do this. Hell, you *have* done this. All you have to do is hit the same shots you've hit before, nothing new, just do them all in the same round..." He held up his hands and let them drop. "And that's what makes golf such an addiction, Leif. It's got nothing to do with fresh air or nice views or handicapping or self-realization. It's that on any given day—"

"This could be the day," a voice behind them said softly.

They both spun around to see who'd been eavesdropping. "Fat Albert!" said Eddie, suddenly grinning. "What the hell are you doing here!"

"Thought you were over at Augusta practicing up for the PGA," Hoogenband said.

"I am," Auberlain replied. "It's only three miles from here. Took a quick break when I heard a rumor this all was gonna end. So? Is it?"

"Yeah," Eddie said.

"Izzat good or bad?"

"Don't worry about it. Gonna be okay."

"You sure?"

"Absolutely. Go on back and work on your game."

"Eddie..."

"Trust me, Albert. Go."

Court reconvened a few minutes later. Bardswith, looking as though he was in the midst of a full-blown psychotic episode, sat at the plaintiff's table, trembling visibly. Trevillian, in a similar state of shock, stared straight ahead from his seat in the third pew behind the bar, looking like he was trying not to throw up.

Eddie entered one more word into his crossword puzzle and tucked the newspaper inside his briefcase.

"Barnyard, you okay?" Judge Howell asked when he'd taken the bench.

Bardswith rose shakily to his feet. "We...um, that is, the two...the parties have reached a settlement, your honor." The stricken attorney was addressing the top of the table rather than the front of the room.

"Say what?" the judge asked.

"Awaiting only the approval of the court," Bardswith concluded before resuming his seat.

Howell bent his head forward and looked at Caminetti, skeptically, over the top of his reading glasses. "You guys *settled?*"

"Yes, your honor."

Howell waved both attorneys to the bench. When they arrived, he said to Eddie, "I best not hear you sold yer client down the river fer two hunnerd bucks."

"I *am* my client, remember?"

"Oh, yeah. Fergot."

Bardswith said, "What two hundred bucks?"

"Never mind," the judge replied, taking off his glasses. "So what's the deal?"

Eddie turned to Bardswith, who was staring desolately at the wood paneling in front of him, then back to the judge. "Pretty simple, really. The Scratch Corporation is going to sell off its inventory, and can conclude deals and contracts already in place. Then, it's going to dissolve."

Howell raised his eyebrows. "You're lettin em put you outta bidniz?"

"That's about the size of it."

The judge looked back and forth between the two attorneys. "Criminy, Caminetti! My opinion, yer winnin the case. Why you wanna roll over so easy?"

Eddie shrugged. "Tell you the truth? It's a bore running a business. Fun to get it going and now I'm not interested in it anymore."

"So why don't you just sell it?"

"On account of then I'd have to see this case through to the end. Nobody'd buy me out with this hangin over my head."

"So why not see it out? Let the jury decide?"

Bardswith, a quaver in his voice, said, "I don't believe it's your honor's place to counsel continuance of a proceeding when—"

"Yeah, yeah. And who can predict what a jury'll do. That what you're thinkin?" he said to Eddie. "So what about the dough?"

"We keep it," Eddie said.

"Keep it? Braunschweiger, you're sayin that's okay with you?"

"What? Oh. Oh yeah. Yes. We're agreed."

"They keep alla their money."

Bardswith's jaws were clamped so tightly shut the muscles in his cheeks stood out like little ropes. "Yes," he said through his grimace.

"Huh." Howell shrugged and put his glasses back on. "Okay. You guys draw up the papers and I'll sign em."

"Thank you, your honor," both attorneys recited.

"So that's it? We're over?"

Again, the two attorneys agreed.

"Fine. Hornswoggle, go on back. I'm gonna talk to this guy alone."

As soon as Bardswith was out of earshot and making his unsteady way back to the plaintiff's table, Howell said, "So tell me, Caminetti. How many-a these balls you got left?"

"Couple gatillion, give or take. Why, you want some?"

"Wouldn't mind."

"No problem. Soon's you gimme my two hundred bucks."

"You'll get it."

"In cash."

"Screw you. You'd make a helluva lawyer, you know that?"

"And you'd make a lousy gambler."

"Whatever. Say, how'd you know that about Agnormo?"

"Know what?"

"That he don't use his own Python clubs?"

"When I played in the Ryder Cup, I heard some guys talking. Then when I played him one-on-one, I looked. Had one Python in his bag and he never took it out."

"I'll be damned."

"Yeah. A real shock to find out one of your athlete heroes would do something like that for money."

Howell shrugged it off. "I don't even pay no attention to that anymore, but you wanna know what still shocks the shit out of me?"

"What's that, judge?"

"Twenty million golfers know Agnormo uses Medalist balls on accounta the company pays him eight big ones a year. And they run right out and buy em anyway."

"This from a guy who just hit me up for a couple boxes-a hunnerd-dollar golf balls?"

"Shit, Caminetti...I don't even play golf! Way I figger it, though, once you boys disappear?" Howell sat back and took off his glasses. "Them balls're gonna be collector's items."

"Why the hell'd you drag this out so long?" Hoogenband asked as he and Eddie stood at the defense table and began gathering up their stuff.

"Had a few things to get off my chest first."

"So let me ask you something." Hoogenband stopped moving papers around and leaned on the table. "You really mean to say that there's no differences in golf equipment?"

Eddie stopped as well, and stared at his co-counsel. "You must be kidding. When did I ever say that?"

Hoogenband, startled, straightened up. "Are you kidding *me*, Eddie?" He waved toward the front of the room, as though indicating the entirety of the case. "Isn't that what your whole strategy was about?"

"Hell, no. I wasn't saying that there isn't *different* equipment."

"Then what were you saying?"

"That there isn't *better* equipment."

Hoogenband, perplexed, didn't respond.

"Look." Eddie sat down and waved his co-counsel onto the other seat. "Only an idiot would say that there aren't any differences. Graphite versus steel shafts, hard balls versus soft... those're real differences."

"So..."

"But one's not better than another. They're just different."

"Then what's a golfer supposed to buy?"

"Whatever's the most appropriate for his particular game, that's what. If he doesn't swing very hard, he needs a more flexible shaft. That kind of thing."

"But there's about two hundred different shafts on the market."

"Different *brands*, you mean. Shit, Hoogenband. There's two hundred brands of aspirin, too, but every damn one-a them's the same. The angle your club head makes with the ground when you set it down is a hundred times more important than what the club head is made out of or what ball you use."

"But people swear by the brands they like!"

"People swear by their astrologers, too. Doesn't mean shit. You show me one guy ever changed his game by changing his brand of golf ball, I'll eat the ball."

Eddie stood up, but Hoogenband didn't.

"All those billions in advertising trying to tell golfers some club or some ball is better than all the others?" Eddie said as he resumed stuffing papers in his bag. "It's like trying to tell you one pill is better than the others without finding out what's wrong with you first." Eddie sighed. "But damned if golfers don't swallow it all up anyway."

Hoogenband still hadn't gotten up.

"So you got, what?" Eddie asked, looking down at him. "A three-thousand-dollar setta plutonium golf clubs?"

Hoogenband looked at his fingernails. "Something like that."

"Sell em on eBay," Eddie said, "and use the money for lessons."

Hoogenband finally stood up and buttoned his jacket. "So what'd you say to Bardswith and Trevillian that convinced them to let you keep your money?"

"I just reasoned with them," Eddie replied as he put away the last piece of paper and snapped his bag closed. "They're reasonable men. Let's go grab a beer."

CHAPTER THIRTY

"**J**ust read the trial transcript," Norman Standish said back in the Scratch corporate offices in Hallettsville. "Sounds to me like you had a good time."

"It was kind of fun," Eddie replied.

The noise of some major commotion from the direction of the entrance lobby rattled the door. Then there was more noise and a ceiling tile came loose, fluttering to the floor in front of Eddie's desk.

"What in God's name is that?" Standish asked, cocking an ear toward the indecipherable yelling coming through the closed door.

Eddie listened for a few seconds, then said, "I had to guess, I'd say it was Fat Albert, absolutely convinced that the entire world just crashed in on his shoulders."

A metal cylinder, several springs and at least four screws went flying across the room. It took Standish a moment to realize that they were pieces of what used to be the door lock.

"It was unlocked," Eddie said calmly to whatever force of nature had kicked open the door.

Standish bent forward in his chair to get a better look, then recoiled instantly.

"How could you do this to me!" Albert Auberlain roared.

"Do what?"

"You know goddamned well what!"

Auberlain appeared to fill the entire doorway as he came through it. Standish unconsciously tried to shrink his entire body so as to become less conspicuous as Auberlain turned to him.

"How could you let him do this, Norm?"

"We got sued, Albert," the physicist replied in a high, squeaky voice. "We didn't ask for it to happen."

"Bullshit! You had them beat! You coulda won that case!"

"Norm," Eddie said, "why don't you give me a couple three minutes with Albert here?"

Standish was out the door before the sentence had half concluded.

"Sit down, Albert, and tell me what the problem is."

Auberlain remained standing. "I'm in no mood for any-a your games, Eddie. We ain't in court and you ain't a real lawyer, so don't let's waste time bullshittin each other, uhh-ight?"

"Fair enough. So let's see here: Your game went into the dumper, you switched to the Scratch, you came in second at the BellSouth, fourth at the Byron Nelson, you won the Kemper, won the Greater Milwaukee, and now you've got the PGA coming up and the company that makes your ball is going out of business and you're worried you're gonna be selling knockwurst on the Lower East Side after missing the cut by twelve strokes." Eddie looked up at the ceiling, thought for a second, then turned back to Auberlain. "That about sum it up?"

Auberlain pursed his lips and lifted a shoulder. "Yeah."

"Bummer."

"Jeez, Eddie. You're a slippery sumbitch but you always watched out for me. How come all of a sudden you so damned hard?"

Eddie laughed and pulled a cigarette out of his shirt pocket. "On account of a smart guy like you bein one of the dumbest bastards I ever did see."

"My career's over and that's what you got to say?"

"Fat Albert." Eddie shook his head and put the cigarette between his lips. "Siddown. Go on, sit."

Auberlain took a seat on the couch along a side wall. Eddie came around and sat on a chair facing him. He flicked a cheap lighter and touched the flame to the tip of his cigarette. "You ever know me to screw over a buddy?" he said after he'd inhaled and blown out some smoke.

"Known you to beat em out of a couple g's hustlin golf."

"That's different. That they expect."

"Give you that."

"So tell me exactly what your problem is."

Auberlain leaned forward with his elbows on his knees. "Eddie, the company goin out of business, how'm I gonna get Scratch balls to play with?"

"Well, I got about two million of em left. Think that'll hold you through the season?"

Auberlain frowned and considered Eddie for a few seconds. "You don't get it, do you?"

"Get what?"

"If the ball ain't bein sold on the retail market, available to any player who wants to pay for em, you can't use them on tour."

Eddie frowned as he thought about that. "Bullshit. Who told you that?"

"Some-a the guys. On the tour. I mean, they should know."

"They don't know shit. Hell, everybody knows the KY 9000 ball Derek Anouilh uses is made special for him. You think when Hymie Pudknocker buys a KY 9000 in the pro shop at the Bumfuck Country Club it's the same ball?"

"That was only a rumor, and besides, Medalist said it was just a cosmetic difference anyway."

"So which was it...a rumor or a cosmetic difference? Cause it can't be both."

"Shit, Eddie, I don't know! But I'm bound to get grief if I play a ball that ain't even made anymore!"

"The settlement agreement says I can sell out our inventory and fulfill existing contracts. Nothing to worry about."

But Auberlain was not to be so easily mollified. "I got a defnit impression you're fuckin with me here, Eddie. You know as well as me I'm gonna get grief playin that ball. People are gonna think, shit, that boy is cheatin. You *know* that's true."

"Yeah. You're right."

Auberlain eyed Eddie. "Which part?"

"About me fuckin with you. I am."

Auberlain sank back on the couch and threw an arm over his eyes. "Then I'm cooked."

"No, you're not."

"I'm nothin without that ball, Eddie."

"And with it, you're the same dumb bastard I just got finished tellin you you are."

"What am I gonna do!" Auberlain whined plaintively.

Eddie drew in a big puff and exhaled a rich blue cloud of smoke. "Guess I might as well tell you. Can't keep it to myself anymore."

Auberlain lifted his arm slightly and peeked out from beneath it. "Tell me whut?"

Eddie stood up and went to his desk. "Tell you about the ball you're gonna be using from now on."

Auberlain's arm dropped, along with his jaw. "I knew it! You got a new ball, don'tcha? You got a new ball for me!"

Eddie smiled and winked. "Yep. Brand new."

"I knew it!" Auberlain jumped off the couch and did a quick jig. "I knew it all along! You were just fuckin with me! Hot damn! Hot *damn!*"

"That's the spirit, Fat Albert, my *man!*"

"Yeah, baby!" Auberlain came to a stop, nearly dizzy from the whirling, and banged his hand on Eddie's desk. "So lessee it! You got em right here, right here in your desk, don'tcha? Hot damn, I just *knew* it."

"Yes I do, me boy-o." Eddie opened a lower drawer on his desk, reached in, pulled out a box of golf balls and threw it on the desk. "With my compliments."

Auberlain stared at the box, paralyzed, even the smile on his face frozen in place. Staring back up at him was a box of Medalist Apex golf balls, the shrink-wrap still intact.

"There's your new ball, Albert." Silence in return. "S'matter? Whyn't you say something?"

Auberlain picked up the box and a pen and slit the shrink-wrap, then opened the box, took out a sleeve, opened it and let a ball drop into his hand.

"It's a beauty, I know," Eddie said. "No need to thank me."

Auberlain held the ball up. "This is the cheapest piece-a shit golf ball there is. You can buy these at Wal-Mart, fifteen for nine bucks."

"I know. Where d'you think I got em?"

Still holding the ball in the air, Auberlain said, "Eddie, I need a Scratch ball."

"You're holding a Scratch ball."

"This is a goddamned Medalist Apex."

"So was the Scratch."

Auberlain stared, but without seeing anything. "Maybe you'd best sit back down," Eddie advised, seeing some teetering motion on Auberlain's part that hinted of imminent fainting.

CHAPTER THIRTY-ONE

"**Are you tellin me,**" Auberlain said some ten minutes later, an untouched scotch in one hand, the cheap Medalist golf ball in the other, "I been playin a goddamn Apex for the last four months?"

"That's what I'm tellin you. With a Scratch logo, of course, and some glitter on the cover."

"Of course. Yeah. Sure."

"Your slump had nothing to do with your equipment. It never does. And I mean *never*, Albert, not for anybody. It's all in your head."

"In my head."

"That's right. And the minute you convinced yourself that the Scratch ball was the answer to your prayers? It was. Just like changing your dental floss would have been, you'da believed in it that much."

Auberlain couldn't take his eyes off the ball. "Damn."

Eddie sat back to let the implications sink in, which they did so quickly Auberlain could hardly control the flow of his questions.

"You meana tell me," he said, holding up the ball for about the thirtieth time, "a million people been shellin out a hundred bucks a dozen for this piece-a shit?"

"It's not a piece of shit. It's a good ball."

"It is?"

"Hell yeah, it's good. They're *all* good!"

"Oh yeah?" Auberlain turned his head slightly and looked at Eddie suspiciously. "What about the KY 9000?"

"Damned good ball."

"*Damned* good? You mean better'n this?"

"No, not better. The same."

"How d'you know that?"

"Because they're the same ball."

"I don't get you."

"They're the same ball. Different logo, different box, one or two dimples a little larger or smaller...but they're still the same ball."

"You're shittin me."

"Wanna cut a couple open and see?"

Auberlain knew there was no need to do that. "But... the box. The one the Scratch came in?"

"What about it?"

"It said it was made out of Dulerium. The middle, anyway, and the cover was Sacrolyn and somewhere else there was... what the hell was it...Sachertortium?"

"Schermanium. What about it?"

"The Apex doesn't have any-a that stuff."

"Sure it does. They just call it something else."

"What?"

"Buna-SG, Surlyn and Molybdechite."

"See? That's not the same!"

"Also known as rubber, plastic and silicon."

"Rubber, plastic—I don't get it."

"What?"

Auberlain already knew that Eddie was telling him the truth. He was just trying to understand how he'd gotten away with it. "How can you do that?"

"Do what?"

"Call stuff something that it ain't! Isn't there a law somewhere?"

"A law against misleading consumers? You can't be serious!" Eddie pulled a cigarette from the pack on his desk. "See this here? The company that makes this makes seventeen different brands. They're all the same. They come right outta the same machines and the only thing different is the package. One of them says it's a smoother smoke and they advertise it in upscale men's magazines. Another says it's lighter and they aim it at women. Another says it refreshes, and another says it satisfies. The ones they send to Asia they call a manly smoke."

"But they don't say it's made of different stuff."

"The hell they don't. They got over eight hundred names for one type of tobacco." Eddie tapped the end of the cigarette on the desktop. "You ever heard of rich Corinthian leather?"

"Sure. They use it in some car."

"You know what rich Corinthian leather is?"

"It's, uh, really good...comes from..."

"It's leather, Albert. Their advertising agency made up the name over lunch."

"How can they get away with that!"

"Get away with what? You make something, or have it made, you can call it anything you want. There's two hundred kinds of aspirin on the market; you think there's any difference? Hang around a refinery someday if you want a real education. You'll see gasoline delivery trucks from a dozen different companies all filling up from the same pipe."

Auberlain absorbed this in silence, then suddenly perked up. "Okay, then...what about you and the professor takin all them balls to Caltech? To that nukular whatsis?" He thought he was on to something and warmed to it. "Yeah, like that reporter said! The one that followed one-a your trucks! Hah!" He slapped his thigh and pointed at Eddie. "What about *that!*"

"That's where we put the logos on."

Auberlain's triumphant expression sagged. "The logos?"

"Yeah. Caltech, they got this machine, it prints some special way... the inks sink way in, steada being just on the surface, and you get this nifty sparkly look to boot. Ever notice the little devil never wears off?"

"Uh..."

"Even if you take sandpaper to the cover she won't come off until all the dimples are gone. It's pretty cool, but it's still a prototype machine and they only got one, and they wouldn't let me move it. So? We went to them."

"But...that reporter, that Trilling guy...he said he heard you and the professor, you know, calling out numbers. Like for the nukular whatsis. Said nobody could understand what the hell you two were talkin about."

"*You* could, Albert."

"Me! What're you, kidding me? Nukular shit? No way!"

"Sure you could."

Eddie stood and went back to the desk. From the top center drawer he pulled out a dictating machine. "Hoogenband got hold of the tape Trilling made. Court order or something, I don't know. Here, listen." He pushed the play button.

His and Standish's voices could be heard clearly over a loud background hum.

"Four." Standish's voice.

"Nine." Eddie's.

"Seventeen."

"Twenty-four."

"Thirty."

"That's a go. Eight."

"Eighteen."

Auberlain jumped up so fast he spilled half his drink. "That's crib!"

Eddie shut the machine off. "Yeah."

"You and Norm were playin *cribbage?*"

"Six hours straight, except for a couple three minutes here and there to help the night crew load more balls into the printing machine."

"You were playin *crib?*"

"I just told you we were—"

"But everybody thought—"

"Not my problem what they thought. I mean, what the hell was I supposed to do, f'shit's sake? Explain a tape a guy made while he was spying on me?"

"Holy smokes..." Auberlain slowly set the drink glass down on Eddie's desk, then plopped back onto the couch. "How'd you get Medalist to sell you all those balls?"

"Through a dummy corporation."

"A dum—wait a minute." Wheels turned. "This wouldn't by any chance be a Chinese company, would it?"

"No. I mean, it sounds like one, but it isn't."

"The one Medalist said they had a deal with?"

"Yeah. Trevillian thought it was an ordinary private label deal."

"Private label? What's that?"

Eddie sat down on the chair behind his desk. "It's when a big company with a famous brand-name manufactures the same product with somebody else's name on it."

"What for?"

"To make money, what else?"

"But is that legal? Isn't it fraud or something?"

"Better not be, or damned near every brand-name manufacturer in America is in a lot of trouble. You go into a grocery store and buy Shopmart string beans? Green Giant made em. You buy Wal-Mart cough medicine? It's Robitussin. BigMart ibuprofen? It's Advil. Not *like* Advil. It *is* Advil."

He picked up a sleeve of Medalist Apex balls. "Medalist churns out these puppies, without any logos, for seven different companies, three of them overseas. One boxes it up with a cover that says 'Longer!' Another says 'Supreme Control!' Another says 'Made with SupraMaxi Findibulized Titanium!' All the same shit. And you know where the titanium is?"

Auberlain shook his head.

"In the paint."

"What paint?"

"Stuff they color the ball white with."

"Why in the paint?"

"Because all white paint has titanium in it. Titanium dioxide. That's how you get it white. Look on any can of paint at the hardware store."

Auberlain was having trouble grasping everything Eddie was telling him. "So they sell the same ball to other companies."

"Hell, they even sell em to themselves."

"Now you lost me."

"They only make four different kinds of balls, Albert. They ship em to their own marketing divisions and they end up in forty different packages."

"Bullshit!"

"Like I said, you wanna cut a couple open?"

Again, Auberlain knew it wasn't necessary. "So what was the name of your so-called Chinese company?"

"Sum Ting Wong. And here's another one for you, Albert. You know those counterfeit balls the FBI found?"

"Yeah?"

"Every one of em was a Medalist Apex."

"Oh, stop! How—"

"I cut a few open, that's how. Trevillian had private label deals all over the world. All those balls were supposed to be sold only in overseas markets. But why do that when you can sell them here for four times the money?"

"I can't believe this."

"Medalist announced sixteen ways to spot the counterfeits—the logo came off with alcohol, the printing on the box wasn't very good—and not one of them had to do with how the ball performed. Why do you think the company never got a single letter of complaint?"

"But how come the FBI still hasn't been able to trace the source?" Auberlain asked.

"Because they spent all their time trying to find out how the fake balls got into this country."

"And...?"

"And, they never left in the first place. Straight from Medalist's factory to the shipping broker, and from there, right to a warehouse in Portland where they packed them up in fake boxes." Eddie held up his hands. "Of course, I'm just guessing on that last bit."

"And all those Medalist balls you bought in the twenty-bucks-off deal? What'd you do with those?"

"Turned them into Scratch balls, what else? Ran the whole lot through an acid bath and recoated and re-logo'd em. Cost us twenty bucks a dozen instead of six, but it's not like our profit margins were tight to begin with."

Something else occurred to Auberlain. "That's how you got Medalist to settle without taking your money, isn't it. They told the world the Scratch sucked next to theirs, and then you told them it *was* theirs."

Auberlain didn't need Eddie to answer. His head reeling, he reached for his drink and took a long sip. "I won the Kemper and the Greater Milwaukee with a Medalist Apex," he said, half to himself. "Oh, mama..."

"You ever look at the tapes, see how you were swinging that day?"

"No."

"You should. It was pure poetry. You coulda won hittin an apricot."

They sat there for a while. Auberlain reached toward the desk and set his drink down. "So what happens now?" he said. "You gave up the company. Why'd you walk away from all the dough you still coulda made?"

"Walk away?" Eddie stood up and kicked his chair back against the wall. "You oughta know me better'nat by now. Me and Normie gonna make about a hundred million each outta this deal!" To Auberlain's confused stare he said, "Come with me, son. Lemme show you something."

In a small office down a hall, they came upon Standish, who was sitting in front of a computer terminal.

"How's it going, doc?"

"Splendidly!"

"Good. Show Fat Albert how this works. Siddown, me boy-o."

Eddie dragged over a rolling chair and placed it next to Standish.

Auberlain sat and looked at the screen. "Hey...that's eBay!"

"Yeah," Standish snickered. "I'm addicted to this stuff. Yesterday I got a pair of Bose speakers for a hundred bucks!"

"You don't have a stereo, professor."

"So what? You know what kind of bargain that was?"

"Quit foolin around and show him, Norm," Eddie urged.

"Sure." Standish's fingers flew over the keys. He created a new auction, titling it SCRATCH GOLF BALLS. BRAND NEW STILL IN SHRINK-WRAP. Then he clicked on a field labeled BUY IT NOW. "What that is, it's—"

"I know," Auberlain said. "Lets somebody skip the auction and just buy it if they pay that price. So how much're you gonna put in there?"

"Two hundred and fifty dollars."

"Two fifty? You're nuts! Who the hell'd pay that kinda dough for a box-a golf balls!"

"Watch this," Standish said, and pressed the enter key.

The newly created auction appeared on the screen. The information box showed that it had seven days left to run, with a "Buy It Now" price of $250.

They sat there. A minute later Auberlain said, "So now what?"

Standish hit the refresh button so they could see the latest status of the auction. The same screen came up, with no changes. "Sit tight," Standish said.

A minute later he hit refresh again. Same screen.

After another minute he hit it again. This time the screen said, "This auction is closed. The winning bidder has used Buy It Now to purchase this item."

"Get oudda town!" Auberlain yelled, as Standish, grinning, turned around.

Eddie clapped him on the shoulder. "How many-a those you done already today, Norm?"

"More than two hundred," the physicist answered. "Over fifty thousand dollars." To Auberlain he said, "I just showed you how one works, but I've been doing them ten at a time. And we've got about a hundred and fifty thousand dozen more."

"And that's only if Sum Ting Wong doesn't buy any more balls from Medalist," Eddie added.

Auberlain, still holding the Apex, dropped his head into his hands. "I don't believe this. People spending that kind of dough for a plain old golf ball."

"Why don't you believe it, Albert?" Eddie asked. "Hell, half an hour ago you'da paid me a hundred grand for a dozen of these balls, am I right?"

"But I thought—"

"And *they* think so, too," Eddie said, pointing to the computer display. "How do you think manufacturers get away with the tidal waves of total bullshit they put out?"

Auberlain rocked his head back and forth. "Fuck *me*..."

"Come on," Eddie said, patting Auberlain's back. "Let's go get a drink and I'll tell you the entire secret of golf."

The three of them stood up.

"*You* stay here, Norman," Eddie ordered. "Work the machines."

"Ah, well," Standish said, resuming his seat. "Just saw a set of mag wheels, brand new in the box."

"You don't have a car, professor," Auberlain said.

"So what? I bet I can get those babies for less than two hundred bucks!"

On the way out, Auberlain said, "Just one thing, Eddie."

"What's that?"

"Back at Swithen Bairn. When you and Norman were telling me about how the ball screws up every once in a while. Which it did, by the way."

"Yeah?"

Auberlain held the door open. "He called it momentary something-or-other failure."

"MGF," Eddie said as he stepped through.

"Yeah. If that ball's really an ordinary Apex, how do you explain that?"

They'd reached the car. As Auberlain walked around to the passenger's side, Eddie said, "MGF stands for monumental golfer fuck-up," then unlocked the doors. "Kind of like a brain fart except it involves the whole body."

Auberlain stood where he was. "What?"

"The ball was fine, Albert. It was you that screwed up every once in a while. Just like I do. Just like every golfer on the face of the planet does."

Auberlain still hadn't moved. "Then how come you told me alla that bullshit about—"

"Because if we hadn't, every time you screwed up you would've either gone to pieces or tried to fix your swing."

"Well, that only makes—"

"No, it doesn't. Your swing is so smooth it's like watching a jellyfish swim. It works ninety-nine percent of the time. And when it doesn't, all you need to do is nothing. You getting in or what?"

Auberlain scratched blindly at the door until he found the handle.

Once they were inside, Eddie held off on starting the car. "But when you blew a drive at the Valley View, you fell apart in front of fourteen million people when all you had to do was forget about it and just keep doing what you were doing. That's usually all any decent golfer needs to do."

"Jeez. I don't see how—"

"Albert," Eddie said, "you came to Swithen Bairn, and while you were telling me how badly your game had tanked, bitching and moaning about how it had all gone down the shitter...you came in four under for the front nine! While you were telling me!"

Eddie inserted the key and started the engine. "So I said to myself, is it possible a kid this bright could be this damned stupid? Well, let's see, I said. And then I pulled that dopey trick, getting you all confused about your breathing. You duffed one shot, okay, I messed you up a little. But all you had to do to kill me was do *nothing*, and instead you completely wrecked your back nine."

Auberlain thought back to that day, and saw no basis for mounting an argument against the force of Eddie's logic. "All I had to do was nothing."

Eddie nodded. "Yep."

They sat for a few more moments. "Hell," Eddie finally said as he put the car in gear and looked in the rearview mirror, "if I could convince every golfer of that, the national average handicap would drop five strokes overnight."

They drove in silence for a few minutes, then Auberlain said, "One more question?"

"Shoot."

"When the professor first came to you with his idea for the ball, he'd just played a round of golf with some guys."

"His first."

"Yeah. He said he'd seen something that day. Something that gave him the idea."

"And he did."

"What was it?"

"Their equipment."

"I figured that. But what was it, exactly? I remember him sayin one guy had a set of customized clubs that cost him over two grand. The other one had some fancy gear as well. He said these guys were all the time buying new stuff out of magazines and had closets full of all the latest gear."

"That's true. But it wasn't about him looking at their equipment."

"It wasn't?"

"No. It was about him looking at how *they* looked at their equipment. Because there was a fourth guy with them that day."

"What'd he have?"

They'd stopped at a light, and Eddie waited until they were rolling again before answering. "He was seventy-six years old. He was using a set of clubs he'd had since college. Wooden heads, the whole bit. His ball looked like it'd been at the bottom of a pond since the Second World War and he had on a pair of sneakers, Norman swore he couldn't tell what was holding the tops to the bottoms."

"So?"

"So, while the other two with the hoity-toity hardware were spraying em all over the course, this old guy shot a seventy-four."

"Huh."

"That's what Norman thought: Huh. For eighteen holes these other two were telling the old guy about how he really needed to get with it, how much the technology had improved, all about spring effects and dynamically balanced shafts and cavity backs and aerodynamic what-the-fuck-evers...neither of those guys stopped for a moment to consider that this old bastard was kicking their asses from tee to green on every hole.

"And somewhere around the fifteenth one of them says to the old guy, he says, 'Hey, why don't you hit a couple with my clubs, see how good they are,' and the old guy says, 'I don't have to hit your clubs to see how good they are,' he says. 'I see how good *you're* hittin' em!'"

Auberlain laughed, imagining the scene.

"And Norman thinks to himself," Eddie continued. "He does that good, you know? Thinking? He's a scientist. He thinks to himself, okay, what's the deal here? I got two guys playing with a million dollars' worth of equipment that are getting killed by an old man using sticks that cavemen coulda used to start fires. And after fifteen holes of getting humiliated it never even occurs to them that maybe...just maybe...the equipment doesn't enter into it.

"So Norm tries a little test. He says, 'Gee, fellas. Seems to me, just looking at it logically, you guys should be borrowing *his* clubs.' After all, from Norm's point of view, if you think the equipment is the key, wouldn't you want the stuff that the guy who's playing the best is using?"

"That's the professor," Auberlain agreed. "So what'd they say?"

"They laughed. Didn't say a word, just laughed, because there was nothing anywhere in their brains that popped up to say maybe Norm wasn't joking. He *had* to be kidding, because who would want all that ancient, beat-up shit? Right in front of their eyes this old fart was on his way to shooting two over par, and even though they'd spent a fortune on all kinds of exotic doodads thinking it would improve their game because an ad in some magazine said it would, here was absolute proof that it had nothing to do with the equipment and they simply couldn't see it."

Eddie swung the car onto Highway 77. "And right there's where he got the idea for the Scratch."

"I'll be damned," Auberlain breathed.

"Yeah." Eddie checked the rearview mirror and eased into the left lane. "Too bad they don't give Nobel Prizes for insight into shit that really counts."

EPILOGUE

They jumped on Albert Auberlain as soon as he stepped out of the club-house.

"Albert! Albert! Albert!" was all he heard as they competed for his attention. It always surprised him, forty people all yelling his name. Did one of them think he'd get picked out of the crowd just for yelling "Albert!" exactly like the other thirty-nine were doing?

He stopped and turned to the crush of reporters and photographers. One of them, a smallish but bull-like man wearing enormous wireless headphones resembling a pair of baby armadillos with an antenna sticking up out of one of them, rudely muscled his way to the front of the crowd and nearly broke someone's nose as he shoved a microphone to within half a centimeter of Auberlain's mouth.

"*Albert!*" the man yelled, even though he was only a foot away. "Joe Finney, Fox News. How do you see this first day going? What about the threat from Licenciados? Do you plan to go out strong or play conservatively?"

Finney didn't need the mike himself, as the headset had a built-in boom that could capture his words even as he was maneuvering the handheld toward his hapless subjects.

Auberlain looked around and spotted a thin, bespectacled young man he didn't recognize hovering sadly at the very outside edge of the huddled crowd. The man was holding a sheaf of papers and mouthing words to himself as he read the top sheet, as though practicing the questions he'd prepared. Then he looked up and let the sheaf drop to his side. He sighed resignedly and held his mike up, pointing it at Auberlain so he could grab a few answers that would be asked by the more experienced reporters who'd out-hustled him.

"Are we gonna see more of that hotdogging you did at the BellSouth?" Finney was yelling. "Is Fleckheimer a serious threat or—"

Auberlain put his hand over Finney's mike and stepped around him.

"Hey!" Finney pushed his boom mike off to the side and released the switch on the handheld. "Where the hell're you—this is fucking *Fox*, goddamnit!"

Other microphones were shoved in Auberlain's face as he made his way through the throng. The thin young man stepped respectfully to the side as Auberlain got through the last of the horde, and nearly panicked when the number six golfer on the PGA Tour grabbed his elbow.

"Jeez, Mr. Auberlain! I didn't—"

"You got some questions for me?"

"Huh? What? Questions? About what?"

Auberlain pointed to the papers at the man's side. "Questions. About the tournament?" The man blinked a few times. "What's your name?"

"My—uh, Peter. That is, uh, Peter Chamlee. KDSM–Des Moines."

"Okay, Peter. Fire away."

As the rest of the reporters shifted their center of gravity to once again surround Auberlain, he said, "Gonna answer some questions from Peter Chamlee here. Y'all are welcome to listen in."

There were some protests in the form of reporters shouting questions anyway, but when Auberlain didn't answer, they quieted down.

"Go ahead, Peter."

The young reporter regained his composure with remarkable speed. Holding up the mike from his shoulder-slung tape recorder, he said, "Mr. Auberlain, you're still using the Scratch golf ball, is that right?"

"Sure am."

"Now, you don't have a sponsorship deal with that company, do you? After all, they don't even really exist anymore."

"That's right, Peter. About me using the Scratch, anyway. As to whether the company exists, well..." Auberlain smiled and rubbed his ear. "Tell you the truth, I'm not too up on that legal stuff. All I know, as long as I can get em, I'm using em." He elected not to add that he was getting ten percent on the sale of all Scratch balls from the company's "remaining" inventory. It wasn't exactly a sponsorship deal: Eddie and Professor Standish had sold him ten percent of the company.

"Well, you might have some competition for that," Chamlee said with professional ease. "After all, you already know two players on the tour were discovered using that brand despite their multimillion-dollar deals with other golf ball companies. Looks like they're going to be gobbling up Scratch balls same as you."

Auberlain smiled a wide smile. "Nothin like a little competition to spice up life, Peter."

"But at some point, let's face it, you're going to have to switch."

"You're right. And when I do, I'm going to hit about ten thousand of every ball in existence and make my choice based strictly on which one plays best." *And when I do,* he neglected to add, *that company's gonna pay me about twenty million a year, long as I keep winning on tour.*

"Lotta folks are going to be watching that decision! Okay, Mr. Auberlain, tell us: How's it looking for your first round of the PGA, the last major of the season?"

Auberlain looked up at the palm trees, down at the deeply hued green grass, out at the searingly blue water of the Pacific Ocean loitering lazily behind the number four green.

"You know, Peter, I'll tell you…"

Fat Albert Auberlain rubbed his stomach, then slapped it and said:

"I think this could be the day."